I0714937

THE RISING

Lilly Maytree

LIGHTSMITH PUBLISHERS
Thorne Bay, Alaska

Lightsmith Publishers
P.O. Box 19293
Thorne Bay, AK 99919

www.LightsmithPublishers.com

Ordering Information:

 Quantity sales. Special discounts are available on quantity purchases by corporations, associations, and others. For details, contact info@LightsmithPublishers.com

Lightsmith Publishers is an imprint of the Wilderness School Institute, a nonprofit educational organization that offers outdoor youth activities in wilderness settings, including training in wilderness skills and nature studies, as well as the publication of curriculum on related subjects, through the Wilderness School Press and their children's imprint Summers Island Press.

The Rising / Lightsmith Publishers / Paperback edition

To our United States of America...the beautiful.

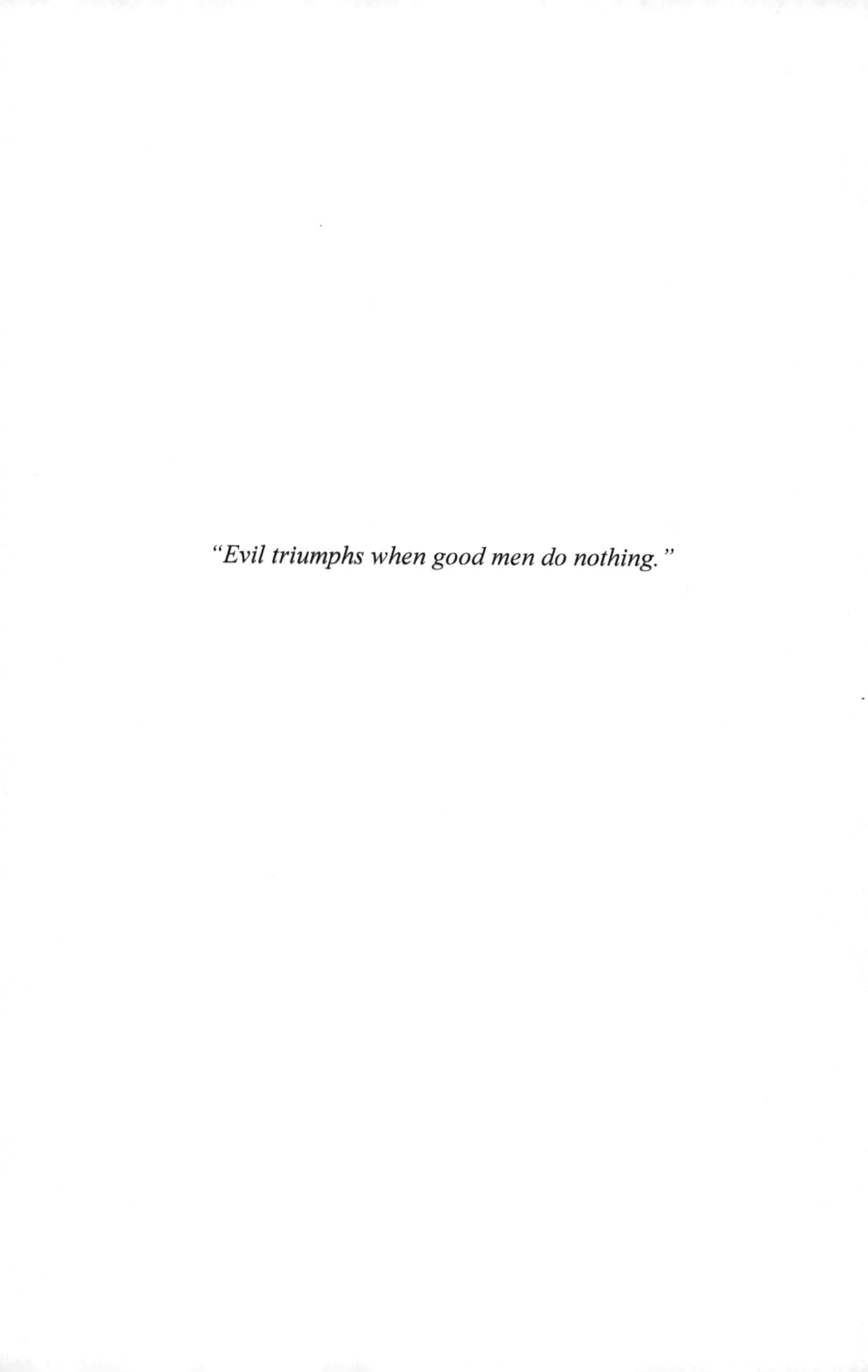

"Evil triumphs when good men do nothing."

1937

Lias Harper's company days were over. Last week, when he collected his pay, they had given him his notice. He raised his own food and could always trade meat or eggs for what little else his family needed. The tobacco crop paid the taxes each year, along with a little extra for store-bought things. But last year it had barely brought more than the expected tax money and a new pair of shoes for each child. This year, even though the crop looked good, he couldn't be sure about it. What if it didn't sell at all? Then again, the economy could change overnight. That's what everyone said. It could be like just after the war. When the coal tipples roared constantly and the money flowed. Back then, they had everything from new cars and trucks to the best clothes money could buy.

Those were the days.

But almost as fast as things boomed, they busted. In 1920, the price of coal dropped and men went from earning fifty dollars a day to barely more than a dollar. There were lay-offs and strikes. The government sent troops in and arrested them all for standing up for their rights. Meanwhile, the company hired gangster thugs from Detroit to act like company guards. Cedar Creek folks were beat every way but Sunday! They even took over Cedarville. Put a company man on as sheriff, let Ainsley elect his self mayor, and they were whipped. Been that way ever since. Cedar Creek wasn't big enough to go against the company and never had been. Not once they come in and bought up everybody's land. All they wanted was the mineral rights to the land...

"They said we could keep our farms and such. But what do you do with a mountain that's been skinned and plumbed? What can you do with it? Spring rain brings floods bigger and stronger every year. Now, even my good bottomland's getting washed away with the mess. So, here we are. Folks say we're lawless. But we're just trying to hold onto the proud spirit this country was found on. The truth is, we don't give up as easy as everyone else does. Maybe standing up here on our mountain we can look down and see the whole world going wild... and it's a heartbreak."

1

Harlan Fleming stepped into the Cedarville post office, set down his suitcase, and had the odd sensation of having somehow stepped back in time. This was not what he expected. It was the turn of the century here... not nineteen thirty-seven, as it had been when he left Richmond, three days ago. After the long train-ride, his well-cut gray suit was not as immaculate as when he started.

He was carrying his jacket instead of wearing it, and his tie had been stashed away in one of the pockets a long time ago. Already the place was changing him, but he was too distracted by the strange surroundings to notice. He had no premonitions. No uncomfortable sense of warning crept in to make him glance behind. If he had he might have seen that — even on that first day—all the bridges of his past were burning.

The few people in line ahead of him did not notice the condition of his suit. What they noticed was that it was "store bought," had a matching gray vest, and that he had the perfectly trimmed hair of a city person. Dark, wavy hair and eyes that were so blue they set off a striking handsomeness. But no stranger—handsome or otherwise—had any right to stare so intently at folks. Especially in a public place.

Harlan looked around. He had heard the people in the hill

"

country were shy of strangers but he wasn't in the backwoods, yet—just this little town on the outskirts. Most places he visited, local folk were eager to direct a traveler to where they could best spend their money. Maybe he could get someone to recommend a good place to eat.

"Warm weather for this time of year," he said aloud, to no one in particular.

The woman in front of him, dressed in a flower print dress, glanced back briefly and then pushed her small son a little farther ahead in the line.

Undaunted, Harlan addressed a grizzled looking man ahead of her who had turned around to eye him curiously. "Is it always so warm this late in September? I just got off the L and M from Richmond. I could use a good place to eat."

Now, all eyes turned to him but no one said a word.

"Next!" the postmaster's voice rang out from behind the iron bars above the counter.

The line moved ahead and everyone looked forward, again. When someone else came up behind him, Harlan turned to face the newcomer, determined this time to at least win the favor of a smile. But he couldn't have been more startled if he had seen someone step out of a painting. For a brief moment, he suddenly found himself caught off guard as much as he had caused the others to be.

There, standing before him, in a blue lace-trimmed dress, and deep red hair that was pulled back from a lovely face with a velvet ribbon – was a girl he was almost certain he had seen before. Even the sweep of those tumbling curls was familiar. And he was sure the fashionable cut of that dress belonged somewhere else he had been, not here.

She had the look of the French – which he knew very well – but that was absurd. He must be more tired than he realized to even think such a thing. Yet he couldn't help the quiet murmur that escaped him, *"It must be a small world!"*

He only realized he had spoken in French when she answered back in the same, *"Indeed, sir, it is."* …As if they had been two friends talking over coffee on the streets of Paris. His surprise must have amused her, because the green eyes sparkled and she smiled—a beautiful smile that seemed to light her entire face.

"Next!" the postmaster's voice rang out, again, and the lovely vision pointed past him to indicate that his turn had come up.

The man behind the counter was frail and balding, and limped uncomfortably as he moved to deposit a few envelopes into the outgoing mailbox.

"I was wondering…" Harlan still felt distracted – he must talk to her, again, before she left – if only to find out—

"Need stamps?" the postmaster prompted, seeing he had nothing to mail.

"Oh, sorry. No, thank you. I was wondering if you could direct me to Tom Bascomb's place. He doesn't live in town, here, but farther up. Somewhere called —"

Cedar Creek," the man finished for him. "On yonder side of the winding river, and just this side of the Wind Ridge."

Finding the explanation far from sufficient, Harlan asked, "But how do I get there from here?"

"Well," the older man said thoughtfully, "you can follow Main Street to Cedar Creek Road... then follow it clear on up past the mines. It's a far piece to walk, though."

"How far?"

"About twelve miles, give or take some. Mailman stops there. You might ride on out with him."

"That would be fine. When does he leave?"

"Left this morning."

For a moment there was silence, except for the buzz of an electric fan and the sound of papers fluttering softly on the counter. "Well, I suppose I could wait until tomorrow," Harlan finally decided. "What time does he usually leave?"

"He only lights out that way once a week," said the postmaster.

There was another silence. This time it was broken by the

long blast of a car horn outside, and an impatient masculine voice shouted, "Bonnie Rae! You in there?"

The postmaster looked past Harlan as if their business had ended, and spoke to the girl. "That package you been waiting for come in, Bonnie Rae."

"It did? Law, Mr. Farnsby—I been just enduring the time waiting for it."

"I'll fetch it," the wrinkled face broke into a smile, as if the pleasure of a package from far away was something to share. "You go tell Joseph Lee to keep his shirt on."

Bonnie Rae…

She hurried to the open door and called, "I'll be along!" before returning to stand next to Harlan, again, this time, casting her eyes down as shyly as the others had. Surely he must have been dreaming on his feet, or had some momentary mental slip, because now her voice rang with that same mountain twang everyone else had been speaking all around him since he had arrived.

"Here it is," the postmaster returned and handed the package across the counter to her. "Come all the way from New York, this time."

"It's a wonderment, ain't it?" she murmured, looking the plain brown wrapping over. There was another long blast from the horn outside and then another as she turned and started for the door.

"Hold up, Bonnie Rae —" the postmaster called her back. "You reckon you could pack this foreigner up to Doc Bascomb's place?"

Now, she stared uncertainly at the handsome stranger.

"I'd be happy to pay for the trouble," Harlan said quickly.

"Law!" she breathed the word as if the offer had been an insult. "I ain't about to take no money, Mister..." She looked questioningly at him.

"Fleming," he replied. "Harlan Fleming. I'm the new— what is the phrase you folks call it out here—government teacher. For Cedar Creek. Tom Bascomb is my uncle and I'll be staying with him."

"The government teacher?" It seemed the title suddenly made him acceptable. That, or the mention of his uncle. "Well, Mr. Harlan, if you can abide my brother's driving, I reckon we can get you there."

"Thank you," He reached for his suitcase. "And thank you, Mr. Farnsby," he added as he followed her outside.

The horn blasted, again, and Harlan saw that the noise belonged to a dilapidated, 'thirty-two, Ford pickup. The engine was running and the back was filled with four children, each holding a bottle of *Coca-Cola*. "How are you all?" he asked politely.

They just stared at him.

Then a ruddy, good-looking young man, with hair somewhere between the color of sunset and sand, stuck his head out of the window. "Howdy." When he smiled, Harlan noticed that he had the same charming smile his sister had.

"This here is Harlan Fleming, J-Lee," Bonnie Rae explained. "He come from off to be the new government teacher. I told Mr. Farnsby we'd pack him in to the Doc's place."

"Doc's place —" The friendly smile disappeared.

"He's my uncle," Harlan added. "It's where I'll be staying for the year."

"Well... shoot, I guess we could do it. Bonnie Rae, you set in the back with the younguns."

"Oh, no need for that," Harlan objected. "I would just as soon ride in the back, myself." He threw his suitcase over the side and climbed in.

A girl around fourteen, with hair a shade darker than her sister's, was holding a freckle-faced boy of five or six on her lap. A smaller girl—not much more than seven, Harlan guessed—had blonde hair done up neatly into two braids. She moved closer to an older brother who was seated nonchalantly with one arm up on the rail. He was wearing a faded gray cap and looked to be older than the rest, but not by much.

"He a foreigner, Rafe?" the little girl asked, staring wide-eyed at Harlan. She sipped on her drink and then spit some back into the bottle.

"Yep," her brother replied.

"I am not a foreigner," Harlan corrected. "I'm an American. Same as—"

The door of the truck slammed after Bonnie Rae got in. As if it had been the long awaited signal for the start of a race, the engine roared, the truck leapt forward with a startling jerk and began to barrel its way down Main Street, entirely too fast for downtown. Harlan had to hold on to the side as he was bounced and jostled with every bump and rut in the road.

When the children's eyes shown with pleasure, he realized they were enjoying the sight of the "foreigner's" discomfort. He won them over, however, when—in spite of their shyness—they couldn't help laughing out loud at the shocked expression he let cross his face when the driver hollered back to them from the open window, "Hang on, now! I'm gonna drive her wide open all the way!"

2

At the corner of Main and Cedar Creek Road, Joseph Lee blasted the horn and waved at the local gas station attendant. He ignored the stop sign and turned sharply onto the dirt road. Dust rose up in a cloud behind them and the truck leapt, bounced, and lurched over ruts and potholes as it leaned into the turns.

It reminded Harlan of one of those fast moving rides at a carnival, only it never seemed to end. He had all he could do to hang onto himself and his suitcase, and he wondered if walking could be any worse. About that time, the truck slid to a sudden stop in a great cloud of dust. The door on the driver's side flew open and Joseph Lee left the engine running as he got out.

"Why we stopping, here?" the boy named Rafe asked, shaking the dust from his cap as he looked over the side at his brother.

"I want to talk to Harlan," Joseph Lee replied. "We ain't even half there," he spoke seriously. "Nothing but this kind of travel for the next ten miles... I know a shortcut..." He looked off into the distance as if studying something he saw out there. "Get us home in six miles. You want I should take it?"

"I wouldn't mind," Harlan admitted.

Joseph Lee looked directly at him then, and broke into his charming smile. "You come on up front with Bonnie Rae and me, Lil Sam," he said, reaching for the smallest child.

"Awww…" The little boy wrinkled his freckled nose and frowned at his brother.

"Come on, now—you can hang out the window."

The front door slammed again and the oldest girl, who had been silent up until now, suddenly said, "What shortcut?"

"I reckon I know," snickered Rafe, his eyes beginning to twinkle with mischief. He's fixing on giving us a wild run down the Devil's Backbone. So, you best hang on to your —"

"Good lord," Harlan breathed, wondering how any ride could be wilder than the one they just had.

"That foreigner swearing, Rafe?" the little blonde girl asked.

"Yep," her brother answered.

"That was not swearing," Harlan corrected, again, slipping unconsciously into his classroom tone. "It was simply an expression of —" The engine roared and the truck lurched forward as Joseph Lee threw it in gear, causing everyone to grab for the sides.

"Joseph Lee!" the oldest girl screamed. She got to her knees—heedless of the sudden tear in her yellow checked skirt as it snagged between the boards. She set up a fierce pounding on the rear window and hollered, "I'm gonna tell Daddy!"

"You do, Lou Ellen, and I'll wale you to a frazzle!" came the shouted reply.

She sat down, again, with a petulant sigh and pushed her long auburn hair back that began to blow wildly about her face. "Gonna tell somebody," she threatened, to no one in particular.

About a half-mile up the road, they turned down a slope to the right. It dropped off so suddenly that everyone's stomach stayed in the air, and Joseph Lee bellowed out a rebel yell that carried across the Appalachian ridge like a wildcat in a bog hollow. The old truck began to gather speed through the sheer force of its own momentum as it plunged down a long, steep decline. The road—if it could be called that—was hardly more than a footpath along the ridge. And though it was hard packed and firm, the abrupt drop on both sides gave the sensation of plunging over a ravine as it descended into a gorge over three successive slopes. The breathtaking, headlong plummet was straight and long enough to allow the truck to reach wildly excessive speeds.

Joseph Lee gunned the engine as they crested each new slope, and the vehicle seemed to take a flying leap of its own accord. On the second one, they were in the air for nearly five seconds. When it hit ground, again, they crashed down with such force that the youngest girl dropped her bottle of cola. She reached for it and tumbled dangerously toward the pitching side and Harlan caught her out of pure reflex. All shyness aside, she buried her face in his broad shoulder and clung to him. Even Lou Ellen had gone pale, clutching the side of the truck with one hand, and Rafe with the other.

They crested another rise and flew into the air with a wild abandon. The girls screamed and even Bonnie Rae could be heard through the open window of the front seat, while Rafe hollered, "Whoa! Whoa!" as if he could calm the truck like a mule. After the shock of crashing down, again, Harlan decided it was time to put an end to the game. He rose up to bang on the back window but by then, they were racing down another narrow decline, and he was shocked to see that they were plummeting headlong toward a raging river. "Hold on, kids!" he warned. "Hold —"

Like the screech of a banshee, Joseph Lee gave another loud yell, and all at once a torrent of chilling water came at them from all directions. The girls screamed, and the truck thumped its way over the rocky river bottom, hell-bent for disaster. But the river was wider than it was deep, and after the first splash, the water bubbled and churned just above the running boards and rose no further. Then, as if Joseph Lee sensed somehow that the foreigner had his fill of such foolishness and was about to become something to be reckoned with, he hollered back through the window with a reassuring smile, "That was the worst of it!" and slowed down.

The rest of the road followed along the ridge, twisting and turning, and in some places diminishing to a width no wider than the truck, itself. At one point, a back tire slipped, and for a hair-raising moment they tottered on the edge of a great precipice. But the young driver was maneuvering the truck with a carefully controlled skillfulness, now. With no sign of panic, he gunned the engine and shifted down to first gear. The truck leapt forward with the usual lurch and they were saved.

The last two miles were peaceful enough. The sun began to go down behind the ridge and they slowed down even more the closer they got to home. The air cooled as they came into the deep woods of the hills. Tall trees rose up on either side of the road and here and there they passed a cabin nestled into a hill. Harlan breathed in the fragrant freshness of the mountain air with a pleasure that overrode the wild ride.

It caught him by surprise—this place he had never been —for he knew these smells and the plants they came from. They were the fragrances and sensations of his youth. Blackberry brakes lined the edge of the roadside and his mouth watered at the thought of the cobblers his grandmother used to bake. He recognized Evening Primrose, Forked Chickweed, Aster and Goldenrod... and memories of his country childhood began to push gently against the back of his mind. Between his university days and five years of teaching in the city schools of Richmond, Harlan had almost forgotten how wonderful the sights and smells of the country could be. It was... invigorating somehow. Refreshing to the mind and senses in a way that a city could never be. How had he forgotten that over the years?

It was "first dark" as they turned into a yard spread out in the front of a large, rambling cabin with a sagging roof and weather-worn shingles. It might have looked shabby if it hadn't been for the neatly trimmed Honeysuckle vines framing the porch and the swaths of blooming Wood Nettle along the fence posts. A thin wisp of blue smoke rose from the chimney into a sky that was lit with only a few, early evening stars, and Harlan felt it must be heaven to come home to a place like this.

A dog ran up to the truck to bark a greeting as everybody climbed out. The screen door banged and a slender, pleasant looking woman in a faded flowered apron stood smiling on the porch. The engine gave way to quiet, and Joseph Lee got out and walked back for his youngest sister, who had fallen asleep in Harlan's arms.

"There's only one thing I have to say to you, Joseph Lee," Harlan began with a mock severity as he handed the child over. "I have never in my life, seen anyone... Then he smiled with an amiable tolerance and finished, "handle a truck the way you do. That was some pretty fancy driving."

The young man grinned at the concession and then offered good-naturedly, "I'll pack you the rest of the way after supper."

"Oh, no need for that," Harlan replied, climbing down, himself. "You just tell me how to get there and I'll walk the rest of the way."

"Well, shoot, it would take me longer to explain than to drive you, Harlan." Then he turned to the porch and hollered, "Mama! You gonna ask this foreigner to supper?"

3

The woman on the porch looked Harlan over for a long, uncomfortable moment and then finally replied, "I reckon," before turning to head back into the house, again.

"For heaven sake," Harlan whispered, embarrassed by Joseph Lee's bluntness. "I'm not going to intrude on her supper."

"Oh, come on," he urged. "You won't hardly taste better cooking nowhere. Besides..." he lowered his voice confidentially, "Bonnie Rae would be disappointed if you said, no."

"What?"

"Shoot..." He laughed quietly, as if he were once, again, taking a pure enjoyment out of making a stranger uncomfortable. "I ain't seen her take on that much about anybody in a long time. What did you say to her back there in the post office, anyhow?"

"Nothing, actually, it's just that—well, I was almost sure it was —"

"Come on," he urged, starting toward the porch. "It's getting cool. I wouldn't want to rile Mama letting this youngun catch a chill after I soaked her the way I done."

Harlan stood quietly for a moment, surprised at the show of concern from someone he had judged careless only an hour before. But in truth, the spray of water felt good after the heat, and they had dried off quickly in the warmth of the sun. As awkward as the situation felt, he decided he really didn't have much choice about the invitation to dinner. No one had told him where his uncle's place was, and it would be even more awkward to wait for Joseph Lee in the yard. So, he reluctantly followed his young host inside.

There was a fire crackling in the large, stone fireplace at the back of the room, casting a warm glow on the painted wooden floors. They were a deep wine color, polished to a waxy shine, with several rag rugs scattered around. An older man with dark hair turning gray, sat quietly by the fire, smoking. He neither stirred nor spoke as Harlan came into the room. After a moment, he tossed the butt of his cigarette into the flames with the quick agility of a younger man and it occurred to Harlan that he wasn't really as old as he looked. He coughed, took a handkerchief from his back pocket and put it to his mouth. He coughed, again, and when he finally withdrew it, Harlan thought he saw a speck of blood on the white cloth.

"Harlan, this here is my daddy, Lias Harper," Joseph Lee introduced them as he laid the sleeping child on an overstuffed sofa. "Daddy? This here's Harlan... he's from off."

"I seen him," Lias replied without looking up.

"Pleasure to meet you," Harlan murmured anyway. His uncle had warned him that these hill people might be difficult to approach, at first, but it was still disconcerting. He had hoped to save introductions such as these for the schoolhouse, when he could take shelter in formalities. That way parents—no matter how reluctant at having an outsider take the position this year—would come by their own choice and he could be prepared. So, he was relieved when Joseph Lee gave him a congenial jab and said, "Come on, let's go out back and wash up."

As they passed through the kitchen, Harlan breathed in the rich smell of fresh coffee, warm bread, and fried pork. He suddenly realized how hungry he was and knew he was about to sit down to the sort of cooking a bachelor such as himself, rarely had the opportunity to enjoy. Bonnie Rae was doing something at the sink as they passed, and—though she didn't turn around or acknowledge him—he felt a sort of warmth pass through him as if she had. He noticed how the soft light of the kerosene lamps made her hair look like slow burning fire, and Joseph Lee's words echoed through his mind, *"she would be disappointed if you didn't stay."* It made him feel drawn to her all over, again.

The back porch was screened in, and in the glow of a single lamp set on a rough-hewn table Harlan saw a bathtub off to one side. In it, sat the largest, most magnificent man he had ever seen. He was almost god-like in appearance and proportion, as if some deity had somehow stole into this far region of hill country and left this uncanny proof that he had passed. He was a perfect man, who when standing—Harlan guessed— must be well over head and shoulders above anyone else. He broke into an easy, ready smile when they came in—that charming, Harper smile. But if there had been light and beauty which shown on the faces of the others; here was the sun from which such light was born.

"Hey, Joseph Lee," he spoke in a deep and resonant baritone, "who's that with you there?"

"This here's, Harlan. He's the new government teacher. Harlan? This here's my big brother, Johnny. Big John, they call him around here." He pumped a few times on an old-fashioned hand pump and then leaned over to splash water on his face from the cool, clear flow before he continued. "The biggest Harper ever was, the strongest Harper ever was... the first born and the first loved..." He reached for a towel. "And the pride of old Lias —"

"That'll do, J-Lee," his brother warned, reaching for a nearby towel and giving a friendly nod to Harlan. "Howdy." He began to rub himself dry.

"Nice to meet you, John," Harlan returned, unable to help noticing a jagged, lightning-shaped scar across Big John's right side.

Joseph Lee moved out of the way and motioned Harlan to the sink. "He's gonna be staying up at the Doc's." He relayed the information to his brother more as if it were a tease than conversation. "Got to pack him up there after supper. Want to come along, Johnny?"

Once, again, there was a long moment of uncomfortable silence, and Harlan glanced back from the sink in time to see the friendly smile fade to what he thought looked like a glimmer of mistrust. "The Doc's place…" John ran a hand through wavy brown hair and looked over at Harlan, again. "I reckon I better," he murmured. Then, as if suddenly deciding there was nothing to worry about, he cast his brother a teasing glance and said, "but I'll do the driving, J-Lee, else we'll have to leave you behind."

Joseph Lee frowned and stalked back into the house.

Big John laughed and buttoned a pair of fresh jeans he had just stepped into. "Don't mind him none," he said to Harlan as he pulled suspenders up over bare chest and shoulders and reached for a gray flannel shirt. "He's just at a time in his life when he's mostly muscle and the rest fool. Nineteen. I was risky in them days, myself. You known the Doc long?"

"He's my uncle." Harlan took in the old pump at a glance and moved the lever up and down until a stream of cold water began to flow. "I haven't seen him since he visited Richmond four years ago. Summer of 'thirty-three, I guess it was. He's the one who told me you all could use a teacher up here. I really had other plans for this year but they were delayed."

"I reckon that means she turned you down," John said with a teasing grin. "You look like the kind could rile up the women folk, all right. How old are you?"

"Twenty-five. And as much as I hate to disappoint you…" He dried his hands and looked at the large man as he replied. "The plans didn't involve a girl."

Big John laughed and tucked in the ends of his shirt. "Well," he took up a wooden comb and turned to a mirror on the wall. "My advise to you is…"

He paused to run a hand over the faint shadow of whiskers, decided not to shave and then tossed the comb back onto a shelf. "Grow yourself a mustache or beard. Something to make them kids show you some respect. Some of them are pretty burly, you know."

"So I've heard."

"They don't take kindly to being forced into book learning when there's other things to do. Know what I mean?"

"I think so."

"They've plumb wore out three teachers, already. Most of last year the school was closed down on account of the government couldn't get no-one else to come."

"I've heard that, too."

"Reckon maybe you got your job cut out and waiting."

"Could be." Harlan leaned against the washstand and suddenly realized how tired he was. It was becoming clear to him that this job was not going to come as easily as his previous ones had.

Besides the usual respect that came with the profession of a teacher, Harlan had a natural talent for dealing with children. It had always made him a ready favorite with students, as well as parents. But he was beginning to realize that—here in Cedar Creek—he was an outsider before anything else. The term seemed to transcend any previous claims to honor or accomplishment. It caused a deep sense of mistrust in these people—he could feel it—from the adults right down to the children. He wondered what it would take to break through a barrier of that kind.

He wondered if he even wanted to.

The door opened a crack and Bonnie Rae stuck her head in. "Supper's ready," she announced. Then she glanced at Harlan and smiled. Once again, it was sweet and refreshing, and to Harlan at that moment, incredibly beautiful. More than just a show of acceptance. It was that same sense of familiarity he had experienced in the post office. For a moment, their eyes locked, and held.

He and Big John followed her inside where the kitchen table was fairly sagging with food, and children were already crowding around. She sat down across from Harlan—between Lou Ellen and Little Sam—and he was glad he would be able to watch her instead of meeting other sullen or mistrusting eyes when he looked up from his meal. He wondered if he would get a chance to talk with her alone and ask her…

Except for a simple prayer of thanks spoken by the father, no one said anything while they ate. Harlan knew his presence was the cause of it. The overshadowing heaviness even put a damper on his own usual ability to make light conversation and set people at ease. Perhaps if he asked some things about the school, and invited the children to come look at it with him tomorrow.

"Delicious meal, Mrs. Harper." He glanced across at the smallest boy – he had always found the youngest the easiest to win over. But before he could put even a word to the invitation, the boy suddenly spilled his milk.

The glass fell from the small hands and tumbled without warning against the edge of the table, splashing its cold contents onto the lap of his older brother.

"For cripe sake!" Rafe jumped to his feet as the milk soaked into his jeans. "That's the second time I got soaked today— and I ain't enjoying it!"

"I'm sorry, Rafe," the younger boy said quickly. "It was the foreigner done it. He give me the evil eye and the glass jumped right outen my hand!"

4

Celia Harper looked at her youngest son with an expression of shocked embarrassment. "Lil Sam!" she admonished, casting an apologetic glance at Harlan.

"He did!" The boy insisted, "I swear it!"

"That'll do, Samuel," came the quiet, authoritative voice of his father. "Stop swearing at the table and apologize to our guest."

"Yessir," the boy responded, immediately contrite. "Sorry, Mr. Harlan."

"Evil eye," Big John muttered, getting back to his meal with renewed vigor. "Where did you hear tell of that kind of foolishness?"

"I nigh onto seen it myself," the boy answered as Bonnie Rae wiped up the spilled milk with a dishcloth and then sat down next to him, again.

"How could you nigh onto see something?" Joseph Lee asked. "Either you seen it, or you ain't."

"Ain't nobody can look straight into a evil eye without something gawd-awful —"

"Lil Sam!" his mother admonished, again.

"Sorry, Mama. Something..." He thought for a moment until he came up with can a better phrase. "Plumb terrible happening."

"Like what?" Lou Ellen dribbled honey across a biscuit with her spoon.

"Like what happened to Jesse Tolliver last week. He was out frogging and run into the old Doc talking hoodoo in the woods behind Cedar Creek. Before Jesse could run off, Doc give him the evil eye! After that, he were blind and deef for three days."

It occurred to Harlan to assure the boy that if his uncle were seen speaking anything to himself in deep woods, it was probably nothing more than a recitation of French poetry while enjoying the beauties of nature. But he didn't. The uncomfortable silence and mistrustful looks any mention of "the Doc" had brought on, already, made him keep the explanation to himself. Meanwhile, there was a long moment of silence as the boy's story evoked a vivid scene in the mind of each listener before a chorus of protests began to echo all around.

"It's true!" Little Sam argued. "You can ask Mr. Tolliver, yourselves, if Jesse weren't gone for three days last week!"

"Aw, Jesse's always going off hunting or fishing for a few days by his self," Rafe explained, having come back into the room with a dry pair of jeans in time to catch the end of the wild story.

"He was blind and deef!" the boy insisted. "And he had to hole up in a cave because he couldn't see his way home. And he nigh onto starved, only his hound dog brung him a rabbit. And he ate it raw!"

"Vow and declare!" Mrs. Harper got to her feet with an exasperated sigh. "If you don't quit conjuring up such lies, Lil' Sam, I don't know what I'm gonna do." She took the coffee pot off the stove and returned to the table.

"I know what I'm gonna do," Mr. Harper said quietly. He pushed his chair back from the table and took a slip of thin paper and a small pouch of tobacco from his shirt pocket. "I'm gonna cut me a strong, young hickory stick and wear a hole in his britches, if I hear anothern."

Yessir, Daddy." Little Sam dug into his unfinished supper with a will after that.

Like a spell that had been suddenly broken, the guarded silence that had hung so heavily before Sam's wild story began, was gone. A relaxed peacefulness settled over the kitchen. The girls washed dishes while the men lingered at the table, talking of the weather, and if this year's tobacco crop would yield so much and sell for so little as last year.

They drew Harlan in with an easy, effortless rapport that made his earlier impressions seem ill founded. They seemed eager to see the school open, again, and it was Mr. Harper, himself, who agreed to let the children accompany him to the schoolhouse tomorrow and help get things ready for the coming first day. He even offered the services of his boy, Rafe, who was a good strong worker, should there be need of any repairs.

So, Harlan pushed his former misgivings aside and decided—once past their first shyness—the Harpers weren't much different from the many other caring families he had shared a meal with over the years. He sat back and sipped on his second cup of coffee, watched and listened to them, and noted the curious ring now and again of Elizabethan English in their phrases.

There was no chance to talk directly with Bonnie Rae, however, and he discretely left any further mention of his doctor uncle out of all conversation. Could it be possible that even after all these years, his uncle was still considered an outsider, as well? At any rate, the Harpers seemed friendly enough now, so, he was content to set further questions aside for another time and simply let the magic of this mountain family enchant him.

After a while, Rafe left the house and returned a few minutes later with an armload of wood for the fire. "Wind's rustling things up something fierce, out there," he announced. "Storm coming." He dropped the heavy load on the hearth.

Lias got to his feet. This seemed to be the signal for everyone to adjourn from the table, and Harlan decided it was time for the "foreigner" to take his leave.

By the time he climbed up into the truck with Big John, lightning had begun to flash and the smell of rain was on the wind. They bounced and jogged along the dirt road—though not as violently as when Joseph Lee had been at the wheel. The hills were in a different mood now. Instead of the quiet peacefulness of sunset, they seemed dangerous—foreboding—and the trees were like evil sentries pressing in all around. The road took them down and down, like a dark winding tunnel, and the headlights on the truck were only bright enough to make their surroundings look even more black and eerie.

"Rough road," Harlan said.

"Yep."

"Can't see much."

"I can see more with my eyes shut," the large man teased. "But don't worry. I know this here road like the back of my hand. I'll get you there in one piece. That's some storm coming, though. Fixing to rain any minute now."

Harlan stared out into the blackness. Richmond seemed far... far away, now. It began to rain. The force of the wind changed the drops into piercing needles and Big John turned on the wiper.

"What's that noise?" Harlan asked.

"River. There's a bridge right up here."

"I thought we just crossed the river."

"Cedar Creek winds all through these hills. Bridges all over the place. Folks call it Cedar Creek, but it don't live up to its name. Most of the time there's so much water coming down out of the mountains, it's a all out raging river. Especially this time of year." The tires began to thud over rough wooden planks as he went on. "It sure don't settle down like no creek ought to. And there's a heap of folks been drowned in it over the —"

All at once a man appeared—out of nowhere—and darted

in front of them. John hit the breaks and swerved, coming dangerously close to crashing into the wooden railing as the truck screeched to a halt. The engine stalled. For a moment, all was quiet except for the rushing sound of water beneath them and the steady pelting of rain.

"Hey!" Harlan yelled out the window as the man ran down the embankment and disappeared into the darkness. "You all right? Wait a minute!"

Big John seemed to be in a daze. The headlights were still on, casting a meager glow across the bridge and partly out over the frothing, white water below.

"I don't think we hit him," Harlan offered. "He couldn't have run off so fast if we had. Looked like he just came up from the mines with that miner's cap on. You all right, John?"

"Looked like Willie Hollis," the large man replied.

"He looked all right," Harlan assured.

"He looked like Willie Hollis," John said, again. He started the engine with a sudden fervor. The wheels spun for a few seconds on the wet planks before the truck leapt forward.

"So?" Harlan looked up in time to see a sharp turn and braced his hands against the dashboard as the truck flew around it on two wheels. "Hey—what's the matter with you, John? Now, you're driving like Joseph Lee!"

"Willie Hollis —" They took another corner at a wild high speed, this time splashing into a mud hole and sending spray up in every direction. "Been dead for two years. Killed in a mining accident just as the shifts were changing. Willie was just fixing to come home when it happened. He used to take this shortcut over the bridge."

"Are you saying that guy back there was —"

"I don't know what that was back there," John answered quickly. "And if I did, I sure wouldn't say it out loud."

In a few minutes, they came to an abrupt stop in front of a cluttered yard with a small tumble down cabin set back against the trees. The windows were dark and there was no sign of anyone inside. A shutter that had lost a hinge was banging loudly, and a dog began to howl somewhere close by.

"Lord of mercy—just look at that place!" John breathed. "Listen, Harlan. Whatever we saw back there on the bridge, I take it to be a bad omen."

"Bad omen —"

"Yep. And from the looks of that place, you couldn't pay me to go in there. This is a witching night, for certain."

Harlan looked over at the large hulk of the man sitting beside him, but it was too dark to see anything but a shadow. "The way your father prayed at supper," he ventured, "I thought you were a Christian."

"I am," came the ready reply. "And a God-fearing one, too. Maybe that's why I can tell a witching night when I see one."

Harlan sat quiet for a moment. He had never met anyone who was pulled so strongly by those two opposing things. He could sense the sincerity though, and didn't want to offend.

"I came a long way to get here, John," he said after a while. Then he looked a little uncertainly at the strange surroundings, himself. Where was Tom, anyway? Did he really live in this awful, run down place? "Are you sure this is the right house?" he finally asked.

"Certain sure. I been here a time and a time and that's the place, all right. Never seen it look so much like the wrath. Storm must have blown things all to... Aw, he's probably off doctoring up on the ridge, somewhere. Don't look good, though."

"Well," Harlan opened the door to get out and a big gray dog rushed up and began to bark wildly at him.

"Go home, Bones!" Big John snapped sharply. "Go on, now!"

The dog backed off and was quiet, except for a low, occasional growl. Harlan reached for his suitcase on the seat between them and climbed down out of the truck.

"Wait a minute." Big John sighed, as if what he was about to say took great effort. "I ain't been here in a couple years, on account of... well... on account of us Harpers don't hold with the Doc no more. I ain't gonna go into the reason. It's over. But being you're his kin, I wouldn't feel right if I was to leave without telling you."

He sighed another great sigh and Harlan began to see why they had been so reluctant toward him. Maybe all those distrustful glances had not been just in his imagination, after all. He stood quietly and waited for John to continue.

"I can't leave without telling you he ain't been acting too right in his mind, lately. I been hearing a few rumors, and, by the looks of this place, I'd say they was true. Anyhow, all I can tell you is..."

He eased the truck into gear and looked toward the shadow of the young man standing a few feet away. "Watch yourself, Harlan."

5

The door to the cabin was unlocked, and Harlan noticed a faint light coming from a back room. It was warm inside, even though a fire on the hearth had long since turned to embers. He set his suitcase down and walked through the darkened living room toward the dim light down the hall.

"Tom?" He called ahead, "Are you in there, Uncle?"

It was a small kitchen, with a low-burning kerosene lamp set on a table in front of a large French window. There were signs of a meal having been prepared but not eaten: a pot of stew still faintly warm on the stove and a loaf of brown bread partially sliced through and not put away. Near a sink with the same sort of old-fashioned pump he had seen at the Harper's, there was a coffee pot filled with fresh water, but no coffee can in sight.

Harlan moved over to the table, where the lamp cast a spectral glow over the dark window, making it seem as if some ghostly replica of the tiny room were beckoning from outside. His own reflection met him as he cupped hands around his eyes and pressed his face to the cold glass to see what was out there.

Nothing but dark shadows and tree branches thrashing in a violent wind.

He turned away and headed back toward the living room,

again. As he retraced his steps through the hallway, he heard footsteps on the front porch. The front door suddenly creaked on its hinge as a blast of cold dampness and the sound of rain rushed inside. A tall, gaunt figure stepped in, wearing a wide-brimmed hat and long open coat with ends whipping in a strong following wind.

"Tom?"

The startled expression turned to instant recognition as the familiar voice filled with a warm fondness responded, "Harlan? Well, it's about time!" He sluffed quickly out of the hat and wet coat and hung them on a wooden peg by the door.

"Hello, Uncle!" Harlan moved into the outstretched arms with a wave of relief to see it was really him; but it was short-lived. Instead of the strong, confident bear-hug he expected, he was caught off guard by the rib and bone he could detect even beneath a heavy flannel shirt. "Hey…" he murmured, unable to hide his surprise. "You starving on your own cooking out here?"

"Ah, I never was much good at it," the older man replied as they started toward the living room. "But it feels like you've put on plenty of muscle since the last time I saw you. What are you walking around in the dark for?" He struck a match and lit another kerosene lamp on a mantel above the large stone fireplace.

Harlan's gaze was drawn first to the familiar painting he thought sprung to life this afternoon, and which now hung in this other-worldly place. He had not been dreaming, after all. Although the exquisite woman pictured before him was the head and shoulders of his Aunt Melanie, the dress he had seen this afternoon had been the same. And while the hair he gazed at now was not the rich chestnut of Bonnie Rae Harper's, it had been swept up in the same fashion as this painting that had hung in his uncle's study ever since he could remember.

This cabin was too small for such luxuries as a study, but looking around, Harlan saw that the main room served the same purpose. It was crowded with books from floor to ceiling on three walls, with his grandfather's large wooden desk and leather-backed chair in the center of them. On this wall, there were two overstuffed chairs covered in green plaid, pulled up close to either side of a stone fireplace, with a large braided rug in between.

"I just got here," he answered finally. "Saw the light on back in the kitchen and thought you might be in there."

"I've been cutting a piece of barbed wire out of a mule's jaw about a mile or so down the road."

"Taken up veterinary practice these days?"

"This far out in the country, a doctor gets called on to do a bit of everything. Besides…" He stirred up the coals with an iron poker and then took a couple pieces of split wood from an old tin washtub next to the hearth. "Belonged to a man who lost an arm in the mines last year, or he'd have taken care of it himself. Most folks are pretty self-reliant around here. Have a seat and let's catch up on things."

Harlan couldn't help staring. The thick brown hair and beard he remembered were streaked with gray, and the once-ruddy face was far too gaunt and pale. "Well, I see it interrupted your dinner. Why don't we talk in the kitchen."

"Sure. I'll bet you're hungry, too." He turned toward the hallway. "I have an Irish stew to warm up – a good one – because it was made by old Mrs. Meecher and not me. Got it in trade for a bottle of rheumatism lineament ."

"I just finished a large supper with the Harpers."

Tom stopped in mid-stride, as if the name had been a closed door in front of him. But only for a few seconds and he didn't turn around as he continued on and replied, "How about some coffee, then? I've been thinking about some all the way home."

"I didn't hear your car drive up."

"I don't have one. Isn't much use when so many live back in the hills and hollows. I have a nice reliable old mule named, Blu. If I need to go into town, there's always someone with a car coming or going."

Harlan followed him into the kitchen and watched as he turned up the wick on the table lamp, then began to busy himself at the stove. A brighter, more cheery glow spilled over the room. Harlan pulled a chair out from the table and sat down.

"Where have you been all this time, son? I've been expecting you for two weeks, now."

For a moment he didn't answer. When his uncle turned and looked at him with an inquiring gaze, he finally said, "I sold the farm, Tom, and it took a little longer than I expected to store all the furniture and settle things."

Tom moved over to the table and unbuttoned the cuffs of his green flannel shirt. He rolled them up thoughtlessly—as if he were preparing for a surgery instead of supper – and then replied, "Did what you had to, I suppose."

"I've always asked for your advice," Harlan said, feeling a twinge of concern at the tone of remorse in his uncle's voice. "Taken it, too, Tom. Most of the time. This time, I had to make the decision, myself."

"Well, it was your decision to make, Harlan," he said quietly. "It's been yours for a long time, now."

"I considered renting it out because it was the family place."

"No, you did the right thing. I could never live there, again. Too full of memories. Too full of Melanie and the folks. Six years staying anyplace but there if you possibly could, I guess you couldn't, either. So, you did the best thing for both of us."

The coffee pot began to boil over and Tom jumped around to rescue it. Harlan smiled. It suddenly occurred to him how much he had missed his uncle during all those intervening years.

"I like this place," Harlan said.

"Thought you might."

"I like the Harpers, too," he began carefully.

"Did they know who you were?"

"Not until I was standing in their living room after Joseph

Lee already dragged me in there. They warmed up after a while, though. I didn't find out until John drove me here that you weren't on speaking terms with any of them. He wouldn't say why."

There was such a long silence that Harlan thought maybe his uncle wasn't going to tell him, either. Finally, the older man set the coffee pot and two cups on the table with a resigned sigh. "Of all the people on this ridge," he murmured, turning back to dish up the stew. "I was hoping we could have a little time before that came up."

"They seemed like a nice enough family," Harlan persisted. "I can't imagine what would cause the sort of rift I felt whenever your name came up. Or the sort I feel in you when I mention theirs."

"It's a long story, Harlan." He sat down across from him. "And a hard one to tell."

"Even to me?"

"Especially to you, son." He looked over at him with an expression that was so full of love and sorrow, that Harlan felt a sudden stab of concern about what he was about to hear.

6

Tom left the stew untouched in front of him and sipped on his coffee. "Lias and I used to be friends," he finally began. "When I first came to the mountain, that family was like a tonic to my soul. The kids especially. That little Bonnie Rae… well, she was something special. And smart as a whip, too. So hungry for learning, she couldn't keep away from my books. Read everything she could get her hands on, even those long dull French histories."

"Are you the one who taught her French?"

"It was sort of an accident, really. She contracted a light case of scarlet fever when she was about ten, and I brought her here so it wouldn't spread to the others. She got bored right away, so I dug out some of those old French pattern books of Melanie's and let her fool around trying to make something. But she was a smart little thing! Memorizing the directions I'd translate for her, and the names for all the pattern pieces. She had a knack for the language. So I drug out the children's stories, too. One book led to another. It was almost as if I'd been carrying those old books of Melanie's around for a reason."

He cast Harlan a glance. "Well, you know how it was back then. I couldn't imagine life without Melanie. All I was hoping for was a big enough job to crowd out any time I might have to myself. I came here because it was as opposite to

Richmond as I could get. I knew there was no doctor. I figured the sheer remoteness of traveling around these hills would keep me busy. I had to keep busy."

He fixed his gaze on the flickering flame of the lamp. "Your grandmother's people came from this hill country. A little farther south but a lot similar. I always remember Dad's early stories of being a circuit doctor in the hills. That's how they met, you know. But his stories were bleak ones. So, I came to Cedar Creek expecting to tackle poverty, disease, and ignorance. That's what he always said was running rampant in the backcountry. But that isn't what I found here. Instead, I found utter hopelessness. These people aren't poor, Harlan, they're exploited. And the diseases they grapple with are the kind that society inflicts upon a people, not nature. As for the ignorance—"

The tired blue eyes suddenly flashed with some of the past intensity Harlan remembered so well. "You'll see it, yourself," his uncle went on. "This is a culture so far from ignorance you'll feel ashamed sitting down with such noble hospitality sometimes. The guest still holds a sort of old-world honor around here."

"I felt something of that at the Harpers," Harlan admitted. "Like they were obligated to be polite even though they didn't want to."

"Says a lot that they were. It's important what the Harpers say about things. They're the largest, most influential clan in these hills."

"Clan?"

"Most of the people up here migrated years ago from the Scottish Highlands. Lot of their phrases and customs come from there. Lot of their strength and stubbornness, too. Anyway, Lias Harper's word carries more weight on this mountain than anyone else around. If he approves of you, it will be a lot easier to gain acceptance from everyone else in Cedar Creek."

"I thought he was just a crotchety old man, at first. Didn't want anything to do with anybody. Then I realized he was just sick.”

“I did that to him.”

Harlan raised a questioning eyebrow in response to the statement. “What – because he didn't respond to some treatment you gave him? Nobody like that would, Tom. I'd say he's got black lung, or something close to it, and it's pretty far gone.”

“Did he come right out and tell you that?”

“He didn't have to tell me. He was coughing enough blood to prove it just in the short time I was there.”

“He's been trying to hide it for a long time, so he can keep working. You always could pinpoint a diagnosis with surprising accuracy, Harlan. You should have gone into medicine, like the rest of us. ”

“It's just a knack that comes from being raised with doctors. I'm a lot better at teaching. But don't change the subject, Uncle. You've had other treatments that didn't work out, either, and you never took the blame for them. No doctor can, or they could never keep doing what they do. Isn't that what you used to tell me? What makes Lias Harper so different?”

“Because this time I did have a hand in it. I guess you could say I brought trouble down on his whole family, and... well... it broke him. Nobody can take the blame for that but me.”

“What kind of trouble?” Harlan asked gently.

Tom Bascomb looked up and realized how much of a man his nephew had become since the last time he saw him. He had grown strong and mature, yet, he was still sensitive and caring. All at once Tom felt a welling sense of pride in him. It was time to tell the story and get it over with. Because if there was one thing he dreaded worse than facing his nephew at this moment, it would be to face him after he heard it from someone else.

“Four years ago,” he began, “the Harpers ran the biggest, illegal whiskey operation in these hills.”

“The Harpers?” It didn't seem to fit.

"Bootleg whiskey is about the only profitable crop you can get off these hills anymore," Tom explained. "Especially when so often it makes the difference whether your kids will starve or not. The Depression's been hard on people out here. For a lot of families, it's their only source of income."

"But the coal mines are operating. Doesn't it help to be a company town?"

"They pay twelve cents an hour, Harlan. And the waiting list to get on there is over two years long. That's a long time to wait for a little grocery money."

"John said he and his father both work there."

"They do now. Before all this happened, they only worked off and on. Their ridge running goes back a lot farther than the coal company does. The Harpers have been known for making prime whiskey for at least three generations on this mountain. And no one could ever catch them at it. Anyway, not until I came along."

A light dawned on Harlan and a flood of relief washed over him. "You mean all this—misunderstanding and hard feelings—is because you managed to stop a business that was illegal to begin with? You can't regret that." He reached for the coffee pot between them and refilled both their cups. "Not if it was the right thing to do."

"I'm not so sure it was, anymore," Tom replied. "And the truth is, if I had it to do over again, I wouldn't do it at all. It cost me the very thing I was doing it for. It cost me the Harpers themselves. And I loved them, Harlan. I loved every one of them! It cost me my honor, too."

"In their eyes, maybe," Harlan assured, "but not in principle. You can't have honor without principal. You taught me that, remember?"

"It was only half a lesson, son. Since then, I've learned you can never trade people for principle. It does something terrible to the very core of your being. It destroys you. Lias Harper offered me his undying trust and friendship, and—in the end— that's what I used against him."

"You did what you had to."

"I was deceived. And if I had as much trust in him as he had in me, I might have realized it in time. But back then I didn't take the time. There were too many lives to save and I wanted to save more of them. I thought I was God's answer to Cedar Creek—arrived in the flesh. I was going to take on the dragon of this town single-handed. And as far as I could see, it spent a good deal of its time with the Harpers."

"I didn't see any dragons tonight when I was there," Harlan offered. "I saw a normal caring family. So, you must have done something right. Whatever hard feelings they still have about it will probably disappear, too. Especially now that they've found other ways to make money."

"I doubt it. They didn't just lose their money. They lost..." He let his gaze wander to the ghostly reflections of themselves in the window. When he went on, it was like an undesirable recital he had been forced to commit to memory.

"One stormy night in the fall of 'thirty-three – just after I visited with you in Richmond that summer, Cedar Creek saw the biggest raid on any still these hills have ever known. Half the Harper clan either killed or drug off to the state penitentiary. It was a nightmare. Most stills that get busted up... just get busted up. The people usually get away and the ones that don't get fined, or a light sentence. But those Federal men had been after the Harpers for a long time."

"That doesn't make you responsible."

"I'm responsible. I'm the one that tipped them off on the location. I told myself it was my duty. The truth is I was just sick and tired of patching up gunshot wounds in kids, or setting bones because they went off some road running from the law. Tired of seeing them die, Harlan. Celia getting old before her time after losing one of her boys. Seth was a couple years younger than John, and older than Joseph Lee. Ran off a road and got pinned beneath the car... drowned in a couple feet of water. Such a senseless death! I was so sick and tired of senseless deaths!"

He shook his head as if to rid himself of the memory and pressed on. "I thought if the Harpers went straight, a lot of other families might follow. Lias is a good man basically. I thought if he had a little push—a little scare—he'd see the reason of it in the long run. Thought I'd get to him through his family because that's where his strongest feelings were. Well, that's what happened all right. Only the whole thing backfired. I never thought anyone would get killed!"

Tom got up, unable to stay still anymore, and began to pace back and forth between the table and the stove. "His father, a younger brother, an aunt and a couple of cousins… all dead in a mere few minutes. The law caught seven or eight of them down at the site and just started shooting. Lias was shot. Took a bullet in the back and it went through one of his lungs. So, later, when he took up work in the mines, again, with a lung that was weak already…"

Harlan sat quiet as the horrible scenario played through his mind.

"Joseph Lee was arrested."

"Joseph Lee? Why, he couldn't have been more than —"

"He was fifteen and a Harper. So, they arrested him. And Bonnie Rae…she was collecting firewood when the first shots came. Lias was close by. He picked her up and started to run but they shot him out from under her. She got away. There were too many others with serious warrants out on them to waste time going after a kid, and luckily, she was gone too quick to shoot."

He answered the shocked expression before Harlan even asked the question, "Yes, they shoot kids right along with the adults if they run off during a raid. Without many repercussions, I might add. Depends on how humane the officer in charge happens to be. Only I didn't know that then. When you look at it from a legal point of view, it's often the kids who take off and bring help back that leads to more killing on both sides. Rules of engagement, you might say, just like in a war. Anyway, that was the end of ridge running for the Harper Clan.

Some are still serving out time."

"What about Lias? If he's the leader, why didn't they keep him in?"

"They never caught Lias. Big John lived up to his name and managed to haul him off into some swamp nobody could follow him through. Brought him all the way back here with a bullet in his own belly at the same time. He was worse off than Lias, but so worried about his dad, he didn't tell me. Found him curled up in a corner, bleeding all over the floor when I finished with his father. God – I almost lost him!"

Tom sank down onto the chair once more, as if even the memory of it was enough to stagger him. "For a long time after that I kept expecting one of them to pull me off into the bushes somewhere and do me in. That's the way they handle things around here. I was pretty sure I'd end up another victim of their so-called mountain justice."

"Why did you stay here then, Tom? Why didn't you come home?"

"Because..." He put his elbows on the table and dropped his head in his hands. "Lias Harper's judgment was to let me be."

In all his growing up years, Harlan had never seen his uncle defeated, or known him to crumble under any one man's opinion of him. What kind of unearthly influence had come over him not to care if he lived or died, or ate or slept any more? This was not the Tom Bascomb he had always known. This emaciated shadow person sitting across from him didn't even look like the same man. And what was this eerie resignation to stay and take whatever the town of Cedar Creek saw fit to dole out to him?

Whatever Lias Harper doled out to him.

"All right, it's a tragedy – I can see that, Tom. I can feel the crushing weight of the thing just sitting across the table from you. But it was a tragic situation to begin with before you ever got here. Can't you see that, too? What makes this so different from any other awful thing you've been through? All those horrible war years! No deaths could be more senseless than Mother and Father's – they were innocent! You didn't give up then, Uncle – I'd be dead if you had! You kept going and you did right until we came out on the other side. Well, I think you did the right thing this time, too. It doesn't matter what anybody says. It doesn't even matter what he says. Lias Harper isn't God."

"Well, he might not be God but he's something." Tom answered the passionate outburst without even lifting his head. "Because I've been dying right along with him ever since."

Such hopeless resignation had a chilling effect on Harlan. It was like the helpless futility one felt when a drowning person lost hold on an outstretched hand and slipped silently back into the deep.

In sight, but still out of reach.

7

Harlan spent the next morning thinking, and tearing down the remnants of an old barn. He was relieved that what had first confronted him as a yard full of violent illogical disarray, was merely an unfinished improvement project that had turned daunting in respect to his Uncle's failing health. He could deal with that. He would have a new smaller one in place before school started.

He even felt confident in his ability to pour renewed vigor into Tom, since—in Harlan's opinion—it was his own neglect of himself that was causing most of it. No more skipping meals, even if he had to hire a cook. Things weren't as ominous as they had seemed last night. How could they be? It was a perfect Appalachian morning. The air was clear, the breeze was light, the sunshine brilliant and the temperature undetectable. He might have worked all day and got a good start on the place if he hadn't had another appointment to keep.

So, he cleaned up—no suit for a working day like today, only jeans and a blue cotton shirt with the sleeves rolled up. It was a little before noon when he set out for an old stone bridge that passed over Cedar Creek, about a mile down the road. Here he had arranged to meet the Harper children. Maybe Bonnie Rae would even come along. Last night, when arrangements were made, he had been hoping so. He wanted to see her, again.

He had known a lot of girls in Richmond and he certainly hadn't come to Cedar Creek looking for one. True, he had never met anyone he couldn't live without. And although he enjoyed such pastimes as dancing, and theater, or dinner with friends, he had always been careful to keep those relationships casual. He had to. He was going to a place where he could not bring anyone else along.

Now, this captivating Bonnie Rae Harper had crossed his path and stirred something inside him that had been silent for a long time. And she had been drawn to him, too. Now that he knew more about her, she had obviously known who he was from the very beginning and been influenced by Tom. Those mysterious looks and unspoken words between them began to take on new meaning. But where could it possibly go? After hearing the long terrible story last night, he couldn't see how it could become anything more than some sort of strange magnetic kinship they shared to the past and his own wonderful Aunt Melanie. No hopes of going farther, considering the circumstances.

Lias Harper might feel an obligation to approve his teaching status in Cedar Creek but that's all he would approve of. The volatile situation between the two families was still not over—Harlan could sense it. He also sensed that his uncle had left something out of the story.

Whatever it was, Harlan had no intention of standing idly by while Tom quietly destroyed himself over the thing. Whatever spell the people of Cedar Creek had cast over his uncle to allow it, was not going to happen to him. If Tom couldn't resolve his conflicts by the end of the school year, he must be convinced to live somewhere else.

Simply giving up was not an option Harlan was willing to accept. This was the twentieth century, not the dark ages. And in case Cedar Creek didn't know it, society no longer had to be a slave to superstitions, or potions, or even feuds that went on for generations. It was a new age of industry and invention, and—here in America, anyway—a person's life was their own to rule and not someone else's. They could waste it if they chose. Because that was their right, too. But no one reserved the right to waste it for them.

Harlan believed in these things.

Yet, looking down on the tumbling waters of Cedar Creek as they rushed under the bridge, and breathing in the intoxicating scent of pine mingled with warm earth, he felt a flash of contentment that was so intense he didn't want to let go of it. But it only moved through his soul like a gust of wind in the trees: gone as quickly as it came. What was that? Where had it come from? It had broken through his thoughts, scattered them, and they were not in the same order when he gathered them up, again.

Now, he felt torn between his compulsion to protect the only member of his own family he had left in the world and some other-worldly desire to step closer to the mystery of Bonnie Rae Harper. How could he be so double-minded all of a sudden?

Of course, the best thing to do was to keep his boundaries strictly within school duties until a sufficient amount of trust could be built. Whatever acceptance he might find here in Cedar Creek beyond that—especially with the Harpers—must be carefully and diligently worked out from there. And as for Bonnie Rae, she was seventeen.

In this part of the country, that was considered way past schooling age.

By the time he heard the excited chatter of young voices, he had fairly well made up his mind. But he couldn't have been more surprised if a flock of angels had come around the bend. The two younger children ran up to him with an open delight and Bonnie Rae's smile was even more lovely and inviting than he remembered. Not that he had ever been such a soft touch for everything beautiful. It wasn't the flowered skirt or lacy blouse that melted his former resolve as much as the fact that...

She was barefoot and carrying a picnic basket.

"Did you see it, Mr. Harlan?" Little Sam asked, breathing hard from his surge to get ahead of the others and be the first to tell. "That fancied up car at the Tolliver place? It's the traveling man's!"

"We got a traveling man, Mr. Harlan!" Jenny Beth fairly bounced with excitement and grasped him by the hand as naturally as so many others who had danced and skipped around him during a playground time. Her yellow braids were tied with red bows and she had a matching red apron over a flowered dress to keep it clean. "He's selling carrot pans but I don't think we need one."

"Not carrot pans, Jenny," Bonnie Rae came up beside them and looked directly at Harlan as she spoke. "Credit plans. Whatever that is. Howdy, Harlan."

"Hello." He smiled.

"Mr. Harlan," Jenny went suddenly serious, "Do you need one of them credit plans?"

"Not me." He matched her tone with equal importance." A credit plan lets people who can't really afford something, take it home anyway—pay a little money each month—and end up spending twice as much as it was worth to begin with."

"Land sakes!" Bonnie Rae's tone was skeptical. "A person would have to be nigh onto a fool to do something like that."

"Well, I'm sure that's not the way your traveling man will explain it," he conceded, "but it ends up that way."

"Ain't but a few half-wits in Cedar Creek," she mused, turning back to look down the road for a moment as if she could see her best friend, Ivy Tolliver, who was probably hearing the glories of such an idea even as they stood there. "I reckon if that's what he's selling, he sure ain't gonna sell much of it here."

She turned around again. "Been a time and a time since we had a traveling man this far back."

"You don't get many up here?" Harlan asked. "There's always one coming to your door, trying to sell you something, in the city."

"Traveling man come through last year, selling house lights," she remembered. "But he didn't get no farther than the Wind Ridge with them, on account of Orey Thompson thought he was a Republican and shot him in the leg."

"For being a Republican?" Now it was Harlan's turn to wonder.

"Just in the leg," she assured. "But I'll vow he'd have killed him plumb dead if he thought he was a union agent. These hills ain't safe for strangers. Specially ones that don't let folks know right quick what they're here for."

"Are we going to the schoolhouse, or ain't we?" Little Sam objected, as he hitched up a loose strap of overalls across his brown bare shoulder. "I want to pick out my desk today!"

"Well, we best get going, then," Bonnie Rae prompted. "Rafe and Lou Ellen had to help the McCords with their sugar harvest, but I reckon we four can take care of about anything we find out there. You younguns lead the way on account of Mr. Harlan ain't never been to the schoolhouse before."

It was the only encouragement they needed to take off down the road with a happy enthusiasm. Harlan watched them for a moment and then reached for the picnic basket. "I was thinking I should probably send you back," he said to Bonnie Rae. "I wouldn't want to be any more of a burden to your family than we've already been."

"I seen right off you talked to the Doc," she replied. "You want me to go back, Harlan?"

"I don't want to make any trouble for you."

"I've had trouble ever since I can remember. You know, Harlan, we ain't had a government teacher that stayed since old Mrs. Farnsby had to move into town three years ago. Last year, they couldn't get no one to come out at all. These youn-guns..." She looked up the road after them rather than into Harlan's eyes as she continued. "They're away behind in their learning. I just can't think of anybody on the Creek wouldn't do whatever they could to help out a new teacher. Just so he'd stay."

"I'm not going to stay, Bonnie Rae," he confessed. "I'm just here for this year. And to try and find someone local who could take the position when I'm gone. The school board thought a local person might have better luck in Cedar Creek than... foreigners."

The look of disappointment that came over her was so obvious that he felt sorry for having told her so bluntly. He had a sudden, incredible urge to touch her—to soften things in some way—which he could only avoid by setting the picnic basket down and turning away for a few moments.

"Would they let you stay if you wanted?" she asked.

"I'm scheduled to open a refugee school on the Burmese border."

"Oh, no, Harlan—" Her tone held the same sort of dread he expected to confront in Tom when the time came to tell it to him. "Not back in China!"

"But it's in a war zone, now, and the paperwork was delayed. September rolls around and I have to teach somewhere. Tom's the only family I have and I wanted to see him before I left. Then when he wrote and told me about the job, here, all doors opened up for me to take it. An answer to prayer, really."

He turned back to her and said, "You see, I love school and children. I have to teach. I especially like teaching in difficult places where no one else wants to be. It's the challenge, maybe, or just being needed. I don't know." He shrugged his shoulders in a gesture of apology. "Anyway, I thought it was time to be honest. Especially under these circumstances. I didn't come here to cause trouble for anybody. Certainly not for you."

"Do you want me to go back, Harlan?" she asked again.

"It isn't fair to put it that way."

"Ain't fair not to, if I'm gonna rightly judge. You just said it was time to be honest. Best be honest all the way."

Harlan had the fleeting sensation that a judgment was

something that held a lot of importance in Cedar Creek, and—whatever the verdict—would probably be final. So, he hesitated. Two months ago he had sat comfortably in an opera house in Richmond, dressed in a suit and tie, in the company of the daughter of one of the wealthiest families in Virginia. But other than a pleasant evening, he had not felt compelled to carry things further. Now, this seventeen-year-old country girl had him second-guessing himself. Yet, she was more than that. As uncanny as it seemed, he felt almost as if—

"Tell me what you're thinking, right now," she said after the silence, "and that'll do."

"I'm thinking you can see right through me but you just want to hear me say it," he replied. "I'm trying to do the right thing for everybody, Bonnie Rae, and you're not making it any —"

"Hey!" Little Sam called back to them from across the bridge. "Are you coming, or ain't you?"

Harlan picked up the basket, again. "We're coming!" he called. When he turned back to Bonnie Rae, she didn't move.

"All right." He laughed and put an arm across her shoulders as he began walking. When she didn't resist but fell pleasantly into step with him, he gave in to the urge to let it linger a moment longer and say, "I was thinking you have the prettiest green eyes, and the loveliest hair, and wondering how we've managed to stir up such close feelings in so a short time. Is that honest enough?"

"Wonderful honest."

"Enough for you to rightly judge?" he persisted.

"Are you teasing me, Harlan? Making fun at the words I said?"

"Never," he assured. "Especially after I've heard you speak French like an aristocrat with absolutely no accent at all. Not that I've known that many, I just happen to have been partly raised by one."

She laughed. "You looked like you were seeing things when I done that!"

"I was."

"I had an idea who you were when you first spoke it. But it wasn't till I heard you talk to Mr. Farnsby I was certain sure. Then I couldn't quit looking. Because… well, I feel like I've known you since my young days, Harlan. Not you, now. But when you were a youngun. Back when I was that age, too. Way back then."

"Tom told you a few stories, I suppose."

"He told me some. But only after I found a Kodak picture tucked away in one of the books he let me read. I thought you were his son, on account of you had the same eyes. He said it was the only thing that kept you from dying of sheer fright when he first come and got you, on account of your mother had them kind of eyes, too."

"Did he tell you why?"

"Just that you seen soldiers do a lot of bad things and been running and hiding for nigh onto a year. Said you must've thought he was another soldier, too, the way he came charging up the hill to the village on some horse like one. I reckon he wanted everyone to know he meant business, if you really were there."

"He meant business, all right. He scared the daylights out of everybody."

"He also said you were about the stubbornest boy he ever made acquaintance with. Just hauling you back to France all that way was a chore. Had to force food down your throat, too, even though you was starved to skin and bone by then."

"The old woman I was staying with said he paid a lot of money for me—probably for eating. So, I shouldn't let him fatten me. That if I worked my hardest, he might keep me alive to do all his chores."

"Land sakes! What a thing to tell a youngun! I'll vow—I never heard that part of it before."

"I'd guess it was because you probably weren't much past a youngun yourself when he was telling it and he would agree with you. He didn't know it, either, until about a year later when I let it slip to my Aunt Melanie. But by that time, she had won me over. Took a while longer to convince me of the uncle, though. He kept squeezing my arm to see if I was gaining weight, yet. Later I realized it was from the doctor's point of view and not a connoisseur's. Then again…"

He answered her startled expression at the use of the word with a teasing wink. "He worked me quite hard when I was growing up, so, who's to say the old woman couldn't have been right as well?"

"Law! Before the raid, there wasn't a mean bone in that man's body! Why, he wouldn't any more scare a youngun than —"

"I saw one last night who seemed pretty scared of him."

"That's on account of Lil' Sam's too young to know anything about the Doc except booger tales and haint stories. Jesse Tolliver don't want kids running around them woods because he's got a still hid back up in there. And I'll vow if he did hear Doc talking hoodoo, it weren't nothing but French!"

"I thought the same thing when he said that. But then the way everyone got so quiet every time the subject of my uncle came up, I decided to leave the discussion to the rest of you. How is it, you didn't straighten things out if you were so sure about it?"

"None of us ain't so much as breathed his name in our house till you come along, last night, Harlan. It goes too hard on my daddy. And everyone else, too."

"Which is why I thought it better to keep things, between us, within the school for a while, Bonnie Rae. At least until people get to know me for myself around here."

"Well, that's where we're headed, ain't it?"

"If it is, why do I get the feeling you're trying to pull me in another direction altogether?"

Now, she was quiet, as if the tables had suddenly turned and he was looking into her thoughts in the same way she had so uncannily looked into his. She retreated back into the safety of her mountain shyness and fixed her eyes on the road ahead of them.

He switched to French, again. *"It isn't fair to stop in the middle of the game, dearest. Did I not share my true feelings with you? Let me hear your judgment, then, as well. What did you decide?"*

"*I decided to leave the past to the past,*" she replied in the same. Then she added in that distinctive Elizabethan English that was beginning to sound more like music to him, "I ain't never seen a light come over the ridge like yours, Harlan. I reckon I'd just like to walk in it for a spell." The words swept through him with another startling wave of sweet sensation.

It was the most beautiful thing anyone had ever said to him.

8

It took nearly an hour to get to the schoolhouse. The two young children played and collected things along the way while Harlan talked literature and history with Bonnie Rae. He switched off and on again to French, though he soon slipped into the habit of calling her *chère*—the French version of dear—even when they were speaking English. He marveled at how she never missed a beat, slipping just as easily from one to the other, and taking as much pleasure in it as he did. It was only at any mention of the raid that she faltered and seemed unwilling to speak about anything other than her earliest recollections of the doctor. Not that dreadful night of betrayal.

Harlan let it go.

At the end of the woods a large open meadow stretched out before them, and in the far corner stood a long rectangular building with windows boarded up. The play yard behind it was overgrown with blackberry bushes, holly, dogwood and fern. There were traces of sassafras, grapevine and sumac, and beyond that—stretching all the way to the river—stood a grove of white pine and hemlock.

"The old Farnsby place is a little ways up the river from here," said Bonnie Rae. "It used to be a sugar farm until Mr. Farnsby died back in the War. Now, nobody lives there."

"Any relation to the postmaster back in Cedarville?" Harlan asked.

"His daddy," she replied. "But him and old Mrs. Farnsby live in town now and the place is set aside for the government teacher. You could live there if you took a notion,but it's a big old place that would take a heap of work to fix up. Not much worth if a person was only gonna stay one year." She looked up at him and sighed. "So, I reckon it'll be turning into another haint before too long."

A haint?"

"A hainted place with ghosts and the like," she explained. "Probably when old Mrs. Farnsby dies."

Harlan was about to venture an objection but remembering Big John's remarks about ghosts and witching nights, thought better of it.

"Other than that," Bonnie Rae started across the meadow, moving her hands against the waist high grass before she walked through to scare any snakes away, "there ain't nothing else for miles around. Still, it's plumb in the middle of Cedar Creek, considering how far the younguns have to walk from the other way."

"Well," he replied, "let's see what a year of standing empty has done to it."

First, they took the boards off the windows to let the light and fresh air inside. Then Harlan began to absorb the atmosphere of the little school. He had five years of teaching behind him: the last two running a small school in one of the poorer sections of Richmond. But from the moment he entered the dusty one room cabin, a different sort of awareness began to stir in him.

Something was different here.

Everything within the four walls looked like it came out of another century altogether. There was a black potbellied stove at the back of the room to give heat in the wintertime, and the walls were lined with desks that had been put there long ago— maybe to make room for some community activity. The desks were old, made of wood on the top and black wrought iron for the legs, cast in fancy flower designs. He put his hand to the smooth, worn surface of one that was nearby and noticed letters just above the inkwell that had been carved with a pocketknife. Calvin sat here. The letter "a" was backwards.

When he asked Bonnie Rae how long the schoolhouse had been there, she didn't know, except to say her father and grandfather had attended. There were several shelves lining the back wall, filled with books, most of them old and worn. In the bottom drawer of the teacher's desk, he discovered a grade book which had entries from eighteen sixty-three.

The past was only a breath away from him. Within these walls he could sense the very heartbeat of a culture that time seemed to have overlooked. He found last year's records— what there were of them. They were incomplete since the school only remained open for two months into the year. There were eighteen students registered. Mostly girls.

Why eighteen? He had been told there were anywhere from fifty to seventy school age children on the ridge. So few of them took the bus into Cedarville that the rural route had been stopped altogether. But if they were not here, where were they?

A sudden vision of the coal pit two miles to the north came to his mind but he quickly dismissed the possibility. There were laws against things like that. He had been told there was a company school nearby, in a place called Coaltown. Perhaps some of them attended there. It was one of the first things he would look into.

"I already know my numbers, Mr. Harlan," said Jenny Beth as she retrieved a box of crayons from one of the shelves in the back. "And pert nigh all my letters, too. I'm gonna write some out for Lil Sam. Want to see?"

"I sure do." He gave one of her braids a playful tug as she passed by. "And when you're done, you can both draw me a picture so I can guess what your favorite colors are."

"You gonna whup all the biggest boys the first day, Mr. Harlan?" Little Sam slipped into a desk beside his sister. Even though it was a smaller one, his feet still didn't touch the floor.

"Think I'll have to?"

Yep," the little boy replied.

While Harlan had been busy with other things, Bonnie Rae had swept the floor and dusted. She and the children had arranged the desks into neat rows, and now everyone was settling into something quiet. Harlan looked over after a while to find them absorbed in Bonnie Rae's telling of some familiar story he had heard repeatedly in his own youth and it suddenly occurred to him why they felt so kindred to each other. She had been influenced by the same man, at the same critical time in her youth, as he had been, and that man had somehow been a shelter for her. Even as he had been for Harlan.

"Is that true, Mr. Harlan?" Jenny Beth suddenly broke into his thoughts. "Have you really seen the learning tree in the old world that story talks about – and do you have a Kodak picture to prove it?"

"I do. If you like, I'll bring it to class when school starts and show it to you."

"Awww, how'd you know it was even the same one?" Little Sam was skeptical. "Might be it was just something a teacher made up so's you'd remember all them hero names. You didn't hear any ghosty sounds, did you?"

"I didn't hear one sound from any of those black-hearts that said no Scottish child was to be given a decent education," he replied. "But the names of every hero who learned from whatever soul who was brave enough to teach under its branches, still ring in my heart to this day."

"Law!" Jenny Beth breathed.

"Considering it's been more than a couple hundred years since all that passed by," Bonnie Rae added, "That'd be proof enough for me that it was real."

"You know we got a learning tree in Cedar Creek, too, Mr. Harlan?" Jenny Beth informed him. "It's how come Sam and I know how to read and write, already, and Rafe has the gift for Latin."

"The gift for Latin?" Harlan asked.

"All them scientific names," Bonnie Rae explained with a confidential wink over the tops of their heads. "They're in Latin. Rafe's got them memorized like he was reading straight out of a book. But don't nobody but old Mrs. Farnsby put much store in such things around here. She even told Daddy she'd take him in at her house if he'd let Rafe attend the high school down to Cedarville. Just so's he wouldn't end up in the pit along with every other—" She stopped short, as if she had suddenly said too much.

"Did he go?" Harlan asked.

"Daddy don't hold to having the family split apart," she replied uneasily. "Said if he was to allow that, next thing he'd be wanting was to get clean off the mountain to go to some college."

"How does Rafe feel about it?"

"He mourned over it some but it's passed now."

"What do you think?" came the next question.

"I think he might get Daddy to think on it again after these hard times are gone. Daddy's of a mind things are hard all over —not just in Cedar Creek—and it's best to stick by family during such times."

"They have been hard all over," Harlan agreed. "But those with an education have a lot better chance of getting a good job than those who don't have one. Because first you have to know something up here." He pointed to his forehead, "before you can feel anything with conviction in here." He put a hand over his heart.

"Could be he might listen to you, Harlan," Bonnie Rae's voice turned hopeful. "I'm sure he don't want to see Rafe's gift swallowed up in them coal pits any more than he did seeing Big John go down there. Or even Joseph Lee."

"How about you? Would you like to go to college?"

"Law—he wouldn't spend such money on a girl child, even if he had it to spend."

"There are scholarships."

"Wouldn't do no good, either, since he thinks girls don't belong no place but home. Nope." She went to where the picnic basket sat and whisked it up as she headed for the door. "Seems my kind's gotta be content with just reading any book I can get my hands on and teaching younguns under trees. Anybody hungry, yet?"

"I am!" Little Sam sang out and leapt up to follow her outside.

Harlan slowly closed the grade book he had been thumbing through and got to his feet. "Coming, Jenny?" he asked the little girl who was still seated at the desk with a crayon in her hand, looking after them with a sad sort of longing.

"She can still be a hero, though – can't she, Mister Harlan? 'Cause she done taught us all how to read and write under the tree!"

"Of course she can, honey." He held his hand out to her as he passed by and she slid down from her desk to take it. "Anyone can be a hero if they want to be."

She sighed with a childlike contentment and skipped along beside him as they walked outside.

They sat beneath one of the nearest tall pines. Jenny Beth picked at her food, though she ate every bite of the "sass cake," —a spicy and delicious gingerbread made with applesauce. Little Sam ate as if he had never eaten before. It wasn't long before the two of them ran off to enjoy the play yard. Harlan sat back against the tree and rested a forearm on one drawn up knee. He felt pleasantly relaxed from the vigorous day. He could hear bees buzzing in nearby clover, and the musical sound of the children as they played.

"Will you tell me something?" he ventured as Bonnie Rae put the picnic things away. "Don't answer if you don't want to. But there's something I'd like to know and you're the only one I can ask."

"It's about the raid, I reckon," she replied uncomfortably.

"Afterward, actually. You see, I can't figure out what keeps Tom here. Four years is a long time. But to him it's like yesterday. Doesn't eat enough, barely sleeps. I hardly recognized him, last night. Seems the tables have reversed between us in some bizarre way and now he's the one who's starving himself down to skin and bones. Why…" There was no easy way to put it, so he said the first thing that came to him. "Why did your father let him stay?"

The look Bonnie Rae turned on him went beyond a girl of seventeen. Once again, Harlan had the fleeting sensation that she was judging—deciding what she would or wouldn't tell him—whether or not she could trust him. Then all at once he realized she was shielding him as much as he was trying to shield her.

"Live, then." He changed the word so there would be no misunderstandings. "Why did he let him live after all that?"

"Some say it's because he seen the light." She looked away from him and out across the meadow as she spoke. "And that's true. Traveling preacher come through not long after. Set up here in the schoolhouse meadow for camp meeting, just like usual. Only that year the revival came and my daddy seen the light. He's been a changed man ever since."

"How changed?" Harlan asked.

"Oh…" She sighed and thought for a moment. "He don't lose his temper near so much as he used to. He keeps the commandments. And he don't hate no more."

"Tom, you mean?"

"Oh, no. He never hated the Doc. That's the trouble, he…" She cast him an uncertain glance and then looked away quickly from the intense gaze that met hers. "You see my daddy stands on his word, Harlan. He's something like the law out here in Cedar Creek. You wouldn't think it to look on him now. But he is."

"Still?"

"Yep. He's been quietsome the last four years, on account of grief, mostly. It nigh onto killed him, grieving so. It would have if the traveling preacher hadn't come by so quick and he got born again. We—all of us—got born again that week. Except for Joseph Lee. He's the only one left of us still seething over it. But Daddy keeps him in line."

"What kept Tom alive before the revival?" Harlan persisted. "What kept him from this mountain justice he keeps talking about? It's like he's still waiting for it. As if dying might somehow pay for those lost lives."

The thought startled her. "My daddy would never let anybody lay a hand on the Doc!" she insisted, then. "A life for a life, he says—and he don't never take back his word, no matter what comes after. We didn't know it was the Doc brought the laws down. Not till after."

"A life for a life." Harlan breathed the ancient words and felt the impact of them to the very depths of his being.

"It was because he give us back Johnny!" The words tumbled out suddenly then and were filled with an emotion he wasn't prepared for. As if some mental door had come unhinged in her mind and the spilling could not be stopped. "After he was—gut shot—in the raid —"

"Bonnie Rae—" Harlan reached out a hand to keep her from going on but she was too caught up in the horrors of the memory to even notice.

"Everybody was dead and I followed Johnny! None of us knew he was shot. He just said, help Daddy – help Daddy! And afterwards, Johnny was—there was blood all over the floor! Doc poured his own blood into him to keep him alive —because Daddy lost too much, already. Everyone was crying—Johnny and Doc—and even Daddy! Then Johnny quit breathing! Daddy said he was dead—just like when Seth died—I thought I'd go crazy! We was all crazy —"

She covered her eyes with her hands as if it were all happening again right in front of her and she didn't want to see. "But Doc wouldn't quit! He breathed his own breath into him! Then he cried and he hollered—live—live! There was blood all over the floor, and I— "

"Don't say anymore, *chère*.." He ran a comforting hand over her hair but she was oblivious to it.

"No—not Johnny! Then he—he breathed, again! It was a miracle! And we saw it! That's why Daddy wouldn't let nobody lay a hand to him, because he—" For a moment she covered her eyes with the back of her hand. "He said God must love that man! He must—love—that—man! So, don't nobody touch him!"

Then all at once she was on her feet and running toward the trees.

Harlan stood up and started after her but had gone only few steps when he felt a small hand pulling back on him from behind.

"Don't, Mr. Harlan," Jenny Beth pleaded, having appeared seemingly out of nowhere. "She don't like for no one to see her bawl like that."

It was all he could do to comply.

He played with the children for a while after that, pushing them half-heartedly on the swing and helping them pick the last of the summer blackberries. But the thought of Bonnie Rae, crying off in the woods somewhere over something he should never have brought up, distracted him and made him feel miserable. It was getting late by the time she finally appeared on the edge of the meadow, and Harlan started across to meet her.

"Law—we got to be getting back!" She avoided his eyes as she passed him. "If we don't get home before supper, we'll—"

He caught her arm as she passed by and brought her back to him, in much the same manner he would an errant student. "I was worried about you. Why did you stay away so long? It's almost dark."

"I went too far, I reckon," she replied. "God almighty, now we'll have to take the shortcut home!" She tugged at him but he would neither follow nor let go of her. "Come on, Harlan. If you get me in trouble the first time out, I'll have to go through fire to see you again!"

At the same time the remark startled, the open unwavering

declaration—coupled with the relief that she was herself, again—melted any more thought about reprimands. Instead he pulled her into an embrace, held her close for a moment, and whispered how sorry he was to have made her cry that way.

And even though she deftly slipped away and chided, "Them younguns don't miss a thing, and they tell everything they see!" the walk back was more charged with intense feelings between them than when they had started.

The shortcut led to a long suspension bridge that swayed nearly a hundred feet above the Cedar River rapids. In Harlan's opinion, it looked far too old to be safe. But Bonnie Rae swept up Little Sam and started across, sidestepping the gaping holes left by missing boards as if they were nothing more than cracks in her own kitchen floorboards.

He followed after her with Jenny Beth. The little girl reached up to him with an eager anticipation when he lifted her and squealed delightedly every time the bridge swayed beneath them. A few minutes later, they were swallowed up in the shadow of deep woods, and an eerie silence settled over the small group. Harlan attributed it to the long day until Jenny Beth hung back, took hold of Bonnie Rae's hand, and held on tight to Little Sam with the other. They all moved closer to him and Harlan felt Bonnie Rae take hold of his arm.

"What's wrong with everybody?" he asked.

"We're coming to the Weaver's cottage!" the littlest girl answered in a half whisper. "We got to pass by real quiet, and if she talks to you, don't say nothing back! Don't look at her, neither!"

"Why not?"

"Because she's a —"

"Shhh!" Bonnie Rae stepped up her pace.

The "cottage", when it came into view, was nothing more than a rather dilapidated run down shack, with no visible signs of life inside. They passed by quickly and solemnly, though Harlan would have liked to see the individual who had commanded such an eerie respect from them all. After a few more yards of silence for the sake of safety, Jenny Beth sang out, "We're almost there!" and dashed off ahead of them with Little Sam still in tow.

"I reckon you think we're all a bunch of scare babies." Bonnie Rae sighed and let go of his arm. "But that Weaver, she —"

"I wouldn't mind if this whole trail was lined with weaver's cottages," he interrupted, "if it would keep you holding onto me that way."

"Law—that's a awful thought!" She cast a wary glance back over her shoulder. "Ain't nothing to make fun of, Harlan—she'll witch you for certain if you do!"

"Being witched doesn't bother me half as much as crossing that old bridge. Do the children use it very often? All those missing pieces, somebody could get killed if they weren't careful."

"Most don't on account of the Weaver. She can make the wind blow, so it will dance. Then it ain't safe for nobody. Saves a heap of time coming this way, though. See that fork in the trail up there? Cedar River Road just past it. Comes out right above the stone bridge."

"When will I see you again?"

"Well, there's a sugar party at Aaron McCord's Saturday night."

"Who's Aaron McCord?"

"He's a good friend of Joseph Lee's. They hunt together."

"Bonnie Rae, I can't just impose on some young person's dance party. That would be worse than showing up for dinner unannounced."

"Law—Aaron ain't no young person!" She giggled at the thought and slipped her arm through his, again. "He's nigh onto seventy. Or, maybe he is already. He's the best tracker in these parts. J-Lee's been tagging after him since he was a youngun. Now there don't seem to be much difference between them two at all when it comes to ranging from one end of this mountain to the other. Aaron's just getting his crop in and it's everybody's party when there's sugar to pull. Work parties about the only kind of party you'll find around these parts any more but they're fun all right. I'll tell Joseph Lee to have him invite you if you'd like that better, though."

"Better than being mistaken for a union agent."

A far off "chick-a-dee-dee-dee" sounded from the deep woods behind them. It was twilight, and the light filtering down through the trees was fading fast. Too fast, Harlan thought.

"You'll like Aaron, he's a friend of the Doc's, too. He wouldn't even mind —"

The familiar blast of a horn sounded in the road ahead and a booming voice bellowed, "Hey—what are you younguns doing out here by yourselves this late?"

"Thunder and hail—that's Big John and my daddy!" Bonnie Rae pulled quickly away from Harlan's as they rounded the bend.

The truck, with its headlights casting a yellow glow over the dirt road ahead, had pulled to a stop at the side of the road. The driver's side door was open and Big John was helping the children into the back. His face was so black with coal dust beneath the denim cap that it reminded Harlan of a theater minstrel.

"I want to sit up front with Daddy—" Little Sam complained, "and tell him about my desk!"

"Daddy's tired tonight, boy." His brother lifted him over the side and reached down for Jenny Beth. "He don't need you jumping all over him in the front seat, now. You can tell him when we get home."

"Wait for Bonnie Rae!" Jenny Beth shouted when he started to climb back into the truck.

Big John turned around in time to see his other sister and Harlan walking toward them from the woods. "Hey, Harlan." he called with a friendly wave. "You don't look too much worse for wear!"

"I'm still here, anyway."

"Well, that's a start, ain't it? You coming along home with

us?"

Bonnie Rae's face brightened.

"Not tonight, thanks," Harlan replied. "I've got to be getting back." He moved closer a few steps and looked into the truck's dark interior. "Evening, Mr. Harper."

"Harlan," the older man said coolly as he struck a match and touched it to a freshly rolled cigarette. For a few moments the brief glow illuminated the haggard black face and went out again. "Get in the truck, Bonnie Rae."

9

The house was dark and quiet when Joseph Lee opened the window in the loft room and returned to his bed. The heat in this upper part of the house seemed stifling. He stretched himself out on top of the blanket and let the refreshing night breezes sweep over him. He had just folded his hands under his head and began to think about things when he heard the squeak of bedsprings across the room and watched Rafe get up. In the dark all Joseph Lee could see of him was a shadowy form with a bush-like appearance where his hair was sticking up. The boy shuffled sleepily across the room and reached for the window.

"Hey," Joseph Lee said quietly, "leave it open."

"I ain't enjoying getting my backside chilled, J-Lee," his brother complained.

"You're gonna have a problem the other way around if you don't leave it alone."

"Shut the window!" Big John growled from the bed on the far side of the room.

Joseph Lee muttered a low curse as he got to his feet, snatched the pillow and quilt from his bed and started for the door.

"Boy," Rafe taunted, "I'd like to hear you say that when

Daddy —"

Joseph Lee stopped the youth in mid-sentence with a sudden forceful swing of his pillow as he went by and stepped out into the hall. He paused long enough to slip into the jeans he had grabbed from a hook by the door, and made his way quietly down the stairway, pulling the dangling suspenders up over his long sleeved underwear shirt. When he passed the girls' room he heard Bonnie Rae call softly to him from inside. He turned the latch and stuck his head in.

"What do you want?" he whispered.

"Come in for a minute," she whispered back. "I got a favor to ask."

He left the quilt and pillow in the hallway, slipped inside, closed the door and leaned against it. "What kind?"

The moonlight was fairly bright coming through the window but he could only see the vague outline of her hair against the pillow as she spoke. "I was wondering could you invite Harlan to the sugar party Saturday night. But don't let on to nobody it was my idea."

"Ain't you being a little hasty?" he asked. "Fun's fun but you best be careful chasing after a foreigner."

"I like him, J-Lee."

His eyes drifted to the window, where the night breeze was gently moving the edges of a honeysuckle branch against the pane. The window was open a little and he could smell the sweet fragrance— and just faintly—a damp earth smell that rose from the bog hollow five miles away, coming on the wind... fresh, invigorating, and calling to him.

"All the trouble Elliot Brown and Ben Sutton have gone to get your attention," he finally replied, "and you're mooning over Harlan after one day." He came over to the end of her bed and sat down.

"I ain't mooning." She moved her feet beneath the covers to give him space. "Ben Sutton's a lazy, good-for-nothing, and Elliot Brown ain't hardly more than a boy. Harlan's a fine man, J-Lee, even if he is a foreigner. Will you ask him?"

He put a hand through the open space of the window next to her and lifted it enough to reach out and snap off a blossom. "He's kin to the Doc, Bonnie Rae," he said. "Don't that mean nothing to you?"

"It ain't like he could help it. And you seen yourself how winning he is, else you wouldn't have invited him home with us in the first place."

"I seen he was good looking and you wanted to get to know him, that's what I seen. If I'd known you was gonna swoon —"

"Joseph Lee!"

"I admit I liked him all right," he relented. "But I ain't about to traipse up to that no-good turncoat's place and ask could I talk to Harlan, if that's what you're getting at. I just ain't gonna do it."

"You could ask Aaron to."

"I could. But then what are you gonna do about —" Lou Ellen stirred and turned over in the bed across the room, and they were both quiet for a few moments until her breathing became steady, again. "What are you gonna do about Daddy?" he whispered.

"Seems to me Daddy liked him enough."

"That's when he was company. Or when he's teaching the younguns their ABCs. But you ask what he thinks about you setting your sights on him—shoot, that's a different story, baby. And you know who's gonna catch fire when he finds out it was me helped you do it. He's looking to catch me at the back of whatever goes wrong around here, anyway."

"Lord almighty—I ain't asking you to stand up for me, Joseph Lee—I'm asking you to get him there! I reckon anything comes from it, I can handle, myself."

"I'll get him there," he sighed.

She settled happily back down under the covers, again. "Thanks, J-Lee."

"Well, it ain't because I approve." He slid the window open wide and climbed through. He dropped gently onto the soft earth below and said, "It's on account of any time you try and handle things, yourself, you get us both in a heap of trouble."

"Joseph Lee Harper..." She leaned out after him as he turned to leave. "Where you going this time of night?"

"Someplace where I can breathe without too much trouble," he replied. "Or get talked into it."

10

When Saturday arrived, Celia Harper sat in the living room braiding her youngest daughter's long blonde hair in the early evening. The setting sun poured in through the front window and bathed them in a golden light. It made Celia's tired face look soft and beautiful. There were wisps of golden curls that had pulled free from the rest of her pinned back hair and sitting next to Jenny Beth, the two looked strikingly alike.

Lias watched them from across the room with an affectionate gaze. "You want to go along tonight, Darlin?"

"Ain't no fun without you, Lias," his wife replied. "Another time, maybe."

"I reckon it's about time I went. Before my best girl forgets how to dance."

She looked up in surprise. "Do you mean it?"

Her husband nodded. "I been doing a lot of thinking, Ceely, and I figure it's time we Harpers start living, again."

"What if..." She paused to think of a careful way to say what was on her mind.

"I ain't gonna cause no trouble. If we're gonna lay down the past, I figure we best get on with it and lay it down."

"He ain't been to no play-parties or holiday feasts, anyway, Lias," she assured. "And it would be a pure pleasure to go. I'll vow, he probably won't even be there."

"He keeps to himself, all right," he replied with a tired

sigh. "Always does."

There was the sound of a car motor and two short blasts of a horn, and Lias looked out the window to where Joseph Lee was chopping wood in the front yard. It was just in time to see a shining, black and white DeSoto pass by, driven by a man in a white suit with a flashy hat to match. Joseph Lee's sweetheart, Ivy Tolliver, sat next to him on the front seat, her loose dark curls blowing wildly in the convertible's open air.

She waved gaily at him as they passed and shouted, "Meet you at the party, J-Lee!" as if they had never made arrangements to go together.

There was a thundering curse that echoed all around with an incriminating clarity. Lias got to his feet. He started across the room at the same time Joseph Lee called out to him from the porch. The screen door flew open with a bang and the two met face to face in the center of the room. Lias, seeing his son meet him straight on without flinching, softened at the sight of the turmoil he saw on the handsome face.

"Did you see that?" Joseph Lee demanded fiercely. "Sitting right next to that good-for-nothing traveling man!"

"Might be she just wanted a ride in that fancy car," Lias offered.

Another anguished swear escaped him.

"Watch your mouth, boy, you got women and children, here."

"Well, I'm gonna put an end to this right now!" He turned on his heel and was halfway out the door when Lias called after him.

"Leave the truck."

"Awww, Daddy —"

"Either walk off that temper or stay and go with the rest of us."

"I'm walking."

The screen door slammed again and Rafe nearly collided with his angry brother on his way up the steps. "Finish chopping the kindling," Joseph Lee snapped.

"We got enough," he argued.

His brother grabbed the front of his shirt and nearly raised him off his feet. "You chop kindling or chew grass, boy!"

"I'll chop it, J-Lee —" the younger boy cowered. "I'll chop!"

Joseph Lee let him go and continued across the yard with eyes still flashing like thunder. Rafe rubbed his throat and waited until his brother was out of ear shot before muttering, "Could at least have some respect for a feller's next-to-best shirt!"

The McCord farm was aglow with paper lanterns by the time Joseph Lee got there and the big gray barn was already crowded with people. Children ran in and out of the darkness, laughing and enjoying the freedom, while the teenagers milled around outside, talking in small groups. There were great vats of maple syrup being boiled down for sugar and a few kettles that had been taken off the fire at taffy stage, cooling and waiting to be pulled. Small bowls were set on long tables pushed against the walls so that the younger children could enjoy themselves making candy-balls.

The women were laying other tables with all kinds of good things to eat and slapping hands that reached too early. The men clustered toward the back of the barn, talking and smoking. A crowd had gathered inside by the time the Harpers arrived and a sudden uncomfortable hush settled over everyone as soon as they saw Lias.

"We don't want any trouble here," said an old man who was seated on a bench against the wall. "Don't bring it here."

"Awww, you can set easy, Uncle Rory," Lias said with a friendly pat to the old man's shoulder. "I done left my troubles at home."

Aaron McCord, a wiry man with a gray beard and an unusually young twinkle in his brown eyes, came up and offered Lias his hand. "I'm God-proud to see you, Lias," he said warmly. "You, too, Ceely."

"Hey, Lias–" someone shouted, "did you bring your fiddle?"

"I shore did," he smiled.

"Well, bring it on up here, then, and let's get this party started!"

Bonnie Rae left an apple salad and a plate of sliced ham on the food table and wandered off to get a better view of who was there: or who wasn't. Lou Ellen spotted a friend and ran to show her the new dress Bonnie Rae had made for her from the pattern-pieces that had come all the way from New York. Little Sam and Jenny went back outside to join the "play party" games in the yard, and Big John Harper took the truck into Cedarville to pick up Sarah Wesley, whom everyone expected him to marry one of these days. She was a shy, soft-spoken girl from town whose family owned the hardware store.

Harlan Fleming was nowhere to be seen.

Bonnie Rae wandered around the yard beneath a cloud of disappointment. She was wearing a pale, yellow dress printed with small white flowers, and her rich coppery hair was tied back with a matching ribbon. Just when she was about to return to the barn she noticed a group of children clustered around someone beneath a large sycamore tree. She started across the grass and began to hear snatches of conversation as she came near.

"Are you gonna make us read every day, and cipher, too?" a black haired boy inquired.

"Probably," Harlan answered. "But whatever we do, I'm sure you can adjust."

"Just about what?" asked a small, curly-headed girl.

"Get along," the city teacher corrected himself. "I'm sure he'll get along no matter what we do."

"He bessen," she replied, "or I expect you'll whup him black and blue."

Harlan saw a flash of yellow out of the corner of his eye and looked up as Bonnie Rae approached. "Hello, Miss Harper." He smiled as she walked up to them. "You look pretty this evening." Then turning back to the children, "Should I ask her to dance?"

A delighted chorus of assent went up and someone whispered, "Bonnie Rae's gonna dance with the new teacher!"

"I'm right glad you came, Harlan," she said as they walked back across the yard.

"I wouldn't have missed it for anything," he replied.

They could hear the music as they neared the big barn and Bonnie Rae recognized her father's rendition of "Cotton Eyed Joe" even though there were a number of other instruments playing along.   Joseph Lee was at the door, his face still clouded with dark emotion.

"Evening, Joseph Lee," Harlan said amiably

"Hey, Harlan.   Daddy's up on the box, Bonnie Rae, better watch yourself. You seen Ivy anywhere out there?"

"No," his sister replied, "Are you sure she ain't inside?"

"I'm sure. That good-for-nothing stranger ain't, neither. Him or his car." He looked up quickly as another young man came around the corner of the barn, humming to himself and straightening his wrinkled shirt collar. "Hey, Tate!" Joseph Lee called him over, "You bring your car?"

"Why shore." The tall, lanky figure cast eyes on Bonnie Rae. "Don't you look fine!" He ran a hand over black, slicked down hair and gave Harlan a quick appraisal.

"This here's Harlan Fleming, the new government teacher," she said coolly. "Harlan, Leroy Tatum."

"How do, there, Harlan," Tate grinned. He was about to stick out his hand for a friendly shake when Joseph Lee interrupted.

"Now that everybody knows everybody, give me a lift into town, will you, Tate? I got some business to take care of."

"I just got here, Ol' Son," he replied.

"Come on, it won't take long. I can tell you that."

"Well, all right. I was fixing to go in later, anyhow." He looked at Bonnie Rae and grinned again. "I got a little business of my own to see to."

"Then let's see to it," Joseph Lee urged, shuffling him

back around the corner again. "Where you parked?"

"Out back a piece." Then he called back over his shoulder, "You all have a good time, now!" as they hurried along. "You ain't never rode in my car, have you, Ol' Son?"

"Once, when you first got it," Joseph Lee replied absently, still casting furtive glances over the yard in search of Ivy. "Couple years ago, I reckon."

"Well, I fixed it up since then. Hey—you want to drive it? Go ahead on, you can tell me what you think. See if you can guess what I done."

"I don't know, Tatum," he hesitated. "Mood I'm in right now, I'm liable to drive like the devil."

"Then I'll feel right to home."

11

Joseph Lee climbed into Tate's car, put the key into the ignition and pushed the starter. The engine roared to life with a satisfying smoothness. "Where did you get any money to fix it up?" he asked.

"I told you," his friend slipped into the passenger seat and slammed the door closed, "I got a little business of my own, now."

"You got it tuned all right, that's for sure." They crept out of the barnyard and halfway to the road before Joseph Lee caught himself and turned the headlights on.

"Old habits die hard, don't they, Ol' Son," Tate observed. He licked the paper on a freshly rolled cigarette and stuck the end in his mouth. "Always did think you were the best driver in the business. Outside of your Uncle Buck, that is. Lookee here —" He turned a switch near the steering column and a loud blast of static came pouring down from a speaker above them. He turned the volume down. "Put it in myself. Let's see what we can find."

"Not much up in these hills. What do you have the switch over there for? I thought they were making them to fit into the dash now."

"They do if you want to give up your ashtray. Couldn't see giving up one luxury to make room for anothern." He continued to move the dial. "Here we go." He tuned in a distant but distinct voice of the popular, Kate Smith.

"Where's your aerial?"

"Built in."

"Built in where?"

Tate put a match to his cigarette and smiled. "Chicken wire in the roof support." He blew out the match. "Sounds good, don't it? Now, ain't that something of a luxury? I believe the next thing I'm gonna do—just for luxury—is paint the whole car black. Two tones just ain't the thing no more, and I never was partial to 'Old Chester Gray' anyhow."

"Since when do you have enough money for luxuries?" Joseph Lee turned onto the road and picked up speed. "Hey— this ain't bad—something of a revver, ain't it."

"Eighty-five horsepower. Got one of them dual-throat Stromberg carburetors—this baby'll do eighty, wide open."

"No fooling?"

"Why shore. Set your eyes on that big, bee-utiful speedometer there and let's have us a run for old times sake. When we hit that long straight piece just before town, you can see for yourself."

"I told you, I was feeling dangerous. Wouldn't want to break nothing for you."

"Never known you to break something you couldn't fix." His friend smiled. "So, let's go, boy."

Joseph Lee put his foot to the floorboard and a cloud of dust rose up behind them. At the same time, Tate reached beneath his seat and retrieved a clear pint-sized Mason jar. They slid sharply around a corner and he waited until the road straightened out again before taking the top off.

"Who you working for, Tatum?" Joseph Lee slowed down to thirty for a hairpin curve that was headed down hill at a treacherous slant. But already he had a feel for the car and took it in stride.

"Myself, Ol' Son." Tate took a long swallow and handed the jar to Joseph Lee. "Tell me what you think."

Joseph Lee sniffed it and then took a sip. "Ain't prime. But it ain't bad."

"Go ahead and take some more. No charge."

"No thanks. My daddy would kick me out for sure if he smelled it on me. You know what he's like these days."

"I do, and I'm purely indebted to him. Yes, sir."

"What do you mean?" The road leveled out and they picked up speed again.

"I mean, if you folks were still running the ridge, there wouldn't be no room for me in the business, that's what I mean." He put the lid back on the jar and braced himself. "Watch it—brakes been pulling awful hard to the left, lately."

"I noticed. I bet you went and bought yourself some of them new disc wheels and put them on a while back, didn't you."

"Yep. I figured I could use anything new I could afford."

"Them wheels are made for those new-fangled hydraulic brakes. Ain't nothing but trouble for these mechanical kind. Least little bit of hard driving you give them and they'll start wearing on your drums."

"What? I shore can't afford that kind of expense—what do I do about it?"

"Change them back," he said simply. "That ain't what's making them pull to the left, though. Just makes it more noticeable."

"What I gotta do to fix that?"

"Can't, really. They all pull to the left. Every last one of them."

"Gonna be some cut in my profits if I have to keep this thing in new wheels all the time." He opened the jar again and took two more swallows.

"I know how to make it more tolerable, though," Joseph Lee offered. "Little trick I learned from my Uncle Buck."

Tate flipped the end of his cigarette out of the partially opened window and turned seriously to Joseph Lee. "Tell me what it is, Ol' Son—you give me the secret —" He raised up slightly and straightened out his right leg to get his hand in his pocket. "And I'll give you twenty dollars, right here and now."

"Shoot!" Joseph Lee laughed. "That's more than two weeks wages. How long you been sipping that stuff, Tatum?"

"I'm serious. There it is right there. Ten, five and… three, four, five ones. Right there. Come on."

"It ain't worth that much. Just a little something I learned from Uncle Buck. Nothing I got a corner on."

"It is to me," Tate insisted. "I got me some big plans, boy. I aim to make me a heap of money real quick. Then be long gone before anybody finds out about it. And you know better than most how good you gotta be to make money in this business, anymore."

Joseph Lee slowed down while they jostled and bounced over another rough section of road. "I'll tell you. Not for no twenty dollars, though. Not when I ain't earned it. Truth is, these mechanical brakes are adjustable. Only most people don't know it. There's these two holes in the cross-shaft lever? You know, where the pedal rod's hooked on?"

Tate nodded.

"Well, it's hooked up to the first hole now. But if you take it loose," he went on with the flicker of a smile, warming to the satisfaction of sharing the little known trick, "and hook it to the second one, it'll brake better."

"Well, if that don't beat all." Tate marveled.

"Pedal won't push down as far, and you'll have to push harder, but it'll brake better."

"Joseph Lee, I do believe, after four years you still got what it takes. Want a job?"

"What—fixing your car? Here comes the straightway— hang on."

"Nope." Tate stashed the jar beneath the seat and put his hand against the dashboard. "I need a driver."

The dirt road opened up before them, left the hills on an easy gentle decline and stretched out straight for nearly three miles. At the end they could just make out the faint twinkle of town lights on the horizon. An announcer's voice on the radio burst into loud clarity as they came into the open and the speedometer began to inch its way toward fifty.

The car seemed to have suddenly taken on wings. It flew over the hard dirt road with less than half the bounce and jostle of the Harper's old pickup. Joseph Lee's heart began to beat faster as the needle continued to move up and the roar of wind inside the cab from the open windows added to the thrill.

"Ooooo—weeeee!" he yelled, "sixty-five and climbing!"

"She ain't done, yet!" Tate hollered. "Come on, baby— come on!"

"Seventy-five! The whole world's going backwards!"

Tate let loose with the loud long cry of the rebel and Joseph Lee flung his head back in sheer ecstasy and cried, "Eighty miles an hour—Ooooww!"

The car sustained the incredible speed for nearly a mile and the two of them whooped and hollered until the lights of the Cedarville gas station loomed close ahead. Joseph Lee backed off on the accelerator. Knowing they would slide out of control if he applied the faulty brakes at such high speed, he made a calculating turn onto Main Street and hit the ridge of pavement at forty miles an hour. It sent the Tudor sedan leaping into the air for nearly thirty yards.

They came down with a forceful crash that smacked both their heads against the roof and sent them into a fit of laughter. Tate smoothed down the back of his hair and reached, again, for the Mason jar.

"Shoot fire!" Joseph Lee laughed. "These V-8 engines are really something, boy!" He gave Tate a playful smack on the shoulder that made the top of the jar fly over the back seat.

"Oooops—hold this for a minute, will you, Ol' Son?" Leroy Tatum handed the jar to his friend and leaned over the seat to reach for the lid. "Got it." He had almost turned around when a casual glance through the back window revealed a police car moving up on them from behind. He squinted his eyes for a better look. "Ho...lee... Gawd!" he moaned, feeling his insides churn. "Where'd he come from?"

Joseph Lee looked over his shoulder. "Here," he said, shoving the jar back to Tate. "Get rid of this and I'll slow down. He must have been parked at the gas station when we come by."

Tate slid miserably down in the seat and faced forward. "Joseph Lee..." He could feel himself beginning to break out in a cold sweat.

"Hey, don't worry. It's Saturday night, he ain't gonna be too hard on us. Especially if I pull over."

"Don't pull over."

"I got nothing to hide, Tatum," he laughed.

"Ol' Son... you got twenty quarts of illegal whiskey setting in the back seat."

"Oh, Jesus."

12

It turned into a hair-raising chase. The kind Joseph Lee still had nightmares about. But something inside him took over as if working the family business had only been yesterday. Down one street after another. In, out and over people's yards until it all finally ended on a quiet residential street on the outskirts of Cedarville.

Joseph Lee peered cautiously between two wooden doors they had hurriedly closed after pulling into an empty garage and turned off the motor. He breathed a sigh of relief. "I think we lost him."

As Tate pushed ahead to see for himself, Joseph Lee felt a sudden weakness in his knees and sat down in front of the car to lean his shoulders against the bumper. The engine was still hot and the warmth of it engulfed him. It mingled with the darkness of the garage, and caused a suffocating illusion of being locked in a small place.

"Open one of them doors," he said miserably as he felt himself begin to tremble.

"In a minute," Tate replied, still watching through the crack. "I just want to make shore they —"

"Open the door, Tatum!" he snapped. "Or I'm gonna be sick right here."

Tate gingerly opened one of the doors and stuck his head

out to peer cautiously in both directions before turning back to his friend. "What's wrong, Ol' Son? That was the best piece of driving I seen in a long time. And ducking into this empty garage? Why, hail—I could of swore ol' Buck his self was setting at the wheel."

A wave of cool air rushed in from the open door and Joseph Lee got slowly to his feet. He leaned his outstretched hands against the hood of the car and hung his head for a moment, steadying himself with long deep breaths.

"You got to drive for me now, boy," Tate could barely contain his excitement as he came up beside him. "I can shore see that! Why, you and me together could —"

"Shut up, Tate."

"No, now listen up. I'm gonna make you a deal, Ol'—"

All at once, Joseph Lee threw a sudden forceful blow to Tate's face that came as such a surprise it sent him flying into the garage wall. He lay stunned for a moment, crumpled on the ground, before rising to his knees to put a hand to his mouth. It was bleeding.

"Gawd!" he bawled, stumbling to his feet. "Day-em! Got some of your daddy in you, too! What'd you do that for?"

"Because you got no idea what happened here, that's why."

"What—do I look like I can't listen?" He pulled a handkerchief out of his pocket and put it to his mouth. "Ain't no call for that rough stuff!"

"What are you thinking—driving through town with shine setting on the back seat? You could have ruined your life with that kind of foolishness—you could have ruined mine! I been paroled once already and them Laws don't take nothin' the second time. Rough stuff. You keep that carelessness up and you ain't gonna live to see rough stuff!"

"I forgot it was there."

"Forgot!"

"I was fixing to sell what I could at the party. You're the one wanted to get in to town so all-fired fast."

"If you were working that's even worse! Anybody works and drinks at the same time's just waiting for his own funeral. That ain't carelessness, it's plain stupid!"

"I don't appreciate them inferences! You been out of the business for four years –I'm telling you it's different now."

"What—because they made drinking legal? It ain't never gonna be legal to make it and sell it yourself. And don't ever think them Laws aren't getting smarter and smarter. They're coming way back in the hills now. Nobody's safe no more. Ain't you even reading the papers?"

"What do I need the papers for?" he sniffed. "They ain't on my tail."

"Shoot, I'm surprised you ain't hung yet!" Joseph Lee walked over and threw open the other garage door. He got into the car and Tate followed after him.

"So, what do you want me to say?" Tate yelled through the closed window. "I'm sorry?"

Joseph Lee rolled it down. "Will you get in the car? We got to get out of here before these folks come home."

Tate went around to the passenger side and slumped into the seat like a pouting child. He reached for the Mason jar and wiped a wetness away from his nose with the back of his hand. "Jeeze—my nose is bleeding!" He finished off what was left in the jar. After awhile, as they drove slowly and civilly down a side street, he looked over at Joseph Lee with watery eyes and said, "You're right, Ol' Son. I've had a lot of close calls lately."

"I ain't surprised. Where you taking this stuff—Ruby's?"

He nodded. "I ain't never been good at running things, my-self, and that's the truth. You got to come in with me, Joseph Lee. I need you! I'll give you all the money you want!"

"You're letting the whiskey talk, now."

"Jesus Gawd—my nose won't stop bleeding! I think it's broke."

"Lean your head back and be quiet."

He leaned back and held the bloody handkerchief to his

face, again. "What do you say, Joseph Lee? I'm trying to make a deal!"

"I say you're drunk and I'm not talking to you no more."

By the time Joseph Lee finished Tate's delivery and headed the car back toward Cedar Creek, the sugar party was almost at an end. To his dismay, The traveling man's car was still nowhere to be seen. He parked in the same spot they had started from, then reached over and shook Tate by the shoulder. "Wake up, Tatum. We're back."

"What?"

"Here," he pulled a roll of money out of his shirt pocket. "You got thirty-five dollars here. I kept twenty because I figured I earned it."

"You earned it, Ol' Son."

"Best head on home, you don't look so good."

"I'm going. You think about what I said."

"I ain't interested. If the Laws didn't get me first, my daddy would sooner or later. I ain't up to either one."

"Think about it."

They heard the sound of another car motor and looked up just as the black and white Desoto pulled into the yard. Joseph Lee had never seen the traveling man's car up close. But even with the brief flash he had glimpsed this afternoon, he recognized it. "I got to go." He flung open the door, "before that good-for-nothing stranger gets away from me, again. See you, Tatum."

"Take it easy, Ol' Son."

Lon Durham—the traveling man—felt it only prudent to make his face known to the people of Cedar Creek at this community festivity before venturing too much farther into the backwoods with his wares. There was pay dirt, here, if he could get past the suspicions. All it took was a few local ladies to give him a good word. He had always been good with the ladies. He reached into the back seat for his suit jacket and hat before starting in the direction of the music. There were children playing in the yard, their shouts and laughter mingled with the music, and an inviting aroma of good food wafted toward him from the barn.

"Hold it right there, mister!" Joseph Lee called out from the darkness behind him as he walked past. "I got something to say to you."

Durham turned, and then slung the white jacket over his shoulder as he started across to meet him.

"Where's Ivy?"

"Well, let me see now..." The traveling man pushed the brim of his white hat farther back on his head with a thumb. "You must be Joseph Lee Harper."

"Yeah, and you're the man's been busting in places you ain't got any right to."

"I wouldn't put it that way."

"Where's Ivy?" Joseph Lee demanded.

"She wasn't feeling too well, son."

"I ain't your son."

"Had to take her home."

"You been gone longer than that takes," Joseph Lee noticed that the stranger looked unusually fit. As if he had gone to great lengths to get that way. His face above the white collar of the shirt had a deep golden tan—the kind a person picked up from being near the ocean—and his hair and mustache were streaked with blonde in a way that only came from long hours in the sun. He was several inches taller, too, and Joseph Lee wondered fleetingly if he would be able to hold his own in a fight against him.

"Sizing me up, are you?"

"Maybe."

"Well..." He grinned, put on his jacket and straightened his tie. "I didn't force her into my car. So, maybe you better take the matter up with your girl, Harper. That is, if she still is your girl."

"If you done anything to her, mister, I'm gonna —-"

"Don't threaten me, kid," the stranger warned in a tone that was suddenly low and serious. "You can't afford it."

13

Harlan and Bonnie Rae were together all evening. They danced beautifully. They moved over the rough-hewn planks of the barn floor in the middle of the crowd, yet with eyes only for each other.

Circle to the left, circle to the right
Promenade, circle back down...

At dinner they sat close. At the candy pulling, they were partners. They had to be touching, always touching. Near the end of the evening, Harlan held her overly long after a dance and brushed the side of her face with a kiss.

"My daddy," she whispered, with a worried glance over her shoulder.

"Come outside," he said.

Out in the yard, the children were growing quieter now. The younger ones were laying on blankets stretched out over the grass, drifting off to sleep to chants of "*The Duck and The Goose*" or "*Red Rover, Red Rover*" still being played by the older children. Harlan and Bonnie Rae walked hand in hand, enjoying the cool breeze against their faces after the warmth from inside. They walked away from the yard and down to the soft banks of the creek. There were no watchful eyes, here, no reason to be careful, and no more reasons to hide the fact that their feelings for each other seemed to have grown even more intense since they had been apart.

Harlan led her into the protective shadow of a nearby tree, and when he pulled her into his arms, Bonnie Rae's heart began to pound at the thought she just might do anything this man asked her if she wasn't careful. But sensing the slight hesitation, he took her face in his hands, instead, and softy kissed first one side, and then the other: the same cultural French familiarity he had been raised with in those childhood days after China.

So different from what Bonnie Rae expected, yet, so endearing. They had known each other such short a time and, yet, something inside told her she already belonged to Harlan. It had come to her by some mysterious force back in her own early days. As if, all her life she had been learning his ways. Brought up in them by the beguiling personality of a woman she had never met but grown to love, simply by looking at the beautiful painted image that hung over the mantle—day after day—from the long ago illness that had taken her to his uncle's house.

She had given the matter a great deal of thought since the day at the schoolhouse, when she had let every feeling she ever knew spill out in front of Harlan. Things not even her family knew. All the old hurts had spilled over and melted away in the presence of this man that—until then—she had only known as a boy and believed in.

Now, he had not only come this long way to Cedar Creek, he had recognized her the moment he laid eyes on her, and drawn her to him. The wonder of it! Suddenly, she could feel nothing but this strong wonderful closeness between them that had begun so many years ago and miles apart and—before she could stop herself—melted deliciously into his arms with complete abandon and proclaimed, "I Love you, Harlan! Oh, I love you, I—"

Then the sound of Rafe's voice came from somewhere

over the hill, "Bonnie Rae—where are you?" He stood on the top and hollered down at them, "Big John's gotta take Sarah home and Daddy's gonna play, again. He wants you up on the box with him to sing *The White Dress.* Everybody's asking for you!"

If Harlan had not let her go and still held onto her hand as they started up the bank, again, she might never even answered! She didn't want to sing tonight – the night was too close to over. Then—as if she had spoken the thought out loud—he replied in French, *"But we're caught, chère, are we not? They'd only come looking if we stayed."*

Which was true. For as soon as they entered the barn, Lias spotted them and called out, "Here she is, folks! And let's bring Adie Pierson in on the dulcimer for this one, too. Come on, Adie—watch them steps, there."

An elderly woman came slowly up on the platform and sat down on a chair someone quickly provided for her. She laid the instrument across her lap. "I could play it a heap better ifen I had me a jack-knife," she suggested.

A man toward the front reached into his pocket and handed one up to her. A hush came over everyone. Lias Harper Looked down on them all with a smile and tucked the fiddle up under his chin. "Kick us off on the mandolin, Virgil," he said to the man beside him. "And we'll all follow right behind."

All at once the air was filled with the enchantment of a long ago waltz as the magic of the harmonious strings drifted out over the crowd. When Bonnie Rae began to sing, the beautiful clear sweetness of her voice seemed to reach out to Harlan. Everyone loved her. The last strains of the song were barely finished when someone shouted a request and the instruments picked it up before the last note died.

After that song, the other musicians drifted back into the crowd and Lias laid down his fiddle to reach for a guitar. He joined his daughter in the center of the platform. He began to pick the strings with an arresting rhythm while she hummed a mournful tune that suddenly changed the mood to things more heartfelt and serious. It was a song that described the bitter trials of a miner's life, set to the music of the mountains. It raged against the injustice and poverty of their times and ended sadly, on a sweetly executed final note which the father and daughter sang together.

Over half the people present worked in the mines and all of them were numbered among the Nation's poor. A long moment of quiet emotion followed. Lias, sensing the atmosphere, looked across to no one in particular and began to talk softly.

"At a time in my life when I had the Laws on one side, and hard times on the other... well," he paused, rested his forearm on the guitar and looked down at the floor. "Well, there ain't a one of you don't know how it was in them days. There's a lot of you folks in this barn tonight that I done a heap of wrong to."

"It's in the past, son," came a voice from the crowd.

"Yeah, Uncle Ted, but sometimes the past has a way of hanging onto you."

"We ain't accounting you, Lias," someone else spoke up.

"I'm beholding to you for that. But I got something I got to say to you all tonight, or I ain't gonna be at peace with myself. And the days of me having no peace with myself are over."

"Amen," came another voice.

"That day in summer when I saw the Light..." Now he looked up with a fervor. "I knew—right then and there—that I was lost! And the Lord himself looked down and says to me, Lias Harper? I seen all them things you done. Lord almighty!" He sighed and shook his head, as if it was still hard to believe. "When I heard that, I figured He was gonna strike me dead right there. I just knew I was that much of a sinner."

He paused and a female voice from the back said, "God be praised."

"But then He says to me, I ain't gonna kill you, Lias. Because if I kilt you, then I'd have to kill every last one of the rest of the folks—from the oldest on down to the tiniest, little set-along child."

"It's true," someone said and several heads nodded in agreement.

"He said, My onliest boy took care of all that some time ago, and the job he done there on Calvary was enough to last all Creation. And if it's enough for Creation, it's shorely enough for the wickedness you done here in Cedar Creek. So, I'm telling you, if you'll bare and bow your head right now—repent—and turn from them wicked ways... then I ain't gonna hold you accountable."

He paused for a moment. "You all know that's just what I done that day. But how many of us know repenting's easy but turning from your wicked ways ain't." He raised his hand in response to his own question.

"Amen."

"You got the truth there, Lias."

"Glory!"

Then he proclaimed with a deadly seriousness, "The past has a way of hanging onto a man. God ain't holding me accountable. And I know—as shore as I'm standing here—that I'm going to Glory when I die. But I been walking around with the burdens of my past weighing so heavy on me, I been like to die. So, in front of God and all you folks, I want to say I'm sorry."

There wasn't a sound in the room as the atoning words settled down on them. Then, as if it still wasn't enough, Lias Harper took a deep breath and proclaimed, "I'm sorry for the fear my brothers and me brought on your homes for the sake of the business. Avery Harris—I'm mortal sorry you lost your onliest boy on account of me. I'm sorry to you, too, Mama... where are you?"

The old woman, wearing a man's battered leather hat over a tangle of white, unmanageable hair, was sitting on a bench along the wall. She covered her face with her apron and began to cry quietly. Lias looked at her and his own eyes began to trickle as he spoke. "I'm sorry for losing Daddy... and Seth... and Little Buck. And for losing Aunt Jenny, too. I apologize for all them that's been drug off to the penitentiary on my account and to the families that's been left behind to fend for themselves in these hard times."

He bowed his head and was quiet for a long time. Bonnie Rae, who had been standing beside her father with her head bowed, too, laid a hand on his arm and tried to slip quietly off stage. But he reached out to catch her by the hand and keep her there.

Aaron McCord stepped up on the platform then, and laid an arm across Lias' shoulders. "It appears to me," he said, "that Lias ain't the only one that needs to lay down the past. I got a sensing in my soul that now is the time for all of us to make things right with God and our brothers."

"Amen."

"Send the Glory!" someone cried out.

"And I'm gonna start off with myself," Aaron went on, "by saying I'm ashamed of the way I let this man carry the burdens of this town for so long after he seen the Light. We all got to share in the responsibility of our ways—ain't right that any man but the Lord bare our sins!"

"I done laid blame on him, too," said another man from the crowd, "and I swear to you all, I ain't gonna account him no more—I'm right sorry, Lias."

"Sing with me, now," Lias called out to them. "Sing with me—*Amazing Grace how sweet the sound...*"

And everyone responded with the lovely melody as he lined each phrase to them. The barn became filled with music again, and the long, eventful evening drew to a close, softly and safely. Like a prayer.

On everyone except Joseph Lee.

14

On Monday, Harlan rode into town with Aaron McCord to meet the two o'clock train from Richmond. A few boxes of his personal belongings shipped from the farm had finally arrived, as well as his most prized possession that—he was sure—a teacher in the hill country would need.

When they pulled into the Cedarville station, the train had not come in yet. Aaron, a thin man who was amazingly fit for the age of seventy-two, climbed out of his well kept 1929 Chevrolet and looked down the long, empty track. "Late, again," he observed, taking a chunk of chewing tobacco from his shirt pocket to cut off a bite-sized piece with a jackknife.

Harlan, his thumbs in his pockets, ambled slowly up beside him and looked in the same direction. "I wonder how long it will be."

"Never can tell," the old man admitted. "You get this far back and it's a long wait if something goes wrong."

"It's a long ride, that's for sure."

Aaron looked at him with a slight twinkle in his eyes. "I don't doubt them belongings of yours will be in better shape than you was when you come in."

Harlan lifted a questioning eyebrow at him, and Aaron smiled as he returned the chunk of tobacco to his pocket and looked down the track, again.

"How is it you would know what shape I was in when I got here?" Harlan asked.

"Well, now. I heard tell you stirred things up some at the post office, then screamed and hollered all the way out to Cedar Creek!" He burst out laughing, as if it were one of the best jokes he had heard in a long time. When he noticed Harlan wasn't seeing the humor in it, he smoothed his gray beard and looked off down the track, again. "Yep, it's a long trip, all right."

"Who told you that?"

"Took it myself once, back in 'twenty-three."

"That's not what I meant."

"Awww, ain't nothing to get riled about," the old man soothed. "We're just pleasuring in your city ways, is all." He started to laugh again, but cleared his throat instead and leaned over to spit a stream of tobacco juice off to one side. "One thing about Cedar Creek you might as well know, right now. Folks around here take a heap of pleasure in everybody's business. And a heap more in telling about it."

"One can at least hope it would be the truth."

"Well, ain't no way you can expect it to be." He laughed, again, this time as if remembering something. "I'll tell you what—town like Cedar Creek—you make too many trips to the outhouse in the morning, your door neighbor will be stopping by in the afternoon to see what you're ailing with, and ol' Doc… he'll be by to bury you that night!" He couldn't help himself this time, and burst out laughing with the sheer enjoyment of his own humor.

"Very funny," Harlan replied. "Here comes the train."

A few people who were waiting on benches stood up and walked to the edge of the platform as the squealing brakes were applied and steam began to shoot from beneath the massive engine as it came to a stop.

"I expect your things will be away at the back," Aaron suggested.

"Probably," Harlan started past the long row of cars. "Aaron? There's something I didn't tell you."

"What's that?"

They stopped at the first freight car where some boxes were being unloaded. "I won't be riding back to Cedar Creek with you—that one there is mine—but I would really appreciate it if you could drop my things by Doc's for me. There's another one. I'll put the boxes in the car for you and Tom will help you get them out back home."

"Shore, I don't mind carting the boxes, Harlan, but —"

"But you would really like to know the rest of my business, right?" This time it was Harlan who laughed.

"Hey, you catch on purty fast, though. For a city-slicker," Aaron smiled. "Well, you gonna tell, or ain't you?"

"Sure, I'll tell. Have to adjust to small town living sooner or later, don't I? It'll be interesting to see what kind of story it turns into by the time I get back. You see, the other thing I had sent was —"

There was a sudden commotion toward the far end of the train and a lineman cupped his hands to his mouth to shout in their direction. "Hey! Which one of you folks down there, does this beast belong to!"

"Excuse me —" Harlan dismissed himself from Aaron and ran off in that direction.

"I got the job of loading and unloading these freight cars, mister," the lineman said, meeting him halfway. "But they sure don't pay me enough to put up with that kind of trouble!"

"Where is he?"

"Second car to the end, and I want him out of there before he kicks a hole through one of them wooden side panels."

Harlan stepped up his pace and ran to where several other railroad workers had gathered to peer in through the open doors of the freight car and watch from a safe distance, the tumult that was going on inside.

"Ain't that fire?" Someone whistled in amazement.

"I never seen such a critter in all my born days!" another

replied.

Harlan squeezed in front of them and jumped up inside the car. "Prince," he said gently. "Whoa, there. Steady, now. Steady..." The angry black stallion, breathing hard and rapid, stood suddenly still at the sound of the familiar voice and perked up his ears. "Easy, boy," Harlan soothed, as he laid a hand on the glistening, dark coat that was still trembling all over. "It's just me."

His saddle and bridle were piled in a corner of the hay-strewn floor, as if they had been dumped there in a hurry to avoid any contact with the horse during the changeover of trains. Harlan went over to straighten out the tangled heap, and as he picked up the bridle and unwound the reins, the horse began to prance and back off, shaking his shaggy, black mane in protest.

By that time, Aaron McCord had finally arrived to see what was happening. "Lord almighty, Harlan!" He poked his head inside. "That wild thing belong to you?"

"He's not wild."

"Temperamental."

"Three days rattling around in a box would tend to make most anything temperamental. I had him sent all the way from my farm." He put the bridle behind his back and approached the animal again. "He'll be all right," he spoke gently to the horse, though he was still talking to Aaron. "After a nice long run to Cedar Creek, he'll be himself, again."

He put his arms around the strong, sleek neck and just stood there for a moment until the beautiful horse settled down and gave him a low whinny of recognition. Then Harlan slipped the bit gently and easily into the animal's mouth and the horse was subdued. The men stepped out of the way so he could lead the beautiful animal out and tether him to a nearby post before returning for the rest of the tack.

"Sorry he caused so much trouble," he said to the lineman as he passed.

Aaron was stroking the soft muzzle when he came back.

"Shore is a sightly critter," he said. "What kind is he?"

"Morgan." Harlan shook the hay out of the saddle blanket and laid it across the animal's back.

"He's some thick in the neck and chest," the older man observed. "Hear tell them kind make good work horses."

"They're known for their endurance. And good nature. Isn't like him to act like he did back there. But then it was a long trip with a lot of strangers."

"I reckon that's what it was. Look at them eyes. Like two chunks of shining black coal." He stroked him again and ran a hand through the long mane. "Had him long?"

"Since he was foaled," Harlan answered. He put on the dark leather saddle. "Tom gave him to me when I was thirteen."

"The Doc?"

"Yes. Tom's a real horseman. I used to think if I could only be half the rider he was…" He paused thoughtfully for a moment. "Half of anything he was. I'd be satisfied."

"Looks like you turned out all right, anyhow," Aaron offered.

Harlan smiled. "I guess so." He took the horse by the reins and they walked toward the car. "You already got the boxes loaded?"

"Why shore, they weren't nothing." Then he added, "I didn't get to be this old by not working."

"Well, I appreciate the help. I was beginning to think the books wouldn't get here before school starts next week. Now, I'm all ready."

"Right down to having the sightliest horse in the county to ride there every morning. Them younguns will be right proud of that."

"I'm pretty proud of him, myself," Harlan admitted. "We sort of grew up together. Prince and I. We've seen a lot of good years."

"Well," Aaron opened the door to his car, "I reckon it'll take you a couple hours to get back."

"Probably." Harlan climbed up into the saddle. "I'm not in a hurry. Thought I'd stop by the Harpers before I go home." He looked down the track in the direction of Cedarville and noticed a large, brick mansion set back among the trees on a low hill. It was surrounded by an elaborate iron fence, and seemed oddly out of place to be sitting on the edge of this quaint mountain town. "What's that over there?" he asked as Aaron got behind the wheel of his car and closed the door.

The old man turned his head to see where Harlan was pointing. "That there's the Owner's house," he replied matter-of-factly.

"The owner of what?"

"Coaltown."

Once again, the thought of school children working in the mines entered Harlan's mind and he asked, "Just where exactly is Coaltown?"

"That's what they call all them company houses down the hill a little piece below the coal works. Coaltown."

"One man owns all of it?" Harlan looked again at the great house with its blatant extravagance.

"Lock, stock and barrel," Aaron answered. "And the people to boot!"

"No children, though." Harlan threw him a challenging look this time.

"Why, shore – a few, as I recollect—everybody's prone to families hereabouts."

"That's not what I meant." Aaron suddenly started the car and Harlan had to raise his voice to be heard above the motor. "I meant do they employ any ——"

"Be seeing you, Harlan!" The old man called cheerily as he eased the car back toward the street, as if he hadn't even heard.

15

Little Sam Harper, with his face washed and hair slicked back, climbed up to the supper table before anyone else and reached into the sugar jar. "Where's Daddy?" He took out one of the cubes and gave it a lick before returning it to the jar, again.

"He's having another one of his spells," Celia bent down to lift a tray of biscuits out of the oven. "So, I want you to be real quiet for a while, till it passes."

"Why's he keep having them things, anyhow?"

"Because he's working too hard, I reckon."

"Big John's been working like a bull ox ever since he was borned—how come he don't have none?"

"Lil' Sam." Celia turned to him. "Why don't you get down from there and go tell everybody supper's ready?"

"I reckon I could get the fellers but them girls take fits ever time I open the door."

"That's because you didn't behave yourself last time Bonnie Rae had her dress makings out," his mother informed him. "I'll get the girls." When she returned a few moments later with her daughters, Lias was sitting at the end of the table with a cup of coffee. "Lias, why ain't you resting?" she asked.

"Don't do no good, Ceely," he replied. "Don't nothing do

no good no more. It's near passed now, anyhow."

The door opened and Rafe stuck his leather-capped head in. "Mama?"

"Take your hat off in the house, son," Celia said. "And wash up for supper."

"Yeah, but you gotta come out here for a minute."

"Will you help me set the table, Rafie?" Jenny Beth asked as she began placing plates around.

"Heck, no."

"Then I ain't gonna be nice to you no more!" His little sister pouted. "I ain't gonna be nice to nobody!"

"Jenny Beth," Celia warned. "Let's everybody get to the table."

The front door banged and Joseph Lee came in with a load of firewood. "Guess who just rode in to the yard on the purtiest critter you ever seen?" He dropped the wood onto the hearth. "Harlan Fleming."

Bonnie Rae's face brightened. "Oh, Mama, could we ask him to supper?"

"Nope," Lias answered for her. He set down his coffee and got to his feet.

"Come on out and see him, Daddy," Joseph Lee urged. "We ain't never had nothing like this here in Cedar Creek."

Bonnie Rae followed.

"Stay in the house," Lias told her.

"But, Daddy —"

"I said, stay," he repeated. "Ceely, go ahead and put supper on and I'll be back in after a bit."

Lou Ellen went into the living room and watched them through the window as Bonnie Rae returned to the kitchen. She sat down at the table alone and tried to fight back sudden, stinging tears of frustration.

"I ain't gonna make no excuses for your daddy, Bonnie Rae," Celia said as she sat down beside her daughter. "If I was to start now, I'd never quit talking."

"But I ain't a youngun no more!"

"He just don't want to see you get to liking Harlan too much. I told you it was gonna be that way."

Outside, Harlan was standing in the dark, holding onto the reins while Little Sam was exalting in being perched on top of the beautiful horse.

"Lookee, here, Daddy!" he called out as Lias came across the yard. "Hi-o-Silver, away!"

"Ain't he something, now –" Lias reached up for his youngest son and then handed him off to Joseph Lee. "Take him in the house, J-Lee."

"Awww, Daddy!" the little boy complained.

"Go on, now. Your mama's got supper on and I'm fixing to have me a talk with Harlan."

"Didn't mean to break in on your supper," Harlan said when they were left alone.

Lias sat down on a nearby wood stump and reached into his shirt pocket for his tobacco. He rolled a cigarette and lit it without saying anything.

"If you would rather I came back some other time," Harlan offered, beginning to feel uncomfortable with the silence.

"Rather you didn't come back," the older man replied.

"Because of Tom?"

"Nope. I done put the past behind me, and I aim to live up to it."

"Why not then, Mr. Harper?"

"Because of the way my little girl looked when she heard you was here. The way you was walking with her that night when I got home from the shift. And seeing how she wouldn't dance with no one but you at the sugar party. I figured I best put an end to this thing right now."

"Mr. Harper, I realize that seventeen is somewhat young to be —"

"Her mama had two younguns by that age," Lias replied. "Folks tend to pair off early up here on the mountain. That ain't it, neither."

All Harlan could see of him was the bright red tip of his

cigarette and the dark shadow of his form. Prince blew out his breath and nibbled at some grass growing up along a nearby fence post. Harlan thoughtlessly ran his hand through the animal's shaggy mane and tried to control the sudden turmoil he felt inside him. Whatever he did he must not offend this man whose word was so final in Cedar Creek. "What is it then?" he asked carefully.

"She's my first girl-child," he replied. "And I take a heap of pleasure in having her close by. Truth is…" He crushed his cigarette out against the log he was sitting on. "I got nothing against you at all, Harlan. Every one of my kids put a heap of store by you, already. I can see you got the gift for that sorta thing, and I'm proud you're gonna be teaching them. But you're a foreigner, boy. And I can see just by looking, you ain't gonna stay." He got to his feet again and leaned his forearms against the fence rail. "Am I wrong?"

Harlan didn't reply.

"First thing I'd know," Lias went on, "you'd be dragging her off somewhere and she'd never see her family, again."

"Don't you think Bonnie Rae should make that decision herself?"

"Nope."

"Mr. Harper," Harlan objected, "there's more to the world than Cedar Creek. Bonnie Rae's bright and intelligent. She deserves to make her own decisions. It's part of growing up. You can't hold her back if you really love her."

"Do you love her?"

Once again, Harlan was startled by the blunt straight forwardness of the man and could be nothing less than honest, in return. "I think maybe I loved her the first time I saw her," he said quietly.

There was another long uncomfortable silence, during which Harlan felt that his very future weighed in the balance. Perhaps if he went slowly. If he could court Bonnie Rae properly, according to their local customs. It was not right that Lias Harper should have him so squarely nailed in this one brief but cutting conversation for which he was not prepared. Now, Lias had forced him to confess something he had little understanding of himself, much less an adequate explanation for.

"Out in these hills," Lias explained after a while, "a man sets a heap of store by his family. He does what he has to—to take care of them—and in these hard times it ain't easy. We ain't got much but we got what we need. I been off the mountain before, Harlan. And I seen folks was starving for what we got the most of out here. Fresh air, pure water and kinfolk. My baby don't need nothing else."

"Maybe she feels differently."

"A man has to live according to his lights."

"Then let Bonnie Rae live according to hers."

"The only light she has, she got out of them books she reads all the time. Or a moving picture magazine. Or from what some foreigner told her. I hope you ain't been filling her head with the glories of life off the mountain, Harlan."

"How is she going to learn how to think for herself," he argued, "if you keep making her choices for her?"

"Girl-child don't need to think for herself," the older man replied.

"That's ignorant!" Harlan accused, and then was immediately sorry he said it.

Lias reached into his pocket for the tobacco again and was quiet while he rolled and lit another cigarette. In the momentary flare of match light, his face looked unbearably tired.

"I'm sorry," Harlan said quietly.

"You're a foreigner," Lias said, again. "That's the only thing I got against you. I look at you and see you got some winsome ways about you. The kind would make a little girl want to up and follow you anywhere. Maybe it ain't right to make her choices for her but I'll answer to my Maker for that. Truth is, I can't find it in myself to let her go. It just ain't in me."

"Mr. Harper —"

"I don't want you to see her no more."

"Please. If you would only think about it."

"No more."

"I told you how I feel. I have to see her."

"If I catch her with you again," he said, and this time there was something different in the tone, "I'll beat the fire out of her."

"What?"

"I'll beat her till she's afraid to even look at you."

It was the last thing he had expected, and the thought was so appalling it was a moment before he could say anything at all. What could he say? "That's your idea of love?" he suddenly demanded. "How could you even say something like that, much less, do it? That is the most unreasonable—contradictory trash—I've heard since I got here! I don't believe it! You wouldn't —"

"Try me."

The response was so chilling that Harlan practically reeled beneath it. He stood there for a few more moments and then turned away. Without another word, he leapt onto his horse and—the spirited animal sensing his intensity—started off at a run. Lias stood and watched until they disappeared down Cedar Creek road.

He rode beautifully.

16

That night when most of the Harper family was asleep, Big John closed the screen door quietly and whispered into the darkness, "Joseph Lee, you out here?"

"Over this way," came the reply.

John could see only a silhouette of his younger brother a short distance away. He was sitting against the side of the house, with one leg dangling over the porch and a forearm resting on one knee that was raised. "What are you doing out here?" John asked.

"Getting some air."

"I got to talk to you." The handsome, favored brother came and sat down beside him. "About Daddy."

"What ain't I done, now?" Joseph Lee sighed.

"Don't be like that, boy. Why you always have a chip on your shoulder for?"

"Maybe it's because every time something goes wrong around here, I'm the one ends up taking the blame."

"I didn't come out to lay blame."

"Well, shoot," He turned his face into the soft, night breeze and leaned his head back against the wall. "You might as well stay all night, then."

"Hey, we used to." Big John sensed his brother's mood and tried to lighten it a little. "Remember? Make tents out of blankets... have pillow fights."

"Remember that time I made your nose bleed?" Joseph Lee teased.

"Ain't you never gonna let me forget that?"

"Can't," Joseph Lee laughed, warming to the memories in spite of himself. "It's the only time I ever got you down. Fair, that is."

"You're turning out to be a fearsome thing yourself, these days." His brother threw him a playful punch. "I don't believe we've taken each other on since... well..."

"Last summer when I told you Sarah Wesley was bow-legged."

"Mmmm!" Big John shook his head. "That riled me, all right."

Joseph Lee laughed, again.

"You don't still think she's bowlegged, do you?"

"shoot, no. I never did, really. I was just feeling mean, is all." His hand brushed against a wood chip and he tossed it out into the yard. "Naw, I like her, now."

"What's ailing you, J-Lee?"

His brother sighed and leaned his head back against the wall, again. "Ivy," he admitted, finally. "She done set my blood to boil running off with that foreigner."

"You talk to her about it?"

"Nope. And I ain't gonna."

"Maybe it ain't like you think."

"It is if it gives me a case of the miseries like this. If I have to worry about her every time a stranger comes to town... go through the same thing all over, again... I don't need her."

"You been needing her ever since you was a baby," Big John reminded him. "Can't turn away after all these years just because she riled you. You been riled before."

"Not like this. Not over another feller."

"You ought to just up and marry the girl." He folded his arms across his chest and looked up at the full round moon and the scattering of stars all around. "That would take care of things."

"Ain't you one to talk."

"I aim to marry Sarah soon as I get that house of mine fit to live in. I sure don't sit around from one day to anothern wondering do I, or don't I. Girl needs marrying if you want any respect, J-Lee. Just hopping in and out of her window now and again ain't where it comes from."

"What's some slip of paper from the local laws got to do with it? She either loves me or she don't."

"Well, it's sort of what the paper stands for, isn't it? The fact you'll own up to them feelings and be respectable to your-selves and everybody else. That you care enough to call each other family. It's being family that makes the difference—that's where the respect comes in. Seems to me you got that girl trailing behind you so long she's starting to disrespect her-self. Ain't any wonder she's in a mood to look around. Boil-ing over don't help, neither. Drop her or marry her. Anything between just gonna hurt you both."

"I was thinking on it before he come along."

"Then you best think harder."

They sat quietly for a while, listening to the frogs in a far off pond and the occasional call of a night bird.

"Shhh!" Joseph Lee straightened up suddenly, so he could listen. "Hear that?"

"What?"

"Whistling Swan," he said softly. "Away off down in the swamp. Ain't this some kind of a night, though?"

"I reckon my ears ain't so good, these days."

"Why not?"

"Too much blasting down in the pit, I guess," he replied.

Joseph Lee sank slowly back against the wall and looked over at the dark form of his brother with shocked disbelief. "Dang, Johnny... don't that rile you?"

Big John looked back at him and shrugged. "If I thought about it enough, maybe. It was just sort of a gradual thing."

"Ain't human what they make you do down there!"

"Better than getting shot dead without ever knowing what hit you. Maybe I can't hear the Whistling Swan five miles down the holler, but I can drive anywhere in the county without having to look over my shoulder no more. And I can sleep all the way through every last night of the week, peaceful."

"Don't seem like a fair enough trade to me."

"We ain't living in fair times, J-Lee." Big John leveled his gaze on his restless younger brother and let the low soothing tones of his voice ease gently into what he had come out to say in the first place. "In a way, that's what I come out here to talk to you about. Seems us Harpers got more troubles ahead."

"What sort of troubles?" Joseph Lee asked warily.

"Company's gonna let Daddy go at the end of the month. We'd never known ahead of time if Bobbie Duke hadn't got one of his fingers smashed between a couple coal cars and was waiting for the Doc up in the office. When he heard the Boss Man talking about his Uncle Lias, he perked up his ears. They know he's took with the Black Lung. So, they're letting him go."

"But I thought you been covering for him."

"Been trying to. But it ain't easy no more. Last week he took one of them coughing fits when we were coming up the shaft to go home. I could of swore he was like to die right there in front of the Straw Boss and everybody. It ain't the work that's behind. It's just he can't hide it no more."

"And when they find out they fire him!"

"Ain't much more you can expect them to do. He sure ain't fit for working."

"Well, he ought to get something for what it done to him. Ain't right they should throw him out like he was nothing."

"They're gonna give him something." Big John grew strangely quiet and Joseph Lee felt a sudden uneasiness creep into him. "They're gonna hold his place open for you," he said slowly, "instead of give it to someone else on the list. That way the family won't have to take such a cut in the weekly pay."

"To me? Do you think he'll make me do it?"

"I ain't speaking for him," Big John snapped. "He don't even know about it, yet. I'm coming to you because I expect you to do what you got to for the family. No matter what way you feel about it."

"Now, just a minute!" Joseph Lee jumped down from the porch and walked off a few paces before turning back to continue. "You know I'm willing to work for this family, Johnny, and we got a prime crop of tobacco sitting out back to prove it! It wouldn't be there if I hadn't done it myself. I plowed and planted and tended it all the time you both been working down in the pit! Shoot – it paid the taxes last year, didn't it? Don't that count for something?"

"The way things are going this year, you might as well burn it."

"I'll do something else, then—I ain't shiftless! You know I can't work down in that hole!"

"You got to try."

"I tried already and it like to killed me!" He started off across the yard in a storm.

"Joseph Lee—you get back here, boy!" His brother got off the porch and started after him. "I ain't done talking to you."

Joseph Lee stopped and waited for John to catch up with him. Now that they were beneath the bright light of the moon, he could see the grim determination in his brother's face and tried to explain it away. "I still get nightmares about them days!" he protested miserably. "The whole world cut off with that black, choking dust... them deep, dark tunnels it takes a whole hour just to climb up from... the blasted faces and the broken bodies. Every day wondering if it's gonna be me next time! You remember how I threw up every blessed day he made me go down there."

"That was four years ago, J-Lee. You owe it to him to see if you can't take it, now. You got any idea what it's gonna be like trying to take care of this family off one Company check?"

"I told you I'd get the money some other way."

"You ain't going back to the business, if that's what you mean," he warned, and Joseph Lee could see the sternness in his brother's face as if it was etched in stone.

He didn't answer.

"All I got to say is, you better not be fool enough to put us all through that, again!" Big John forced down his own anger and spoke levelly, "Now, you got a couple weeks to get used to the idea."

Joseph Lee cursed under his breath and turned away from him.

"Then I want you ready and waiting at the truck first of the month," he pressed. "Without Daddy having to ask you. Maybe just once in your life do something without kicking and fighting about it."

"Maybe I got a reason for kicking and fighting," Joseph Lee returned. "Maybe I'm sick and tired of paying for everybody else's sins!"

"Everybody pays, J-Lee. Seems to me you're the only one taking miseries over it. I ain't proud it worked out this way, you can believe that. But you be there. First day of the month, hear? Just be there." Big John turned away then, and headed back toward the house without waiting for a reply.

Joseph Lee watched the door close behind him and then stood for a while in the middle of the yard, alone. He heard the sad sweet quaver of an owl somewhere deep in the woods and suddenly he found himself trying to choke back all the rising turmoil inside him. It seemed to be coming at him from every direction he turned. He looked for a long moment at the house with its dark windows and closed doors.

Then he turned and walked away from it.

17

Tom Bascomb climbed up the ladder to the loft room and set two steaming mugs of hot chocolate on the wooden floor. He looked around the three-walled room with its sloping ceiling and long front side that opened onto the living room below. He was amused at how fast a place could take on the characteristics of the person who lived there.

Harlan had been here only a little over a week, and already it had become distinctly his. He had built bookshelves from planks he had taken from the old barn, and the wall at the far end of the room was already lined with books. The bed was covered with a richly colored quilt that his grandmother had made for him, years ago, and there was a small painting of the Bascomb farm on the wall. It was an old one, showing a stand of woods in the background where now the outskirts of the city of Richmond bumped up against it.

"Saw your light was still on," Tom looked over at his nephew, who sat quietly at the foot of the bed with an unopened book in his hand. "Thought—with the first day of school tomorrow—you could use a little something to help you sleep."

"Is it Swiss chocolate?" Harlan asked with a smile.

"Ah, I wish it was, but it's just the domestic variety." His uncle turned a chair away from a narrow wooden table Harlan used as a desk, and sat down. "That woman sent us Swiss chocolate—faithfully—for nearly fifteen years."

"Every year at Christmas," Harlan remembered.

"Even after the accident, she never quit thinking of me as one of the family. All the way up until she died a couple years ago."

"I remember her. Not very well, but I remember how clean and inviting her farmhouse in France was. Especially the kitchen. And she smelled absolutely wonderful. Like flowers."

"The French and their perfumes," Tom laughed. "Even the older ones."

"What was her name again?"

"Yonic Dubois."

"No wonder I didn't remember it. Since she was Aunt Melanie's mother, she said I could call her Grandmama. And she was very kind. Everyone was kind to me, there."

"You were a sorry sight when we first brought you back. Head all shaved, nothing but skin and bones. She made it something of a personal quest to fatten you up during that year. And she did, too. I'm telling you, your parents would have been shocked at the way their so-called fellow workers were treating their son. I was shocked."

"There was a war on, Tom," Harlan reminded him. "And they were endangering themselves to hide me."

"So they said. And you were just young enough to believe anything they told you. Personally, I think if it had taken me any longer to get there, you would have been dead."

"I still owe them something."

"You don't owe them anything!" He set his cup down on the desk with a bang and reached into a shirt pocket for his pipe. It wasn't there. "Sometimes I think you're more stubborn than your mother ever was! You don't know how relieved I was when they turned down your visa again. Now with another war on over there, maybe you'll realize—"

"It wasn't turned down. Just delayed," Harlan finally confessed the news he had been keeping to himself since he arrived. "They're letting me appeal."

"Good Lord," his uncle breathed. "How in heaven's name did you manage that? They've been pulling Americans out of that country for the last ten years!"

"I found one of the few organizations left that wasn't complying," he admitted, "and joined up with them."

"Not the Mission."

Harlan's silence as he sipped on the warm sweet drink was all that was needed for an answer.

"I can't believe you did that." Tom shook his head and then looked over at him, as if he could figure it out by looking harder. "It isn't like you to compromise your stand. That's what you had to do, wasn't it?"

"I did. But it was the only door open to me. And they weren't principles, they were only personal differences. I don't drink, or use tobacco. All I had to give up, really, was going to dances. And two nights a week for meetings. Sure, I miss the dances and the big bands but if that's all that's keeping me from—"

"Two nights a week sitting with those stuffed shirts!" His uncle interrupted. "Thinking they're so much above the rest of humanity. You of all people, Harlan! You couldn't look down on another human being if you tried."

"In a way, I've been looking down on the Mission folks, Tom. I've been rejecting them as a means of getting where I wanted to go, just because they did things poorly when my parents worked for them. Anyway, I took a long hard look at myself and decided I didn't have the right to set personal differences above my obligation to the people."

"The people!" Tom breathed disgustedly. "China has a barbaric, backward culture—and if they're not at war with another country—they're warring among themselves! They kill your parents and fifteen years later you still feel obligations? I don't understand you, Harlan."

The next phrase Harlan spoke was in perfect Chinese, and it angered Tom so that he only realized he understood it after he burst out, "I can't let you go back to a place I nearly killed myself trying to get you out of!"

"You do remember," Harlan whispered.

"Of course, I remember," his uncle admitted. "How could I forget the most constant phrase you ever spoke to me for the first year we had you? All you wanted to do was go back."

Tom ran a hand through his graying hair and sighed. "I thought it was pretty much licked—that old longing. Especially since you graduated and took so well to teaching. And since you so loved America and everything it stands for. Hasn't anything I've taught you taken hold?"

"Of course it's taken hold, Uncle," Harlan set his empty cup aside and looked at him earnestly. "It's the reason I have anything worthwhile to give. Freedom—and the worth of the individual—those are principles every downtrodden nation of the world needs to grasp hold of. And those of us who teach, have the obligation to do just that."

"But you don't have to go back to China to do it," the older man persisted. "Why can't you do it right here in Cedar Creek? God knows we have enough downtrodden people here to —"

"Why was I born there? Why did I spend the first ten years of my life in China? There had to be a reason, Tom."

"You weren't born there. You were born in that farmhouse you sold last month, and I personally carried you on my shoulders through the Richmond City Museum when you were two years old. It wasn't until that zealot Scottish father of yours talked my sister into joining the Mission that they took you over there. Until then, you were as American as the rest of us Bascombs. Even if your last name is Fleming."

"It was for a reason," Harlan insisted. "I still dream about the river and the people. I learned about people there."

"You would have learned about people wherever you were, Harlan. It's your gift. You've turned into a fine teacher and I'm proud of you. I just hate to see you waste it, that's all."

"I'd be doing the same thing, Tom. Just in a place no one else can go."

"Don't kid yourself. You'll end up a refugee all over, again. Just like before. What kind of school can you have with starving children on war-torn roads? I can't imagine the Mission would even consider sending you. They might be letting their people stay but they have no right to send any more over."

"I already knew the language and the customs," Harlan explained. "And the couple who ran the school last, were killed during a —"

"For God sake, Harlan—doesn't that tell you anything?"

"It tells me they have an incredible need there," he replied quietly. "And it seems I remember someone else who was looking to fill a need… and came here."

"I didn't have to join the Mission to do it."

"You joined something, though. This mountain society, or whatever it is. It looks like you've swallowed all of it – the good and the bad together. Its religion and its spells, the blessings and the curses. Not so different from the Mission, if you ask me."

"Harlan." Tom got to his feet and began to pace, his tall frame nearly brushing the low ceiling boards. "I can't argue with you, you've got too good at it over the years. Twisting the very things I tell you around and throwing them back at me again. You should have been a politician!"

"I'm sorry."

"Or, a diplomat." The older man was quiet for a few minutes as the realization sank in. He looked into the intense blue gaze—the image of his dead sister's eyes and the only physical trait they both shared – and wondered if he would ever get over feeling the loss of him. Or the incredible sense that Harlan's life was a fleeting treasure, redeemed merely to be spent in wild extravagance on the destiny of others.

It suddenly flashed through Tom's mind to forbid this

crazy thing. Then he just as quickly realized it was a grown man sitting across from him and not a young boy, anymore. "Well," he finally said with a resigned sigh, "At least you came when I needed you, son."

"I am glad I came, Uncle. And we still have this year."

"We do at that." He collected the two cups and started for the ladder, "But I was hoping this place would get to you somehow. The way it got to me."

"I do like it," Harlan admitted. "The people and the place, itself. But I don't like this old world anarchy they seem to live by out here. You know they shot someone last year just because he was a Republican?"

A glimmer of humor came into Tom's eyes but he tried not to smile. "A traveling salesman, as I recall. I removed the bullet from his leg. Little misunderstanding, is all, and I believe Orey Thompson ended up buying one of his carbide lighting systems just to make up for it."

"Isn't anyone afraid of the law around here?"

"Law doesn't come back this far very often. Federal men, sometimes, but they're interested mostly in raiding stills. Sheriff will come out and pick somebody up for murder if it's so obvious he'd lose face if he didn't. Other than that, Cedar Creek is pretty much left to itself."

"And Lias Harper."

"Yes. And Lias Harper."

"Does he always do what he says?"

"Why, did he say something to you?" Now a look of concern came over Tom's face and Harlan had second thoughts whether or not he should confide in him.

"He told me to leave his daughter alone," he said finally.

"Have you been seeing Bonnie Rae?"

"I have been seeing Bonnie Rae Harper—waking and sleeping—since the moment I got here," he confessed. "She's wonderful, Tom. I know this is hard to believe, but she makes me think of Aunt Melanie. Almost like she was back with us, again"

"Well, it's no wonder. Between her old dress patterns and her cookbooks she's been following in the same footsteps for years. Which is my fault. Since I selfishly indulged myself in the pleasures of her education. She was someone to speak French and talk literature with, in a place that seemed horribly devoid of refinements during those first few years. Anyway you've got to stop."

He set the cups down and returned to the wooden chair again. "Especially after what you told me. There's nothing that could come from it. And she certainly doesn't need anymore trouble from this family."

"I love her."

"For heaven sake—you've only been here a week!"

"I don't understand it, either. I just know that I do. I want to marry her, Uncle."

"Harlan Fleming!"

"And I was willing to—court her, or whatever they call it around here—to do things right. Only Lias wouldn't even give me a chance! Not because of you, Tom, but because I was a foreigner! He just doesn't want anyone to take her off the mountain."

"Can you blame him?"

"Blame him—of course, I blame him. He wasn't thinking of her welfare when he said it, he was thinking of himself."

"Are you thinking of her welfare, Harlan?" Then he asked the bitter question that Harlan had been turning in his own mind all evening. "What about China?"

The younger man sighed and ran a tired hand through his dark, wavy hair in much the same gesture his uncle had a few minutes before. "I don't know," he murmured. "All this has hit me when I was least expecting it. I don't know why, or what for. Except that it feels right. And she feels the same way about me."

"Wait till you tell her you're leaving. And you'd better tell her, Harlan!" His voice took on some of the firmness of earlier days. "Because that girl's been like a daughter to me."

"I told her already," his nephew assured. "I told her the first day we spent together. But I certainly never told Lias. He just... looked right through me and saw it. People have got some mysterious ways around here.They seem to operate on an instinctive sort of inner level. Even the children. I don't know what it is. But when Lias Harper looked at me then... I didn't have a logical argument to stand on. I just felt everything I thought I was sure of start to crumble."

18

The next morning, Harlan went to the schoolhouse early to make sure everything was in order for the first day. He started a fire in the old black stove to take the chill off the air and moved the smaller desks a little closer to the warmth. Children began to appear in the yard almost an hour early.

At nine o'clock he opened the door and—like magic—two lines formed in front of him. One of boys, and another longer one of girls. He stepped aside and the girls' line filed by first. Everyone seemed to know where to go and what to do. Even though he recognized about half of the faces from the sugar party, they were strangely subdued. The thought crossed his mind that they looked more like they were marching to a funeral rather than going to school. The tallest boy near the end of the line smelled faintly of corn liquor. Without saying anything, Harlan put a hand on his shoulder and held him back while the others entered ahead of him.

"Shee-ut!" the youth spat irritably. "I ain't even walked through the door, yet!"

Harlan quietly closed the door on the other children and looked him in the eye. "How old are you?" he asked.

"Sixteen. And I ain't about to get knocked around when I ain't done nothing, yet!"

"Nor will you get the chance," Harlan informed him. "I suggest you find something else to do today. You can come back tomorrow if you're willing to follow rules. If not, don't bother. There will be no swearing in my school. And don't tempt me by showing up drunk, again."

"What are you gonna do?" He sneered and tossed his head so he could see through his overly long blonde bangs. "Tell my pa?"

"I wouldn't take the time," Harlan replied. "You come here this way again, and I'll turn you over to the sheriff."

The boy's mouth dropped open with a startled concern. "You ain't gonna tell him this time, are you? I'd catch fire if I brought the Laws down on the house, mister."

"Not if you leave quietly today," Harlan answered. "And show up tomorrow, cleaned up, and ready to learn something."

"You mean you really ain't gonna let me in? I'll get skinned if I get kicked out the first day!"

"Sorry." Harlan went inside and left the surprised youth standing on the porch.

There was a hurried scuffling as he entered—telltale signs that the other children had been crowded against the window—waiting to see the oldest boy get "whupped." The teacher smiled, inwardly, and walked over to his desk at the front of the room. He looked at the small crowd of faces, all looking back at him. Some were obviously afraid of him, some were arrogant, but most were merely looking. He unbuttoned the jacket of his light gray suit, sat down on the corner of his desk and said, "Well, let's get to know each other."

There was an almost visible sigh of relief among them, and some of the younger ones even smiled. He noticed the typical seating arrangement: back rows filled up first, the youngest children toward the front, and off in the farthest corner, a cluster of the oldest boys. Rafe Harper was among them. Harlan let each student stand up to say their name and age.

There were seventeen between the ages of six and sixteen. They were dispersed among five families and six of them were

Harpers. Where were all the others? Once more the possibilities of where they were began to bother Harlan, and he wondered if the parents of Cedar Creek could be so indifferent toward education that they would simply let their children stay home.

Perhaps most of them didn't expect him to last very long at the job, either.

During the course of the day he passed out books from an old set of McGuffey Readers. There were four editions ranging from a first reader filled with folk tales, to one for the fifth and sixth grades that contained Norse myths. There was one that was simply a collection of stories and some poems. Three-fourths of the children could not read past a third grade level. But Harlan was surprised that the others could not only read well—they could figure long math problems without the aid of pencil or paper.

This smaller group had an unquenchable thirst for learning. They attended the school for several years beyond the point at which they mastered the available material, and they held a record-breaking excellence in any subject up to the eighth grade. They had also gathered a startling amount of information from an outdated set of encyclopedias that was missing a few volumes.

Now, it became clear why Bonnie Rae had been so voraciously drawn to Tom's library. Having done much of his medical training in Europe, and even remained there throughout the war years, Harlan's Aunt and Uncle had gathered an impressive collection of books by the time they finally moved back to Virginia in 1924. So, it was not surprising to discover that not only were all of the Harper children working above grade levels, but Rafe Harper – besides having his "gift for Latin"—held the record for the highest marks of anyone who had ever attended the school.

Sometime during the lunch recess, six-year-old Corrie Peterson was stung by a "waspie" but duly "doctored up" by Lindy Pearl McCord, who was fifteen. Later on, Harlan surprised the younger ones by joining their game of "Blind Man's Bluff" —playfully allowing them to blindfold and spin him around. And finally at the end of the day, he selected twelve-year-old Joey Luke Wilson for a ride on Prince, for being the best-behaved student of the afternoon.

His beautiful horse was well trained in the role he was supposed to play in this activity. It was a game that stretched back past a long successive line of Harlan's students, to his own childhood days when he enjoyed showing off for friends. At the sound of the familiar whistle, Prince came running across the field where he had been grazing all afternoon, to stand alert at Harlan's side. The teacher went on talking to the group of children as if he hadn't noticed, until the horse gave him a persistent nudge with his head. Harlan turned with a mock severity and said, "Prince, you're interrupting. Don't you have any manners at all?"

The horse replied with an exaggerated shake of his head, which brought a chorus of laughter from the children. Harlan lifted the saddle and tack from the low hanging branch of a nearby tree, and prepared the horse for the favored rider. "Now, I want you to give Joey Luke a good ride, Prince. No playing around, understand?" The horse seemed to ignore him. "Prince—I'm talking to you—are you going to behave?"

The animal nuzzled his master with the velvet softness of his nose, and gave him what could only be described as a wet slobbery kiss on the side of the face. The response brought whoops and hollers of enjoyment from the onlookers. Joey Luke was motioned over and given a boost up into the saddle.

"Feels awful high up, Mister Harlan," said the boy with a nervous smile. "He ain't gonna run off with me is he? I ain't never rid much before."

"Prince," Harlan asked, "you're not going to run off with Joey, are you?" The horse shook his shaggy black mane in reply. "There, you see?" Harlan assured. "He said he wouldn't. Besides that, I'll be controlling him with a magic rope."

"Awww, you're fooling," one of the older boys spoke up

from the crowd.

"No, I'm not." Harlan made motions with his hands as if he were uncoiling a long rope. "I have it right here."

After that, the teacher—who was taking just as much pleasure in the demonstration as the children—made an elaborate show of tying a pretend rope around the horse's neck. He fed it out slowly as he walked backward some twenty feet, with his hand outstretched as if he were holding on to the other end. He gave an obvious tug, and the horse moved forward—as if led.

Then, to everyone's wonder and amazement, Prince—responding to the familiar signals of the outstretched hand—walked, trotted, and finally broke into a gentle lope in a circle around Harlan. He kept the same precise distance away from him at every angle, adding to the illusion of being put through his paces on a common lunge line.

The children were fascinated. Some of the younger ones could not be convinced that the performance was anything less than real magic. And the older ones couldn't help but admire the skill and obvious affection shared by the horse and the man. Such an unusual display caused an open acceptance from the younger children. Though the others were still somewhat hesitant, they were quick to proclaim Mister Harlan as the most "wondersome" teacher that had ever come to Cedar Creek.

Harlan stayed at the school long after the children had gone that first afternoon, looking over their work and wondering—after five years of teaching—why he had been so emotionally moved by them all. There was something strong and long-suffering about these children who had chanced to be born in such hard times. The more he learned about them the more he longed to make their lives more tolerable in some way. If for no other reason than to turn the schoolroom into a place of safety and acceptance, instead of harsh rules and "whuppings".

He expected a few more to filter in during the first week,

but probably nowhere near the twenty to thirty others he knew must live somewhere out there on the ridge. He wondered why none of the former teachers had bothered to report such a large discrepancy in the records. Why hadn't they been just as disturbed about it as he was? Well, this year, Harlan Fleming was responsible for the education of the children of Cedar Creek. If they did not want to learn, he could deal with that. If they were wild and rebellious, he could deal with that, too. On the other hand…

Not knowing where they even were was something he had never encountered before.

19

A few days later, the first stars of evening were beginning to appear in a darkening sky when Harlan started home from school. He took the shortcut. Not over the suspension bridge, but one he and Prince had discovered themselves. It followed a game trail off the east end of the school meadow and meandered through woods, up and down over some steep hilly areas, and finally came out where the trails crossed just before Cedar Creek Road, at the back side of the Weaver's cottage. It was not one to be enjoyed on foot, but for riding it was pleasant and peaceful.

It gave him time to think about things.

Such as why his uncle had been so evasive when he had asked how many students attended school in Coaltown. Besides being the nearest doctor in times of emergency, Tom was responsible for running a small clinic there for the workers and their families one week out of every month. His work for the company was what had brought him to Cedar Creek in the first place and still provided the only "cash money" his uncle had coming in at all. The local people usually paid for his services with goods or produce.

However, when asked about the school in Coaltown, Harlan was met by another of the long, telltale silences that were becoming more and more familiar since his arrival in the hill country. So far, they had all proven to be forerunners of subjects his uncle was either ashamed or embarrassed to tell him about.

"There is no school in Coaltown," the older man admitted finally, one evening after Harlan had pressed the point. "It's been closed since nineteen twenty nine. When the wages all dropped."

"And it was never reported?" Harlan asked.

Tom shrugged. "There were all kinds of problems back then. Malnutrition—children dying by hoards of the bloody flux—they converted the building into a clinic. The one I work out of when I'm there. It's been that way ever since."

"So, none of them send their children to school?"

"There's a woman by the name of MacKelroy who teaches the youngest ones how to read and write out at the community center. But it's not a real serious thing and students come and go. Won't get much out of her, though, because she's married to one of the guards."

"What's that got to do with anything?"

"Plenty. The Company keeps most of its business within its confines, including the clinic and that little school. They even have a grocery store. With high prices and paycheck accounts that have made the people depend solely on them. They run their own regular world up there." He held up a hand to stop Harlan's next question before he even got a word out. "That's because they're running on the shy side of the safety regulations. Sad but true."

"What about the older Cedar Creek students? They drop out on the slightest whim and no one seems to care. None of them are going on to college. A higher education seems to be the last thing on anyone's mind in these hills."

"Sure, some of them are working in the mines. I don't deny that. But there are dropouts in any district you work in, isn't that right? Let me tell you something." They had been talking at the kitchen table after dinner and Tom slid his chair back and began to fill his pipe. "You keep doing what you're doing out there, and—believe me, Harlan—the kids will start coming out of the woodwork around here. You'll see."

"That could take months."

"Months well spent. You have to give people time to get used to things out here. If you don't, they'll just clam up and you'll never see any change. Or—worse—they'll go against you."

"I at least have to do the job I was sent here to do, Uncle," Harlan pointed out. "I certainly can't wink at fifty names missing off my enrollment records."

"I'm not asking you to ignore them. Just give folks more than a few weeks before you go telling them how to raise their kids. We've had hard times out here."

Harlan agreed to try.

Whether, or not, the Company had shut down their school was really not his affair. It was a private school and the state was ultimately responsible for the education of the children in Cedar Creek. But for that company to illegally employ minors... now, that was Harlan's affair.

It was obvious there were more than a few working over there, or everyone wouldn't be trying so hard to keep him from finding out about it. Suddenly, he felt angry at such ignorance and stupid reasons. Toward his uncle, as well. Hard times and poverty – how could they justify doing something that was wrong, when it was impossible for anything better to come out of it? His uncle was tired of fighting and had given up: Harlan could see that. And the Company was like any other rolling machinery that operated on greed, doing things no one individual would take responsibility for. He could understand that, too.

But the parents who would permit such things—those were the ones he did not understand and had no explanations for. He did not blame any of the children. They would do what they were told. Or, what they wanted, if no one told them anything. Vulnerable to whatever wind might blow against them.

He was riding along, trying to make sense of all these things, and still feeling the echoes of strong attachment that always took hold of him when students were drawn to him for a shelter. Suddenly, he noticed that the "weaver" was out in her yard this evening. He stopped at the rickety rail fence and looked over at her.

She had skin that was dark and wrinkled, and long black hair that hung loose around her shoulders. There was not a strand of gray in it. She reminded him of some of the old Chinese women he had seen in his boyhood. She was wearing a man's hat and leather-fringed jacket over the top of a long calico dress. With no shoes. And she was smoking a pipe.

There was something unusual about her eyes. After looking at them for a long moment, Harlan decided they were animal-like: a woods deer or squirrel, maybe. They were as black as her hair and incredibly bright and alert. Seated in a straight-backed cane-bottom chair, she seemed to be looking him over with the same scrutiny that he was giving her.

"Fine evening we're having for this time of year," Harlan began casually. "Wouldn't you say so, ma'am?"

"Harlan Fleming," she replied.

Obviously—like everyone else on the ridge—she already knew everything there was to know about him, so he thought he might offer her some of the same.

"I hear you're a weaver by trade," he ventured, "and that you command a lot of fear and respect from my children."

"The little wheels spin and spin, Harlan Fleming," she answered, "but it's the big one turns them around."

"I beg your pardon?"

She got to her feet with a strange and chilling sort of dignity. She seized the back of her chair by one of its upright hickory posts, tilted it slightly forward, and began to turn it around and around with only one leg touching the soft earth.

He watched her, wondering if she expected him to respond to the strange ritual. But she turned away from him without another word and returned to her little shack, dragging the chair along behind her as she went.

Well, Harlan thought as he started down the path again, the poor woman was obviously a little mentally touched. That sort of behavior was just the kind to make people label her as a witch. Not surprising, considering the way these mountain folks tended toward superstition. There had been something unnerving about her bearing, though. And what a strange thing to say to him. Maybe it had something to do with weaving.

The little wheels spin and spin
but the big one turns them around...

The rhythm of it echoed in his mind almost like a song... and he found himself repeating it over and over again, all the way home.

20

The teasing heat of Indian summer was gone from Cedar Creek as quickly as it came. Granny Harper was aware of it almost before she opened her eyes the following morning in her tumble-down cabin which was nestled away safely in the depths of the Bog Hollow. Her old bones were announcing the approach of cold weather several hours before it finished descending into the hush of deep woods where she lived.

She sat up slowly in the "off-the-floor" bed she had slept in for over sixty years, and waited for her eyes to focus in the early morning darkness. She was fully clothed. The way her "rumitiz" was kicking up these days, she couldn't see making herself ache with the efforts of dressing and undressing any more than she had to. She reached for the man's hat on the night stand beside her bed, plopped it onto her disheveled heap of gray hair, and set her feet onto the cold floor.

She slipped a stocking foot into one of the homemade leather brogans Big John had made her last year at Christmas. They were the kind without laces so she wouldn't have to bend or tie. Then she shuffled toward the stone fireplace at the far end of the cabin. All at once, she gave a sudden startled gasp when she saw the familiar form stretched out on the hearth. She stood still and quiet for a long frustrated moment, trying to remember what time it was.

The old woman looked toward the window and peered out at the gray dawn breaking through the tangled branches of tall balsam firs that clustered near her front porch. Morning. A crisp fall morning and Zeb must be out at the early chores and Buck was still asleep. Been out all night again, no doubt. Better make breakfast.

She reached carefully over the sleeping figure and unearthed the banked coals with a small black shovel. She carried a few of the red glowing embers across the room to the old wood burning stove and placed them gently in the firebox where she already had wood and kindling waiting from the night before. She lifted a large iron skillet from its peg on the wall and set it on the stove to heat. When the coffee was on and the biscuit-bread nearly done, she broke ten eggs into hot bacon grease, salted them lightly, and gave them a liberal sprinkling of black pepper. Then she listened to the pleasant pop and bubble of their cooking sounds and sighed contentedly.

"Hey, you setting rounder!" She called in her cheeriest voice. "You best be stirring yourself before your pap gets back in!"

Joseph Lee sat up with a quick obedience that was more reflex than response, and tried to blink the sleep away. He breathed in the fragrant smell of a warm breakfast and looked over at his plump unkempt grandmother bustling around the wooden table with plates and mugs. He ran his hands through his red-gold hair and got to his feet.

"What time is it?" He sat down at the table.

"Past time, for certain," she replied. She set the large pan of eggs in front of him. "Now I'll just fetch the bacon and biscuit-bread. Got a touch of gravy, too, this morning."

Joseph Lee looked at the large number of eggs in the pan and then noticed that the table was set for three. "Who else is eating?" he asked. "You got company?"

"You'd think so, the way you and your daddy swallow down one egg after another of a morning. I declare, Buck

Harper! You'd think you was —" She came back to the table then and looked him straight in the eye. "Why, Joseph Lee— how long you been here?"

"Most of the night, I reckon," he said carefully.

The old woman looked out the window, again. She looked toward the fireplace. "Been sleeping at the hearth?"

"Yep."

An expression of grief suddenly flooded over her face. She set the plate of bacon and biscuits down and slowly reached for the extra plate, holding it close up against her while she carried it back to the cupboard.

"Granny —"

"I done forgot what time it was," she mourned. "And where they all gone." She brought back the pot of coffee and sat down across from her grandson. "I reckon you was looking so much like him in the half dark, I just..." She wiped her eyes with the corner of her apron.

"I'm sorry, Granny!" Joseph Lee got up from the chair and gave her shoulder a pat. "I shore didn't mean for nothing like this to happen."

"It ain't no fault of yours, son," she replied. "Your ol' granny's just getting low in her mind, is all. Done seen too many of my children go. I hope the good Lord takes me home before ever I have to go through it, again. He was my youngest boy!"

"I know." He bent down and gave her wrinkled tear-wet cheek a kiss. "He was the best of us all. But let's don't think on it no more, it's too hard. Hey—you want me to chop you some wood?"

"You're so like him," she replied. "You can chop me some after breakfast. Fetch my pipe before you set back down, will you, J-Lee?"

He walked over to the stove and reached up on the warming shelf where she kept it. He opened the firebox and lit the end of a thin stick of kindling as he tamped the loose tobacco down into the bowl with his thumb. When it was lit and drawing properly, he returned to the table and handed it to her.

"Thankee. Now set yourself back down and eat before all these fixings get cold." She cast a self-conscious glance into the enormous pan with ten eggs inside. "What in tarnation am I gonna do with all them eggs?"

"All what eggs? Don't you reckon you can eat two?"

"Why shore, but —"

"Then we ain't got too many. I eat eight every morning myself, regular!"

"You do?"

"Yep. Ain't no need to waste eggs when you got me around! I just naturally figured that's why you fixed them."

"Naturally," She began to brighten. "I recollect that's why I done it. Want some coffee?"

"Shore do. Got any sweetening?"

"You want the long or the short?"

"I'll take short for the coffee, and long for the biscuits."

"I'll vow!" She got up to reach into the cupboard for the maple sugar and the clay honey pot. "If you ain't your grand-pap all over, again!"

"You know, Granny," he said, "way I figure it, you got fourteen boys left—counting the grandkids. And as long as even one of them is still around... well, you ain't really lost any. Not really."

"How do you mean?" She sat down again and slid two of the eggs onto her plate.

"I mean the others ain't really gone," he explained. "Because each of us that's left has a piece or two—of them—hid right down inside us."

"Why, Joseph Lee Harper!" she breathed in amazement. "Them's the purtiest words I ever did hear!"

"Well, they're the truth." He flashed a winning smile that sent a comforting warmth all through her. "And as long as we're all walking around with pieces of each other inside, then it don't make one heap of difference which of us is setting down at this here table. You're gonna have your boys around you for the rest of your born days, some way or other."

"Praise the Lord! That warms me clear through to my bones! It purely does." She sat quietly for a moment, just savoring the thought and picking at the eggs, before looking back at him with a sudden worried expression. "You ain't got yourself into no trouble have you, Joseph Lee? I can't think of any other reason to wake up and find you on my hearth of a morning."

"Naw, I ain't in no trouble. Just had me some thinking to do, is all. That house of ours is a might crowded to be doing much of that."

"Well, I reckon." She put three heaping spoons of sugar into her coffee and stirred it slowly. "How's my boy?"

"Not real good," he answered, knowing she meant Lias.

"Help me put some things together, will you, son? I reckon I'd like to come home with you for a spell."

"Shore, Granny, I'll help. But I didn't drive the truck part way, like usual. We can get you all packed, then I'll go home and bring it back for you. What do you want to take?"

"Oh…" She looked off distantly, "something I can't quite recollect where it is. You could try looking in them shelves over next to the fireplace."

Joseph Lee shoveled the last egg into his mouth and dutifully got up to look. He stared for a long moment at the rows of neatly arranged jars of various shapes and sizes. "What's it look like?"

"Powder… it's a powder. Kind of red-brown color."

"This it?" He held a jar up for her to see.

"Nope. That there's ground up sassafras bark. But we best bring it along because it'll be right helpful."

"I don't see nothing else looks red-brown."

"Well," she thought a moment. "Maybe I still got it drying up in the loft room. We best both go up there."

21

Joseph Lee helped his grandmother climb the steep wooden ladder in the corner of the main room. Unlike the rest of the house, everything was spotlessly clean and organized up in the loft. There were shelves along the walls displaying all manner of dried roots and herbs. Small bundles of others were tied together and hung from the low rafters to dry. The loft room had always interested Joseph Lee. As a child, he had even slept there, occasionally, and he always remembered the vivid smells of the place. Strong herbs and spices mixed with sulfur.

"Might be I stashed some in this ol' chest, here." His grandmother pointed toward a trunk off in one corner. "Can you open it, J-Lee? Hinge is a might rusty."

He opened it with a little effort and the rich smell of cedar enveloped him as he looked inside.

"Law! I ain't seen this stuff in years!" She bent down beside him. "Why, here's my wedding dress... and a cup left over from my mama's chiney she brung over from the old World."

"Right purty."

"What's this? Lookee here... family birth papers. Teared right out of the Good Book my ol' grandpap used to keep. Here's me. Ellie Mae McFerson. Born April ninth, eighteen fifty —" She gasped. "Tarnation! I'm getting nigh onto middle age!" She folded it back in a hurry and tucked it away again. "Well, it ain't in here, neither. Course I ain't used any since Aunt Evie needed it away back in ninety-two."

"What's it called?" He let his eyes continue to wander over the room. "Maybe I could dig some for you."

"Don't even recollect. Did a heap of wonderments, though. I'll just have to use the belladonna. Have to be right careful with that, though. It's one of them nightshade herbs." She shuffled over to another row of shelves and picked out a jar. "Kill a person plumb dead if you don't use it right."

Joseph Lee closed the old chest and sat down on top of it. "Didn't you use to sell this stuff for cash-money sometimes, Granny? You shore got a heap of curiosities up here."

"Oh, you can still sell it for cash-money. But what do I need cash-money for? I used to back when I was younger. But my ol' bones ain't up to all the traipsing it takes no more."

"What sort of cash-money does it bring in?"

She moved to a narrow wooden table at the far end of the room and began to measure the medicine into a smaller jar. "There's folks over the Wind Ridge make enough to bread their whole family through the winter."

"Are you fooling me?"

"Nope. But it takes a heap of work. Most of it outside. You got to gather your plants, clean them real careful... dry them. Then, it ain't till they're nigh onto ready for market that you can figure just what they'll bring."

"Just say some of this stuff you got up here."

She cast him a wry glance. "Joseph Lee, what are you thinking?"

"I was thinking maybe I could turn my hand to Wild-crafting if it paid good enough." He got to his feet again and reached for a bunch of drying roots hanging from a nearby nail on the wall. "Mmm..." he breathed the familiar fragrance in deeply. "Sang root?"

"Yep." She took them back and replaced them carefully on the nail. "But don't you get no idees, now. All this up here shows for a lifetime of herb-hunting. Some of this stuff I couldn't never get back, again, at my age. Even if I do know where it grows. I'm too old. I figure what I got left here is enough to keep me for doctoring folks on this ridge. But I ain't got as many to care for since he came. He don't do nothing much different than me, excepting he uses store bought drugs where I use crude – and folks think he's next best to God!"

"Don't think about him, Granny," Joseph Lee said quietly. "You done a heap more doctoring on this ridge than he'll ever do. But I wasn't thinking on selling any of yours. Say I was fixing to start ranging on my own, would you help me with what I don't know? I need something to start bringing money in regular."

"I'll help you," she replied. "But don't go figuring you'd get no money right off."

"How come? I'm willing to work hard at it."

"Because it's the kind of thing that has to dry and cure. And there ain't no way on God's earth, Joseph Lee, to hurry up drying and curing. Then again..." She sighed and looked wistfully out of the little loft room window a few feet away. "You can't never be certain what the demand's gonna be at the wholesaler. Sometimes you work months on something they don't need right then—and they don't buy. You got to cart it back home and wait till they have a need. But sometimes..." She shifted the stem of her pipe from one side of her mouth to the other and looked back at him again. "Sometimes they need just what you got. And that's when you can make enough cash-money in two or three trips to see you through any kind of winter the good Lord wants to send!"

"Shoot—that's something!" he said.

She giggled and her eyes grew distant. "Times there was when these hills were covered with revenuers, J-Lee. They looked up and down the holler again and again, but we all just laid low. Didn't nobody come or go from corn-planting time till the first snow. They took the Miller still up on the Wind Ridge, that year... the Muskadee... and a whole heap of others.

Never did find the Harpers. Biggest operation in these parts, and they figured if they couldn't find us—they could at least starve us. Ooooo!"

She laughed again and winked at him. "But they wasn't ready for a old granny-woman like me, carting her wares to market. Oh, they stopped me every time—they stopped me. But there ain't no law against Wild-crafting, so, they had to let me by. Now, you ask your daddy, boy, and he'll tell you that was the best year us Harpers ever lived through! The men-folk not doing nothing but hunting and fishing, and the women-folk glorying in just having them around. Everybody living their lives out safe and natural. Why, there was six new Harper babies born that year!"

"Well, shoot," he marveled again.

"And one of the peacefulest things I recollect, was ol' Uncle Sedley, laying down in his own bed—of his own notion—and dying of natural causes."

"Granny—that's just the way it ought to be!"

"That's what I'm praying for, son," she said fervently. "You want to pray with me on it? We can get down on our prayer bones this here minute and the good Lord will give ear to us, Joseph Lee. Come on, I need to see this family in peace and plenty before I go!"

"Well..." He hesitated. "I ain't much for praying. But I'm all for learning this here Wild-crafting trade. I'm made for this kind of thing—I just know it. I love the outside. I can't stand being shut up nowhere. This way, I wouldn't have to be. And no boss-man would be telling me what to do."

"Won't bring no quick money, boy," she warned again.

"Then in the meantime," he replied with a grim resolve, "I'll think of something else to get me by."

22

Joseph Lee was still thinking about wild-crafting when he left the little cabin an hour later and headed down into the deeper regions of the Bog Hollow. A morning mist was rising up from the damp earth in great wisps of slow moving swirls as he pushed his way through the thick jungle-like tangles of undergrowth. He noticed a few red leaves on a sour gum tree and farther on, a poplar bore some that had turned to gold; tell-tale signs that autumn would soon be flaming across the steep mountainsides and deep into every hollow. The ground began to grow soft and spongy beneath his feet as he passed close to the marshes, and the distinctive "oongka-choonk" of a swamp bittern came to his ears.

Ahead of him, a white-tailed deer sprang from the trail and escaped into the sheltering brush. It was all these things—the sights, the sounds, the smells—that made him love the outside. Sometimes he felt more kin to the wild things that lived here than to people, simply because he understood them better.

The enormous breakfast he had forced down was beginning to sit like lead in his stomach as he moved along in the cold, crisp air. He was not headed toward home. Instead, he was making his way deep into the bog hollow: a wild tangle of swamp and marshland that lay in the very heart of Harper land.

There were only a few family members left who knew the trails and traces well enough to find their way in and out of it. Few outside the Harper clan would even dare. With bog holes that could trap and drown a grown man in thick, oozing mud faster than a fellow traveler could devise a way of helping him out, there was little of the threatening place that was appealing. Even for Harpers.

But Joseph Lee loved it. He loved its wild sounds and eerie silences, and the great protective solitude that kept everyone else away. He jogged along the familiar trails in the same way he would have jogged through his own tobacco field, even though he had not set foot in this particular part of it in nearly four years. He stopped to drink from a cool clear spring, and heard the angry chatter of a squirrel who was not happy at his intrusion. When he got to his feet again, he looked down the narrow trail. It disappeared into the brush, farther down, but he knew the turnoff was only another twenty yards ahead. He dried his hands on the front of his shirt and kept on.

At the sudden rustle of greenery ahead of him, he stopped instantly. There was a loud crack of gunfire, and a bullet thumped into a nearby tree... dangerously close.

Hey!" He jumped into a tangle of underbrush as if it could somehow protect him. "What do you think you're —"

Another shot rang out, this time so close to his head it made his ears ring. A wild, unfamiliar laugh drowned the string of profanity that escaped him, and after a moment, a young man wearing a miner's cap and carrying a Winchester, stepped onto the trail in full view. His right arm was in a sling. With a wry, half grin, he brought the rifle up with his left hand and—to Joseph Lee's horror—shot from the hip, sending another bullet winging toward him with an unnerving closeness.

Just then, Leroy Tatum came bounding down the trail with his dark hair sticking out in all directions and only a single suspender strap pulled hurriedly up over one bare shoulder. He ran bold and barefooted up to the crazy youth, yanked the Winchester away and gave him a shove that sent him sprawling. "What in hail do you think you're doing, boy?" he hollered, pouncing on the startled figure before he could get up. Tate yanked the cap from the youth's own head and began hitting him furiously with it. "You nigh onto killed yourself a Harper, you half-wit!"

The young man covered his head with his one good arm to ward off Tate's blows and whined, "He called me every kind of bad name he could lay his tongue to!"

"That was after you shot at me!" Joseph Lee emerged cautiously from the bushes, even though his assailant was obviously subdued. "Near kilt me!"

Tate straightened and looked over at him apologetically. "I'm purely ashamed about this, Ol' Son... you all right?"

"Well, I ain't shot," he answered.

"I'd have had him the first time if my shooting arm weren't all busted up!" the young man on the ground got slowly to his feet.

Joseph Lee looked at him in astonishment and then turned to Tate. "Who is he?" he asked.

"Willie Hollis Jr." His friend slapped the hat back on the young man's head and prodded him to move along the trail ahead of them.

"I want my gun back," Willie sulked, looking back over his shoulder.

"I've a mind to keep it!" Tate snapped. "The trouble you got us into with it, just in the last two days—get on back to camp first and cool off some!"

Joseph Lee could smell the still before they actually came to it. The pungent odor of fermentation mingled with woodsmoke and the hint of something else... burnt coffee? A dog growled as they neared the secluded spot and then ran to greet them in recognition. The actual equipment was not the same but the surroundings were so familiar that the hair on the back of Joseph Lee's neck began to rise. A picture involuntarily flashed through his mind...

A well-built, robust man with sandy blonde hair, and an uncanny resemblance to Joseph Lee, sat comfortably on a wood stump pulled close to a low burning fire. He held a tin cup half full of coffee in one hand, and a cigarette burning close down to his fingers in the other. "Mean looking sky," he had said. "Fixing to get us a storm of rain any minute, now."

"You reckon you better drive?" Joseph Lee asked.

"Nope. We'll leave things just like we planned. You're ready." His Uncle Buck had looked directly into his eyes then, and smiled. "The way I figure it —"

He never finished. One moment they were sitting there, talking quietly together, and the next, the whole world seemed to explode into a cacophony of shattering glass and gunfire. His uncle flew ten feet across the clearing and landed blood covered and motionless, with his arms outstretched and the cigarette still burning between his fingers.

The rest of the memory was a confusion of blood and noise, during which he tried to staunch the incredible flow of blood pouring from his uncle's chest. It began to rain. In a mere few moments, the downpour drowned out the fire and left them all in darkness. Somewhere, his Aunt Jenny was moaning and sobbing. Then, as hand-held lanterns came bobbing toward them through the trees, somebody knocked him to the ground and wrenched his hands painfully behind his back to cuff him. They held his face against the wet earth and he couldn't breathe...

"Joseph Lee?" Tate gave him a nudge with his elbow. "What's wrong with you, boy? Ain't you heard a word I been saying?"

"What?" He forced himself back to the present and looked over at his friend. "I reckon not. Sorry. It's just this place gives me the miseries. I didn't think it would be this bad." He ran a trembling hand through his hair and walked over to the fire.

"Here, Ol' Son," Tate handed him a metal cup. "Drink some of this."

Joseph Lee took a swallow, choked and spit the rest out on

the ground. "That's the worst stuff I tasted in all my born days!"

"I never was too good at housekeeping," Tate said. "But it ain't bad for being a few days old."

"Tastes like you scooped up ash from the fire, stirred it in the pot and called it coffee."

"Well, shoot," Tate grinned. "Ain' t that how it's made? Sit down and I'll put on some fresh."

Joseph Lee sat down on a large rock and looked around anxiously. "Where did he go?"

"Willie Jr.?"

"Yep. I don't trust him."

"Ah, he's probably off pouting somewhere because I took his gun. He'll get over it."

"If he don't," Joseph Lee warned, "he's liable to come back and shoot both of us."

"Naw. He's just high strung is all. Especially when there's trouble brewing."

"I'd say he's crazy but I reckon that's your business. What kind of trouble you talking about, anyhow?"

Tate dumped the old brew out of the soot-blackened pot and poured water from a bucket into it. He reached into a large canvas sack and clattered around until he came up with a coffee can. He popped the top off with the edge of a pocketknife, took out a handful of grounds, and threw them into the pot. "We stole a little business from the Manifees last week." He wiped his hands on his pants, and turned from the fire. "Big Otis got riled up some."

"Are you fooling me?" Joseph Lee asked.

Tate shook his head. "I figured they had so much going for them, they wouldn't hardly notice if I sold a couple or three cases to that little speakeasy just over the county line. Then they came busting into the back room down at Ruby's, last week." He sighed and shook his head again, as if he still couldn't believe it. "Before I could pay them off and make things right by the ol' man, Willie got het up and fired at Big

Al. Didn't do nothing but graze him on the forehead, but I thought the whole lot of them was gonna blow up right there. Weren't any reasoning to be done then."

"So, what happened?" Joseph Lee prompted. "How come you both ain't dead?"

"Little operation like ours ain't no threat to them big boys, really. I reckoned they figured on giving us a lesson. Shot Willie in the arm and give me a black eye is all. I been sweating out the last two days hoping they wasn't gonna bust up my still."

"I'm surprised at you, Tatum," Joseph Lee admonished. "I mean it ain't like you don't know how things are in the Business."

"Easy money... gets to me every time. I was trying to make enough to get out of here before winter. My days are numbered in this business, and don't nobody know it better than me. I just ain't got what it takes to out-figure everybody. The longer I'm in it, the sooner I'm caught."

"Where you gonna go if you could get out?"

"I heard there was still some jobs left in Dee-troit."

"Shoot –" Joseph Lee threw a twig into the fire he had thoughtlessly picked up off the ground. "There's always still work around, somewhere else."

"Yeah, but I heard them automobile factories ain't doing so bad."

"Well, I sure wouldn't move off the mountain and halfway cross the country to find out."

"Way I see it, I got no choice. I been on the Company list now for three years. I'd be starving right now if it hadn't been for the still. They're laying off and cutting back hours as it is, they ain't gonna get around to calling me." He sighed and moved the coffee pot over a higher flame. "Ain't no time to be in a fix like this."

"Ain't no time to be in a fix like this and be careless, that's for sure."

"Trouble is, I never see things careless till I look back on them. Then, I wonder where I left my head last."

"So, what are you gonna do now?"

"What do you mean? Right now I'm just waiting for the next run-off and glad my still ain't been busted up before I get it."

"See?" Joseph Lee straightened up and pointed a finger at him. "That's just what I'm talking about, Tatum! You shouldn't to be waiting here like a setting duck. You should be moving the still."

"I ain't got the revenuers on my tail, J-Lee, why should I go to all that trouble?"

"Listen..." He lowered his voice and looked at him seriously. "Just listen to me for a minute. You got revenuers."

Tate jumped to his feet. "Is that what you come for? To tip me off? Gawd—now what am I gonna do? I'll bet that ol' man Manifee let a word slip to them because of what I done!"

"Set down." Joseph Lee pulled him back down by the arm. "What I mean is, the whole county's crawling with them. So, you might as well figure you got them."

"Now, what did you do that for?" he said irritably. "Nigh onto scared the fire out of me!"

"That's the way it ought to be. You just ain't serious enough. I bet you don't even know where they are."

"What do I care where they are, long as they ain't after me?"

"They're after you. They're after every last person on this ridge that has anything to do with making or running shine. And don't you forget it. They're tightening up, too."

"They are?"

"Yep. All you got to do is read the papers to find that out. I told you that last time I saw you."

"I been busy."

"Busy getting yourself in trouble, looks to me like."

"So, where are they?"

"Like I said, they're everywhere. Two days ago, they busted up a hooch gang just over the state line. Clapped every last one of them in the local jailhouse, waiting for the penitentiary. And you know what them G-men are doing now?"

"What."

They're going back over all the old locations. They busted up the Chaney still that way three weeks ago, and another one over the Wind Ridge before that. Next thing you know, they'll be poking around the old Harper site."

"I got to move my still!" Tate jumped to his feet again and began to pace. "Help me think of someplace to move it to, J-Lee. I ain't ready for no penitentiary!"

"Bear Lick. Halfway up Sugar Hill."

Tate stopped in his tracks and looked down at him in surprise. "If I didn't know better, Ol' Son, I'd say you already had things planned out."

"I might."

"You coming in with me?"

"I was thinking on it. Just to get me through the winter. Nothing permanent."

"Boy—that's all I need!" Tate said. "I just need one good year!"

"But that was before I found out you got the Manifees riled. Now, I ain't sure. You can keep yourself from the revenuers. But you get on the wrong side of them local boys, and they'll catch you wherever you're hid."

"We'll move the still, just like you said."

"Don't think they won't find it. But if you leave their business alone, they might cool off by the time they did."

"Oh, Harper..." came an almost musical voice from the surrounding brush.

Joseph Lee looked up in time to see both barrels of a shotgun pointed directly at him from behind a tree. His face paled.

"Willie Jr.!" Tate roared, "You get on out here right now, boy— and quit fooling around!"

The gun disappeared slowly and Willie began to laugh to himself as he came out into the open to join them. He looked over at Tate. "Weren't loaded," he snickered.

23

Lou Ellen Harper felt like she could walk a hundred miles. Maybe she would. No one in the family seemed to realize she wasn't a youngun anymore. With all her mother's talk about hard times and saving money, she didn't even know the value of perfume. Why, Lou Ellen had seen bottles at the drugstore that cost at least fifty-five cents! To not let her accept one that was offered—absolutely free—could only mean one thing.

Her mother didn't think she was old enough.

She could cook, or clean, or pull weeds, or watch younguns, all right, but she didn't need any perfume. How could she not need perfume when she didn't have any? A little something for the young lady, the man said. But her mother had stopped her just as she reached out to take it. It was so mortal embarrassing she had to leave the house just to keep her temper. She might have to walk all the way to Cedarville to keep it.

She had gone half a mile before she realized she still had her apron on. It was covered with tomato stains because she had been helping with the canning this morning. She took it off and stashed it behind a bush at the side of the road, where she could pick it up on the way back. They had made her do most of the cleaning up afterward, too, since Bonnie Rae had quit early to take some of the jars over to the Tollivers. No doubt, if her older sister had been offered the perfume, her mother would have allowed it.

Lou Ellen pulled off the rubber band she had used to keep her hair back during the canning and shook her head like a spirited pony. Then she screamed. Which was why she didn't hear the car motor until the black and white DeSoto slipped up beside her and slowed down enough to keep pace. Without a word, the traveling man held the coveted bottle of perfume out to her. She hesitated only a moment. But when her fingers finally closed around the cool smooth glass, he didn't let go.

"How about a smile, darlin? Face like yours…" He let her have it, then. "… is way too pretty to stay clouded over that long."

"Thank you, Mr. Durham. I —"

"Don't mention it. Company allows giving samples away from time to time. It's how we get regular customers. Women who like the perfume usually like other things that go with it."

"What other things?"

"How much time do you have?"

She giggled at the absurdity. "Law! Time I got plenty, it's money I don't have enough of. So, maybe you best save this for someone else." She held the bottle back out toward him.

He didn't take it. Instead, he smiled, pushed his hat farther back on his head with a thumb and asked, "Got anything to trade?"

"Not unless you'd like a jar of homegrown tomatoes," she replied with a hint of sarcasm.

"Honey, I love homegrown tomatoes. Tell you what. You look like the picture show type to me and I've got a new shipment of a make-up line called *Hollywood Secrets.* Should be coming in any day now. You meet me here – at this very same time – on Saturday and we'll do some trading."

She hesitated.

"That is, unless you already have a date lined up for Saturday."

"Law, Mr. Durham – you can't be serious!"

"Sure I'm serious. Thing about being on the road? A man ends up with lots of money and nobody to spend it on. Truth is…" He stopped the car and turned off the motor. "I thought I just might be able to talk you into seeing that new picture show that came out last week. what was the name of it?"

"*The Jungle Princess*? With Dorothy Lamour?"

"That's the one."

"I don't reckon my folks would let me."

"Well, now…" He smoothed down his blonde mustache and cast an obvious glance at the perfume bottle. "How is it I get the feeling you're not the kind of girl to let a little thing like that stop you?"

Later, that evening. Bonnie Rae was having similar thoughts as she took a stack of plates out of the cupboard and began to set them around the table for supper. She thought how she had not lived seventeen years in this family without learning how to get around Lias Harper. Now—after days of trying to think of a way to see Harlan—she had finally come up with a good plan. Joseph Lee thought otherwise. After pointing out its shortcomings, he reluctantly agreed to help. But only because—in his opinion—she was headed for trouble without him. So, a secret meeting, unknown to Harlan, was devised.

She wondered how he would respond to seeing her after all these days. Every day since school started, she had looked for some message from him sent through the younger children. But one never came. What natural-born man wouldn't risk a little trouble to see a girl if he really cared enough about her?

What if he didn't care anymore?

But if it turned out that he loved her as much as she was sure she loved him, she was prepared to do anything to be with him. Even if it meant running away off the mountain. Why, she was even considering —

"Bonnie Rae," her mother said as she stirred a little more salt into her simmering stew, "ain't you listening? I said, there's only gonna be seven of us tonight, counting Granny. Rafe and Lou Ellen's staying over with friends and Big John's going in to town to eat with Sarah."

"Oh." Bonnie Rae had the same response the second time she was told and took the three extra plates back to the cupboard, again. "If I was Sarah," she said, "I'd get awful tired waiting around for him to marry me."

"Could be that's why you ain't Sarah," Celia replied.

"What's this, Mama?" Bonnie Rae suddenly noticed a yellow tin box set back in the corner of the counter top.

"Ain't that purty?" her mother smiled. "I got it today from that traveling man. It's a breadbox. And look here..." She came over and opened it. "See that little shelf right on top, there? What do you guess that's for?"

"I can't imagine."

"Pies," Celia looked quite pleased with the thing. "A place to put left over pies."

"We don't get many leftovers of nothing in this family," Bonnie Rae pointed out a bit skeptically. "It is awful purty, though," she added quickly, seeing her mother's disappointment. "Especially the color."

"I thought you'd like it. It's been a time and a time since we had anything new in the house, and—well, I just couldn't pass it by."

"Must have cost a heap," she ventured. "I seen those things in Cedarville a few times and they was nigh onto three dollars apiece."

"My," Celia laughed and turned back to the stew. "This one didn't cost me but one dollar now, and thirty cents a week."

"Mama!" Bonnie Rae gasped. "You ain't saying you got took in by that new-fangled credit plan!"

"Bonnie Rae Harper! Ain't right you should talk to me that way."

The door opened from the back porch and Lias came in with his face half covered with shaving soap and a cigarette in his mouth. He was still holding a straight razor. "You sassing your mama, girl?"

"No, I ain't, Daddy," she replied. "It's just that Harlan said —"

"You seeing him behind my back?"

Well, she was planning to, but she hadn't yet, so she said, "No, I ain't," and turned back to the table so she wouldn't have to look him in the eye. "The day me and the younguns took him to the schoolhouse, we was passing by that traveling man's fancied-up car, and Harlan made mention that a credit plan was something to trick a body into paying twice what a thing's really worth."

Lias stood quietly for a moment, taking the thought in, before looking over at his wife. "How much did you pay for that thing, Ceely?" He gave the bright, yellow box an estimating glance.

"Like I already said," she snapped, "I didn't give no more than a dollar for it. What's wrong with you two? You think I ain't seen enough traveling men in my day? I'll vow! He told me first off it was gonna cost three dollars —"

"Three dollars —"

"Just let me finish, Lias, unless I get so flustered I can't think!"

He took the cigarette from his mouth and slowly blew out the smoke. "All right. I'm listening."

"Well, I says to him—law, Mr. Durham, you know what kind of hard times these are. Ain't a body in these parts would have three extra dollars laying around just waiting to spend. So, we argued and dickered some. And that's when he come down."

"What did he come down to?" her husband asked.

"One dollar."

"But Mama, you said —"

"And thirty cents a week," she finished.

"How long for?" came the next question.

"Just three months. I said, three dollars I ain't got, Mr. Durham, but thirty cents a week ain't gonna break me. And then's when he —"

"Lord almighty!" Lias exploded suddenly. "You know what that figures to?"

"Whatever it figures to, Lias," she replied coolly, "I know I got it."

"That ain't the point! Listen here, Ceely. By the time you're done, you'll end up paying four dollars and sixty cents for something you could have bought down at the drugstore for two ninety-eight!"

"The point is," his wife argued, "I never would have done it!" She snatched a potholder with a frustrated sigh and opened the oven door. "I just never would have put out that kind of expense for no kitchen-purty!"

"Did you hear me when I said it's gonna cost you four dollars and sixty cents?" he asked.

"I heard."

"Don't that show you something?"

"It shows me..." She set the tray of biscuits in the center of the table. "That men don't have the same sort of reasoning inside their heads that womenfolk do."

"This is starting to rile me," Lias said more to himself than Celia. He brushed at a trickle of wetness dripping down his neck from the shaving soap and went back onto the porch for a towel.

For a moment there was a dead silence. Finally, Celia turned to her daughter and snapped, "Go tell everybody supper's ready!"

When Ljas returned to the kitchen, there was no one but Celia hustling around, putting things on the table with a fervor.

"I got one more thing to say about it," he said, "then I'm gonna leave it lay. The next time you want a kitchen-purty, or any other kind of foofaraw a woman likes to put up around the place, you just come and ask me. You hear me, sugar babe?"

She stopped bustling and looked at him. "Am I supposed to believe you'd get it for me?" She put her hands to her hips and looked at him some more.

"I guarantee it."

"Lias Harper, what kind of trick you pulling, now?"

"Ain't no trick at all. You see, it just occurred to me how even if it might hurt me some to spend the money now, I best grin and bear it. Because I'm liable to go dead broke paying for it later on!"

"Vow and declare, Lias! I'd rather you —"

"That water in the kettle on the boil, yet, Ceely?" Granny Harper's voice could be heard in the hallway before she shuffled into the midst of the quarrel. "I got the mixture right here. Don't go nowhere, son," she directed when she saw Lias heading for the porch again, "this ain't gonna be worth spit lest you drink it hot."

"What's it gonna do to me, Ma?" Lias looked with suspicion at the steaming mug she pushed at him.

"Ain't gonna do nothing but give you a good night's rest," the old woman prompted. "Now go on."

"I reckon I could rest just fine without it," he replied. "That onion poultice you put to me three days ago liked to kilt me."

"You ain't had a spell since, have you?"

"Good thing," he insisted. "Because I'd been dead if I had to suffer both them miseries together."

"Well..." Granny Harper shook her head sadly and took it back. "I can fix it for you but I shore can't force it on you."

"Oh, give it here," he relented. "One thing I don't need is another woman around this place that's riled at me!"

She handed it back to him and watched contentedly as he drank it down.

"Lord!" He gasped, taking a deep breath. "That's the most miserable tasting stuff you give me, yet!"

"It's the fish oil, I reckon," she explained. "But then some of them herbs is right bitter. Can't make it all taste good."

"What's it gonna do?" he asked, again.

"I told you it's gonna give you a good night's rest. Tomorrow night."

"Tomorrow?"

"Yep. And a good cleaning out, tonight."

He banged the empty cup down onto the table. "You mean to tell me that was a purge?"

"Ain't any sickness on God's earth, Lias," his mother said sweetly, as she took the empty cup to the sink, "a purge don't make better."

"Well, I've had me about all the doctoring I'm gonna take!" He sat down at the table. "You hear me, Ma? That's it! Whatever I got is a heap better than you torturing me dead!"

The sound of an engine and a flood of lights through the living room window, made a reply unnecessary as Lias got to his feet, again, to see who was there.

"Just Aaron McCord," Joseph Lee called into the kitchen as he thundered down the stairway and headed for the door. "We're going hunting tonight. And Bonnie Rae's coming along, too."

24

Bonnie Rae was surprised at how easy it was. For once, she was glad she had grown up with brothers who allowed her to tag along with them—even if they did tend to give her the worst chores when she did. Her parents were not suspicious. Her interest in hunting left over from her tomboy days, led to an ability to work with furs that was becoming sought after in Cedar Creek. Requests for her winter coats and jackets sometimes even provided welcome extra money at Christmas time. Lias and Celia were proud of the things she made. Thinking on it, just now, made her feel a twinge of guilt as they drove toward the Doc's place but she pushed the feelings aside.

She would have done anything to see Harlan, again.

Aaron went up to the door while the others waited in the truck he left running farther down the road. That was as close to Tom's place that Joseph Lee would consent to go. It was Harlan who answered his knock. "Howdy, Harlan!" The old man stepped inside with a grin.

"Things are all right at home, I take it," said Tom, as he came up behind them with his reading glasses still perched on his nose. "Or you wouldn't look so pleased with yourself."

"Well," Aaron replied, "I always did like getting outside on nights like this. Thought maybe Harlan, here, would like to try his hand at a little coon hunting. What do you say, Harlan? There's me and a couple others out in the truck."

"Well," Harlan hesitated, "I don't have a gun. And I —"

"Loan him a gun, Doc," said Aaron.

Tom smiled indulgently and went to the closet. He took out an old ten-gauge shotgun and a box of shells.

"I couldn't shoot a raccoon with this," Harlan objected. "Why, it would blast the poor thing to —"

Aaron took it from him and peered through the sights in a mock attempt to examine it. "Awww, this here's an effective widow and orphan maker. It'll do." He handed it back. "Especially if we see something bigger. Want to come along, Doc?"

"I think I'll sit this one out," Tom replied. "I've got some research to do on a difficult case I came across last week. But you all go ahead and enjoy yourselves."

It was merely an expected courtesy that Aaron had asked. Tom hadn't participated in anything other than his doctoring duties for the last four years.

"Who else is going?" Harlan buttoned his tailor-made gray wool jacket as he and Aaron started out across the road in the moonlight. "Isn't that the Harper truck?"

"Yep. But don't worry, I'm driving. On account of last time!" He laughed and reached for the front door on the driver's side.

"Hey, Harlan," Joseph Lee called out to him with a friendly wave. "Just climb up in back, there."

The back was filled with three barking dogs and one other person that Harlan assumed—judging by the overalls, heavy jacket and hat—wasn't Rafe, but someone around the same size. He laid the gun down and pushed an overly inquisitive hound out of his face as he climbed in and settled himself for the bumpy ride he had no doubt he was about to get. "Howdy." He offered a polite hand to the silent stranger as the truck shifted into gear and leapt forward. "Name's Harlan Fleming."

An unusually soft hand returned his shake in the darkness. "Bonnie Rae Harper," came the reply.

He pulled her hat off with a startled surprise, and a torrent of red-gold curls spilled down over the boyish jacket. "Bonnie Rae," he breathed, "if you didn't look so good to me, I'd send you right back home!"

"Oh, I done wrong." She leaned her head back against the cab. "I knew it was wrong, but..." She looked searchingly at his face, dark and handsome in the moonlight. "I just couldn't help it! I don't know what come over me."

"Well, it looks like you had help in the scheme."

"I had to do something, Harlan. Seems to me I was gonna grow old waiting for you to call on me, again. I was worried Daddy scared you off with all that—"

"I was trying to give him some time to change his mind about me. But the way it looks, now, I might as well —"

"God's bones, Harlan—you'd have to wait till hell froze over before he changed his mind about anything!"

"Bonnie Rae," he admonished, at the same time pulling her toward him, "what am I going to do with you?"

A shimmer of emotion ran all through her. She forgot her decision to be more dignified than the last time they were together, when she had told him she loved him before he had even said it to her. Instead, she melted into his embrace and said, "Kiss me, Harlan, kiss me like you was gonna before —"

He kissed her. He buried his hands in the cool silkiness of her hair and drew her face against his in a way that sent that same wonderful longing through her all over, again. "Marry me, Bonnie Rae," he entreated then. "Marry me and come away from here after the school year."

Move off the mountain! The sudden seriousness of it caught her off guard. "But that's a long ways away. We've got plenty of time, yet, before then. Don't you want to—"

"I don't want anything to happen to you," he admitted. "I need some time to figure things out with your father ."

"I can handle my daddy, Harlan."

"You shouldn't have to." He kissed her, again, and then spoke the next words in French. *"Will you marry me, dearest?"*

Joseph Lee glanced through the back window, hoping to see the expression on Harlan's face when he found out who he was sitting next to. But he didn't look long before politely having to turn around again. "They sure ain't wasting any time," he muttered, his air of fun giving way to a vague irritation.

"It was your idea," Aaron reminded him.

"Yeah, well..." He glanced backward, again. "I only got one thing to say." He returned his eyes to the road. "He sure enough better do right by her. Step on it will you, Aaron? They got all the help from us they're gonna get!"

"Boy, you'll be worthless for hunting if you're gonna worry about keeping them two in your sights all night."

"Well, shoot. He don't look like no backwards boy to me. Way Bonnie Rae was talking I thought he was gonna be like Big John and take three months to ask her out for a soda." He cast another worried glance through the glass. "By the looks of it back there, we're gonna have to either break it up, or take them into town and stand up with them. Ol' Lias would take the hide clean off me if I done that!"

"If you would quit fuming long enough to use your head..." Aaron's eyes began to twinkle with an idea. "We maybe could redeem the situation."

"Ought to dump him on the side of the road and let him walk home! Trouble is, I sort of like him, myself. Besides I'd have to gag and tie Bonnie Rae to do it."

"I said use your head, not yore muscle, boy. Listen up, now, because I got an idee."

"Well, let's hear it, Ol' Man."

"We take them around behind the ol' Credence Mines. Down by the Big Lick."

"What do we want to go there for? That's a haint. I ain't about to go snooping around no haint on a night like this. Just look at that moon up there. Big and bright as it gets."

"Lordy, boy!" The old man gave a disdainful shake of his head. "I been down there a heap of times and look how long I lived to tell about it."

"You have?" Joseph Lee cast him a calculating glance.

"Why, shore. Ain't nothing down there." He was coming up on a hairpin curve in the road and took it fast, with such an easy competent control that Joseph Lee was sure he had done it on purpose, just to give their passengers in back a reason to have to reach for the sides.

"All that about the Singing Bone?" Aaron went on as if he were telling a story in his own living room instead of driving a truck down a snake-like road on a witching night. "Ain't nothing but the wind whistling sort of eerie-like through them tall pines. Ain't no little baby girl out there got buried with one hand sticking out the ground, neither."

"Maybe you didn't look good enough." Joseph Lee paused for a few skeptical moments. "I heard that hand ain't nothing but one little piece of parched bone, now. And when the wind blows through just right, it sings out, on account of she was a murdered child. Some folks seen her at bends in the trail, too. Wearing a bloody dress. Specially on nights like this."

"Ain't nothing but wind in the trees," Aaron said, again. "And folks that scared theirselves into thinking they seen her." He looked over at his young companion and smiled. One of his upper teeth was missing off to the side, and in contrast to his light gray hair and beard beneath an old battered hat, he gave the chilling impression of a jack-o-lantern the way the moonlight shown through the windshield just then.

Joseph Lee looked uncertainly at him. Then after thinking over the possibilities for another few moments, he began to grin.

"Now, the trick to the whole thing," Aaron went on, "is gonna be how serious we can play it. You know, straight-faced. They got to be set up right. Just follow along with me and I'll do most of the talking."

"What if Harlan ain't the kind to believe in them things? I mean, what if he ain't scared of ghosts or hainted places?"

"Awww, ain't a man alive ain't scared of something," Aaron reasoned. "Set him up right, get him wandering around in the dark with strange noises, and he'll think up something to be scared of all right. Can't you just see city-slicker Harlan, running around in the dark? Lordy!" He began to laugh. "Scare the Holy Ghost right out of him!"

Joseph Lee couldn't help laughing, too. "Shoot, Aaron, you sure sound like you're gonna be enjoying this!"

"Boy, it's my kind of fun. Hey —" he gave into a sudden loud guffaw.

"What?"

"I just thought of something. Oh, lordy! I just thought of something would scare the bejeezus out of Gabriel!"

The remark sent them both into peals of laughter until the tears began to roll and Aaron straightened up and said, "Get serious, now. Get serious!" before taking another fit and giving into it, himself.

"Get serious—you get serious!" Joseph Lee crowed. He gave him a playful knock on the shoulder. "That's what I like about you, Ol' Man—you ain't never growed up!"

25

When the truck finally rolled to a stop near an old deserted tipple that had once been used to load tons of coal into transport trains, the dogs jumped out, barking and trembling with excitement. Aaron and Joseph Lee sauntered up beside them just as Harlan was helping Bonnie Rae climb down out of the truck.

"What in God's thunder we doing here?" Bonnie Rae turned suspicious eyes on her brother.

"Ain't for a girl to pick where the fellers are gonna hunt." Joseph Lee cast an expectant glance at Aaron.

The older man stood calm and quiet in the center of the braying dogs, patiently shaving off a piece of chewing tobacco with a jack knife. Now, the pale glow of the moon flooded full over him, this time turning his gray beard to a snowy white, and making him look—-not like a jack-o-lantern—but like some ancient Biblical patriarch. He tucked the rest of the plug back in his pocket and looked over at them. "Might as well tell you right now," he said in a low serious tone, "this ain't gonna be no ordinary hunt."

Joseph Lee turned his back on them and walked a few yards away. He let his eyes wander over the eerie lay of the land and tried not to listen to his friend's carefully droned ex-

165

planation.

"Just what kind of a hunt is it going to be, Aaron?" Harlan asked wryly, beginning to sense another prank coming on that he was obviously going to catch the brunt of.

"Well, I'll tell you. The boy and me been trailing this big ol' gray for nigh onto… how long has it been now, J-Lee?"

"Oh…" The accomplice had to clear his throat before he could successfully call back over his shoulder, "least a month, I'd say."

"I reckon it's been that long." The old man reached for the rifle he had leaned against the truck fender. "Yep. Anyhow, this ol' gray has been giving us the slip every time we try, by high-tailing into them trees, just past that old shaft, there." Aaron leaned over to spit, smoothed down his beard a little and thought for a moment before going on.

His two victims weren't looking as vulnerable as he had hoped. "Course it was on account of the rumors," he finally continued, "that we never followed him in. But after watching that ol' gray come out week after week—just tempting us—we decided there was only one way to chase that critter down. We had to come back with someone that ain't so easy swayed by rumor. To tell the truth, Harlan, we needed a God-fearing out-lander."

"And why is that?" Harlan asked. There was something about Aaron McCord that did not fit his image of age and dig-nity.

"Outlanders," the old man explained, "well, now they don't tend to be so scared of these rumors as us mountain folk that's been raised on them. Course, we could of brung that Durham feller. But the boy here has a grudge against him. Be-sides that he ain't God-fearing. Everybody knows only God-fearing folk got the power on the supernatural. That leaves you."

"You seemed pretty God-fearing to me at the sugar party," Harlan reminded him.

"Yep. But like I said, I was raised in these here hills and

brought up to live in mortal fear of hainted places. A man don't get over them ways easy. I didn't live this long by chasing down rumors."

"We sort of figured it would work out mutual," Joseph Lee rejoined the circle. "You could spend a little time with Bonnie Rae, and we'd get the big gray to boot!"

"Yep," Aaron nodded, "that's the whole of it, right there."

"It don't pleasure me none to go traipsing around in no hainted places," Bonnie Rae objected.

"Now, that right there is just why we brung you," said her brother. "We figured any self-respecting spirit would think twice before getting you riled. On account of it's common knowledge you can out holler and out swear any man in this here county!"

"Joseph Lee Harper!"she fumed indignantly. "If that ain't a low-down, good-for—nothing —"

Harlan directed a few softly spoken words in her direction that neither of the others understood and she abruptly quieted.

"Shoot fire —" Joseph Lee marveled. "I ain't never seen nobody could shut her up like that, before."

Bonnie Rae retreated a few steps away from them to sit down angry but quiet on the truck's running board. Harlan's remark to her in French, of *"Quiet, dearest, or you'll prove him right,"* spoken so calmly, made her achingly aware of her shortcomings. Why was it that the harder she tried to act like a mature and dignified lady around this man, the less she seemed like one?

"What did I tell you," Aaron replied approvingly. "He's got the power!"

"Let's just get one thing straight," said Harlan in a tone that was good-natured but firm. "I know you're both having a wonderful time with my ignorance of all your mountain ways. But considering the last couple of weeks I've had, staying late at school every night to start things off right, and even—ritualized, or whatever it was—by that weaver of yours —-"

"Lord almighty—you mean she witched you?" Aaron

asked aghast.

"Something like that, and I haven't had a decent night's sleep since. I have to get there early tomorrow, and I don't mind saying I would be very irritated if you just happened to lose me out here so I'd have to find my way home on foot."

"Now, just what sort of neighbors do you take us for, Harlan?" Aaron asked. "We know what kind of hard work it takes to get kids back in a mind for school when they ain't been in so long. Why it's on account of that we brung you here. To sort of get your mind off things for a spell."

"That's right," Joseph Lee agreed. "And if it'll make you feel better, I swear I won't move that truck for home till every last one of us makes it back here."

Harlan hooked his thumbs in his pockets and looked at them both with a careful scrutiny. He turned to look at Bonnie Rae, still seated disconsolately against the truck. The gentle tug he felt on his emotions settled his decision. "All right," he gave in. "Let's start looking for your phantom coon." He went to get his gun.

Joseph Lee and Aaron looked at each other and smiled.

The four of them started down a narrow trail that led into a stand of pines. They walked along in silence for a while, glancing ahead and all around. The moonlight's pale silvery rays filtered down onto the trail and cast ghosty shadows in every direction. Bonnie Rae clung tightly to Harlan's arm but he was sure it was more out of fear than affection. The possibility of having any type of serious discussion with her was—for the moment—out of the question. And it began to dawn on him that her escorts had planned it that way.

"See anything?" asked Joseph Lee.

"Nope," Aaron replied. "Can't hear nothing, either. Dogs are gone but they'll get noisy when they find something." He slowly pulled the hammer back on his rifle and looked cautiously down the moonlit trail. Then he held up a hand to stop everyone and whispered, "Shhh! What's that?"

"Just an owl," Harlan identified the low rhythmic tones

somewhere off in the distance.

"Shoot," whispered Joseph Lee. "I might of known one of them would be snooping around somewheres."

"Let's wait and see what he does." Aaron still stood at the ready. "Could be he won't come near at all."

"So, what if he does?" Harlan felt Bonnie Rae's grip on his arm tighten. He looked down and noticed her eyes were closed. "Owls aren't dangerous."

"Don't mind us, none," Aaron explained. "Just another one of them mountain rumors. Some folks say they're in the service of the devil. Spies, sort of like."

"That's ridiculous," Harlan pronounced.

"They say, if they fly off to the left," continued the old man, "bad luck's in store. To the right, you got good luck coming. But Lord help you if they fly directly over, because that means death for certain."

"Generally..." Joseph Lee looked around uneasily. "I think it's best not to offend them, myself."

"Don't you go running off, now, boy." Aaron cast him a warning glance. "We didn't come this far just to—"

"Listen, Ol' Man, I thought you said—"

"Awww, I was just funning," he replied with a teasing grin. "Personally, I don't believe a—"

There was sudden movement in one of the trees up ahead of them, and all at once the great horned bird appeared—gliding low on silent wings—to swoop down close and menacing in their direction.

"Here it comes!" yelled Joseph Lee, viewing the ominous approach with dismay.

Bonnie Rae screamed. Within seconds, Aaron raised his gun and sent forth a shot that met the frightening intruder with a resounding blast. The large owl crumpled onto the trail in front of them in a lifeless heap.

"Well, I guess you personally took care of that rumor," Harlan criticized.

"I wouldn't have bothered," Aaron answered. "But the

dern thing was headed right for us!"

Now, the wind began to bewitch the topmost branches of the pines to cause a vague stirring that seemed to trouble the air all around them. Then they began to hear the faint but unmistakable sound of a young voice, thin and high, blending like music with the wind in the trees.

"It's her!" Bonnie Rae's voice quavered fearfully. "Oh, it's the singing child—I can hear it plain as day!"

"Aaron," Joseph Lee switched his rifle to the other hand and wiped his sweating palm on his shirtfront. "I had just about all of this I can take."

"You got a point, there," the old man brushed a trickle of tobacco juice from the corner of his mouth with the back of his hand. "It's either a ghost, or a witching. One or the other."

"Now, just a minute," Harlan reasoned. "Obviously, someone else is out there."

"Hear that?" said Joseph Lee. "Even he ain't denying it. One more sign like that, and I'm gone!"

"Let's get out of here, Harlan!" Bonnie Rae pulled on his arm, again.

"Look," he reassured, "there's got to be a logical—-"

Suddenly, off in the distance, the dogs began braying and barking wildly.

"Dogs got something," Aaron said. "Just up ahead, there. In that birch grove, sounds like."

"You couldn't pay me to stand next to a white birch on a witching night!" Joseph Lee protested. "I shore ain't going in."

"We got troubles, then," said the old man. "Because it's gonna take more than a whistle to get them hounds back once they got something treed."

"Yeah, well, maybe they ain't got nothing treed. Maybe they're barking at a little girl spook with a bloody dress."

"Don't say it out loud, J-Lee!" Bonnie Rae gasped. "It'll bring her for certain, and I'd just die if I saw her!"

"Don't talk like that, now." Harlan put a protective arm

around her.

"It ain't spooks—it ain't spooks!" Aaron insisted. "Hounds are scared of them things. If it was—why, they'd be howling and trying to run off home with their tails between—"

There was a sound like the crushing and breaking of brush —and all at once—the barking increased to a frightened high pitch as the hounds came running back toward them.

"Look out!" someone shouted.

Joseph Lee and Aaron jumped off the trail and took to the brush in what seemed like a blind panic. Bonnie Rae screamed and tried to follow, but she was held back by Harlan, who had a strong hold on her, and wasn't budging.

"Let me go!" she cried. "Let me go before—"

"Not until—"

Suddenly all the noise and confusion was engulfed by a loud, ferocious roar. He let her go and spun around. The dogs and an enraged bear were closing in behind them in a tangled jumble. Harlan's mind snapped with an acute clarity. Everything around him was captured into a dreamlike slow motion.

The startled bear reared up on its hind legs at the sight of them in the middle of the trail, threatening and snarling at the unexpected intruders. Harlan raised the shotgun slowly—too slowly—he would never get it to his shoulder in time. Then he felt the oncoming weight of the black, shaggy beast against the muzzle of his gun and pulled the trigger. At the same instant, the bear's paw struck the side of his head with a deafening smack that knocked him off his feet and slammed him onto the ground.

26

"Wait a minute!" Joseph Lee dropped to his knees and tried to catch his breath. "That was a gunshot."

Aaron came stumbling up behind him, wheezing and coughing. "Probably just Harlan." He eased himself down next to his young friend. "Shooting at spooks."

"We better go back. Might be something serious. We can't just leave them there. Bonnie Rae probably don't have spit left, by now."

"I'll bet my bottom dollar they'll be back at the truck before we are."

"What if they ain't?"

"Then, we'll go fetch them. Lordy—I need a rest first. I didn't live this long by running myself to death!"

"There ain't time," Joseph Lee got to his feet again. "If there's trouble —"

"Don't worry yourself none," the old man consoled. "I know a shortcut back to the truck. Get us back in about five minutes."

"Must be some shortcut."

"If they ain't there, won't take no time longer to hike back in and meet them on the way out."

"I think maybe we carried this thing too far."

"Whose carrying? That was the real thing, boy. I quit funning a long time ago."

"Dangit, Ol' Man—you mean, I just run off and left my little sister in a real, honest-to-God haint?"

"I reckon."

"We got to get back there!"

"All right. All right. Give me a hand up."

Joseph Lee pulled him to his feet and waited impatiently while he stretched and straightened his spine. The old man took several long breaths, as if preparing to dive into deep water and when he was finally ready, the two of them walked for a mere few minutes before they came to a small clearing in front of an old mining shaft.

"What are we doing, here?"

"This here's the shortcut." Aaron walked over to inspect an old coal car that looked stark and abandoned.

"I can't do it," Joseph Lee said warily. "I ain't putting a foot in there no matter how much faster it is. Not in no deep, dark tunnel."

"Not the tunnel, boy—the car—we're gonna shoot the spur."

"What?"

"Used to do it all the time back in my day." He put his rifle inside and crawled into the small iron car that had been used for carrying coal in and out of the low tunnels. "Leads right down to the old tipple where we're parked. Shove us off and jump in."

"I don't know." Joseph Lee rested the stock of his rifle across his shoulder and held onto the barrel with one hand. "You sure look silly in there."

"I ain't in here to get my picture took." He withdrew the tobacco plug from his shirt pocket and began to shave off another piece. "Course if you'd rather take time to hike down..."

"Oh, all right." He put his rifle in beside Aaron and went around to the back of the car to push.

"Lordy—ain't them muscles of yours good for nothing but

show?"

Joseph Lee turned around and put his back against the cold metal. "Thing hasn't been moved in years."

There was a screech and a moan and the old car started to move. When the track began to slope down and wind its way around Credence Hill, the car picked up speed and began to move by itself. Joseph Lee jumped in. The moon shown high and bright above them. Not as huge and golden as it had been earlier when it hung so low. The stars twinkled and looked close in the crystal-crisp air.

Joseph Lee sat with his knees pulled uncomfortably up against his chest and his arms resting at shoulder level on the sides of the car. He looked at the hillside slipping by on his right—almost close enough to touch—and then at the steep, sloping embankment falling away to his left. They were moving at a speed that he was sure he could beat walking. Aaron was sitting with his back to him, relaxed and comfortable, seemingly enjoying the sights.

"This is some dern shortcut, mister," said the young man impatiently. "We ain't gonna make it by morning going this speed."

"Awww, don't get your dander up. She ought to be picking up speed directly. Little more of a slope just around this next bend, if I recollect right. Best check that hand brake behind you and make sure it ain't set."

"How come you didn't say nothing about that when I was breaking my back trying to start this thing? Now, look at that." He rose up and kicked the steel lever twice before it clanked down. There was an immediate rush of speed. "Dern thing was half on."

"Now we're moving!" Aaron laughed. "Lookee there, boy!"

"Ooooweee! This is more like it!" Joseph Lee slid back down behind the old man and noted with satisfaction that the landscape was now rushing past them in a blur. "Hey, Aaron—funny thing, I don't recollect seeing any track laid down by that old tipple."

"You know how it is," Aaron hollered back over his shoulder. "They's always pulling them old spurs apart and..." He trailed off in mid-sentence, shocked by the realization even as he spoke it.

Joseph Lee caught the inference at the same time and couldn't help exploding into a barrage of profanity when he realized they were now moving too fast to jump out. He stood up part way to attempt it, but the high speed and dizzying height was too much and he sank back down, again. Aaron, having the same thought, rose up and sat down, again, too.

"The brake—the brake!" The old man hollered as the car began to sway from side to side with mounting speed.

Joseph Lee grasped the steel lever with both hands and, remembering how rusty and reluctant it had been before, gave it one abrupt heave with every ounce of strength he possessed. The lever snapped off in his hands.

Aaron heard the chink of iron and turned around to see his young friend staring at the disconnected bar with his mouth open. "We're up salt creek, now, boy," he said with disgust. "Nothing to do but hang on and hope we don't lose our heads on the first roll!"

The two of them tried to scrunch down below the rails, but it was a tight squeeze. Joseph Lee's face was squashed so close against the smooth, worn leather of Aaron's jacket that he was engulfed with the strong smell of tobacco. After only a few moments, the old man peeked his face up over the front to see what was in store for them and gasped, "There's the end!" and ducked down, again. "Lordy —if she don't stop before the next bend—we're going over the side!"

"You—crazy, ol' man—I am never gonna—"

The small car hit the end of the track, bumped and jostled over fifty feet of rock and shale, and then began to plummet headlong down Credence Hill. It was stopped three-quarters of the way down by a stalwart, towering pine, where both of them were thrown out on impact. Joseph Lee was first to get to his feet.

He made his way in a daze toward the old man, who was moaning miserably from within a clump of nearby brush. "Aaron—" He fell to his knees beside him. "Aaron, are you broke somewheres?"

"Nope—" came a feeble reply. "But get me some—water—my middle's afire!"

"Can't give you none if you're bad hurt, Ol' Man. It'd be worse on you."

"I ain't bad hurt." He reached out for a hand up. "Just got the wind knocked out of me. But I—I swallowed my dern plug!"

Joseph Lee got up and pulled him to his feet.

"I'll live, I reckon," Aaron said. "Once I get down to the clear lick over there and get me a long, cold drink. Lordy, boy—your head's bleeding something fierce."

Joseph Lee brushed a warm wetness out of his eye. "Probably looks worse than it is." He tore the end off his shirttail to use as a bandage while he trudged toward the stream. "Lucky we ain't dead, is all I got to say. If that hill was any steeper, we would be."

When they reached the stream, Aaron leaned uncomfortably against the trunk of a nearby tree and belched blatantly. "Oh, Lord—" He moaned and bent down for a drink. "I hope this don't stove me up permanent!"

Joseph Lee plunged his head into the icy stream and then tied the piece of flannel around it. "Well, if you wouldn't have been so all-fired certain—"

"Don't be too hard on me now, boy," Aaron defended himself. "Not when I'm took with the miseries."

"I'm gonna be took with something else if anything happens to Bonnie Rae. We got to find them!"

"All right, all right. Truck can't be too far away from here."

Harlan and Bonnie Rae were not at the truck. All joking aside, the two adventurers started down the trail again with a grim determination. Halfway down, they met Bonnie Rae and Harlan—along with the dogs—making their way back, themselves.

"Where in the world you been, J-Lee?" Bonnie Rae called out as soon as she saw them. "Harlan shot a big ol' bear, while you two were off enjoying your play-party games! Why, he got knocked clean off his – Lord, almighty—what happened to you?"

"Nothing serious," Joseph Lee answered quickly. "Where's the bear—is he kilt?"

"Kilt—he's got a hole in him bigger than a window," she boasted.

"Not quite," Harlan said, quietly. His ears were still ringing from the bear's forceful smack and he had a trickle of blood coming from a long scratch on the side of his face. "Did you bring a skinning knife?"

"Sure." Joseph Lee flashed him an admiring smile. "I never would have run off if I knowed it was a bear. It was just this dern haint! And that crazy ol' man over there, thinking he could – now where did he go?"

"Over here," came the faint reply from where Aaron was sitting a few yards off the trail. "And I'll thankee not to —" he was interrupted by another resounding belch. "Oh—Lordy!"

"What's ailing him?" asked Bonnie Rae.

"Swallowed his plug, that's what," said Joseph Lee.

"What'd he do a fool thing like that for?" she persisted.

Awww, it's a long story," her brother hedged. "Just leave him be for a while, he'll get along. Let's get back to that bear or we'll be here all night."

It wasn't until the skinning was done, the meat shared out, and they were all piling back into the truck to go home that Aaron came to life with a sudden concern. "My hat—where's my hat?"

"Probably off in them bushes somewhere up by the coal car," said Joseph Lee.

"I ain't budging for home without my hat."

"Oh, I'll get it," Joseph Lee relented. "God forbid you should go home without your hat, Ol' Man. You all wait here."

"I knew he'd understand," said Aaron, watching him disappear up the dark hillside. "That's what I like about that boy. He's got a feeling for what's important."

Harlan glanced over at him. "Well, I hardly think —" before being interrupted by a loud belch and another moan of, "Oh, Lordy!" that made him give up trying to talk to the old man altogether.

Joseph Lee found his way back to the place where the coal car was tipped over, and got down on his hands and knees to feel around for the hat. The moonlight would have been helpful but was being obstructed by the wide boughs of the towering pine they had crashed into. He could barely see anything. After a few minutes of searching, he found himself in a deep, lush bed of something that had a familiar smell to it. He touched careful, sensitive fingers to the leaves and stems before realizing with a sudden thrill that he had somehow come upon the largest patch of ginseng he had ever seen in his life.

He moved back and forth in every direction, measuring out the size of the bed, and his heart began to pound. There hadn't been a discovery of this size on the ridge for years. If he tended it right, and kept the location secret, it would keep him supplied for a lifetime. And it was well hidden from those who would dig the entire patch all at once for temporary gain.

This steep hillside on the fringes of a local haunt made it a true wild-crafter's dream. It made the whole night worthwhile. When he finally found Aaron's hat—considerably battered—Joseph Lee had a sudden burst of benevolence and decided to buy the old man a new one. Yes, sir.

That crazy old man had been good luck to him ever since he could remember. And as for Harlan… maybe he wasn't going to be so easily scared off by what really went on in these hills, after all.

27

Harlan felt like he had been up all night when he dragged himself out of bed for school the next morning, and he very nearly had. It was past midnight when he finally got home. Although the wild night was unlike any he had ever experienced, seeing Bonnie Rae again had settled his uncertainties and convinced him that his feelings for her were deep and true. He hadn't meant to ask her to marry him so suddenly – at least not without first having a plan.

It at least had to make sense.

But whether it made sense or not, whether it had been only a few short weeks or long years, Bonnie Rae Harper fit into the empty place in his heart like a glove on a hand. It didn't seem to matter how long she had been there, she was there. He still had no idea how he was going to handle the situation with her father. Not that he was afraid to make a stand. He simply didn't know exactly where he stood at the moment. That was something altogether new to him.

At any rate, he was committed to be here for the school year, so he would have plenty of time to work things out. The truth was, this mountain code the hill people seemed to live by was beginning to intrigue him more than put him off. He wasn't so sure he was ready—or willing—to condemn it without looking a little closer. There was something more to it than he had seen at first. And last night was a good example.

Bonnie Rae had gone against her father to see him but something told him it was only a symbolic thing. Something Lias Harper might even expect. And even though her brother had gone along with her in the deception, his presence had made any real seriousness between them impossible. In fact, considering the shenanigans of last night, he had been a better chaperon than Lias, himself, would have been.

And what of Aaron? The old man seemed as at home with his young friends and their capers as he might have been trading stories on the front porch with people his own age. There was an unusual bond between him and Joseph Lee... and no secrets. Right down to the fact that he was aware of some grudge the young man had against the traveling man.

The air was crisp and invigorating as Harlan rode to school earlier than usual that morning. There were lingering traces of frost that had crept into the low places in the still-cold hours before dawn but, now, in warmth of morning light, the schoolhouse meadow looked aflame with fall. The surrounding woods were a riot of scarlet oaks and bronze-colored beeches. The sweet gum tree with its star shaped leaves boasted colors that ranged from pale gold to purple. The giant poplar that shaded the schoolyard had magically turned to gold that rained down on the play area with every stirring breeze.

He had forgotten how lovely fall was in the country. Though his farm always seemed loveliest then, its sparse trees and flat places with their surrounding Richmond skyline in the distance did not hold a candle to this vivid display of nature in the hill country. And it was clearer here. He hadn't realized how dingy and factory-smudged the air of the city had become until he left it.

Sensing the children were as stirred by the new season as he was, Harlan changed the schedule to accommodate them. How could he expect them to sit for long quiet hours in their seats when they were probably feeling twice the way he was?

So he surprised them by declaring the first of what he called, "Mr. Harlan Holidays."

Recesses were extended, and a play was introduced—of which he had a collection to choose from to fit any occasion from Christmas to Election Day— that would be presented before parents at the next holiday program. He had learned early on in his teaching career to use program activities on restless days, especially putting the more rowdy students to work on such vigorous activities as stage construction and set design.

He had always called them "Mr. Fleming's Holidays." except the polite but affectionate "Mr. Harlan," he had been labeled with here in Cedar Creek, charmed him somehow and he had no desire to change it. So, he pulled out of his collection a play called, *"Are You For Independence?"* and set them to work on it so delightfully, they barely noticed the writing, reading, and math calculations that were involved in its production.

The day seemed to fly.

But as soon as the children were gone in the afternoon, Harlan saddled Prince and started down the path at a fast canter, his mind returned like a magnet to more serious matters. He had a reason for getting to school early this morning. It was to do some of the work he usually saved for the late afternoons. Because this was the afternoon he was finally going to Coaltown.

There was something about Coaltown that had been bothering him ever since he came to Cedar Creek. He didn't know exactly what he was going to do there outside of talk with the lady teacher and have a look around, but he felt oddly anxious about it. As if—like so many other things in this hill country— there might be something formidable and treacherous lurking behind quiet places.

If he did discover his missing boys in Coaltown, today, at least he would know the truth. Exactly what he would do about it, he didn't know yet. But whatever the outcome, it would certainly explain a lot of the evasiveness he had come across since he had arrived. As polite as everyone had been toward him since the sugar party, he was still the "government teacher," and a representative of the regulations of that government.

At Cedar Creek Road, he turned right instead of left and started the two-mile ride to the Black Star Coal Works. The closer he got, the more uncomfortable he became, and his mind began to return over and over to something he dreamed last night. A nightmare of sorts, possibly brought on by the late night and disturbing experience with the bear, and the many troubling thoughts that had plagued him lately. Maybe it even had something to do with that strange encounter with the Weaver.

Whatever it was, his sleep last night had been restless and fitful. He tossed and turned and dreamed meaningless dreams of children with black faces and spinning wheels whirring. He was in the schoolroom, standing behind his desk with his hands raised in the air. "Everybody together, now, *Oh beautiful for spacious skies...*"

There was a sea of faces before him: all of them black—black—and the youngest ones kept falling out of their chairs. He tried to put them back again, but there were too many of them. Off in one corner of the room, the Weaver sat spinning at a giant wheel, and chanting:

> *The little wheels spin and spin*
> *but the big one turns them around...*

"You'll have to leave," he said to her, "you're scaring the children." She just sat there spinning, and the big wheel was whirring around and around. He couldn't take his eyes from it. Suddenly, it wasn't a wheel anymore. It had changed into a miniature version of a coal-breaking machine that was used deep in the mines. One of the little girls screamed and cried out, "It's the crusher—the crusher!"

A panic ensued.

Children scattered in every direction like in the playground games. Strange, but Harlan had thought the "crusher" was some sort of mythological beast they had made up to run away from. It never occurred to him that it might be something real. He had wakened from that dream with a chilling dread, along with the terrible knowledge he had known deep inside himself all along.

Most of his missing students – not just the oldest boys—were working "under the hill" as it was referred to in this region. They were illegal employees of the Black Star Coal Works. Tom was aware of it and didn't want him to stir up trouble. But such information, if it could be proved, could not be excused even by the consent of parents. No matter how poor or ignorant they were. And if Harlan, as an employee of the government, knew of such information he was obligated to report it. He wondered how anyone with an ounce of moral standard could do otherwise.

He passed a peaceful looking cabin set back into the trees, and the rustling as he went by caused a Chimney Swift to dart from its rooftop with lightning speed. He slowed Prince to a walk. Even after these few weeks the beauty of Appalachia still took his breath away. He wondered then, why the most beautiful places on earth always seemed to be riddled with the most corruption. His thoughts began to wander again to the many contrasts of Cedar Creek. The wild beauty of it, the people that could stir the very depths of his emotions with their mannerisms and bearing. Even the children seemed to know who they were and what they believed in, from an early age.

Even the children.

He was thinking of the children when he first heard the sound of muffled crying from somewhere off in the trees. Just ahead of him there was a leafy path that seemed to lead to a portion of the rushing creek that ran alongside the road. Harlan stopped. Now they turned to heart-wrenching desperate sobs and he could not bring himself to pass by. He tied Prince to a nearby tree and began to pick his way quietly down the trail.

The banks of the creek were steep and rocky here, and the end of the trail came out above a swirling eddy of black water that formed a deep pool behind a large granite stone. On top, sat a girl with her back to him. Her hair was dark and tangled, her red dress dirty and torn in places. She would pause between sobs to gulp from a slender blue bottle. Then she put the back of a hand to her mouth as if to keep it down before giving into the emotional weeping, again. As Harlan neared her, she let the bottle slip into the water, and swung her legs over the side of the stone to jump in.

"No!" He moved quickly and caught her by the arm just as she went down. The pull from the eddy was strong. He managed to drag her back onto the bank, drenched and choking. "Whatever it is—that won't help!"

She tried to get up—got only so far as her hands and knees – and then stared at him in amazement from between the thick, dripping curls plastered against her face. "Teacher!" she gasped. "Can't help me—I drank—"

He leaned down and held the back of her head with one hand while he forced a finger down her throat with the other. In a few moments she had lost most of whatever she drank. She collapsed into another frustrated fit of sobbing, as if he had struck her rather than saving her life. He pushed the hair away from her face to see who she was, and noticed it was bruised and swollen, and that one of her eyes was black.

"I'm going to take you home," he decided.

"No!" A look of terror crossed her face.

"With me," he assured. "Where you'll be safe and we can sort things out."

She shook her head and staggered to her feet. "No – you— you get away from me, teacher – you —" Her red dress clung to her trembling frame like wet paper, and she suddenly sank to her knees. "I can't move my..."

Harlan took his jacket off and wrapped it around her. He lifted her into his arms and her head dropped onto his shoulder, as if she could no longer hold it up. "Try to stay awake," he coaxed as he carried her back up the trail. "Can you tell me your name? I have a bit of coffee left in my thermos."

"I'm—so—cold!"

"What was in the bottle?"

"He didn't take any."

"Who didn't?"

"He tricked me!"

Harlan set her down against the tree Prince was tied to and took his thermos from one of the saddlebags. There was little more than half a cup left. She was drifting off by the time he turned back to her, but he tipped swallows into her mouth anyway. It was warm but not hot, and enough to startle her awake again. She looked up at him as if he had only just got there.

"The schoolteacher!"

"Yes. And your name is..." She didn't answer. He stashed the thermos away and lifted her up into the saddle. "Come on, then, and we'll—"

"The horse..." She leaned forward to lay her head against his neck and close her eyes. "I heard of... this horse..."

"No sleeping, now." Harlan climbed up behind her and drew her back against his chest as he took the reins. "Or I'll have to stop at the first house we come to and ask who you are."

He felt her stiffen against him.

"Don't, Mr. Harlan—please don't!"

"Give me a good reason why I shouldn't."

"Somebody might tell Joseph Lee!"

28

Big John Harper was tired as he drove home from his shift that night. Not physically tired. For some reason, he had been endowed with the strength and endurance of three men rather than one and even a ten-hour shift at the Black Star Coal Works could not exhaust it. No, he was tired of the way things were. Tired of situations that kept people he cared about so far away from each other.

Tired he couldn't come home to Sarah and live with her in their own little cabin behind the tobacco fields. But it wasn't ready, yet. He was still trying to save up enough money for the window-glass, which wasn't easy when the rest of the family needed so many things. And he was tired of seeing his father fall into a dead sleep in the seat beside him on their way home every night.

Big John was especially tired of driving past Tom Bascomb's place, knowing if they would all swallow their pride, his father might live longer under the skilled doctor's care. Why should the Doc pay longer for his mistakes than any of the rest of them were paying for theirs?

Everybody makes mistakes.

True, some could never be made right, and maybe this was one of those. But lately, a strange notion had been nagging at him. He kept thinking if he were bold enough to make the first move… to actually walk up to that door once more and knock on it… that just maybe the same caring man they had all known and loved so long ago would answer it. He might give him something for Lias. Maybe not something that would cure but would at least make the suffering times more tolerable. Maybe it would help the whole family, too, and not just his father.

What a strange notion to be thinking on while his Uncle Jimmy was still sitting out his time in the penitentiary in Princeton, and his Aunt Lyla cooking in a crowded diner day after day, living in a tumble-down apartment on mean city streets, just so she could be close enough to visit her husband on Sundays. He was due up for parole in the spring of next year… but still. Maybe some mistakes could never be made right, no matter how many people wanted them to be.

If there were only some way he could know.

The horse and rider stepped out into the middle of the road and stopped there. The glow of his headlights picked them up in plenty of time to slow down and pull over to the side. Big John set the brake, left the engine running, and then eased out of the door quietly so as not to wake Lias. He had heard plenty about Harlan's horse but never seen it. Now, as the young teacher slipped as easily down out of the saddle as a boy, and walked toward him with the huge magnificent creature following behind, he couldn't help but be in awe of them.

"I've been waiting for you, John," Harlan said as they neared each other. "I didn't think I should come by the house but I couldn't let it go until tomorrow. It's not something to write in a note for the children to carry."

"Something wrong with the Doc?"

"No. With Ivy Tolliver. She's been beaten badly, and tried to kill herself this afternoon. But she won't tell us anything, just keeps asking for Bonnie Rae. Doesn't want to be taken home."

"I better find Joseph Lee."

"She won't see him, either. I thought you might be willing to bring Bonnie Rae. Tom and I – we'll just busy ourselves out in the barn while both of you are there and maybe we can make all this right."

Make all this right.

"I'll drop Daddy off and bring Bonnie Rae back as soon as I can." But he just stood there for a moment instead of heading back for the car.

"I wouldn't have asked," Harlan's tone was apologetic as he answered the still questioning eyes that were looking down on him from that coal black face. "Except she's still terribly upset and will only talk to Bonnie Rae."

"You done right to ask. Them three been like family ever since they was younguns. It just took me by surprise—you and that horse—coming out of the dark that way. Right then. When I was thinking on some things."

Later, when he had cleaned up some and successfully evaded the questions of the rest of the family, he and Bonnie Rae climbed back into the truck and headed toward town on a pretext. He told them he needed her to measure Sarah for a Christmas coat he wanted her to make. Not that he wouldn't buy everything she needed and have her make one —even if it meant digging into his window glass savings. Big John was not one to say something and not do it.

He wasn't as successful with Joseph Lee. He had not been home for dinner and no one had seen him all day. Finding him wouldn't be easy. The way his wild brother ranged deep into every swamp and holler on the mountain at the slightest whim, made it almost impossible. He would find him, though. Because whatever was wrong with Ivy –

"I said there's any number of different furs to make a collar with," Bonnie Rae finally broke into his thoughts, "not how many do you want on it. Law, Johnny – what's ailing you? Something wrong with the truck? We been driving for ten minutes and you ain't even out of second gear!"

"I'm looking for that little road just after the Giles place that leads out past the old mill. Must be grown over but it ought to be right around – there it is." He turned into a stand of tall grass and bushes, then went bumping and plowing on through. "We're not going to town, Bonnie Rae. We're taking the back roads to the Doc's place. And this time, we're going in."

For a moment she didn't answer; just held onto the door and the dashboard as they bounced over the rough trail. "It'll kill Daddy if he finds out we done it," she finally said.

"He's dying right in front of us, anyhow, ain't he? Could be Doc might give us something that would ease things up for him a bit."

"If it ain't a potion, you'd have to say where it come from. And maybe Doc won't give us anything. Maybe he won't even open the door when he sees us standing on his porch."

"He'll open his door. He's expecting us."

"What?"

"Ivy's there. Somebody's beat the fire out of her and she ain't talking. Just keeps asking for you."

"We gotta find J-Lee!"

"She don't want to see him. So, if you got any idea where he is you better tell me." He looked over at her then, with an expression she had never been able to look into and lie. Not that she could see it as much as feel it in the little bit of moonlight that found its way into the truck.

"He wouldn't do such a thing, Big John—no matter how mad he got at her!"

"I know that. But I got an idea who did, and why she don't want to see him right now." The road smoothed out as it intersected with the mill road that looped back around toward Cedar Creek. "I think he's headed back for the business, again, and Ivy's got a hound on her tail."

They parked at the gate and made their way slowly across the yard. Not because it was cluttered. It had been cleaned up since John saw it last and there was even a new shed-row where the tumbledown barn had once stood. He could see lantern light coming from inside. Bonnie Rae hung back until he took her by the coat-sleeve and hurried her along.

"Come on, ain't no one but Ivy inside. They're out in the barn, so, there's nothing to be scared of."

"I ain't scared, I—feel like I'm about to bawl just being this close!"

"You don't have to see him if you don't want. I'll talk to him, myself, after we find out about Ivy."

"Why didn't Harlan stay?"

"I reckon he don't want to make trouble between you and Daddy. So, behave yourself and show some respect. Ain't no time to fool around." He opened the door into the little cabin and then stood back for her to step inside.

Bonnie Rae entered hesitantly, as if the room alone, with its crackling fire and book-lined walls could conjure the past up all around her, again. Her eyes automatically sought out the painting of Melanie Bascomb above the hearth. It was more beautiful even than she remembered. Big John took the lead and started back toward the bedroom next to the kitchen, where he knew Ivy would be. He rapped twice and went in without waiting for an answer.

The usually feisty, beautiful girl Joseph Lee had not been able to resist even when they were children seemed lost somewhere inside a large pair of man's pajamas and a colorful patchwork quilt. She looked up at them through tear-filled eyes and whimpered, "I just don't want to live!"

"Ivy—" Bonnie Rae put her arms around her. "Darlin! Ain't nothing bad as that!"

"You lead that traveling man up onto the hill, Ivy?" Big John asked the direct question without any preliminaries.

"I met him coming back down—" she confessed. "And he told me—he—he would wait in the car!"

"What'd you even take him that far for?"

"He wanted whiskey and we needed the money. He acted like he didn't know nothing. Like he was scared to go any-where around here his self. I was in a hurry on account of J-

Lee was waiting for me at the sugar party! He followed me up there, and—and then he wasn't that way at all no more!"

"What way was he?"

For a moment, she didn't answer.

Bonnie Rae looked at her brother and motioned for him to leave the room. When John turned to go, Ivy said, "Wait."

He stopped.

"He grabbed me off the trail and drug me into the bushes. Put a hand over my mouth so I couldn't holler for nobody. Said he caught me red-handed and we was all going to jail, if I—if I didn't—"

"Didn't what," John asked.

"Didn't tell him when the Harpers would be getting there!"

Big John stiffened at the words. The only way rumors would be circulating about his family being back in the business, again, was if Joseph Lee were working for someone already.

"If I brung the laws down on everybody, again—" Ivy began to sob miserably, "well, I just don't want to live!"

"It's been near two weeks since then," he pressed. "Why'd you wait so long to tell us?"

"Daddy and Jesse was afraid I'd run to Joseph Lee about it before they got the still moved. Had me locked up in the corn-crib over a week! I was hurting so bad I liked to died in there. But they don't even care what that man done to me! Said I deserved every bit of it bringing a stranger that close. That I cared more about you all than my own kin!"

"When J-Lee hears that," Bonnie Rae fumed. "There's gonna be some —"

Ivy clutched her friend's hand to stop the tumble of words. "Can't nobody tell J-Lee! He'll come looking for daddy, sure, for using his name, and—don't you see? That's just what that Durham feller's waiting for!"

"You mean J-Lee ain't working for you, at all?" John asked.

"No, sir, he never was. When Jesse brung food and such

out to the corncrib, he told me Daddy started them rumors, his self, long about last Christmas. After his product got better. Way things are between me and Joseph Lee, I reckon people believed him. But I never knew nothing about it. I swear!"

"Jesse went along with leaving you locked up like that?" Bonnie Rae couldn't hide her surprise. "To think I believed him, yesterday, when I come looking for you and he said you was off up the hill helping at the still!"

"He was scared as Daddy about Durham being a law. He is—but he sure don't act like one! I been blinder than Eve when she ate the apple!"

She made a sudden effort to sit up and drew her friend close to whisper, "Bonnie Rae—don't let that man catch you alone, honey—you hear? Nor any of your other girl folk! He's —he's just like the devil!" She sobbed and caught her breath for a moment. "He near choked the life out of me when I said he was—crazy if he thought he could get off this mountain alive after what he done!"

"Oh, Ivy!" Bonnie Rae gasped and held her close.

"Then he hit me—so many times I thought I'd die! But then he just quit. Of a sudden. Like he never had no real feelings at all—neither good, or bad. He just said, real cold-like… now, let's see if this won't catch us a Harper!"

John whispered a low curse, turned away for a moment, then did his best to keep quiet until she was finished.

"That's when I knew he was a law. Just—waiting for Joseph Lee to show up. I was dying every day thinking he might! Then I was dying every day thinking he won't. Maybe seeing me in that car, he won't want nothing to do with me."

She leaned her head back against the pillow, again, as if the telling had used up whatever strength she had left in her. But after a few moments of silence, as the others were taking it all in, she declared emphatically, "If J-Lee don't want me no more—if anything happens to him on account of me—I just don't want to live!"

"Thunder and hail, Ivy!" Bonnie Rae suddenly felt her

own feelings spill over. "Killing yourself would only make things worse!"

"But if I was dead, he wouldn't have no reason to come looking for me, no more. And maybe the laws won't find our new place. That's how I planned it all out."

"How'd you get yourself out of the corn crib?" she asked.

"Run off from Jesse, this morning, after I talked him into letting me warm up by the fire. He brung me the laudanum, too, or I'd have died the first night. Wouldn't do no good for me to be gone and J-Lee still looking for me around the still, though. That's why I went for that place in the river runs past the mines. So, somebody would find me quick."

"Ivy——-Ivy!" Bonnie Rae gasped, again, at the horrible thought.

"But then that teacher of yours come along. So fast, it was like somebody told him! Doc and him been pouring coffee down me all day—made me walk from one end of this place to the other so many times—I gone near a hundred mile!"

"What makes you certain Durham's a law?" John finally spoke up. "Could be he just doesn't want you to tell what happened."

"On account of he never did take the whiskey," Ivy reasoned. "Didn't put no personal store in it, at all."

29

Harlan glanced again toward the lighted cabin. They were still inside. By the time they finally did come out, he and Tom had put the finishing touches on the new tack room, which was the last part of the shed-row that needed to be completed before winter. Not only would Prince and the old mule have a smaller, warmer place, the project had been a good reason for the two men to spend time getting to know each other, again. It had become such a pleasant habit to come out and work together in the barn every night after supper that the construction of it had turned into more than just a necessity.

But tonight, Harlan was distracted with Bonnie Rae being so close and Tom being so quiet. His uncle had sunk deeply into his own thoughts as soon as the two arrived and hardly said a word. It was a relief to finally hear the front door close in the distance and—while he had already decided not to talk to John until Bonnie Rae returned to the truck—he suddenly found the temptation to meet them as they walked across the yard almost overpowering. As if there were some invisible force tugging on him. When they turned toward the little barn instead of the gate, it was all the invitation he needed.

They met halfway. The look in Bonnie Rae's eyes was so troubled and apprehensive that it was a natural response to put a hand behind her head and draw her against him. She buried her face in the comforting closeness and clung to him as if it were possible to draw any strength and reassurance she needed in those few fleeting moments. If John was surprised, he didn't show it, and—as it had been when they were with Joseph Lee —Bonnie Rae seemed to make no effort to hide their feelings from this brother, either.

"If he's willing," said Big John, "we'd like to talk to the Doc."

"I'll see what I can do." Harlan returned to the barn to find Tom standing next to Prince with a currycomb but not using it. "They want to talk, Uncle."

When he turned around, Harlan detected some of the same apprehension he had seen in Bonnie Rae. Tom went to the open door and stopped there. The others stood still, waiting for some sign. When the doctor spread his arms, slightly, in a gesture of futility, the two began to move toward him as if drawn by a magnet. It caused a chain reaction.

Tom's eyes filled and spilled over, which caused Bonnie Rae to fly into his arms with tearful relief, and Big John to enfold both of them against his broad strong chest while he leaned his forehead down onto the graying brown hair and held onto them for long moments. It occurred to Harlan then, as he looked on, that he had misjudged them all. They had not so much been torn apart by hate and betrayal as held together by love in spite of those things.

He did not intrude. Instead, he remained in the open doorway until they turned back long enough to draw him into their circle and toward the house with them. The four years began to fall away, and with each moment, the radiance in Tom's face returned by degrees. Until Harlan could see with a startling clarity the way things had been between them. Tom had been a shelter to these two in their young days, the same way that he had been for Harlan. The way Harlan, himself, had now become for others. Could anything worse befall a man when such dependence rested on him and he could not come through?

Where did Lias fit into it all?

Had he and Tom clashed over the welfare of the children and ultimately lost everything in their thrashing? There were no winners on either side. But at this moment—at least for these three—there was enough hope in just picking up pieces. So, when they sat down before the fire to decide what should be done, it seemed only natural that Bonnie Rae made herself at home in the kitchen to fix hot chocolate for everyone before returning to the bedroom to talk more with Ivy.

Harlan leaned against the doorframe and watched her for a few moments before she noticed he had followed her there. "Did her father do that to her?"

"Her father's a no-account, all right, but it was the traveling man done it." She explained without effort to hide anything from him. "If he is a traveling man. He caught her up at her daddy's still but she wouldn't talk. Ivy's stubborn like that. He nigh onto killed her, though. Now, she's afraid she brought the laws down on everybody, again."

"It's a dangerous rotten business no matter which side you're on." He pronounced. "We'll have to keep a close watch on her for a while."

"She'd be dead already if you didn't happen by, Harlan. What were you even doing up there? Ain't nowhere near the school."

She put a saucepan on the stove to heat and went out to the back porch to dip cold milk out of a pail. She handed him the tin pitcher to hold while she did, and then replaced the lid on the milk-pail when it was filled. "It was a miracle out of scripture you even found her. Besides what you done."

"Any decent person would have done the same." They went back inside.

"Not many would have known to do that." She poured the milk into the pan, then added powdered chocolate and several spoons of brown sugar from a set of wooden canisters, nearby. "Would've gone awful hard on Joseph Lee if you hadn't got to her in time. Hard on all of us."

She looked over at him as she stirred the warming mixture, and a sudden expression of amazement came into her eyes. "You stopped death, itself, Harlan! Same way you did that big ol' bear, last night. It's like you got… saving grace… shining all around any place you go."

"Saving grace." He repeated the lovely phrase and gave in to the temptation to run a finger over the smooth softness of her upturned face. "You're looking at me like I just stepped down out of heaven, honey."

"You did, seems to me like."

"Then I better take some of the mystery away for you before it gets out of hand. When a person's raised by two doctors and a nurse, who had an office right there at home, it doesn't take many years to see almost every emergency there is. Knowledge like that comes in handy, now and again, that's all. I make my share of mistakes as much as the next person."

"I sure ain't seen any." She returned her attention to the chocolate.

"I'm probably making one right now, as a matter of fact." He put his arms around her waist as she stirred, and noticed as he looked over her shoulder that she had managed to find a familiar set of several Austrian mugs. He hadn't seen them since his Aunt Melanie made eggnog one holiday season. So many years ago. Another feeling of complete contentment swept through him. "Letting myself enjoy you like this just when I was going to try not to see you for a while. At least not until—"

"But I gotta see you!"

"Shhh."

She let go of the spoon and turned within his embrace to whisper emphatically, "I can't wait the whole school year just so—"

"Did I say the whole school year?"

"I can't even wait till Christmas! Or next week!" She stood on tiptoes to put her arms around his neck, and by reflex, he lifted her off her feet and held her there as she declared, "Or even tomorrow! If you love me as much as—"

"Love you—I'd marry you, right now, if I could."

There was a sound of footsteps coming down the hall and she quickly pushed away from him to turn back to the stove. Harlan moved over to the sink and as John stepped into the kitchen, their eyes met. A flicker of knowing passed between them.

Harlan was determined to be nothing if not honest with him. "John, I—"

But he was interrupted by a disarming smile and the dismissing statement, "Now, here's what we're gonna do."

Then, while Bonnie Rae murmured something about a potholder, her brother reached over and lifted the hot, iron-handled saucepan off the stove with one hand and poured the dark liquid into the colorful waiting mugs before she found one.

"I'm gonna take Ivy into Princeton on Saturday and settle her in with Aunt Lyla. Least till things cool down here on the mountain. Meanwhile, you go back in there, Bonnie Rae, and see if you can't get her to meet up with Joseph Lee first, or we'll have a time leaving her to herself, again, anywhere. He's the only one ever could talk any sense into that girl. We—all of us—got to keep our heads about things till we find out what Durham's gonna do."

30

It was obvious to Big John that another raid was in the offing. And even though the few Harpers that were still ridge-running were working for others and not themselves, it bothered him that there were still people from outside that couldn't leave well enough alone. Hadn't they paid enough? It also bothered him that he had probably pushed his younger brother in that direction, himself, by insisting he return to the mines. In spite of Ivy's insistence that he did not work for the Tollivers, John had always found rumors to contain some measure of truth in them, somewhere.

Joseph Lee was a throwback from the old days. A wild, restless spirit who was not only incapable of staying indoors for very long, but who must also constantly roam from one end of the wilderness to the other. Being in the blackest dark every day—shut out from the sun and wind—had almost killed him once before. Facing that a second time would make even the hazards of the business his only acceptable option. Now, there was this longer than usual absence from home and John's own nagging premonition of what his brother was up to. He had never found such feelings to betray him, yet.

Exactly what he was going to do about it was another matter.

By the next night, he had worked a plan out to the last detail. It had come to him when he was arranging to borrow Aaron McCord's car, to make that trip to Princeton. From here on out, he would assume that Joseph Lee had returned to the business. In that case, no one must know his real errand, other than those already involved. The next step was to create a diversion. Big John Harper had learned early that there was no better hiding place for a thing than the middle of a good diversion.

So, he decided to get married.

All he had to do was convince Sarah. He didn't expect too much opposition from her. Other than the fact that she would be giving up a family wedding, they were both so tired of waiting it no longer seemed much of a sacrifice. But he wasn't taking any chances. He would dress up in his finest, come bearing gifts, and—under the circumstances—make it as festive of an occasion as possible.

He made quite an appearance when he stepped into the Cedarville Drugstore, just before dark, on Saturday evening. Mr. Laurence had already turned the soda fountain over to his nephew and was headed upstairs where his wife had a pot roast cooking. At the jingling sound of the bell on the door, he looked down to see Big John Harper walk in, wearing a pressed white shirt beneath a finely cut leather jacket with a matching cap. That Bonnie Rae was getting to be quite a hand with leatherwork these days.

Mr. Laurence returned to the counter and watched the large, magnificent man move through the isles with that arresting grace that so characterized the familiar stride. John picked up a box of chocolates from one isle and a jar of perfume from another as he passed by (without even a glance to choose which kind) and headed for the counter with a telling smile. "Sort of a special occasion," he replied to Mr. Laurence's curious gaze.

"There some kind of a shindig going on tonight I ain't heard about?" The older man pulled his glasses down from the top of his head to peer at the register numbers. "Your sister was in here a while, ago, and she looked dressed to—"

Big John's face went serious and he stopped counting out his money. "Bonnie Rae shouldn't be running around town tonight." He spoke with a flicker of irritation. "Was she with the school teacher?"

"Wasn't Bonnie Rae, it was Lou Ellen. That'll be a dollar and ten cents."

"Lou Ellen?"

"You know I don't like to carry tales, John," the storekeeper replied. "But I figure a girl Lou Ellen's age shouldn't be let to run around with older men. Especially when nobody knows much about them."

"I know plenty about that school teacher, and he wouldn't never—"

"Not the school teacher. She was in here with that new traveling salesman."

"God almighty!" he whispered furiously.

"Not that it's any of my business. It's just that he near cleaned out my whole housewares isle last week. I'd like to know what kind of company lets their sales folk do business like that. No way they can make any kind of profit on it. Why he paid—"

"How long ago were they here?" Big John interrupted.

"Twenty minutes. Half hour ago, maybe." He handed over the bag and change.

John shoved the money back into his pocket without counting and hurried out the door like a gathering storm. Mr. Laurence sighed heavily and pushed his glasses on top of his head, again.

"How come you done that, Uncle Bob?" His husky-voiced nephew stood watching from a few feet away. "You know what he'll do to that Durham feller, now. How come you done it?"

"Because I got a feeling Durham's up to no good, that's how come," his uncle replied. "And that there's the man who can find out what it is."

"Ain't like he cares anymore."

"He cares."

Big John tossed the chocolates and perfume onto the back seat and listened as the Chevrolet's engine roared to life. He took a mental—almost subconscious—assessment of it as he pulled away from the curb, and felt the past four years drop away as if they had been nothing more than a long dream.

All the old instincts came into play so smoothly, he barely noticed it was happening. Much less the rapid deductions that pointed him in the only direction Lon Durham would have gone. With an uncanny accuracy that came from years of practice, he homed in on the traveling salesman like a hunter drawing a bead.

He was not surprised to catch sight of the black and white DeSoto in a roadhouse parking lot on the outskirts of town. And though he felt a slow rage pulsing inside him, it was not out of control. Saturday nights the place was crowded. But he had visions of himself telling that foreigner to step outside.

That was the last thing he remembered clearly.

Thirty seconds later, he heard the frightened cry of his sister—realized they were still in the car—and was seized by a blind all-consuming rage. It was over in less than a minute.

He yanked open the door on the driver's side, hauled Durham out by the collar, and delivered a single smashing blow to the man's jaw: dropping him in an instant. The man was out cold. He lifted him off the ground and as he shoved him back inside, a wallet dropped out of his coat pocket. John picked it up and would have tossed it back in with the owner, except that it had fallen open in front of him. What he saw there made his blood run cold.

It was the official looking badge of a Federal officer.

Quickly, he reached over the crumpled form and dragged a hysterical Lou Ellen across the seat and outside before slamming the door closed, again. The longer head start they had before anyone found out what had happened, the better. His young sister's first response was to cling tightly to him with an almost desperate relief.

"Are you hurt, baby?"

"Just—scared—" she sobbed. "He wouldn't let me out, Johnny! He kept asking about you and J-Lee! Every time I give a answer he didn't like, he—he—"

"Well, he didn't seem to have no trouble getting you in there! Just look at you! Gone and painted yourself up like a hussy!"

When Lou Ellen realized he was pulling into the first stand of woods they passed instead of heading straight for home, a sudden dread washed over her. But no amount of crying or pleading could stop him. He yanked her out of the car again, snapped off a hickory switch, and nearly wore it out on her. At home, he only stayed long enough to turn her over to his father, who met them out in the yard. After a brief explanation, Lias cut a switch of his own and proceeded to repeat the same punishment over again as his son drove away.

Little more than an hour had passed since Big John entered the Cedarville drugstore, but his world had suddenly changed. Now, the pleasant anticipations of his special evening with Sarah Wesley had been replaced with old fears.

All at once he felt hunted, again.

He tried to dispel those feelings with the logic that he had nothing to hide or run from anymore. The man had been taking advantages with his sister! Yet, in a moment of heated temper, he had reverted to the old ways. Now, he had the nagging dread that he might have killed that foreigner. That he might have killed an honest-to-God Federal officer. The thought made him break out into a cold sweat.

There would be no justice in this town if he had killed him, no matter what Durham had done to deserve it. The Sheriff of Cedarville had wanted the prestige of incarcerating a Harper ever since he first took office, two years ago. Now, it seemed after four years of working hard and honest, Big John Harper may have lost it all in a few moments of blind, unchecked temper. The same kind he had been worried about in Joseph Lee.

He still didn't know where his brother was. He had been gone for three days. What else could be doing this long, if not working some still hidden in deep woods?

Well, Big John wouldn't stand for that. Not for one minute he wouldn't. He would get to the bottom of this and set things right, no matter what he had to do to get there. He was not about to stand by and see his family brought low a second time. And once Big John Harper made a decision, nothing in this world could stand in his way.

Except maybe going to jail.

31

Joseph Lee Harper could not remember a time when he hadn't lived by his instincts. He finally came home on Sunday afternoon. Not because it had been arranged. But because some inner clock told him it was time to harvest his tobacco. His mother was looking at the first flecks of rain beginning to spatter against the kitchen window when she caught sight of him coming from the farthest stand of trees that fringed the fields. He was too far away to see his face but she didn't have to. The form and familiar stride were all she needed to recognize her son.

It was not unusual for him to disappear for long periods but—for some reason—she felt worried about him. The rain began to drum the window with a steady pelting. Knowing that Joseph Lee would be soaked by the time he reached the house, Celia set the knife she was using to chop vegetables aside, and went to get him some dry clothes.

As she was rummaging through his drawer for a clean pair of socks, her hand brushed against a red, two-ounce tin that once held *Prince Albert* pipe tobacco. She heard the familiar rattle of change and a dark apprehension began to creep over her. She picked up the little can and opened it, wishing it could be filled with tobacco or some other boyish vice, before the true contents spilled out into her hand. Ninety-three dollars and forty-seven cents.

Her world began to crumble.

By the time she heard the screen door bang on the back porch, she had put the dry clothes where he would be sure to find them and was back at the kitchen counter, chopping vegetables, again. The rain was pouring down in fine torrents, now, and running in steady rivulets along the windowpane.

He tapped on the back door window and grinned, waving the folded clothes at her in a gesture of appreciation before shedding his wet ones. Oh, there was a sweetness about him that made her want to cry. When he finally came inside, he said, "Hey, Mama," and somewhere between getting a coffee cup and heading for the pot on the stove, he squeezed her tight and gave her a kiss on the cheek. He was still cold from outside, and he smelled like the pine forest and the crisp, autumn air.

"Where you been, honey?" she asked.

"What's wrong, Mama?" He gave her a second, more careful look.

"Oh," she sniffed and pushed at a stray wisp of hair with the back of her hand, "It's just these onions set my eyes to crying."

He sat down at the table and dropped two cubes of sugar into the dark steaming liquid and began to stir. "I been ranging, mostly," he answered finally. "You know I can't take too much inside before I got to feel the outside for a while."

"Joseph Lee... something wrong between you and your daddy?"

"Not lately," he replied. "Why?"

"Just making sure. You know it seems to me things been getting better around here. Like maybe the worst was over."

He ain't never been a bad man to live with, long as he gets his way." He sipped on the coffee. "Looks to me like he's just been getting his way."

"He's a changed man, son."

"The day we disagree and he don't beat the fire out of me,

is when I'll believe it. But I reckon I'll just get tired of him one of these days, and—"

"Joseph Lee!"

"Don't worry. I wouldn't never hit him back. I'd walk away, though. And if I do, I ain't never staying under the same roof with him, again."

Celia set the knife aside and sat down across the table from him. She looked into the golden face, handsome in its young manhood and asked, "Is that what the money's for?"

He looked up at her quickly, was tempted to lie, and then sighed. "Naw. I ain't fixing to run off. Big John's been getting on my back about signing on with the Company, again. I'm tired of hearing him talk about me not doing my part."

"But you got enough money in there, already, to... Joseph Lee?" Her eyes were wide with anxiety. "Where you getting that kind of cash money?"

Seeing her so distraught made him sorry he had caused it. He turned his face away from her for a few moments and thought carefully before he lied. "I got it from Granny. I been taking some of them drugs of hers to market. Where is she, anyhow? Got some things to talk over with her."

Celia was baffled. "Big John took her home day before yesterday. But she ain't let nobody sell her goods for nigh onto ten years, now."

"Well, I made sort of a deal with her. She's gonna teach me wild-crafting, and I'm gonna put back what I take. Range for it and cure it, myself. I ain't cutting her short. And I'll have it all put back by next year."

"She didn't say nothing about it when she was here."

"She's just getting forgetful, that's all," he assured. "You can ask her about it, yourself, next time she comes. I wanted to make sure I had the cash money before I told Big John, because I could just see him putting a stop to it. I tell you, Mama, he thinks everyone ought to be working down in that pit the way he does. Ain't nobody gonna put me down there, again— no matter what kind of times we live in. Not for no twelve cents a hour! I'd die, first."

"Joseph Lee."

"I would," he insisted. "I ain't even gonna stand burying when my time comes, that's how bad I hate being shut up. You're all gonna have to tie my bones up in a tree, like some ol' Indian. I swear!"

Her eyes began to twinkle and the hint of a smile crossed her face. Seeing he was beginning to get the best of things, he flashed her a winning smile that he knew she couldn't resist, and said, "Don't worry. You didn't raise no bad boys."

But the deception weighed so heavily on him he could no longer sit still. He got to his feet, added more steaming coffee to his cup, and then headed down the hallway. Bonnie Rae was reading when he stuck his head in her door.

"Joseph Lee Harper!" She tossed the book aside. "Where in God's world have you been! All hell's broke loose around here! I sent Aaron out to look for you but you must have been clean out of the county. He couldn't even find a sign."

"I been busy." He sat down on the end of the bed and leaned back against the wall to sip on his coffee. "What sort of hell I been missing out on?"

Now that she was facing him, it was hard to tell. When she hesitated, trying to decide how to begin, he warned, "If Ivy done set you up to something, it ain't gonna do no good. That girl's got to learn I ain't no—"

"Ivy's in Princeton with Aunt Lyla."

"What?"

"Big John drove her there, yesterday."

"What for?"

"It wasn't like you thought, J-Lee." She pushed the loose red curls off her shoulder and looked intently at him. "She was so worried at making you wait at the sugar party, she took the traveling man near right to the still to get him some whiskey."

"She wouldn't do that."

"Well, she might as well have. He said he'd wait in the car but instead he followed her all the way up there, and then—"

Joseph Lee breathed a low curse and set his coffee cup down on the floor.

"Then he… did every bad thing he could do to her, and..."

He got to his feet and began to pace back and forth as she talked.

"Said if she didn't tell him where the Harper still was, he'd—"

"The Harper still—where would anybody get that idea?"

Bonnie Rae hesitated, again. "I guess it's on account of Tolliver's been telling everybody you're working with them, J-Lee. Brings more money that way. Made Ivy think Durham's either a law, or working for them. Else why would he go to all that trouble to sneak around? He didn't even take the whiskey when he left."

"Why didn't she come tell me? She knows I'd have—"

"Old man Tolliver wouldn't let her. Locked her up in the corncrib till he could get the still moved off somewhere you wouldn't know about. For over a week she was in there! And her hurting so bad she was still black and blue when we saw her. He said she deserved every bit of it, and to—to quit squalling and bawling over..."

"Go on," he said with a sudden and chilling quiet.

"Over something she'd been doing with, Joseph Lee Harper, for the longest kind of a time, already."

"That no-account father of hers! And Durham, too—I'll take care of both of them! But Johnny's got some nerve taking her all the way to Princeton without even—" He stopped in mid-stride and turned riveting eyes on his sister. "What ain't you told me that you're being so all-fired careful about?"

"She tried to kill herself, J-Lee. On account of when you found out what Durham did to her, you might come out of wherever you..." She spoke the next phrase carefully. "… really are working… to keep him from taking her to jail. Then Johnny would have to turn his self in and— "

He didn't wait to hear more, but stormed out of the room in a burst of temper. Bonnie Rae sighed heavily when she heard the backdoor slam. She leaned her forehead against the cold glass of the window to catch a last glimpse as he moved out across a corner of the yard. Why hadn't she waited until Johnny got home to handle things?

Because then Joseph Lee wouldn't have had enough time to get his own story straight before having to face his brother.

32

Joseph Lee ran through the rain in a blind rage and reached the Tolliver place just as it was getting dark. He stood in the yard and called into the lighted house for Ivy's father to come out. The family was at the supper table when they first heard him. Tolliver—a huge man with curly white hair and close-set eyes—quickly slid his chair back and went for his gun.

Ivy's mother, who had been sick with Malaria for two years, was dressed in the same gown and bathrobe she had worn for many days. Her hair was disheveled and in tangles because her daughter had not been home to fix it for her. Though she sat at the table she had not eaten. She merely watched the others.

Jesse, a heavy, usually slow-moving young man, followed his father into the living room. "What's wrong with you!" He snatched the rifle from the older man's trembling hands. "You shoot him, we'll have another blood war on our hands!"

"He knows!" Tolliver was so unnerved he didn't notice a splash of bean soup that trickled from his chin. "Just what do you want me to do—let him get to me first?"

"Go out the back and I'll keep him busy."

Joseph Lee heard the familiar squeak of the back door just as Jesse stepped out onto the front porch to talk to him. Without waiting to hear what the younger Tolliver had to say, he darted around the house. Too fast for the heavy young man to do anything but follow.

Joseph Lee Harper caught up with Tolliver half way to the wood shed, grabbed him by the shirt in mid stride and threw him furiously to the ground. Before the older man could struggle to his feet, the young Harper picked up a stick of wood and began to hit him over and over with it.

"That's enough—that's enough!" Jesse yelled as he came up on the scene. "You're gonna kill him!" He grabbed for the stick and Joseph Lee spun around to strike him, instead.

"I know what he done, J-Lee!" Jesse backed off quickly with his hands raised in submission. "You had a right—but he's a old man!"

"He set the laws onto my family, again!"

"It was all that cash money from people thinking you was working with us!"

"Working with you!"

"You gotta understand! He's a beat old man and he was broke!"

"Broke—everybody's broke!" Joseph Lee dropped the stick and yanked the older man's whimpering form up by the shirtfront and began to shake him fiercely. "You brought the laws out here!"

"Stop!" Jesse reached for his father in a half-hearted effort to defend. "He's bleeding all over! Leave him be! He's my kin, J-Lee—my kin!"

Joseph Lee let him go, and the sudden weight of the sobbing man against Jesse knocked them both into the mud. He looked long and hard at the two of them wallowing there, and then warned, "Either one of you ever use the Harper name, again, I'll kill you!"

His anger was long spent by the time he reached home, leaving only a dull tired sadness in its place. He entered the back porch quietly, reached for his father's tobacco pouch on the wooden shaving stand, and sat down on the floor with his back against the wall. He rolled a cigarette with trembling fingers, and as he struck a match to light it, Rafe opened the door from the kitchen and whispered into the dark, "That you, J-Lee? You missed supper and we're all—"

"Tell Johnny I want to talk to him," his brother replied.

Big John came in a few minutes later and lit the lamp. "I don't know about you," he began as he adjusted the wick so that a pleasant glow flooded over them. "If you ain't roaming the countryside like some wild thing, you're sitting in the dark like one." He turned to face his younger brother, then, and saw he was dripping rain and blood onto the wooden floor. "Lord almighty," he whispered. "You shore didn't waste no time."

Joseph Lee took a long pull from the cigarette and breathed in deeply before answering. "Looks worse than it was. But old man Tolliver ain't gonna be crowing about selling Harper whiskey no more. Don't know where Durham is, yet, but I'll find him."

Big John folded his arms across his chest as he sat down on the edge of the wooden washstand. He was still dressed in his good clothes and had only been back a short while after dropping Sarah off at the cabin. "I found him in the roadhouse parking lot with Lou Ellen Saturday night."

"That no good—"

"Only hit him once. Caught him just right. Never even saw me coming. Miserable low-down varmint was crawling all over her! Felt his jaw give way. The way his neck snapped back, thought maybe I killed him."

"Did you look back at the hotel?"

"Did that when I hit town, again, tonight. Seems he checked out yesterday morning. Nothing in the papers, though, and his car ain't anywhere around. So, maybe he ain't dead. Just limped off somewhere and we seen the last of him." Big John took the leather cap from his head and ran a hand through his hair. "Come to find out, he ain't no traveling man at all. Looks to me like I nigh on to killed me a law officer."

"What kinda law does them kind of things?"

"What. Worming information about liquor operations out

of kids and womenfolk while he's selling them the same things they can buy cheaper down at the drugstore?"

"A federal man?"

"Yep. I'm guessing one of them undercover kind from the looks of the badge I saw. Maybe he's seen enough by now to realize no Harper's left in the business to speak of these days."

There was a few moments of silence between them.

"Ain't that right, J-Lee? Or is there something I should still be worried over. You have any ideas how such a rumor got started around, and lasted so long?"

"Tolliver's been using our name to sell shine. I don't know how long for. I reckon it's been ever since I told Jesse the only way to upgrade that rot-gut of his was to quit using bad water and jury-rigging his still with old car parts. Ivy sure never said nothing about it."

"Ivy didn't know till Durham come along. And if you hadn't been so all-fired quick to think the worst of her..."

"What did you take her so far off for, Johnny? I wouldn't hurt her, no matter what she done!"

"Because—whether it's true or not—them laws are just waiting for you to slip up! So, don't go losing your head over this. Give things some time to blow over."

"What did Daddy say about it?"

"Ain't told him any of it. Way he's been feeling lately. He thinks I went off to marry Sarah, last night. Spread it around town, too, cause I didn't want none of this to leak out. But it like to put the fear of the devil in me when I found out Durham was a Law. We gotta watch our step."

"Must be some big raid coming down, again."

"Yep. Ain't no time to be ridge running, that's for sure." He threw his brother a hard calculating stare. "And I sure better not ever catch you at it."

Joseph Lee crushed his cigarette out in the folded cuff of his wet jeans. He leaned his head back against the wall and closed his eyes. He could not look at his brother anymore.

"Best get out of them wet things," John said. "Else everybody's liable to wonder what you been up to. All I can say is, you better be smart enough not to go looking for Durham that way. There's other ways to end up in the jailhouse besides ridge running."

"When I think what he done that would make her want to kill herself, I—" His voice caught in his throat for a moment. "If I lost her, Johnny, I—"

"Aw, she'll be all right," his brother spoke more gently. "And safer out there with Aunt Lyla than up here, right now. Give her a couple weeks to get over it, then go fetch her back. We ought to know something sure by then."

"She needs to know I don't blame her, none."

"That's what she was afraid of. That you'd come looking to rescue her, like always, and she wouldn't be able to keep the laws off you. Don't many come that tough, boy."

Big John got to his feet. "Now, you best get into something respectable, on account of I'm about to invite you all out to the cabin for a wedding celebration."

"You mean you really done it?"

"Course I done it. I was past waiting, anyhow, and it was a good excuse."

"That'll be the talk of the town, all right. No matter what crimes been going on, lately. You are some cool operator, Johnny."

"Still got the fireplace to finish off out at the cabin and some windows to set before the cold comes in. But I took Sarah home to it and she's happy enough."

"Well, shoot." Joseph Lee got to his feet and began to un-button his wet shirt. "Shoot—that's the best news I heard in a time and a time. Hey—" He glanced toward the back door and realized how unusually dark and quiet it seemed inside. "Where is everybody?"

"Getting the barn ready for the tobacco harvest this week. Looks like you came back just in time."

"Well, I ain't never missed a harvest."

"No, you sure haven't. Thought I'd have Rafe and Lou

Ellen finish up tomorrow morning, on account of celebrating tonight. Sarah's got a cake baking."

"Could be I might get that girl to dance with me, yet," Joseph Lee teased.

"Better watch yourself," his brother threw him a playful punch as he passed, "She's family, now, boy."

"About time."

33

At the edge of a meadow a quarter of a mile beyond the tobacco fields, stood the little cabin Big John had built during most of his free time, last year. It was nestled beneath a stand of tall pines that grew at the base of a steep towering mountain known as Sugar Hill. The Harper family dressed in their best "go to meeting clothes," piled into the truck, and drove along the well worn path that led to the cabin at the farthest end of Harper land. For over two hours they ate cake and sang and danced, and called Sarah "Mrs. Harper" to her heart's content.

With the weight of tradition on his side, Joseph Lee finally got to dance with the shy brown-haired girl with the angelic voice, who had artfully eluded him at every opportunity. But tradition also demanded that he give up his playful chase and accept her as kin. He did it so sweetly, she found herself wondering why she had ever felt nervous about him in the first place.

Everyone had a chance to dance with the new bride, including Little Sam, who would not be left out simply because of his size. Even Lias persuaded Big John to relieve him on the fiddle while he took a turn with his first daughter-in-law. They danced until he began to cough, and then Celia had to insist he sit down, again.

The little cabin already looked homey. There were quilts hung over the two remaining windows without panes, and the large fireplace—though still in need of a proper hearth—accommodated a comfortable fire that cast a warm cheery glow over the simple furnishings. While Celia and her new daughter-in-law talked about curtains and recipes, and the men sat by the fire, Bonnie Rae slipped out onto the front porch, feeling strangely low for such a special occasion.

She sat down on one of the steps and wrapped her wool sweater around her drawn up knees to keep away the chill of rain. It was still drumming away on the shingled porch roof, and blowing an occasional spatter up onto the steps. After a while, a gold sliver of light spilled over the porch and then disappeared as Joseph Lee came out to join her.

"Hey." He sat down at the other end of the step. "Don't tell me, besides hunting and fishing with the fellers, you took up smoking with them, too."

"Law, I ain't never had a cigarette in my life!" She watched him roll and light one, reminding her of Lias as he did.

"And lying, too."

"Corn silk don't count," she insisted. "Besides, I was just a youngun back then, and you made me do it."

"What did I do, wrestle you down and stick a pipe in your mouth?"

"You know what you done."

He laughed, leaned his forearms across his drawn up knees and looked out over the dark and shadowy fields as they bent and swayed in the storm. "You never could resist a dare. I bet if I dared you to do something right now, you couldn't pass it up. No more than you could back then."

"Neither could you."

"Remember that time I took you up the mountain? All the way to the top of the Eagle Wing? I don't reckon you were any more than nine years old, back then. Shoot, I'm lucky I didn't get you killed."

"You double dared me to do it."

"But I thought you'd be begging to come down way before we got to the top. Only you was the stubbornest little thing I ever knowed." He cast her a teasing glance. "Still are."

"I was scared nigh out of my head though," she admitted with a smile. "If you hadn't helped me get back down again, I reckon I'd still be up there."

"And if you hadn't snuck that piece of Scotch Heather home, I wouldn't have got the fire beat out of me for taking you up that high, neither."

"How was I supposed to know Daddy would recognize it? Mama didn't."

"Daddy seen it before, that's why," he replied. "That white kind don't grow nowhere else except up high, like that. More common in the Old Country. They use it for good luck in weddings. Has another meaning to it, too, though."

"What kind of meaning?"

"Sign of protection. Uncle Buck brought some home once, for Granny, to let her know he was still alive. Revenuers were looking for him for weeks. With dogs and everything. He snuck back one night and left some of that Scotch Heather on her mantel over the fireplace. She knowed soon as she saw it he was all right. And just where he was hiding out."

"How come the revenuers never looked up there?"

"Too steep. Flat, craggy face makes it look like nothing could live up there. A few folks have climbed the face all right, just to do it. Couple even fell off. But don't nobody but one or two Harpers, left, that know about the Eagle Wing. That little piece of high meadow just behind the peak has been a secret place for nigh onto a hundred years. You're the only girl that knows. Outside of Granny."

"How come you told me?"

He shrugged and tossed the end of his cigarette into the dark. "I don't know. How come you told me about Johnny figuring I was back in the business, today?"

She sighed and wrapped her sweater more tightly around

her legs. "Didn't want you caught off-guard, I reckon. You know I ain't never been able to keep nothing from you, J-Lee. Seems I been talking my heart out to you since I learned my first words. Ain't nobody in this world stands by me like you."

"Well..." He pulled up a long blade of grass that was growing near the step and stuck the sweet end in his mouth. "I always did feel the same about you."

"You reckon it will stay that way? We ain't changed much since we grew up."

"Maybe there's some things about people that don't change, no matter how old they get to be. How come you been so quiet, tonight?"

She leaned her head back against the smooth wooden handrail beside her. "I got the blues, real bad. Seeing Johnny and Sarah so happy makes me want to up and marry Harlan. More than anything!"

He was quiet for a long moment. "You want to leave the mountain?"

"He wants me to."

"Ain't what I asked."

"Well, it would make me mortal sad to leave the home-place. I would if it was the only way, though. My feelings get so stirred up when I'm with him, I reckon I'd do just about anything he wanted. I can't even pretend I wouldn't. Is that wrong, J-Lee?"

"You're asking me? Shoot, you're talking to the boy that's been climbing through windows since he was twelve. I got no feelings for right and wrong when it comes to loving somebody."

"I don't want to leave the mountain," she admitted quietly. "Truth is, I'd like to visit them other places, like Paris, and all, but I shore don't want to live there. I reckon I'd do anything if I could stay, right here, and marry Harlan, both. Only he don't want to."

"You could get him to stay, if you really wanted."

"How?"

"Help him give in to his longings, that's how. Show him he needs you. Set him up right, and I guarantee you can get him to do anything you want. Man's fallen hard for you, Bonnie Rae. It's written all over him."

"Suppose he ain't longing?"

"He's longing."

"Harlan's got some rightsome ways, though," she explained. "His folks were missionaries in China somewhere. They were killed during some war over there. It took the Doc nigh onto a year just to find him, then he brung him home and raised him to do what's right. Suppose he don't want to give in to his longings, like normal folks?"

"Ain't a man alive, baby, that don't want to. No matter what he believes in. Why, I could let you in on a little secret, right now, that would set any boy on fire."

"Even, Harlan?"

"Even, Harlan."

34

The first thing that told Harlan he was nearing Coaltown, was the noise. He could hear the familiar sound of trains and whistles, and—every ten minutes, or so—a tremendous crashing sound that he couldn't quite place. Farther on, he began to notice dust in the air. A half-mile before he actually reached the Black Star Coal Works, he found himself passing through two long rows of jerry-built unpainted shacks which had obviously been put together with unseasoned lumber. Now the buildings were sagging and disjointed, with black dust laying thick over every inch of roof, railing and porch. Any attempt at sweeping in such a constant pall would be a lost cause.

There were lines of electric wire strung up behind the houses, with a single strand running to each place. But the number of outhouses was a telltale sign that there was no plumbing of any sort. Not that such luxuries existed in Cedar Creek. They didn't. But there seemed to be something undignified about it here. Maybe it was the way the shacks were crowded so close up against each other. It looked like a person could sit down on one porch rail and prop their feet up on the one next door. There had to be at least seventy houses in a brief quarter mile. So, this was Coaltown.

It reminded him of the slums of Richmond.

After a while, he saw that the deafening roar he had been

hearing from so far off came from a coal tipple, as it dropped its loads of fresh coal into waiting railroad cars at the end of the street. The cars then rumbled along the spurs to the main track, where they could be attached to trains. It was a noisy, nerve-racking process that must go on most of the time. He studied the giant ugly tipple as it loomed ahead of him. It was functional—and necessary—but what a curse to have to live beneath its shadow.

He wondered why they had built Coaltown so close to it. Obviously, this was where most of the dust came from. It was the result of the constant dumping of coal from small tunnel cars into the tipple's giant hopper, then being dumped, again, when it was released into the waiting railroad cars below.

At the base of a hill beyond the tipple, stood a clapboard building known as the "storehouse." He had heard about it. It was a company-owned commissary and the sole source of trade for the residents of Coaltown. Even though the prices could be up to twenty-five percent higher than those in Cedarville.

Beyond that was the company office: a small one-room building elevated on stilts that faced the entrance to the mining shaft. It was mid-shift, and not too many people were around, outside of a few who were waiting for the shaft elevator and some others coming or going on various errands.

No one paid much attention to Harlan, except to give Prince a second glance and quickly size him up as an outsider. He tethered his horse to a nearby post and climbed the few wooden steps to the office. There were two desks inside, one facing the door as he entered —which was empty—and another along the wall in the far corner, occupied by a young woman in the final stages of pregnancy.

She was wearing a heavy sweater and even though there was a small electric heater at her feet, there was also a fan sitting on the desk, blowing full force against her face. Papers were weighed down sufficiently with various objects: a book, a mug, an apple, or simply tucked beneath the four corners of her old *Royal* typewriter. She looked up as he entered and flicked off the fan to talk to him.

"Good afternoon," he began. "I was wondering if I might talk to someone about... employment."

"They ain't taking anybody right now," she replied. "But there's a paper you can fill out if you want your name on the list."

"I don't mean to work here," he corrected himself. "You see, I'm the new government teacher for Cedar Creek, and I'm trying to... well... update the enrollment records."

She didn't say anything, only kept looking at him, waiting for him to continue.

"Quite a number of the older boys have quit school and come to work here, so they tell me, and I was wondering if I might be able to get a list of their names and ages. For the records."

"You a union agent, mister?"

"No, of course not. I just told you, I'm the —"

"I heard. But it don't make much sense, seeing as Coaltown has its own school."

"Yes, I'm aware of that. But the point is —"

"I reckon you better wait and talk to Mr. Perkins. He's the foreman and he'll be back in a minute. I don't work here regular. I'm standing in for Willa Forbes, that's been out sick."

"I see."

"There's a chair over next to that filing cabinet there. I got to get back to my typing and turn the fan on, again. Smell of cigars makes me sick since I been childing." She flicked on the switch and turned away from him.

Harlan sighed and sat down quietly in the chair that was off in one corner and practically hidden by the cabinet. A few minutes later he could hear voices outside the door, talking over some sort of disagreement. One of them was calm and too diplomatic. He figured it must belong to Mr. Perkins.

"It was fifteen pounds off," someone complained.

"Was it?" Mr. Perkins replied. "Well, I shore will have it

adjusted, boys."

"We want a different checkweighman."

"It'd take a change in policy to do that."

"Then change it."

"Well, let's not be unreasonable, now. These things can all be worked out in time. You know the Company's always interested in the best for its employees. Always is."

"This is the second time it come up in three months," the first voice insisted. "We want a new checkweighman. We voted on it, and we want one of our own boys on them scales."

"Well, now just a minute!" The diplomacy was rapidly vanishing. "Taking a vote without proper authorities present sounds like the sort of thing we don't need around here. I told you we'd adjust the scales and we will. Anything more than that constitutes a change in policy."

"How do we do that?" a different voice broke in. "Changing the policy, I mean."

"You start by filling out a formal complaint." The door opened a crack and a cloud of cigar smoke wafted in. "But I'm telling you, these things take time to go through the proper channels."

"We'll wait. Every man getting cheated out of fifteen pounds of every day's labor ain't nothing to spit at."

"Those are awfully strong words, Farrel," Perkins answered coldly. "But it's your right to decide."

"I believe we'll make one of them formal complaints, then," Farrel decided.

"Fine," came the curt reply. "Step over to the window and I'll give you a form."

He came in and shut the door abruptly behind him. He was a large, burly man with a sweat-stained white shirt and a huge cigar dangling from his mouth. He passed by Harlan, without noticing him, and reached into his desk drawer for a long blue sheet of paper. He handed it out through a sliding window on the opposite side of the room and bent over to stick his head out. "Just write your complaint on the bottom line there. Doris

Jane will fill the rest out for you."

"You do it, Angus," the Farrel voice said. "You got a better way with the words."

There were a few moments of silence while the task was being accomplished and Doris Jane turned from her desk.

"Mr. Perkins?" she ventured.

"Just a minute, Doris Jane," he said, waving a hand back at her. "Can't you see I'm busy?"

She cast Harlan a nervous glance, then returned to her work.

"That ought to do," Mr. Perkins pulled the paper back in through the window. "Now, you all go on back to work. And don't worry about it. Everything will get taken care of."

The voices faded as the small group disappeared. Mr. Perkins returned to his own desk and deftly dropped the paper into the wastebasket before sitting down.

"Strange looking proper channels," Harlan spoke wryly from the corner.

Perkins looked up with a startled expression and abruptly pulled the cigar stub from his mouth. "Now, just who are you?" He turned back to the secretary with an obvious annoyance. "Doris Jane—why didn't you tell me he was here?"

"I tried, Mr. Perkins, but —"

"Nevermind." He turned back to Harlan. "You own that horse out there?"

"Yes."

"Who are you and what do you want? We ain't got work— I don't care whose relative you are."

"That's not why I came," Harlan assured. "I'm here to find out the names and ages of any school age boys from Cedar Creek you might have employed here. I'm the new government teacher and I have to update the records."

"Well, you ain't gonna update them here, mister," Perkins said in a low, threatening tone.

"What?"

"You listen to me." He pointed at Harlan with the same

hand that held the cigar. "I know a union rat when I smell one, and I'm smelling one, right now!"

"I've got nothing to do with the unions," Harlan got to his feet and began to feel his own patience wane before the accusation. "And I'm not asking for anything I don't have a legal right to see."

"Well, you just take your legal backside out that door and don't let me see you on company property, again! Hear? This company provides a law abiding school for its children and we don't need the likes of you poking around in it."

Harlan couldn't believe such audacity. At the same time, he was talking to the most important man on the premises and didn't quite know where to go from here. "I'm sorry for saying what I did about the paper, Mr. Perkins," he spoke finally, trying a new tack and hoping to redeem the situation enough to at least get a little information out of the man. "Really, that's not what I came here for."

"Out."

"And I certainly didn't mean to upset you. So, if you don't mind, I'll just look around by myself, a little and—"

Perkins got to his feet as if Harlan had just given him the worst insult of his life. "I said get out! And if you look any direction but forward on your way out, mister," he warned with the stub of his cigar dropping ash on the desk as he pointed, "I'm gonna have you arrested for trespassing!"

<h1 style="text-align:center">35</h1>

That evening, Harlan stayed longer out in the barn than usual after bedding Prince down. Though it was almost November and the nights were crisp and frosty, the snug little building was comfortable. Especially with the horse and mule inside to add the warmth of their bodies to the small area.

Last winter had been hard on the old mule with the great barn so broken down and drafty. It had been an unusually cold year and even the chickens fared badly, dropping Tom's flock of ten to six. Now, the chicken coop was a smaller affair. It was attached to one end of the shed-row, with a large, wire-covered window that opened up into the stall area to catch the added warmth of the large animals.

Harlan lit a lamp and cleaned out the stalls. He threw fresh straw down from the little loft above, and refilled the water buckets. It was peaceful working around the animals. When the outside door opened from the tack room and a draft of cold air wafted through, he looked over to see Tom, carrying two huge ham sandwiches and the coffee pot. His face lit with the easy, ready grin that Harlan remembered so well and was beginning to show itself more and more since the night John and Bonnie Rae had come by. But it faded when their eyes met.

"You look like you lost your last friend." His uncle set the things down on a nearby shelf and withdrew a mug from each large pocket of his wool jacket. "Something go wrong at school, today?"

"I made a mess of things over in Coaltown, " Harlan admitted, as he continued to brush Prince's thick shiny coat. "Now, nobody over there will talk to me, much less let me look around."

"So, that's where you've been." Tom sighed and filled the two mugs, slowly, watching the steam waft up toward the ceiling as he poured. "I guess it's time for some explanations. Whether you're ready for them, or not."

"Ready for them—did you think I was going to become so enamored with this place I could overlook the fact that nearly half my students are working over there?"

"I think tolerant is the word. I was hoping for a time when you could at least be more tolerant."

"You said, yourself, they were running on the shy side of safety, and I'm supposed to be tolerant?"

"Before you jump to any more conclusions —"

"Do they—or, do they not—have at least thirty of my boys down there?"

"Yes. They do," Tom turned a bucket upside down and sat on it before he went on. "They have—to be exact – thirty-two boys. And three girls that work in the slag heap with the younger ones."

The words struck Harlan like a physical blow. The steady—almost angry—strokes he was brushing his horse down with, came to an abrupt stop as he reeled under the thought. Three girls, working with the younger ones... "It isn't right!"

"Harlan."

"And anyone that can turn their back and just look the other way—"

"Harlan Fleming," his uncle warned in a tone he hadn't heard since he was a boy, "you just listen to me for a minute!"

Prince nickered low and pleading before Harlan realized

he had a tight and furious hold on the horse's mane. He let go and tossed the brush aside.

"It isn't right all by itself," Tom began. "But in view of everything else that goes along with it... the poverty from wages too low to live on... labor problems..."

"Labor problems—there's more men out of work on this ridge than ever before! You told me yourself there's a two year waiting list to get on there. What kind of craziness is it to use children when there are so many able-bodied men around?"

"The kids get four to five cents an hour: the men get twelve. You figure it out."

"If that isn't an abomination before almighty God!" he accused. "How could you even think I would tolerate something like that, Uncle—how could you?"

"It isn't any of my business."

"Injustice is everyone's business."

"You can't fight injustice, son. It's not tangible. It's one of those ethereal things that lead a man on when he should be doing other work. It's like wrestling with the devil."

"Somebody's got to wrestle with him," Harlan reminded him. "Or we'll all end up being destroyed. Might for right. Wasn't that the magic phrase you used to read to me when I was young?"

"There's a difference here. It's not like grappling with flesh and blood, you know. The devil is a many sided beast that has no qualms about using his full strength on one poor mortal such as you."

"I believe in standing up for what's right," Harlan insisted. "Even if it means standing alone."

"Some things you can't stand up to. You pick a fight with child labor, and you'll end up struggling against poverty, indifference, greed and corruption. None of which you can ever really lay hold of because it's like trying to catch the wind. Those things are eternal, Harlan, while you're just a mere... drop in the sea of time."

"That's the most depressing thing I've ever heard you say,

Doctor Bascomb," he replied slowly, unable to hide the note of sarcasm that showed through when he spoke the title. "I've always thought that profession of yours elevated a man's standing to more noble things. Now you sound like nothing but some self-preserving pessimist."

The look of hurt on Tom's face caused a twinge of remorse and Harlan wished he hadn't said it so bluntly. He moved out of the stall and shut the gate with a distracted carelessness, forgetting that Prince would open it himself unless it was locked.

He moved over to where Tom was and sat down, leaning back against the gatepost with a sigh. Tom handed him one of the mugs and for a moment, they simply sat there and drank quietly. Tom looked at him hard, as if seeing him for the first time. He was still wearing the brown suit and pressed shirt he usually wore to school. Even though he had taken off the jacket, rolled up the sleeves and stashed the tie somewhere, he looked strikingly mature in the well-cut vest and slacks.

Yet, he could see the determined set of his jaw and the slight, almost undetectable tremor in those hands that only one who knew him well could read. Telltale signs that the sensitive and tender-hearted boy he had once been was still inside that full grown man somewhere. The small recognition caused a wave of affection to sweep over Tom that eased some of the hurt of those harshly spoken words.

He had always loved the boy.

"There's a big space between the way things are, and the way they ought to be." Tom finally broke the silence between them. "Sometimes," he said carefully—he must choose his words carefully if they were to be received, "it can be a sea too deep to cross."

"I have to try."

"I know you do. Maybe that's why I couldn't just come right out and tell you. Then again, I don't really know how to tell you. How can I explain something I don't quite understand myself? Cedar Creek is..." He paused, searching for the right word.

"The most backward," Harlan supplied for him, "maybe even the most barbaric place I've ever seen. And I have seen many."

"It just looks like it," his uncle insisted fervently. "Look deeper, Harlan! Don't cast the unwashed rags aside before you realize they were the same ones Jesus wore. If they were, you'd take them to your heart and cherish them, wouldn't you? Well, wouldn't you?"

Harlan looked up with a startled expression at the analogy. Tom saw the vulnerable spot and pressed further.

"Don't be like me and find out too late. Cedar Creek might just be the last shreds of anything decent that's left in this country, Don't be like all the rest of us and walk on them."

36

After school the following day, Harlan made the long ride into Cedarville. Perhaps he wasn't the only government teacher that had faced such enrollment problems. A conversation with a non-resident official of Cedar Creek might prove enlightening. A talk with local authorities was the very least he could settle for. In fact, the school board would settle for nothing less. That much he was sure of. As ignorant as Harlan might be of custom and culture in the hill country, he had an accurate and educated understanding of the government. Local, or otherwise.

He was sure that the sheriff and deputies of this county were governed by the same systems of order and law enforcement that functioned across the rest of the Country. Together, such systems formed a strong, unified network that complied with the federal government to protect the rights and civil liberties of the people. And though he had some hesitancy as to how to approach this particular sheriff, he had no lack of faith in the system, itself. It was America. It had stood for nearly two centuries with the high and noble standards of "Liberty and Justice For All."

So, he found his way to an old brick building on Main Street with a black and white sign above double doors which read: TOWN HALL. The Cedarville police department consisted of several rooms at the back. As he entered the room marked "Sheriff's Office," a middle-aged efficient looking woman behind the counter glanced up at him.

"I'd like to speak with the sheriff, please," said Harlan.

"Is he expecting you?"

"Well, no. Should I have made an appointment?"

"That depends. Certainly if it's an emergency..." She looked at him with an expression that clearly meant he should explain himself.

"I'm not a union agent and I don't work undercover for the government," Harlan clarified. He had seen that look one too many times since he arrived. There was a distinct glitter of amusement in her eyes and he detected the slight hint of a smile. "That sounds ridiculous, doesn't it," he confessed.

"Well," she laughed, "we don't get too many of those types in here."

Harlan was relieved at the normalcy in her tone and he realized it had been a long time since he had been in the presence of such a rational human being. "I'm the new teacher for Cedar Creek," he explained. "I haven't been here long. Some problems have come up with the records and I need to talk to someone about the community without having a shotgun pointed at me while I'm doing it."

Another smile of amusement crossed her face. "Let me see if he's busy." She got to her feet. "With elections coming up next month it's been hectic around here, but I'll see what I can do."

She disappeared into another room and he walked over to look at a bulletin board that was covered in press releases and wanted posters. In a moment, she returned to point him through the same door she had just come out of. "Sheriff Harrigan, this is..." She looked blankly at Harlan.

"Fleming," he finished for her, extending a hand to the man behind the desk. "Harlan Fleming."

"Well, sit down, Harlan," the surprisingly young man

replied. "Gracie, here, says you're the new teacher for our little stretch of the backwoods." He flashed Harlan a wide, practiced grin and motioned him to a chair.

"Yes," he answered as the secretary left the room and he sat down. "And I'm finding these are difficult times for outsiders in Cedar Creek."

"It's always difficult times for outsiders in Cedar Creek." The sheriff reached into his desk drawer. "Want a cigar?"

"No, thank you."

"Let me tell you something." The young, dark-haired man paused to strike a match and leaned back in his chair. "Not much more than a year ago. . ." He lit the cigar and puffed on it for a few moments. "I sat at this very same desk looking across at the last Cedar Creek teacher. She hadn't been there but two months and one of the older boys got to pushing her around some. I told her just what I'm going to tell you. This county doesn't pay me enough for the time and deputies it would take to —" The phone rang and he paused. In a few seconds, the secretary stuck her head in the door.

"Mrs. Waverly from the Women's Auxiliary?" she asked.

"I'll take it," he replied. "Excuse me, Harlan." He picked up the receiver from the black phone on his desk. "Mrs. Waverly? Yes, it sure is. Looks like it's going to stay that way for a while. We'll have snow soon enough without wishing for it. Yes, I sure do. What's that? The fourth? Well, now, just a minute and I'll take a look at the calendar." He fumbled in the drawer, again. "Here it is. Let me see, the fourth... yes, it's open. More than happy to, sugar. Three o'clock for the Auxiliary tea. Yes, I sure do. Thank you for calling."

He hung up the phone and scribbled himself a note in the proper calendar square and looked up at Harlan with another campaign smile. "Can't turn down speaking engagements this close to elections. Where were we, now?"

"You were talking about the last teacher but I'm afraid I haven't explained myself very well. You see, I'm not having any discipline problems. Things in the classroom are going fine."

"Then, what is the problem?"

"I only have sixteen students."

"Isn't that enough?"

"No, it isn't, really. I should have between thirty-five and forty... allowing for about the same number that should be attending at Coaltown."

"You aren't a glutton for punishment, are you?"

"I beg your pardon?"

"I mean, it seems to me," he laughed, "sixteen of those hell-raisers would be about all one man could handle."

Harlan sighed and looked toward the nearest window. It was bordered on both sides by posters that sported an over-sized reproduction of the campaign smile with the slogan "Let Harrigan Care Again" printed beneath in dark, bold lettering. "Sheriff Harrigan," he began, "I came to Cedar Creek to run a government school and I can barely scrape up enough students to fill a single classroom. I've done a little looking into the matter and found that over half of the school-age boys – and even some girls—are digging coal instead of going to school. I'm sure I don't have to tell you anything about that being illegal. There are other things going on that aren't right, too. But my main concern is with the exploitation of minors. My minors, Sheriff Harrigan."

The sheriff was quiet for a minute. He leaned back in his chair and thoughtlessly tapped the pencil he was still holding on the edge of the desk. He looked at Harlan with a contemplative gaze and then leaned forward, again. "I'm going to be perfectly honest with you, Harlan. Cedar Creek is nothing more than a boil on this town's backside. I know that sounds strong but you just sit back and let me tell you why I feel that way. How long you been here, now?"

"A little over a month."

"A month. Well, then I'm sure I don't have to tell you that's a whole different kind of people up there on that ridge."

"They're different," Harlan agreed, "but I haven't quite

figured out why, yet. I think a lot of what they are is a result of how they've been treated."

"Only one way to treat a renegade."

"Renegade?"

"That's right. They're uncivilized, simple as that."

"Sounds like an odd description for a group of people who still speak Elizabethan English."

Harrigan shrugged. "Saying and doing are two different things. I got files that show a steady thirty percent of them in the state penitentiary, ever since this town hall was built sixty-three years ago. That means if I got two to three hundred people back up in those hills, I've got sixty to a hundred of them that I'm hauling to the jailhouse, all the time. And you know what for?"

"Moonshine, I suppose."

"Nope. Oh, I've got my share of the blockaders, all right. But what we've got an epidemic of up there —and always have had—is cold-blooded murderers."

37

"It's the truth," the sheriff went on. "I got one back there right now, waiting for the judge to come out from the county seat." He shuffled some papers around on the desk until he came up with a file folder. "Here it is right here. Cooper, Rufus J. Picked up last week for shooting some Irish miner out in Coaltown that called him a bad name the day before. Now, if that isn't cold-blooded, I don't know what is. Half the time we're bringing them in for killing a member of their own family. Including women. I tell you, they're uncivilized. No respect whatsoever for law and order."

"Maybe the laws have been too harsh."

Harrigan laughed and tamped out his cigar in an ashtray that was half full already. "They haven't been harsh enough. Most of those murder charges are changed to manslaughter because they're done in something the courts call 'a sudden heat of passion.' Two to five years later those criminals are back in the county and I have to deal with them again."

He sat back in the chair with a sigh. "No, Harlan, the law isn't too harsh. Truth is, they've only had the law up there for the last fifty years, or so. You know what they were doing before that? Feuding, that's what. Regular wars going on between families and neighbors. Nope. If you ask me, I think the trouble's in the blood."

"Well," Harlan looked toward the window, again, and noticed this time that the dark of evening was creeping across the sky. "All I know is, the Black Star Coal Works is employing children in a hazardous occupation and I want to file a complaint. I've already tried going to the Company, but there's a Mr. Perkins—he's some kind of a foreman —"

"I know Henry. He's a cousin of mine on my mother's side. They all come from Chicago. If there was anything wrong going on out there, he'd let me know."

Harlan felt a vague sense of shock at the response. This was the sheriff of Cedarville. It was his duty to look into any and every complaint that was reported, criminal or domestic. "Are you trying to tell me," Harlan leaned forward in his seat, "that you're not going to look into it because Perkins is related to you?"

"No." Harrigan's voice was calm. "I'm not going to look into it because I don't feel there's any need to."

"But I just told you that company's operating illegally out there."

"Let me tell you something about that company. We don't need any misunderstandings, here. Got to keep the facts straight. Situation like this, things tend to look a little hazy from the outside."

"Things are getting clearer by the minute," Harlan commented wryly.

"That's a mighty hasty judgment when I'm taking my time and doing my—you know, you look awful young to be—are you a registered voter?"

"Yes," Harlan answered. "But I don't see —"

"What party? We're all mostly Republicans around here."

"Well, I... usually try to look at the issues, and... Sheriff Harrigan, I honestly don't see what this has to do with anything we've been talking about."

"I just wanted to find out how—and if—you're politically minded. So much of what's happening these days is political.

Everything's political, Harlan." He held up a hand just as Harlan was about to interrupt, signaling his reluctant listener to keep still. "Now, about this company. Like I told you before, Cedar Creek's been nothing but a burr under this town's saddle since the Indians left. Then along comes the Company, and it's been the first and only thing that's ever been able to put the reins on those Mountaineers.

"Before that, they didn't need anything, or anybody. They were ornery and stubborn. You couldn't deal with any of them. Now they've got used to their payday and their store-bought things, and the law has a little bargaining power. Simple as that."

"But it's out of hand," Harlan argued. "They've grown dependent on those paydays, and they don't go far enough anymore. Because of that, they're sending their kids into the mines to make up for it—and that's what I'm here for! It isn't right, and it isn't fair."

"It's better than what it was. Can't expect much more out of those situations."

"Children shouldn't be part of those situations," Harlan reminded him. "And I think any court of law would agree."

"Cedar Creek doesn't have children, Harlan. It just has little renegades. I'd rather see them doing an honest day's work for the Company, than learning to run whiskey or shoot at the Law. I'll admit it's a tragic thing—it's a desperate thing. But desperate times call for desperate measures." He reached for another cigar.

"In other words, you're punishing them."

"We're controlling them."

"Sounds to me like the method sort of outweighs the purpose."

"Is that what you think? Let me tell you something else." He bit the tip off his cigar and spit it out. "They killed the last man that held this office. What do you think about that?"

"I think maybe they're tired of being punished."

"Well," he struck another match, "you wait 'til you've

looked down the barrel end of a shotgun with a crazy person at the other end. See how it makes you feel."

"I already have. They're so used to everyone taking advantage of them out there, half of them will draw a bead on you just riding up to their front door. But I haven't been shot, yet. And it never once made me feel like torturing a child."

Harrigan slowly took the cigar out of his mouth and blew out the smoke. "You got an awful smart mouth, boy."

"I take it that means you aren't going to do anything about my complaint."

"You come back after you've been here for three more months, and see if you still feel like making that complaint."

Harlan sat quietly for a moment, feeling a wave of disgust churn and surge into anger. "I wonder what the owner of the company would say," he said levelly, "if he knew part of the profits he's enjoying are being made from the blood and sweat of children."

"Maybe you should ask him. Ol' Beauford comes from these parts, too, and he thinks idle hands are the devil's workshop. Just like everyone else around here."

The secretary tapped lightly on the door and poked her head inside. "Mr. Giles is here from the *Daily*," she said.

"Send him right on in, Gracie," the Sheriff answered. "Harlan and I have gone about as far as we can go in here. Isn't that right, Harlan?"

"I suppose we have," Harlan replied.

"You stop by and see Beauford, sometime. He's out of town for a few days right now, though. Big political rally up in Raleigh this week. Did you know he was the mayor of Cedarville?"

"No."

"Well, he is. Beauford T. Ainsley's been mayor of this town for—"

The door opened, again, and a man in a suit and tie appeared. Sheriff Harrigan got to his feet and grinned. "Come on in, Charley, be right with you."

"Thanks for your help," Harlan said as he got up and started for the door.

"Why, it was no trouble at all," Harrigan replied. "And give Beauford my regards when you stop by. He's an uncle of mine. On my father's side."

<h1 style="text-align:center">38</h1>

Lou Ellen flung herself backward onto a great mound of hay with the dramatic declaration that she had nothing to live for. She waited for a response to the confession, but except for her brother's rhythmic raking and the occasional cluck of a chicken, the barn was quiet. She hung her head over the edge of the hayloft and looked down at him. Her long auburn braids dangled in the midair, and her rustlings made hay straws flutter down onto the hard packed, dirt floor. "Did you hear me, Rafe? If they're gonna work me to death for what I done, I may as well just die and let them bury me!"

"So, go ahead and die," he replied, without slowing his strokes. "But if you don't get busy and help me down here, like J-Lee told you, I'm liable to kill you, myself."

She sighed and threw a clump of hay down on top of him. He shook it off his cap, put it back on with a casual arrogance, and ignored her. Seeing he would not even respond to teasing, Lou Ellen crawled to the farthest corner of the loft and made herself a nest to lie down in. It was soft and comfortable for a minute before she decided it needed more of a pillow, and began scooping hay from all around her into a large pile. Suddenly, her hand brushed against something flat and smooth.

She pulled it out from under the hay with a vague curiosity and discovered that it was a magazine. Not a movie magazine like she enjoyed but a fairly recent copy of *Popular Mechanics*. She thumbed through it half-heartedly, looking for pictures of movie stars. When she was about to lose interest, a page that had been torn out fluttered onto her lap. There was a large picture of a half naked man flexing his muscles, and above him in bold letters it read, "*How To Make YOUR Body Bring You FAME Instead Of Shame!*" The caption near the picture said, "*Charles Atlas as he looks today from actual, untouched snapshot. Holder of title, "The World's Most Perfectly Developed Man."*"

There was another smaller picture at the bottom of the page. It was a book. The cover showed another man —more naked than the first one—and he was kneeling beneath the weight of a large globe (the kind Mr. Harlan had brought to the schoolhouse). A paragraph beside it read, "*Send for my FREE BOOK now… this is your quick way to get the best-built, huskiest, handsomest body of any fellow in your crowd—so don't delay! Rush coupon to me personally for your copy of EVERLASTING HEALTH AND STRENGTH.*"

Lou Ellen looked at the telltale hole in the page where the coupon had been and giggled. She crawled back to the edge of the loft and dangled the page at her brother. "Hey, Rafie... look what I found..."

"Lou Ellen, if you don't get down here—" He looked up impatiently and then recognized the ad. His face turned red.

His sister laughed triumphantly and crowed, "I'm gonna show —" before he dropped the rake and bounded up the ladder after her. She screamed, dashed off to the large open window, and tossed it out. She would have liked to watch it float and flutter and land in the soft, oozing mud of the pigpen below. But Rafe was nearing the top of the ladder and she barely had time to escape. So, she grabbed onto the long rope that was attached to one of the rafters, and used it to let herself out the window.

Big John had put it there years ago, to enjoy the fun of swinging out over the pigpen in wide long arcs. An idea that had created an enduring pastime for all the Harper children that had come after him. Now, Lou Ellen made her way down as fast as she could without getting a rope burn.

When she was about ten feet from the ground, she suddenly began to feel the rope swing and jostle, and she looked up to see Rafe at the top, shaking it as hard as he could. "Hey—stop—you're gonna make me fall! Rafe! I'm gonna tell —"

"You ain't gonna live to tell!" He gave the rope another fierce yank that dropped her with a splat into the thick strong-smelling mud below. Then with all the skill of having done it a thousand times before, he took the rope and jumped out the window himself.

He was after her in an instant.

"Look what you done!" She dragged herself to her feet and flew at him in a rage. "It's in my hair! You —"

He had expected her to run. Caught off guard, he was knocked swiftly off his feet and landed flat on his back with his sister on top of him. She began hitting and hollering like a crazy person, leaving him no choice but to defend himself. After withstanding, several painful smacks, he delivered a quick and accurate left hook and tried to wrestle her down.

She was stronger than he thought.

They tumbled and rolled, choked and fought, while the two razorback hogs hugged the fence, squealing and grunting their annoyance. The younger children had been playing nearby, and hearing the commotion, came to stare through the fence with their mouths open.

"Go get J-Lee!" Jenny Beth ordered.

"You go get him," Little Sam swung a leg over the bottom fence rail to make himself comfortable. "I want to see who wins."

By the time the little girl had dragged her older brother up from the tobacco field where he had been harvesting, the two had nearly worn themselves out. They were still wallowing in the mire and making halfhearted attempts at revenge when

Joseph Lee climbed over the fence and pulled them both up by their mud-caked collars.

He dragged them off to the little stream that ran by the south end of the house, forcibly threw them in, and made them stay in the icy water until they rinsed themselves clean. Each of them hollered and complained that it was not their fault and, by the time they were finished, their lips were blue and they were shivering uncontrollably.

The washing revealed that Lou Ellen had the beginnings of a terrible black eye, due to Rafe's original left hook. As she trudged up the bank and into the house for dry clothes, Joseph Lee turned a condemning eye on his younger brother.

"You don't understand!" Rafe recognized the threatening expression. "You know what she —"

"You don't never hit a girl that way, no matter what she done."

"But, J-Lee —"

"And you know it." He pointed to the woodshed.

"Doggone it!" Rafe cried, breaking into frustrated tears. "You don't even care what she done to me!"

"Right now, I'm talking about what you done to her. Besides that, when I give you a job to do..." He gave him a shove toward the woodshed and started after him. "I don't expect to have to stand over you with a stick to get it done!"

39

The next morning, when the early mists still clung to the damp earth and the sun was just beginning to pour its brilliance over the mountaintops, Lias Harper sat quietly on a small hill overlooking his partly harvested tobacco crop. He had rolled and started a cigarette but hadn't smoked much beyond getting it lit. Now it was burning down low and close to his rough, coal-creased hands and he hadn't noticed.

His Company days were over.

Last week when he collected his pay, they had given him his notice. He had expected it. Especially the way the sickness was beginning to creep up on him to where he couldn't control the spells anymore. But he hadn't expected this terrible aching awareness of how little time he had left in the world.

Keeping the family on one company check was not going to be easy. Nor could he expect Big John to support the entire family when he and Sarah had already set up housekeeping on their own. It didn't take much to live in this part of the country but there were a limited amount of ways to earn that living.

With their farm being mostly bottomland, the Harpers were better off than most. They raised their own food and could always trade meat or eggs for what little else they needed. The tobacco crop paid the taxes each year, along with a little extra for store-bought things. But last year it had barely brought more than the expected tax money and a new pair of shoes for each child. This year, even though the crop looked good, he couldn't be sure about it. And what if it didn't sell at all? Then again, the economy could change overnight. That's what everyone said.

Lias wasn't worried about his family starving. But what about all the little extras the company checks enabled them to have? There weren't many these days. Certainly not like after the War, when the coal tipples roared constantly and the money flowed. Back then, they had anything and everything from new cars and trucks to the best clothes money could buy. Why, he could remember a day when he wore a white silk shirt down under the hill, just because it pleasured him to. It hadn't been much good afterward but he could always get another from the *Sears And Roebuck*. And he did.

Those were the days.

But almost as fast as things boomed, they busted. In 1920, the price of coal dropped and men went from earning fifty dollars a day to barely more than a dollar. There were lay-offs and strikes. That was when the Harpers went into the moonshine business in a big way. Whether they were in coal or whiskey, his family had always had the best of things.

Even after the raid, they hadn't done too badly with two of them working for the company. Two of them would still have to work for the company. He dreaded having to tell Joseph Lee. And he didn't feel up to the confrontation he knew it would take to make him do it. The boy had always been afraid of closed in places.

Lias wondered if he hadn't been wrong to let him quit after a brief trial when he was fifteen. Maybe he could have overcome that fear, instead of letting him give into those longings to roam back and forth over the mountains like the wild thing he was getting to be. The only thing that kept Joseph Lee Harper from taking off altogether, was his feeling for family. It was his greatest strength and strongest weakness. Lias knew.

He knew it because he was that way, himself.

And for some reason, he had always been hardest on this son that was the most like him. Things had grown steadily worse between them since the raid. Still, Lias knew how to subdue that wild heart with the force and accuracy of an arrow. These days, it saddened him when he had to do it. But at the moment, he couldn't see any other way. He wanted to get it over with last night only Joseph Lee was already gone by the time he got home. He'd be back today to finish the harvest, though. Because as rebellious as that boy was, he always finished his work.

Later that morning, when Rafe sneaked out to the barn for a smoke before breakfast, he was startled to find Joseph Lee asleep in the hayloft, dangerously close to his secret stash of tobacco. He tried to back off quietly but his brother stirred and looked over at him before he was halfway to the ladder.

"What are you up to, squirt?" Joseph Lee asked drowsily. "As if I didn't know."

"Nothing."

"So, this is where you disappear to every morning, huh?"

"Some folks would like to know where you been disappearing to every night," He pushed his denim cap back on his head and sat down a safe distance away. "Especially at tobacco time."

"Yeah, well..." His brother sat up and brushed the hay straws out of his hair. "Long as I'm here for the work days, shouldn't much matter what I do with the nights."

I know what you been doing at night."

Joseph Lee gave him a calculating glance and stuck the end of a hay straw in his mouth. "What do you think I been doing?" he asked.

"Tate's brother, Matty, says you been ridge running." His eyes began to flicker with the hint of a smile. "And I reckon if that ever got back to the folks, you'd be getting your hide tanned for a change instead of tanning everybody else's."

"If it did get back to them," Joseph Lee warned, "I'd know just who to beat the fire out of, afterward."

"Well, it ain't gonna be so easy one of these days!"

"One of these days."

Rafe got to his feet and started for the ladder.

"Hey," his brother called after him when he was halfway down, "you forgot what you come up here for."

But Rafe knew when he was being set up and kept on going.

Later that evening, he didn't do so well. The last of the crop had been brought in and only a little work in the barn remained to be done. He swept the trash from the cutting and sorting into a pile while Big John and Joseph Lee finished off the tying and hanging. Everyone else had gone into the house to help with dinner.

"You swing that rake any slower," said Joseph Lee, "and you just might get out of the rest of the work, altogether."

"I been doing my share of the work!" the boy snapped back irritably.

"What's wrong with you two?" Big John tossed a fresh bundle of leaves onto the rack with the same agile accuracy he had started out with, even though he had been doing it since early morning. "You been needling each other all day."

"Ask him," Rafe pointed an accusing finger, "he's been looking for a good reason to whup me since morning! Shoot, my britches ain't even cooled off from the last time! He ain't been nothing but mean since—"

"Since what?" Joseph Lee watched him with a threatening coldness.

"Since you been… ridge running for Leroy Tatum!"

Joseph Lee jumped over the rack he was working behind and went after Rafe with a vengeance. The boy dropped the rake and tried to run off, only to be caught and held fast by Big John, who was staring with determined, thundering eyes at

Joseph Lee.

"Daaa-dee!" Rafe called loud and long as he struggled to pull himself free from the iron grip. "Daaa—"

"Shut up," his oldest brother clapped a giant hand over his mouth to quiet him. "Just set down over there and don't move!" He shoved the boy onto the pile of trash he had raked and turned to Joseph Lee. "Now, what's going on, prodigal boy?"

"You heard him."

"Well, it looks like we got you signed onto the Company just in time. Before you get dumb enough to get the rest of the Harpers killed or hauled off."

"I ain't going to work tomorrow."

"You think you ain't."

"I got more than a winter's wages saved up right now," he said, still kindling eyes at Rafe. "I figure that ought to give me a right to pick what kind of work I do."

"That right don't include dragging this family back into the business, again. Especially with the laws looking over our shoulders, already." Big John moved in close and gave him a shove backward. "You hear me? Maybe you got no respect for yourself, but you at least ought to have some for the rest of us!"

"Ain't no respect in crawling!" Joseph Lee felt a surge of anger at being pushed. "Ol' Lias crawled to God and you crawled to the Company. I'm telling you, it's gonna be a cold day in—"

Big John shoved him again and this time, Joseph Lee raised his hands in a gesture of surrender. "I ain't gonna fight you, Johnny. You think I'm stupid enough to give you reason to beat the fire out of me, you're crazy!"

"You're stupid enough." His brother shoved him so fiercely this time that Joseph Lee fell backward onto the floor. "If you ain't smart enough to know when to quit."

Joseph Lee breathed out a curse with such vengeance, Rafe felt a frightening tension as he watched his brother get up slowly, again. "I've busted my back for this family! And I ain't—"

He was hardly up before Big John threw a stinging blow to his face with the back of his hand that knocked him down a second time.

The boy's insides suddenly began to churn.

"Leave me alone, Johnny!" Joseph Lee tasted blood and put a hand to his mouth. "I'm tired of this stuff!"

"Boy," Big John pulled him up by the collar and held him against the wall, "you can leave, anytime."

"Let go of me, then!"

"Anytime you can get past me."

Joseph Lee knew he would not get past. But he also knew his brother's most vulnerable places. And though he did not have the strength or stamina to overpower him, he would not make it easy. So, like a sprung coil, he suddenly flew at Big John with a fierce and formidable rage to hurt, if not bring down.

The violent response was what his brother was waiting for. As if it gave reason to his madness, he unleashed his own churning emotions, letting go of the long pent up need to thrash some sense into this wayward brother who had openly scorned their father in so many ways. Big John knocked Joseph Lee to the ground and hammered him with one blow after another.

"Stop it! Stop it!" Rafe hollered over each blood-chilling thud that tore agonized gasps from Joseph Lee. When that didn't work, the boy threw himself against Big John's bull-like back. "You're killing him, Johnny! Let him go!"

Only to be knocked away so suddenly, he was picking himself up off the ground several yards away before he realized what had happened. After that, he staggered to his feet and ran outside, unaware of the warm gush of blood that began to pour from his nose. "Daaaadeeee!" he called as he bounded onto the porch and reached for the door. "Come quick! Hurry!"

"Lord almighty, boy!" Lias came face to face with him at the open door. "Set down right there and lean that head back. You're bleeding all over."

"Daddy!"

"Fetch a wet towel, Bonnie Rae," his father called back inside before steering Rafe toward one of the porch chairs.

"What happened?" Celia stepped up behind them. "If you boys been—"

"It ain't me—it ain't me!" Rafe pushed the towel away with their concern and burst into frustrated tears. "It's Big John! He's—out in the barn—beating the life out of J-Lee!"

Lias handed the towel to his wife and headed down the steps at a determined pace.

"Hurry, Daddy!" Rafe cried, "before he beats him dead!"

40

Lias started off without a word and the rest of the family followed. "You all get back in the house!" He bent to pick up a stick from the woodpile as he passed.

"Lias—" Celia protested. "Lias!"

But he didn't answer.

He heard scuffling before he even entered the barn and had to hit his oldest son twice before he could push him away from Joseph Lee.

"You can expect more of that every time I see you, boy!" Big John hollered over his father's shoulder as he felt himself being shoved toward the door.

"Go on, get out of here!" Lias gave him a final authoritative push. "I'll talk to you back at the house."

Joseph Lee lay motionless on the ground for a few seconds, feeling fiery stabs of pain with each hesitant breath. When he saw the dark form of his father standing over him with the stick, fear washed over him with such dread it broke his last efforts at control. "Don't do it!" he sobbed. "Don't—"

Lias felt his heart wrench at the desperate response and tossed the stick aside. It was the first time he had ever seen him break. "You look pretty done in, already," he replied. "Ain't but one thing I know would get Johnny riled like that."

"Don't worry, Lias—" It took all his effort to trade words for unchecked emotion. "I'm leaving! Just as—as soon as—as soon I can get up!"

"Joseph Lee." His father felt a wave of sadness sweep over him. "There's other ways to work this out. Don't go, son."

"Shoot, I—" He rose to his knees and winced at the pain that shot through his ribs. "I—ain't never gonna turn out like you want. Should have left a long time ago. Lord—I swear he broke me somewhere!"

"Come on in the house."

"No—you heard him. You heard him!"

"I reckon he's cooled off or gone home. You can't go nowhere like this. Gonna need some stitches over that eye, too. Here." He pulled a handkerchief from his pocket and held it out to him. "Hold this against it to slow the bleeding up."

"I need some air." Joseph Lee got unsteadily to his feet, instead, and staggered toward the door. Lias put a hand out to help but the young man refused it and warned, "Don't push me, Daddy. I—I've had it with all of you! And—" He leaned his forearms against the fence rail just outside the doors and hung his head. "I'm so tired of trying!"

Lias looked away from him for a moment and tried to think of how to put what he had to say. "I'm surprised you lasted this long. I figured you'd either see the Light or go back to the business way before now."

He returned the handkerchief to his pocket, again. "I was hoping you'd see the Light." He looked back at him earnestly. "Son, if you could just open yourself up enough to let a little of the love of God inside. You got to be willing to let it in—ain't you willing, boy?"

His son could only shake his head in reply.

"Ain't nothing but the love of God can—"

"Don't—talk none of that trash at me, anymore!" Joseph Lee leaned over enough to spit out some blood before letting the pent-up words tumble out. "Where was the love of God when I needed it? Where was it when Buck was getting himself shot dead right next to me and I was praying he wouldn't die! Where were you?"

"Boy—"

"You left me..." He whispered it so quietly Lias almost didn't hear. But even the barest utterance of the accusation that had lain hidden in his heart for so long was enough to cause a fresh and painful torment. Joseph Lee leaned his head back and cried out from the very depths of his being, "Jesus Christ, Daddy—you left me!"

The words fell on Lias Harper like such a crushing weight he had to reach for the strong fence rail and hold on until the wave of emotion swept past. "Don't do no good to confront me with my failures. I ain't never forgot them."

"Maybe God's love don't mean nothing to me, but—I swear—I'd of died ten times over if I thought it would make you love me the way you love Johnny! You never would have left Johnny!"

"I know I been awful hard on you."

"Hard on me!" He repeated the words. "It's like you had it in for me since I was a baby! I tried, but it was never enough. Maybe I never seen the Light but I tried to do right. I tried for you! Now, when I done wrong—I done wrong, Lias—why ain't you beating fire out of me so I can walk away easy?"

Lias didn't answer, and Joseph Lee spoke the next words with a frustration that was almost desperate. "Why do you have to be so—good—when you ain't being mean!"

"Can't you see I'm trying to make a change, son?" His father tried just as desperately to explain. "I seen a better way. Only natural for me to want the same for you. What else do you want me do?"

"Let me go."

"Boy, I ain't never gonna let you go."

"Then at least let me go my own way."

Lias looked at Joseph Lee and saw that he would be dealing a crippling blow if he refused him one more time. In that moment he also saw—with an almost divine clarity—that even though the wild young spirit was broken, it would surely die if he sent him back to work in the mines, again. Yet, there was little hope his son would survive long on the other side of the law. His name alone would make him fair game and a worthy prize for any over zealous law officer.

And they seemed to be all over the place these days.

Lias gave a resigned sigh and looked up at the waning moon. "That road you're on might look good to you, now," he warned quietly, "but I been up and down it a hundred times over. I found it to be full of holes. And them holes…they get mighty deep."

Joseph Lee didn't reply or look over at him. He continued to lean against the fence rail with his head still bowed and Lias standing such a short distance from him. For a long time neither of them moved.

"Why don't you come inside and let your Ma have a look at them cuts before you go," his father offered one last time.

Joseph Lee shook his head.

"Well, then...watch your tail, boy. Don't let them catch you asleep. He moved away after that. And as he did, a sudden heartrending sob escaped his son. He stopped and turned back to him, again. "Joseph Lee?"

But the young man waved him away without looking up.

Lias honored the request even though it wrenched something deep in him to do it. He started slowly back to the house. Even so, the quiet weeping of his only lost boy followed him. For a moment he had the most overpowering urge to turn around, take that son in his arms, and tell him he did love him.

But he didn't do it.

41

It was still dark when the mine whistle blew for the early morning shift the next day. Big John poured cold water into the washbasin on his back porch and was gingerly splashing it over his bruised face when Sarah peeked in.

"Rafe's here," she pulled her flowered housecoat more snugly around her against the outdoor chill and whispered, as if the hour was still too early to speak in a normal tone.

"Something wrong at home?" A twinge of worry pricked at him.

"No. But I think you best talk to him."

"All right." It occurred to him then that she looked just as pretty to him in the morning, with her cheeks rosy from sleep and her long, brown hair tumbling down, than she did in the daytime when she was all dressed up. Maybe even prettier. But he had better be more careful about getting up on time. He had been late twice, now, and he had hardly been married a week.

He was dressed and lacing up his boots before he realized his brother had silently slipped out onto the porch and was watching him from a chair in the corner. The boy's hair was slicked down beneath his faded denim cap and he was holding a dinner pail on his lap.

"Where do you think you're going?" Big John asked.

"With you."

"What about that schooling you been so fired up about?"

"Don't need much book learning to work under the hill," he replied too easily. "I figured I best take the job while it was still open. Start helping out with the family."

"Bit young, ain't you?"

"Budwing's been working down there for nigh onto a year now, and he ain't but six months older than me. Besides, J-Lee was fifteen when he went down."

"Look. I'm sorry you had to be part of all that, last night. But just because you seen it don't make you accountable to stand in for J-Lee. He's the one ought to be going to work with me this morning."

"Maybe he would have, if I hadn't squealed on him."

"You done the right thing. He could have brung every Law in the county down on top of us, sooner or later. We'd never known what hit us. Them laws don't ask many questions and one Harper's good as another." Big John felt an anger rising up in him all over again – even at the thought of it—and jammed his cap down onto his head with a will. "It's either the business or the family, Rafe. That's just the way it is now. If he thinks he can sashay in after a few days and everything will be blowed over… well, he's got another thing coming."

"Daddy said he's gone for good, this time." Rafe looked out into the darkness and could see nothing beyond the small circle of light cast by the glow of the oil lamp on the wash table. "Oh, Johnny! I was just riled at him for whupping me the other day! I wanted him to be the one to catch it for a change. But I shore didn't mean for all this to happen!"

"So, you're sorry. That don't mean you got to take his place."

"I want to try."

"What about the folks?"

"Daddy give me these here boots of his for this week. Says they'll have to do until he can get me a pair that fits better from the *Sears And Roebuck*. Is it wet down there, Big John?"

"Yep." His brother put on a coal-blackened denim jacket and then gave his young brother a hard calculating appraisal. "What about Mama?"

"She cried some but Daddy said to go ahead on."

"Well, let's go then."

They went back into the cabin and paused in the kitchen long enough for Big John to kiss his young wife goodbye and pick up his dinner pail. The truck was parked in the yard. The roar of the engine caused a momentary shattering of the peace and solitude of the woods before it disappeared into the pre-dawn morning.

The trip to the mines was not long. Most of the slopes around Coaltown were denuded of tall trees, and covered instead with a scrubby second growth. Here and there, the headlights picked up barren outcroppings of rock ledges, making the distinction between Company land and Cedar Creek, stark and obvious.

"Hills around here look sort of naked in the dark, don't they Big John," Rafe observed as they rode along.

"Yep, I reckon they do," his brother replied. "Company bought up all the timber rights for miles around when they first come. They shore did skin the mountains. But you can't mine coal without timber."

"They used nigh onto all of it."

"Well, besides propping up the ceilings under the hill, they needed railroad ties… tipples. Not counting what it took to build Coaltown and Niggertown. All them buildings and all them trees."

"They're killing them, ain't they, Big John. The mountains, I mean."

John looked over at him, somewhat startled by the observation. "I never thought on it that way, Rafe. But I suppose that's what they're doing. Law of nature, I reckon. I'd say it goes all the way back to Adam and the Fall. Seems like after that first sin, something was always having to die for man to make his living. Just the way of things."

They parked the truck and arrived at the driftmouth a little after five o'clock, and already the shaft elevator was filling up for the second time to carry the workers down to what was called the main heading. Together the tall brawny man and the boy stepped into the wooden lift and began the long dark decent into the shaft. The cables rumbled, and each time they went over a brace, the lift thumped unsteadily. "Don't worry." Big John noticed the uneasiness in Rafe's expression. "It ain't gonna fall."

"Shoot," said a man standing across from them, "it only falls at the end of the week. Never on Monday."

When they finally reached the bottom, the small group of men stood around for a few moments to light and attach miner's lamps to their caps before they climbed into several small, electrically powered coal cars. This was the "mantrip": used to carry the miners two and three miles down the main heading to their respective "work rooms." The rooms were nothing more than tunnels bearing off to the left or right, at approximately hundred foot intervals.

"That lift the only way out of here, Big John?" Rafe tried to control a sudden sensation of being trapped.

"There's passageways that lead to other levels." He fit a lighted lamp to his brother's cap. "The ones that go down are called winzes and one that goes up is called a raise."

"You mean we ain't on the bottom?"

"Almost. We're down near a mile, but there's still two more tunnels underneath us. Now, listen here. You got to watch your lamp all the time. If it starts to burn down low; that means you got chokedamp—or black damp. Ain't enough fresh air circling in from the fans. So, you got to get out and get somewhere where there is some."

"Does that happen a lot?"

"Not too much. But if it gets to burning high—means there's firedamp in the air and you got to get out altogether. Firedamp causes explosions with hardly no warning at all. There's something else called afterdamp, but that only gets in the air after a mine fire or explosion. Either way, you got to get out."

Rafe stared back at him with a serious expression. The realities of being a working man were having a sobering effect on him.

"Do you understand everything I told you, boy?" Big John asked firmly. Rafe nodded. "All right, let's go, then. We got another half hour's ride in one of these coal cars before we get to our work room."

"Don't I have to sign no papers to start working?" The boy followed his brother into a waiting car that already had two other men in it.

"Office ain't open this early. We'll take care of everything before we go home tonight. Sit up on the edge there, and keep your feet inside. And watch your head. Tunnel gets low in places and you have to duck now and then. Mind you don't touch none of them naked cables you see hanging from the roof, neither. They can kill you plumb dead."

Rafe hunkered down low and ducked his head down.

"Shoot, you don't have to sit like that."

"But you said –"

"I'm just telling you the hazards so you'll watch out for them. No need getting heated up over any."

42

Rafe and Big John began their ride down the long tunnel, which was lit by single light bulbs hanging from ceiling wires at the mouth of each adjoining tunnel. The other two men got off first and twenty minutes later, the two brothers stopped the car and got out at the head of a tunnel that stretched some hundred and fifty feet off to the right.

After the loud rumble of the car, the silence seemed to carry weight. They started down the cold passageway that became darker the farther away they got from the single bulb that burned at its entrance. Soon, they were walking by the feeble glow of their lamps alone. Rafe tripped once over one of the rough-hewn railroad ties laid down for the coal cars to travel on and his foot slipped into a puddle.

"Try not to step in them big puddles if you can help it," John said, when he heard the splash. "Some of these tunnel walls got sulfur rocks in them. Water trickling down over them makes acid. Chew a hole right through your boot if it gets strong enough."

Their workroom was simply the end of the tunnel. Picks and shovels were lined against the tunnel wall—or coal rib, as it was called—along with various tools and timbers.

"First thing we got to do..." John looked over at Rafe and noticed he was shaking. "You cold?"

"Little," the boy replied. "Scared some, too. But I don't know how come."

"You'll be all right once we get busy." The deep voice softened to one that had an immediate effect on Rafe. Ever since he could remember, that tone had meant safety and protection, backed up by—in his estimation—an unlimited source of power and brute strength to prove it.

Big John smiled reassuringly and then, as if he could read Rafe's mind he said, "Ain't no mountain can keep me down in its gut. If this whole place was to go right now? Shoot, I'd bust on out like a regular locomotive. Take you and a couple others right along with me. That's on account of when I was born..." He winked confidentially."God give me a steam engine instead of a heart."

Rafe couldn't help grinning. Not that he believed such stories anymore. But he had to admit he felt a whole lot better seeing those huge muscles bulge reassuringly beneath the shirt when Big John shook off his coat.

"Come on, now," his brother urged. "First, we got to set these long timbers. See them over there? Set them things as close to the face as we can. That's what we call this whole wall of coal here. The face. Set them timbers close, so the roof don't sag later on."

So, the workday began. They set the timbers in close, and drove wedges in between the roof and the prop ends. Next, they strapped thick rubber kneepads on and knelt down in the wet slush of the slate floor to pick out a "cutline" that started about eight inches above the ground. It would run twelve to fifteen feet wide, and be as deep as the picks would reach.

When this was done, and they had raked all the fine coal out of the cutline, Rafe held an iron spike against the coal—about chest height—while Big John used the sledgehammer to pound it in. For every strike the man made, the boy gave the spike half a turn. They drilled an entire line of holes this way.

"That box over there," Big John pointed. "Full of powder and fuses. Bring it over. And while I'm shoving the charges into the holes, you come along behind with the dead men—them long paper things filled with dirt—and stick one in each hole to tamp it."

All at once the tunnel shook with a tremendous roar. Bits and pieces of rock and shale broke free of the walls and ceiling, and skidded onto the ground like tiny avalanches. "God almighty!" Rafe cried. "We got to get out of here, Big John!"

"Not so fast."

"But that was a explosion!"

"That was just a man-made explosion," he explained as he continued working. "Coming from the next tunnel. We're fixing to make one ourselves here in a few minutes."

"Ain't it dangerous? What about the damp?"

"That's what you got to watch your lamp for. Everything's going just fine. Now, let's get this done. The Shot Firer ought to be coming along any minute to check these charges before we set them."

"What's he got to check them for?"

"Because he's the Straw Boss, that's what. He'll be checking to make sure nobody's wasting time, too. All you got to learn is how to make coal and you're asking enough questions to run the company. Let's get a move on."

When everything was ready, they removed themselves and the tools to a safe place near the mouth of the tunnel, and waited. In a few minutes, the foreman—or, Shot Firer—came along, and shortly after that, another resounding blast that left Rafe's ears ringing, roared through the tunnel. They waited a little longer until the circulating air blew away the acrid powder fumes before returning to the work site.

When they got there, a huge mound of coal had been thrown into a glittering heap on the floor of the mine. Their next job was to extend the track for the coal cars the ten to twelve feet it lacked from touching the mound of coal. This was done with steel rails and wooden ties that had been stacked and waiting for them. Lifting and carrying the heavy pieces was the most hard labor Rafe had ever done in his life.

Big John noticed he was slowing down and made him go sit awhile as he laid the last four feet of track alone. Just before they broke for a brief half-hour lunch, an underground train came along that left an empty car at the head of their tunnel, which John brought by hand down the long corridor, and pushed as close up against the pile of coal as he could.

"Well, little brother…" He sat down next to Rafe and leaned back against one of the wooden beams, "That's about all there is to digging coal." He reached for his dinner pail. "Take us the rest of the shift to shovel that heap out of here. When we leave for the outside, the work room won't look no different than it did when we come in. Except it'll be about ten feet longer. Shoot, I shore have made a lot of tunnels in my time!"

That second part of the shift seemed ten times longer than the first. Rafe shoveled coal and more coal and pushed the loaded cars that were so full they were rounded over, down to the mouth of the tunnel. He went back and forth so many times, he lost count. His feet began to drag and his arms felt like they weighed more than the coal he was shoveling. John told him to slow down several times and made him quit early.

By the time they walked to the main heading to catch a man-car for the outside, Rafe felt like he was dreaming. He barely noticed the ride back up in the lift. When they stopped off at the office to get him on the payroll, his brother had to tell him twice to sign Joseph Lee's name instead of his own. It was already dark by the time they got in the truck and headed home.

The day was over and he had never seen the sun.

This time, as they passed through the barren hillsides, he was hardly aware of them. His tired body was growing heavier by the minute and he looked longingly at the glove box where he knew his father kept an extra pouch of tobacco and a small stash of thin cigarette papers to role them with. He looked over at his brother. "Big John?"

"Yeah."

"You know I been smoking since I was nine."

"I know."

"I shore could use one before we get home." For a long moment there was no reply. "Ain't being disrespectful. Just asking."

"Well, I reckon any boy does a man's job shouldn't be denied a man's pleasures. Go ahead on."

"Thanks, Big John." Rafe's muscles were beginning to stiffen and he could feel a growing soreness in his hands and arms. He had never felt so tired. By the time he fumbled around and finally got a cigarette made and lit, they were pulling into the yard.

John turned off the motor before he even noticed they were home.

"Shoot ."

"Come on, you can set on the back porch and finish it while I talk to Daddy a minute before I go home. Good hot bath and some lineament, little bit to eat, and you're going to bed."

"What about the firewood?"

"You don't need to worry about no firewood, tonight."

The tub was already filled with steaming hot water and waiting for him. Lias had brought the liniment, and Celia was just coming in with clean clothes when Big John walked in. They looked anxiously at him.

"He's pretty beat," he answered without them even having to ask. "But he filled your boots, Daddy."

<h1 style="text-align:center">43</h1>

It took three days for Harlan to realize Rafe Harper was no longer attending school. With the harvesting of local crops, many of the children were absent for several days while they helped with the family work. Knowing that tobacco harvesting took even more time because of the cutting, sorting and drying involved, he didn't start to wonder about his best student until the younger Harpers came back without him. He made a mental note to talk to Lou Ellen during the first recess but he didn't have to wait that long to find out.

When Jenny Beth finished her morning reading assignment, she occupied herself by drawing a picture with crayons until the other children were done. As Harlan moved between the rows checking papers, his eyes fell on her picture and were riveted there. She had drawn a person with a black face, and underneath she had painstakingly written four uneven letters in blue that spelled... Rafe.

"Is that good letter writing, Mr. Harlan?" the little girl asked when she noticed he had been standing there for a long time without saying anything.

"Why hasn't Rafe been coming to school, honey?" He tried to control the sudden, desperate urgency that crept over him. The Harpers knew Rafe was his most promising student. They had even talked about scholarships. Certainly his family would not send him to work in the coal mines when he had such a worthwhile future ahead of him.

"Because." She continued to color as she talked. "This here's the liniment Daddy's been putting on him, see? The bottle's green."

"Is he sick?"

"Nope. He's a working man, now, Mr. Harlan. Just like Big John."

He wanted to send everyone home, ride his horse through the woods as fast as he could, and lash out at Lias Harper for giving in to everything he had ever stood against. He wanted to face him—if it had been anyone but Lias—if it had been anyone but Rafe!

"Can I read next, Mr. Harlan?"

"It's past recess, Mr. Harlan."

He tried to keep control of himself and the routine but the rest of the day was a blur. He sent a note home to Lias, by way of the children, asking to see him that evening. But how would he be able to keep from offending the man's honor when so much was at stake?

They met at sunset.

On a small hill above the Harper home, Harlan tied Prince to a tree and sat down on a fallen log to wait until Lias got there. He knew he would come. In spite of their ongoing disagreement about Bonnie Rae, the man was dependable. Especially when it concerned his children. Harlan thoughtlessly pulled off his tie and stuck it, by habit, into the pocket of his gray suit jacket. He ran a hand through his dark hair, noticed how long it was getting, but didn't care.

His mind was crowded with everything he wanted to say. He knew they were going to come head to head over this and worried it would ruin any chance he had left for winning the man over. He had been trying so hard these past weeks! How many times he wanted to give up on Lias Harper! The man was never going to accept him and—at the moment—he was leaning toward persuading Bonnie Rae to go away with him. Then something would nudge gently at the back of his heart. No, that was not good enough. Wait... wait...

And he would think of Bonnie Rae in all her loveliness and open longing for him. He had the feeling she would do anything he asked. But if that were so, he had to be—oh, so careful—of what he asked. Much of who she was belonged to her family. To break those ties would surely cause wounds that could only be buried rather than healed. He couldn't do that lightly. Maybe he couldn't do it at all. Yet, when things were particularly hard, he only had to think about her before a sweet peacefulness came over him that felt so right and appealing.

He had even thought of marrying her secretly. At least then there would be no more guilt to weigh so heavily upon him about meeting without permission. Her family may, or may not, get used to the idea but the decision would no longer rest with them. Still, something told him that wasn't exactly the right thing to do, either. At least, not yet.

He must think of something, though. Lately, the most intense longings for their own life together swept over him when he least expected it. Then he would force himself to do something else—anything—just to get her off his mind. Too much of that and he wouldn't be able to keep his thinking rational. It was hard enough, already.

"Harlan?"

He hadn't heard Lias approach and was startled to find him standing so close to him. All of his planning and precaution slipped away in the unguarded moment as he looked directly into the tired green eyes. "Why, Rafe, Lias?" he blurted out miserably, "Why Rafe!"

A flicker of remorse shown in the older man's glance before he sighed deeply, and sat down on the other end of the log. "It's these times, I reckon. Just these pitiful hard times."

"It isn't fair—it isn't right! I can't stand the thought of him down there!"

"You think it ain't hard on his mama and me?"

"You could have stopped it and you let him go! Just like all the other parents in Cedar Creek. Child labor doesn't turn right just because everyone's doing it. For the love of—God, Lias! It's illegal!"

"Child labor's what kept a lot of Cedar Creek kids from starving over the last few years. Nobody's proud of it, Harlan. But with wages so low, we don't have much choice. The waiting list is another reason. It's two years long, already. But if a family member gets hurt or killed under the hill —"

"Oh, no."

"Then it's sort of a general practice to let another boy from that family take the job. No matter how old they are. There's families on this ridge that would have been starved out a long time, ago, if it hadn't been for the payroll one of their kids was bringing in."

"But you've got two working for the Company, already. Isn't that enough?"

"They laid me off, last week."

The news took Harlan by surprise and sensing some of the man's burden, he felt a little of his own anger slip away. "I'm sorry, I—I didn't know."

"Ain't right for Johnny to be carrying the whole load. Especially now that he done married Sarah and ain't living at home no more. Burden falls to Joseph Lee. Only he run off."

"I can't believe he'd do that." Harlan studied the careworn face for a few moments but it gave nothing away. "The way he is with the children, and all."

"I'm hoping he'll see his way to come back. I reckon that's the reason I let Rafe stand in for him at the company. He wanted to do it. I didn't twist his arm, if that's what you're thinking."

"But don't you see?" Harlan spoke fervently, "He's too young to know any better. It was a noble gesture that will take everything he's got to keep. Maybe even more. Parents should protect children from doing those things, not encourage them."

"I can see you never had to send no baby to bed hungry. Do that a couple times, and see how you feel."

"I don't mean to be disrespectful, sir, but it seems to me with that good bottom land of yours..."

"Shore, I could turn it back into a truck farm and keep us all pretty good," he agreed. "Might even do that next year. But it don't grow overnight, boy. We done got used to the pay day, and store bought things." He reached for his tobacco but there didn't seem to be enough in the pouch to even roll one. So, he looked out over his land, instead.

It was the most beautiful land, with its trees and purple hills. He had almost forgotten how beautiful it could be beneath a setting sun. He returned his gaze to Harlan. "Younguns like them new-fangled *Wheaties* now, instead of oatmeal. They listen to the radio more than they sing, and they got to have them electric lights you got to pay cash money for. We can turn back to the old ways, all right. But it takes a while."

"That's still not a good enough trade for child labor," Harlan stubbornly tossed a stick he had been holding aside.

"You got any better ideas?"

"A lot of things would be better. Taking the children out and putting men back in, for one thing. Or collective bargaining for a higher wage, so it wouldn't be so advantageous for the company to use them. Strike if you had to. And if that didn't work, appeal to the federal government for help."

"Shoot, Harlan." Lias shook his head and replaced the tobacco pouch in his pocket. "Now, you're talking like every other outsider I ever knew, who thinks we're all a bunch of half wits living back up in these hills."

"Well, what can you expect? While the rest of the country's trying to find new and better ways of working things out—legal ways—you people are still shooting at everybody up here."

Lias got up and walked a short distance away.

"You're not leaving, are you?" Harlan worried.

"No. But I'll admit, you're starting to rile me."

"Then explain it to me, Mr. Harper. That's all I ask. Just explain it to me."

44

Lias Harper turned and looked at the young man who was looking so earnestly back at him, and felt —in spite of himself—a crumbling in the wall between them. For a moment he looked past the city suit and the handsomeness and saw genuine sincerity, instead. "It was Lias, a few minutes ago," he pointed out with a half smile. "Or, did I slip a notch."

"No, sir," Harlan assured, "I hadn't realized."

"Most folks call me, Lias—if it ain't Uncle, or Daddy—I reckon that'll do."

Harlan brightened. Could this be a step toward acceptance? A glimmer of hope passed through him.

"You think we ain't tried all them things you just said?" Lias began. "We ain't still shooting at people around here, boy—we've gone back to shooting at them—and there's the difference. Cedar Creek..."

He sat back down on the log again, as if the explanation were going to be a long one and Harlan was going to get it. "Ain't big enough to go against the company. Never has been. Whole town went on strike back in twenty-two. Know what come of it? They built Niggertown and brought in cheap black labor, that's what. Company don't really need Cedar Creek and never has. Once they come in and bought up everybody's land. That right there sort of shoots the fire out of collective bargaining, wouldn't you say?"

"What about the unions?"

"Tried that, too. One of Aaron McCord's boys wrote a letter to the United Mine Workers Union that Lewis feller started, and derned if they didn't send a bunch of communists back up here to organize something. Well, we're all of us red-blooded Americans, boy. We don't hold to none of that Marxist trash."

"But the government—"

"The government sent troops in and arrested us all for standing up for our rights. Meanwhile, the company hired gangster thugs from Detroit to act like company guards. To sort of keep order, if you know what I mean. We was beat every way but Sunday! They even took over Cedarville. Put a company man on as sheriff, let Ainsley elect his self mayor, and we was whipped. Been that way ever since."

He let his gaze drift out across his land, again. "They let Cedar Creek folks trickle back into the company, now and again, and we been grateful for that. Otherwise, we'd have starved, Harlan. We'd have plain laid down and died."

There was another long moment of quiet, during which a night bird called plaintively from the nearby stand of trees. It was getting dark quickly now, and the two men were no more than shadowy forms against the hill.

"I don't know what to say," Harlan murmured after a while. "I'm shocked. I... just don't know what to say."

"Don't none of us know what to say." Lias sighed. "It ain't like we never saw hard times in these parts. We've had more than our share of them. We fought thirty years of Indian wars when we first come, just to hold this land. Weren't no government around to help us in them days. We was on our own and we turned strong because of it. Then, when we did get a government, they wanted our boys to go fight in the War Between the States. And we did. Shore, we did. Then come the call for progress, and we gave to that too."

Harlan listened to the oration with a sense of awe. He was

a teacher and had more than an average interest in such events. But he had never heard anyone speak of historical things so personally and possessively before. What kind of attachment to the land did this place breed, when each man could feel the echoes of those who had gone before him, so acutely?

Lias laughed a little sarcastically as he thought about it all. "Progress. Shoot, all they wanted was the mineral rights to our land. Said we could keep our farms and such.

But let me ask you. What do you do with a mountain that's been skinned and plumbed? What can you do with it? Nothing, that's what. It's dead, boy. Ain't a thing it's good for no more.

"Spring rain comes and we get floods that are bigger and stronger every year. Even my good bottomland's getting washed away with the mess. So, here we are. Folks say we're lawless. But we're just trying to hold onto the proud spirit this country was found on. And the truth is, we just don't give up as easy as everyone else does."

He looked out across the dark land with a resigned sigh. "Maybe standing up here on our mountain we can look down and see the whole world going wild. And it's a heartbreak."

When he looked over at Harlan he was surprised to find him sitting with his head in his hands. He reached out to the drooping shoulder and said, "This is going awful hard on you, ain't it. Maybe you'd be better off back in Richmond, after all."

"No," the young man protested. "I've never felt so sure about being somewhere in my life. I believe I'm here for a reason. I've got to be! I admit this is the most terrible situation I've ever heard of. But it can't stay this way—it just can't. I'm going to write a letter to the National Labor Relations Board, and—"

"We tried that, too, Harlan. That NLRB don't have no more power to enforce nothing than a company paid sheriff."

"But what about that case a few months, ago, when the FBI made an investigation for the Justice Department? The one that was ordered by Attorney General Cummings."

"Didn't hear nothing about that."

"He ordered it to seek evidence of a possible conspiracy to violate national labor laws. Lias, they indicted twenty-two coal companies, twenty-four operators, a sheriff, and twenty-two of his deputies, for conspiring to deprive miners of their civil rights!"

"Lord almighty—where was this at?"

"Frankfort, Kentucky."

"Did it stick?"

"It happened near the end of the summer and I had to leave before it went to trial. But the point is, the government has finally shifted from civil to criminal indictments for these situations. I think it might mean something."

Lias studied Harlan with a flicker of respect. "You know, you just might have something there. We shorely got us one of them situations, all right."

"I'll write to them. And, if anything comes of it —anything at all—will you stand with me, Lias? As far as the proof goes?"

"If there's any hope at all, we'll stand. But I'll tell you right now, it would be something if you could pull that off."

"I'm going to try," he replied firmly.

Lias could sense the determination in his tone and knew that he meant it. "You got grit, I'll say that much. Tell me, Harlan, what makes you so willing to walk through fire for Cedar Creek when you ain't even gonna stay?"

"I don't know. Looking at this place is like watching something die, I guess. It breaks my heart. And the children… they need me. I'd do anything I could to help them. When I found out about Rafe, today, I—oh, Lias, he was my real hope for this year! We didn't want to tell you until it came through, but I've applied for the scholarship."

"I ain't ready to take him out of the job, if that's what you're getting at."

"But he has so much potential!"

"Boy's got to stick by his family, first. But, if J-Lee comes home, I'll send him back to you."

"What if something happens to him in the meantime? That's why we've got to get him out. And not just Rafe—all of them that are too young to be working under the hill. If the company's at the bottom of this, then—I swear—I'm not going to quit until I find some way to prove it!"

"That Company don't work by no laws but their own, Harlan," Lias warned. "And they done a heap of things to prove it to folks around here."

"Well, somebody's got to bring honest law to Cedar Creek. The only way to get it here is for someone to be willing to holler thief when he sees a thief. Well, I'm willing. And—believe me—I'm going to holler good and loud."

"Just don't get yourself kilt while you're doing it, boy."

"I'm not afraid of them." His face lit with a sudden zeal. "I don't have to be. I don't need their jobs, and I'm not starving. Maybe I could light a fire under that company like no one else could."

45

Lightning flashed and thunder boomed out a response that seemed to echo from all around. Joseph Lee stood looking out through the small window that was hazed over from years of neglect and watched the shadowy forms of the tall pines whipping and bending in the violent winds. There was a sudden hiss and spatter behind him and he quickly turned his attentions from the approaching storm to the coffee pot that was boiling over. Cooking over an open fireplace was something he hadn't quite figured out, yet. For three days now, he had either burned or undercooked everything.

This little cabin where he was staying was a hunter's shack nestled high up on the Wind Ridge, in a crevice of the towering cloud-wrapped mountain called Sugar Hill. It had been built by his great-grandfather, nearly seventy years ago. It was his now. Though it was used occasionally by other Harper men for hunting or getting away, it was his by reason of use. It belonged to him in the same way it had belonged to his Uncle Buck before him, and his grandfather before that. It had never belonged to his father. Nor had it belonged to the many other men in the family who were as much Harpers as anyone else.

The cabin belonged to those few Harpers who were so bound to the mountain wilderness, that they spent most of their time in it. The ones who had inherited the mysterious attributes of the true mountaineer. They were the ones who knew—by feeling—when to plant and when to reap, where to find hidden caches of the precious secret herbs, or how to ferret out the feeding grounds and resting places of the mountain game.

They had a keen inner instinct of when to fight and when to run. But most of all, they were men who needed the land — their land—and it had to be far-reaching and rugged. They were the restless ones who were constantly ranging over that land, drawing their strength from the very heights and depths of it. So, it was Joseph Lee's cabin now, and had been called his ever since Buck had been shot dead in the raid, four years ago.

He had come here often, for one day or two. But he never had the time or freedom to stay longer because of the family and his responsibilities at home. It was too far away to stay just overnight. Granny's place had been good enough for that. He had always longed to move up here one day. Now, for some reason, it seemed small and confining to him and he felt terribly alone.

He pulled the coffee pot off the fire and swore when it burned his hand. He was wondering why no one had taken the time to put a decent cook stove in the place when rain suddenly began to pour down onto the roof in a fierce deluge. He hoped someone back home would have the sense to start a small drying fire on the floor of the barn to keep the tobacco from getting damp. Then he chided himself for thinking about home, again, and returned his attention to the coffee.

All at once, there was a rap on the door. Before he could turn around or say come in, a blast of wind and rain blew furiously through the room as someone barged through.

"Just me, Ol' Son." Tate shook the water from his rifle and removed his coat and hat. "Thought I'd get here before it let loose but it opened up on me before I got in."

"Everything go all right?" Joseph Lee stood to his feet.

"Smooth as glass."

"Anybody see you?"

"Nope. But I don't see what difference it makes. Pay somebody to haul a couple hundred pounds of sugar and grain, and any country fool's gonna know you ain't baking biscuits."

"Well, you just keep thinking on it, Tatum, and maybe the logic will come to you one of these days."

"You shore sound friendly, tonight."

"I feel rotten."

Tate put his dripping hat back on his head and reached for his coat, again. "I reckon I'll just meet you at the still in the morning." He started for the door.

"Tate—" His friend turned back to him. "Hey, I didn't mean it. Why don't you stay awhile."

"Looks like you still need some time to yourself."

"I'm sick of myself. I could use some company. Come on, take them wet things off and I'll give you some—well, shoot, I burned the coffee—but it won't take long to make more."

"I don't need no coffee. But I'll admit I was looking forward to a dry place to sleep tonight. Only bad thing about having the still so far up on this ridge, you can't go home every night. And you're taking your life in your hands shutting both eyes with Willie Jr. around."

"I wish you would pay him off and get rid of him, Tate. He ain't nothing short of crazy and you know it."

"Yeah, but..." He took off his things, again, and went over to stand by the fire.

"But what?"

"Feel sort of sorry for him, I reckon."

"You can't run a business on them kind of feelings."

"His family's pretty bad off."

"Ain't everybody's? How come he didn't take his daddy's place at the company?"

"He did. But they fired him after the first week for stealing explosives, and—"

"Shoot—didn't I tell you he was crazy?"

"He does all right when you stay on him, though. And you know yourself, he ain't half bad in a fight."

"If he can figure out what side he's on. Man's a half-wit, Tate. He sets my flesh crawling every time I'm around him."

"Still."

Joseph Lee went and sat down on one of the beds in the corner of the room and leaned his back against the wooden wall. "You know what I think?" He reached for an old guitar that was lying beside him.

"What."

"I think you got something going for that sister of his."

"Opal's a nice girl." Tate turned his back to the fire to warm the other side.

"She's a miners' lady. Especially around payday." He began to pick out a soft, plaintive melody on the strings.

"You got a jug around here, Ol' Son?" Tate asked suddenly. "I need something to get the chill out of my bones. Jeeze, I'd rather have snow than freezing cold rain like this."

"Buck used to keep one on the bottom shelf of that pantry over there. If there's anything left in it, you can be sure it's prime because my granddaddy made it."

"Oooooweeee..." Tate's eyes widened. "You shore you don't want to save it for something special?"

"Naw, go ahead on. If this ain't a drinking night, I don't know what is."

Tate hesitated, feeling somewhat startled by the generosity.

"Go on, I mean it." He insisted with a smile. "We'll celebrate."

"Celebrate what."

"You and me being the only one's left on this ridge that's got any sense."

Tate went over to the pantry and rummaged around until he came up with a gallon jug that had been pushed far into a back corner. He gave it a gentle shake. "More than half full," he marveled. He pulled the cork and sniffed the contents. "Lordy, Lordy," he breathed rapturously. "It's gonna kiss like a woman and kick like a mule!"

Joseph Lee laughed. "Give it a try," he said.

"No siree," Tate crossed the room to hand over the jug. "This is your heritage, boy. Only right you should have the first swallow."

Joseph Lee set the guitar aside and sat up straight. "Can't do it lightly, then." He thought for a moment. "To my grand-daddy... and his granddaddy before him... and to the treasured memory of my Uncle Buck. Who was a true ridge runner and the wildest son of a whiskey man this county ever seen!" He tipped the jug slowly, holding and savoring the swallow in his mouth for a few moments before letting it go down.

"Well?" Tate asked expectantly.

"Prime," Joseph Lee pronounced. He handed the jug back to him. "Pure, prime."

So, the two friends sat before the fire, passing the jug between them while the rain poured down in torrents outside the door and the roof began to leak steadily onto one of the corner beds. But neither of them noticed. They sang and talked and drank, and sang some more, until the whole world got lost in a comfortable haze. After a while, their innermost feelings were as ready on their tongues as the thoughts that passed so fleetingly through their heads.

"This ain't a bad place you got here, Ol' Son," Tate tried to roll himself a cigarette but succeeded mostly in making a mess on the floor.

"I used to think so."

"You mean, you don't no more?"

"I been feeling so low lately, don't nothing look good to me no more. You ever felt that way, Tatum? I mean you ever felt like just giving up altogether?"

"I tried it once. Giving up." He crumpled the first cigarette paper he had mangled, threw it into the fire and reached for another to try, again. "Most disappointing thing I ever done."

"What happened?"

"Nothing. That's just it." He shrugged. "Not a blessed

thing. One day I says to myself—that's it! I had enough of this no good, lousy world! I ain't gonna take no more and I'm giving up right here and now! Grabbed my gun and went down to the river, fixing to shoot myself dead and be done with it." He twisted the end of his cigarette, touched a lighted stick of kindling to it, and breathed in deeply to start it.

Joseph Lee waited for him to continue but Tate was absorbed in smoking, now, and seemed to have lost his thought. "Well—did you do it, or not?" he asked impatiently.

"What, Ol' Son?"

"Shoot yourself. By the river, like you was gonna."

"Shoot myself—you ever try to kill yourself with a rifle gun when you was dead drunk?"

"Nope."

"You can't do it. Lookee here..." He pulled the front of his shirt open so abruptly two buttons popped off and rolled onto the wooden floor. He pointed a dramatic finger to a ragged scar on his underarm, just below the shoulder. "See that? Missed my derned heart altogether. But you think that didn't hurt? It hurt so much I threw myself into that cold raging river and cried, Lord, take me to your bosom, this boy's coming home!"

"How come you didn't drown?"

"Hail, how should I know? I couldn't even do that right. I'm probably the only poor fool on this mountain jumped into that river on purpose and got spit back up on the bank, again. My little brother found me, next morning. Hadn't lost too much blood on account of that cold, icy water. I was just as alive then as I am now. Excepting I had more miseries staring me in the face than I started out with!"

"Never tried it again, huh?"

"Nope. But I learned a powerful lesson from it, that's for shore."

"What was it?"

"I learned no matter how you live—or what you live like—you're gonna keep right on living..."

Joseph Lee waited another few moments but Tate was

drifting, again, and didn't go on. "That shore don't make spit for sense," he pronounced finally.

"Will you let me finish?"

"So, finish."

"You're gonna keep on living right up 'till... the day you die."

It was quiet for a second before their eyes met and they both broke out into a sudden fit of laughter. Joseph Lee threw a pillow across the room at his friend and accused him of lying. Tate took another long pull from the jug and admitted the untruth.

"How did you really get that scar?"

<h1 style="text-align:center">46</h1>

"My ma shot me." Tate gave another loud guffaw as if the thought were absurd even to him. "Can you believe that?"

"Shoot, that lie's worse than the last one."

"It's the truth, I swear. See, she had this purty little twenty-two she got out of the *Sears And Roebuck* one year. Used it for hunting squirrel. I tried to take it away from her once when she was gonna use it on Ol' Pa and the thing went off. Got me right there." He pointed to the scar through the sagging opening of his shirt and shook his head. "Scared her something fierce, though. My ol' ma was hard but she weren't mean. Said she'd rather live with a bunch of good-for-nothings for the rest of her life, than have one she murdered come back and haint her for all eternity."

"Didn't' she die last winter?"

"Yep."

"How you all getting along out there?"

"Ain't but three of us left no more. Me, Matty and Ol' Pa. He's near all the way blind, now. Compensation from his accident run out last spring. That's why I got into the business."

"That's rough."

"Shoot, it's rough all over, ain't it? You know what I think the trouble is?"

"Trouble with what?"

"Everything."

"What is it."

"Too many people in the same place, doing the same thing, going after the same little bit. And there plain just ain't enough."

"Could be."

"That's the truth. They're all still trying to hold onto them old ways. Live a good life and everything will turn out right. You can't do it that way no more. Because it's all different now. Got to take what you can and get because yesterday's gone, boy. It's gone."

Joseph Lee stretched out on the bed and propped his head up in his hand. "I knew this ol' guy once." He gazed into the warm glow of the fire. "Lived away back in the deepest part of the holler. Name was Curtis Dodge. He died a few years back but he was old. Shoot, he was old when I first met him. Said he fought in the War—knew General Lee personal. Anyhow, I remember him saying happiness is free, along with most everything else a person really needs to live on."

"Well, that sounds reasonable. I mean it weren't 'till the furiners come in and started grabbing up what rightfully belonged to the rest of us, that things started getting scarce. Then they turn around and tried to sell it back to us for money we ain't got. That's the trouble."

"Yep, I reckon," Joseph Lee conceded. "But ol' Curtis was a friend of mine."

"Times like these, I think maybe them folks that's gone, got something over us," Tate spoke philosophically. "At least they made it through life without having to see the whole world gone crazy. Man, I don't think nobody—young or old— can rest peaceful after they seen that. Fearsome thing is, there ain't nothing you can do about it." He tossed the end of his cigarette into the fire. "I used to think I would just make a lot of money real fast and quit this crazy place. But you know what?"

"What."

"I think it's crazy all over. I think maybe there ain't no peace left in this world nowhere."

"Aww, there was never no such thing in the first place," Joseph Lee reasoned.

"Well, gawd! How can you not believe in peace? That's purty low. I mean, I could see not getting religion, or maybe even denying the Almighty. But to just not believe in peace..."

"Yeah, well I heard a lot of people talk about them things but I never seen any before. I don't think nobody else has, neither. You take my brother. Now, ain't he known around these parts for being a peace loving man ever since he got religion? But back him into a corner—or get him good and riled—and dang! He's still worse than most of them."

"I always did think Providence was taking a chance giving so much muscle to one man." Tate shook his head shamefully. "Mmmm!"

"That ol' peace loving boy liked to kilt me last week. I ain't been able to lift nothing heavier than a coffee pot, on account of he stove in one of my ribs."

"Don't I know? I mean you looked like death warmed over, a few days ago. Still look a little green and purple around the edges."

"I worked hard all my lifetime—and for what? A kick in the pants from some peace loving man, and a don't come back again. Ain't no such thing as peace. Ain't no such thing as God, neither."

"Ooooo, Lordy!" Tate marveled. "I wouldn't go so far as to say that!"

"Well, it's true. Folks just too scared to say it. Too scared to admit He ain't nothing more than a good excuse for things not working out for them that ain't tough enough to live in this world."

"If that's so, then we shore had a flood of miserable folks down at the schoolhouse meadow last year at revival time, making fools out of theirselves for something they thought was Gawd."

They was fools. You didn't see none of the smart ones down there getting religion, did you?"

"Your daddy."

"My daddy was a beat man. If he didn't find God for a excuse, he'd a laid down and died, instead. He's wore out."

"Half the town did the same thing."

"Just shows you how easy folks are to lead around. I think it takes a pretty lot of gall to talk year after year to something that don't talk back to you. Who needs it."

"Well, I'll tell you, Ol' Son, I'd shore take it if I could get it."

"Why for?"

"Because it sounds good. Especially that part about Gawd loving everybody individual-like. I think it would be right fine if that was so."

"So, how come you wasn't out there with the rest of them, jumping and hollering and getting religion?"

"I tried. I went down to that meadow every blessed day of camp meeting, waiting to see the Light. Or at least have the Spirit come on me. Nothing ever happened. Whole thing was a bust."

Joseph Lee sat up on the edge of the bed and looked over at his dejected friend as he sat cross-legged on the floor. He reached for the jug and took a swallow while Tate sniffed, wiped his nose with his hand and stared into the dying fire. "That's the most pitiful thing I heard in a time and a time," Joseph Lee said after a while.

"Story of my life." Tate reached for the jug, himself, then. "Like they say... no love for the ugly."

"Hey, don't that just prove it ain't real? I mean, if it's love you're after... well, shoot, that ain't too hard to come by."

"Maybe not for you. But you ain't got my looks. Nope, Ol' Son, I'm the kind of person don't nobody notice. Not girls or no one else. I hear tell it's a sin to be bad and a burden to be good. But if you ask me, it's a curse to be stuck somewheres in the middle. You wouldn't know what it's like. Why, hail, girls talk about you from one end of these hills to the other. Anything you do, you do good. You got brains and you're a Harper to boot. People notice you."

Tate sighed and made another cigarette. "Nobody knows nothing about me. If I'm lonely, or mad, or feeling good... who cares? I ain't too smart, I'll admit, but I make a few mistakes and get by with them. Know why? Because don't nobody care. I don't get in nobody's way because I ain't on nobody's mind. If I hate everybody—who cares? If I say I love everybody, don't nobody care about that, neither. I ain't on nobody's mind."

He paused to light a cigarette that looked sorrier than his last one and was only half long. Then he blurted out with a sudden rush of emotion, "I'm a loser all the way round, boy! And as far as Gawd goes, I'm a sinner that ain't worth coming after!"

"You know, Tatum?"

"What's that."

"I think maybe you just got kicked."

"How do you mean?"

"You said this here whiskey was gonna kiss like a woman and kick like a mule. Well, I think you just got kicked. That's the trouble with this stuff. You get to thinking it's gonna show you a good time, then when you got a belly-full, it starts beating you over the head with everything you ain't, or ain't had."

"Shoot, boy, whiskey's my best friend."

"Yeah, I think we seen enough of it for one night. Next thing you know, you'll be crying like a baby."

"I'd cry like a baby, right now, if I thought it would save me!" Tate insisted.

"We done talked all we need to about religion, too. Anymore and we'll be saying prayers before we go to bed."

"Hey!" Tate got unsteadily to his feet and looked up at the ceiling. "I'm gonna make a prayer."

"Shoot, I knew it was coming to this. It's worse than sitting around scaring each other with booger tales and haint stories. Somebody always gets the spit scared out of theirselves!"

"No—I'm serious, now—I'm fixing to pray."

"Well, I'm fixing to bank the fire and go to bed." Joseph Lee got to his feet.

"You want I should ask for something for you, while I'm addressing Gawd Almighty?"

"Yeah, you can ask him what he's doing up there on his fancy throne while all hell's breaking loose down here on the rest of us."

"I hope He didn't hear that."

Joseph Lee went over to the fireplace, reached for the iron poker, and began to jab at the coals while Tate stood in the center of the room with his head bowed.

"Dear Lord," he began, in ernest, with his eyes screwed tightly closed, "I would not pre-sume that you'd take much store in the likes of me. But I'm addressing you on behalf of my best friend, here... Joseph Lee Harper."

"Oh, for —"

"Whose heart is hardened toward yore mercies. But it ain't a bad heart, Lord — it's just hard on account of it's been broke so many times!"

"Tatum."

"Gawd!" he cried out in a voice that cracked with emotion. "He ain't seen nothing but wrath since he was a baby! He don't even believe in peace no more!"

"Stop that, now."

"Lead him to those green pastures, Lord! Show him them still waters! Oh, Father which are in heaven, with a halo by thy name! Take him, Lord. Heal all his broke parts with your word and don't let no bitterness or heartbreak keep him from yore glory!"

"I swear—if you don't quit—I'm gonna —"

"Bring him to his knees!"

"That's it! You no-good—" Joseph Lee grabbed the hearth broom and swung it at him but missed when a sudden pain shot through his chest for doing it.

"With liberty and justice for all!" Tate finished hurriedly as he dodged another half-hearted swing. "And don't let no federal man shoot me dead. Amen! There's a end to it, Ol' Son."

"About time." Joseph Lee favored his right side as he moved slowly back to the bed.

"You keep playing round with them busted ribs..." Tate headed for the bed in the opposite corner. "You gonna be stove up longer than you have to be."

"I been stove up long enough. Couple days after the next run-off, I want us to make a trip into Princeton."

"Princeton?" Tate turned around and stared as if he had suddenly gone delirious. "There's plenty places to unload whiskey without having to go that far away."

"You can't be filtering shine through the same sources all the time, Tatum. It's a dead give away."

"But what about all them State Troopers they got along that highway?"

"I want to go get Ivy."

47

Several days later, Lyla Harper was wakened out of a sound sleep at one o'clock in the morning by a persistent knock at the door of her upstairs apartment in Princeton. She fumbled into a faded blue housecoat, pushed her bright red hair back from her face, and trudged sleepily toward the door. For a moment she forgot she was no longer in Cedar Creek and it never occurred to her it would be anyone but a family member. Her many years in the whiskey business made her take unexpected callers in the middle of the night, as routine.

"Joseph Lee!" She swung the door wide when she recognized the familiar form, "I didn't think it would be too long before you showed up at my door."

"Hey, Aunt Lyla," He bent to give her a kiss. "You getting along out here in the big city?"

"Just tolerable. I'll shore be glad when they let your Uncle Jimmy out, next spring. Law—but you're growing up handsome and sassy as ever!"

"I come for Ivy," He closed the door behind him as he stepped inside.

"Well, come on in and set down while I wake her, but..."

"But what?" He sank into a big gray couch that dominated the entire living room.

"But she ain't got no intentions of going back, that's what." She sat down next to him and tucked a fallen lock of hair back into a loose comb. "And to tell the truth, son, I don't blame her. Now, you must be plumb wore out after that long drive. Why don't you stretch out on the couch here and talk to her in the morning."

"Wake her up, Aunt Lyla."

The small, middle-aged woman looked at him with tender-hearted understanding. She sighed and patted him on the knee. "All right, darlin, let me see what I can do."

She disappeared down a narrow hallway while Joseph Lee let his eyes roam over the little living room and wondered how people could be content to live out their lives in such close quarters. Not that his Aunt Lyla was content. She had moved to Princeton to be near her husband so she could visit him on Sunday afternoons. Prison was not easy for a mountain man. In a few minutes, she was back again.

"Well…" She was apologetic. "I'm afraid she just plain, ain't up to seeing you."

He got to his feet. "She'll see me." He started for the narrow hallway, himself.

"Joseph Lee—I don't want no trouble, now—the last thing that girl needs is —"

"I know what she needs." He reached for the door handle. It was locked. "Ivy —" he called irritably, "Open the door, or I'll bust it down!"

"You won't do no such thing!" his aunt pronounced with the same authority she had wielded over him since he was a child. "You so much as lay a hand on that girl, I will come after you with a—" She was interrupted by the click of the lock and the door swung slowly open into the dark room. "Well, I'll vow," she marveled more to herself than Joseph Lee. "I reckon I'll go put on some coffee while you two talk things over. Maybe cook up some bacon and eggs."

Joseph Lee stepped inside, closed the door quietly behind him and leaned back against it, waiting for his eyes to adjust to the dark. In a few moments he could see the familiar outline of the girl silhouetted against the faint light from the window. She was wearing only a light, cotton slip and her dark hair looked deep and luxuriant in the moonlight. "How you doing, baby," he asked gently.

"Oh, J-Lee, I—I —" They met halfway across the room, and he folded her into his arms as she sobbed. "I thought you wouldn't want me no more after you found out! I didn't want nobody coming after you on account of me! I just wanted to die! I was sick afterwards. So mortal shamed of myself!"

"Ivy." His tone was almost pleading. "He was a stranger. Why did you even get in his car, or be alone with him in the first place?"

"He was so polite and shy-like, at first." She sniffed. "Everybody knew he come onto the mountain to sell housewares. He said he just needed a little whiskey to help pass the weekend with. He was gonna give five dollars for it!"

Joseph Lee swore under his breath and stifled the surge of anger that threatened to spill over.

"Said we'd be back in plenty of time to drop me at the party," she went on quickly. "Never made no sign he was interested in me that way. We mostly just talked about you and Johnny."

His insides churned at the words and he let her go to move near the window. "Didn't that strike you as strange he should be so interested in us?"

"It did later on. But I shore didn't see it coming," she mourned.

She was quiet for so long he turned back to look at her again. When he did, she threw herself on the bed, buried her face in the pillow and gave way to long, heart-rending sobs.

"Hey," He came to sit beside her run a hand through her hair. "It's all right. Didn't nothing come of it."

"I wish I could just die!"

"Well, I'd go stark, raving crazy if you did. You hear me? Don't you never try nothing like that, again. And don't never run off, again, neither. Not from me, anyhow. Never from me."

"Oh, J-Lee..." She moved over to lay her head in his lap. "I done it because I love you so much! And I was afraid he'd find you if you came looking for me. I..." Her voice became hardly more than a whisper. "Didn't think you could love me anymore after what he done."

"Can't stop loving somebody on account of what happens," he answered. "It riled me you went off in his car that way, though. I thought you liked him, driving by in his car that way."

"I'm so sorry, J-Lee!"

"Well—way I see it – taking him up on the hill was the only thing you done wrong and I reckon you found that out the hard way. But the other... don't see as how you could have done nothing to stop that. I'm mortal sorry I wasn't there when you needed me, Ivy. I'd have been up here to fetch you sooner, too, but I been having a few troubles of my own."

"Joseph Lee?" She put a soft hand over his to stop it moving through her hair. "I ain't going back to Cedar Creek. I can't face it. The way Daddy and Jesse treated me, I don't never want to go back, again!"

"Listen, to me."

Aunt Lyla got me on at the diner and I been thinking I could maybe —"

"Stop."

"I could make a new life for myself, and —"

"Stop right there." His voice was fervent. "You think I'd ask you to come back if I hadn't took care of things? Ain't I always took care of you?"

"But my daddy would—"

"He ain't never gonna make you do nothing again. I swear."

"You stood up to my daddy for me? Oh, J-Lee!" She clung to him with such sudden fierceness that his heart began to pound. "You're the only one in this world really cares about me!"

"Baby, I love you." He bent down to kiss her hair, and the side of her face, and then her mouth with a tender longing. "I ain't living at home myself, no more. I'm staying up on Sugar Hill. You'll be safe there. Don't nobody go that high on the mountain unless they're invited. You gotta come back with me, Ivy, I need you with me up there."

"J-Lee…"

"In the morning and at night." He kissed her again. "All the time. Get your things together, now, and I'll wait in the kitchen."

"Not, now. I been thinking a lot about it, J-Lee, and my mind's made up," she insisted. "Isn't anything you can say to change it."

"Come on." He got up and pulled her to her feet beside him. "We'll have something to eat before we go and afterwards…"

"I said I ain't going."

"Don't you want to hear about afterwards? You're gonna like it."

"What am I gonna like?"

"Close your eyes."

The words sent a shimmer of excitement through her. It had become a traditional phrase that preceded small gifts and pleasures he had given her over the years. It could mean anything from a taste of store-bought chocolate to some new wilderness place he had found for them to build cabin of their own, someday.

When she closed her eyes with delicious anticipation, he gently leaned his forehead against hers and whispered, "Afterwards, I'm gonna wake up the first Justice of the Peace I can find, and make you a Harper."

48

Every year before the first snow, Tom made a long journey out to the farthest reaches of the little community of Cedar Creek. It was a trip that took nearly a month, covering the most remote edges of the ridge and the deepest most tucked away hollows. He visited, and rendered services where needed.

In the eight years since he came to the mountain, the people of the ridge had learned to look forward to his comings and goings, and there were always things saved up for him to do. It was usually the best time of his year. But this year, he was reluctant to get started. He had a nagging discomfort about leaving Harlan alone, even though he could find no logical reason to substantiate it.

So far, Harlan had confined his actions toward the company to a few letters written to various government agencies, and a report to the local school board. Whatever might come from those things would take weeks or even months to happen. In the meantime, something almost magical was happening at the school. The children of Cedar Creek were being drawn to the new teacher like magnets. Since the first school program, when even those who didn't have children attending came to "see what the new teacher was like," children had been trickling out of the hills to attend.

Not the ones who worked for the *Black Star Coal Works*.

But those who had been kept out for various other reasons that ranged from just "being needed at home" to their parents simply having no faith in the school anymore. Suddenly – almost miraculously—the children, themselves, wanted to come.

The program Harlan presented to the community with his students was a convincing display of the cooperation and respect a good teacher generates. But it wasn't as if Cedar Creek never had good teachers before. Something else was emerging. The first community program of the Cedar Creek School had been a surprising glimpse of the simple, unguarded affection "Mr. Harlan" had for "his" children.

He was an unexpected haven from the frightening tides of change and unrest in their troubled world. And he took them all in. He offered them not only the opportunity to learn; but also a sense of peace, safety, and self worth. Things they were hungry for. He had twenty-seven students, now. But he wanted them all.

Could Tom dare to hope the place might finally be winning him over?

Secretly, he had hoped his nephew would grow to love Cedar Creek as he did and choose to stay. Discovering his plans to return to China had been a terrible shock. It made the thought of Harlan working in some far off state where visits were infrequent and brief seem trifling. And as much as he had wanted him to stay in Cedar Creek before, he now openly prayed that he would go anywhere else, if only it would keep him from returning to war-torn China.

Harlan's memories of the place were shielded by the protective veil of innocent youth, and God had mercifully surrounded him with tender friends. But Tom's memories were haunted; beginning with the last letter his sister would ever write to him. Desperate, frantic lines she had written in haste. War had broken out in the province. Her husband was killed and her boy lost. He had been away on a visit with friends when it had all happened.

The last lines read, *"Please come, Tommy. I am stricken*

with grief beyond anything I have ever known and I must find him! Come quick. I know you will." It was shortly after the end of the World War. He and his wife, Melanie, had been living in France and still working in the hospital there. He left as soon as he could make the arrangements. But it wasn't soon enough.

Travel between countries was a slow process back then, especially with so many soldiers to return home. It was nearly a month before Tom found himself in the remote little province where his sister and her husband had been working. He did not speak any Chinese. And it had been one of the most shocking experiences of his life to ask for his sister – through interpreters—and be taken to a grave. She had been killed in a raid only days after writing the letter. But there were rumors that Harlan was still alive. The fighting had not spread as far as the next province where he had been visiting.

The next few months were a tortured existence for Tom. By the time he reached the village Harlan was supposed to be in, it had been burnt out already. Most of the people had fled to the mountains but, yes, there was a boy with blue eyes with them.

For eight months Tom went from place to place, and everywhere it was the same. "You pay much money?" people would ask with greedy smiles. "You pay much money?" He nearly gave up several times. His hopes would rise, then fall, then rise again. He traveled hundreds of miles on some shred of evidence, only to be disappointed and then led on again. Twice he was nearly killed, himself.

Finally, when he had grown weary with his efforts and distrustful of every clue, he came to a remote village where he was received like the Messiah. At first, he thought it was only another commotion over his own blue eyes. All the Bascomb's had unusually blue eyes. Then to his utter amazement, they brought him... his boy. And Tom Bascomb swore in that moment, if life never yielded him another good thing, this would be enough.

Seventeen years later, it was still enough.

Tom had always been proud of Harlan. Outside of typical boyhood pranks he had been a pleasure to raise. And in spite of the scars of those refugee days, he grew up strong and up-standing. He became the son he and Melanie had always longed for. Their time together as a family, back on the farm in Richmond when the folks were still alive, were his happiest memories.

Tom still went back there sometimes… in his mind.

The first few years were the best. After the war years and that long terrible search through the many provinces along the Yangtze River was behind them. Harlan had not wanted to come with him. Not that the boy could have been expected to have any recollections of him. Or even his own grandparents. But it was Melanie who made all the difference.

Just getting him back to France had been a chore. While travel restrictions had eased some by then, Harlan's refusal to speak English – even though he was sure the boy understood every word he said – had caused Tom to resort to firmness out of pure exasperation. Melanie's techniques were the opposite. She enveloped the boy in gentleness, spoke only to him in French, and enticed him with new worlds of culture and learn-ing that were "right outside his doorstep." Wherever his doorstep might happen to be. By the time they reached Rich-mond the following year, Harlan was not only won over, he was devoted to them both.

The three of them had returned to America to help Tom's father with his general practice while he recovered from a stroke. But he never fully recovered enough to handle every-thing himself, again. Harlan grew to love his grandparents, as well. And for six wonderful years, the Bascombs enjoyed life on the family farm. Melanie made the difference there, too.

Besides all her nursing duties for the practice, she drove the old doctor to and from the hospital so that he could make his rounds, or make house calls to any homebound patients. Though he had lost most of the use of one side, the other served well enough, and people had built up too much trust and confidence in him over the years to give up their physician very easily.

Melanie and the old doctor became a team. Tom always believed it was more her lovely French accent which sped that along. She and Tom had met—and fallen in love—working in the same hospital during the war and her gentle, musical words effected him the same way.

In the meanwhile, Tom handled his more serious cases and continued to advance his own career as a surgeon at the city hospital. Between farm life and what the nearby city of Richmond had to offer, Harlan grew up with the best of both these worlds. When it came time, he enrolled at the university, discovered his passion for teaching at an early age, and had already stepped into his own future the night Tom's world fell apart.

It happened suddenly, when an unexpected heart attack befell his normally feisty mother. It was just this time of year: no snow but icy cold. With everyone preparing for the holidays. They were looking forward to Harlan coming home for a visit. Tom was not home from the hospital, yet, and while the senior Dr. Bascomb was working on some case notes in his study, Melanie and his mother were enjoying themselves making Christmas candy in the kitchen. Two hours later, the symptoms that had been declared as "too much exertion" had developed into a full-blown emergency.

Against many protests, Melanie and the old doctor bundled the small, precious woman into the backseat of the car and headed for the hospital, where they could at least make her more comfortable in an oxygen tent. She died on the way. And it was the sudden, heartrending response of her husband that turned Melanie's head and caused her to take her eyes off the road for a moment. She missed the detour sign directing traffic away from some recently washed out bridge.

Tom could not make himself continue living alone at the farm after the funerals. A few weeks later, when he heard of an opening for a company doctor in a mining town several hundred miles away, he couldn't take it fast enough. He signed over the farm to Harlan and planned never to return there, again. The times he and his nephew had visited since then, they had both opted to meet somewhere else. For a while, Harlan made half-hearted attempts to spend summers there, but he usually ended up living close to wherever he was teaching, with Prince boarded somewhere nearby.

When the opportunity to teach for a year in Cedar Creek came up, Tom really hadn't expected Harlan to take it. The fact that he did was almost too good to be true. Tom was unbearably lonely, these days. The rift between him and those he cared for most on the ridge seemed to become more difficult as the years dragged on.

Having Harlan come had been a healing thing.

In the weeks they had been together, Tom was surprised to discover that—in many ways—Harlan had deeper insights than he had. He had grown beyond him in so many things. He had developed into a man of strong convictions and certainly did not need the protection and guidance of his uncle, anymore.

Why did he feel so reluctant to leave, now?

Unable to shake the those feelings, he kept postponing his trip, day after day, on one small pretense after another. A broken harness that needed a mend, another ride into Cedarville for some forgotten necessity. Finally, when there was nothing left to do, he went over all the precautions, again.

Don't drink the water if you do any visiting–only coffee or tea–to be sure it was properly boiled. This because some of the hill people were careless in the places they chose to fetch water. Malaria was common. The intermittent, it was called around here.

"You've told me that, Uncle," Harlan replied. "I'm careful."

Then he went into a long dissertation on the hazards of home remedies in case he should fall ill. Some of them were out and out poison. Especially those doled out by local herb doctors. He even went so far as to relate a long ago story of how Granny Harper had killed one of her own brothers with her primitive doctoring methods, after he had been shot in a blood war. That made an impression.

"Blood war," Harlan murmured.

"Feuding," his uncle explained. "That's what they call it around here."

"Will you stop worrying?" Harlan admonished, then, as if he were the elder and not the other way around. "This is the busiest time of year at school. I'm going to have my hands full right up until the holidays. I'm not going to make any unannounced visits to people I don't know. More importantly, I won't be organizing my students to picket the *Black Star Coal Works*. That's what's really bothering you."

"Well, it is actually," his uncle admitted. "Promise?"

"Promise. I'm going to be the perfect model citizen until you get back."

Why couldn't Tom believe it?

49

Hardly a week after the doctor had gone, the loud long wail of the mine whistle shattered a late fall afternoon and carried its cry of disaster over the hills and hollows of Cedar Creek. People from all over the county threw picks, shovels and blankets into the back of cars and pickups and barreled along the winding roads at breakneck speeds to help with the emergency. Lias stood impatiently at the edge of his yard and looked down the empty road. He paced back and forth twice before finally exclaiming, "God almighty, where are they? Where are they!"

"Don't hear them, Daddy," replied Little Sam with a quivery voice as he strained to see down the road.

"Tell them I started walking," Lias said to the boy. "I'll catch—"

"Here they come!"

Aaron McCord's nineteen twenty-nine Chevrolet came flying around the bend in the road and slowed down in front of the house just enough for Lias to jump onto the running board and hold on through the open window. He shoved the things he was carrying inside, and braced himself for the fast ride. Several other men had been picked up along the way and the solemn group traveled the fifteen minute route to the mines without speaking a word.

The whistle had blown five times and stopped.

The mine whistle had called them to emergencies so many times throughout their lives each man's thoughts were the same. And the seats were filled with more picks and shovels, and blankets to wrap the wounded or dead with. There was one for each family member that had been working the shift that day. The long shadows of late afternoon were spreading across the earth as they parked the car and joined the crowd that was gathering at the secondary entrance to one of the shafts.

Henry Perkins stood on the edge of a partly filled coal car, addressing the people with a half-smoked cigar in his left hand. "All the fans are operating," he called out over the crowd. "We sent the rest of the shift back to work and we can thank God it wasn't anything serious."

"What about Jared Henderson?" Someone spoke up.

"He's got a broke leg and we're doing all we can to keep him comfortable till we get him dug out from this side. The others that were with him have walked down and come out through the lower tunnel."

"Any others hurt?" Lias called.

"Like I said, Jim Wheeton got a crushed hand and a few more had cuts and bruises—but we only had one string of workers on this level today—we were lucky. We still need help to dig Henderson out, and any of you that can stay, Mr. Farris here, will be organizing work parties."

Harlan had been among the first to arrive. He had taken every shortcut off the road that he knew of, and ridden Prince at a wild and thundering pace through woods and pastures and low places. They had jumped fences and climbed hills. Throughout the long run, his mind was crowded with nightmarish pictures and terrible imaginings of the disaster. Now, he looked away from Perkins with a feeling of disgust. Lucky no one had died. They were giving credit where there should be blame.

The company was operating below standards and there could have been fifty injuries instead of five. There could have been hundreds. Besides that, they had sent the company workers back to their jobs to keep up with production, using only volunteers to dig out the man who was still trapped inside the collapsed tunnel.

It would take several hours to get him out and it was getting dark. He glanced back to where Prince was tied to a bush, wondering if he should choose a better spot to leave him. As his eyes scanned the area for a suitable place, he noticed that there was no one at the main shaft elevator.

No one.

He looked back at Perkins. The foreman was no longer standing on the coal car but seemed to be engaged in conversation with someone nearby. The crowd was moving into a tighter cluster around Mr. Farris in order to hear what he was saying about the work parties. Everyone had their attentions on the task at hand and even the bosses were busy.

Harlan backed off quietly and moved—unnoticed —toward the main shaft. So... the shifts were back at work. His decision was quick and determined. Without hesitation, he stepped into the unattended elevator and started it on the long, slow decent. A chilling dampness enveloped him as he neared the first tunnel. There was a single light dangling from the entrance but it seemed deserted and quiet.

He continued on.

When Perkins finally satisfied himself that things were well in hand, he headed back to his little office that faced the main shaft. He had a lot on his mind and would have been oblivious to almost anything. Anything except the snorting sounds of a horse blowing out its breath as it grazed. He looked toward the muffled sound and—recognized the animal immediately. He turned to head back in the direction he had just come from.

"Warren!" he called out to one of the guards, standing on the outskirts of the crowd. "Come on over here a minute!" He stopped and waited until the man reached him.

"Yes, sir?"

"You remember that government teacher that was out here a couple weeks ago?"

"The one that belongs to that horse? Yes sir, I sure do. That's some horse."

"Yeah, well, I don't want him around here and I told him that once, already. Now, I see his horse over there and I want you to look through that crowd till you find him. Tell him to get out of here. If he gives you any trouble at all, get Baker or one of the others, and escort him out. Know what I mean?"

"Yes, sir."

"Hurry up about it. I don't want him under the hill no matter who we got trapped down there. Hear?"

"He union or something?"

"He's something." Perkins went back to his office but he couldn't get anything done. He kept going over to the small window to stick his head out, only to find Prince still tied up to the bush. When the guard came back and told him Harlan was nowhere to be found, he swore under his breath and could feel small beads of sweat beginning to break out on his forehead. "He's under the hill, then," he muttered. "This is the last thing I needed, today."

"What's that?" asked the guard.

"I said he's under the hill!" Perkins yelled in sudden anger. "Probably seen an eyeful by now! Get him out of there—hear me? Take two others down the main shaft —find him—and get him back up to this office if you have to hogtie him to do it!"

"You want I should take Luther along?" the guard asked.

"Take Luther."

The secretary sat at her desk, quiet and pale, wondering if she were going to receive the brunt of Perkins' outburst. Her mind went involuntarily over the day's tasks, hoping she had done none of them haphazardly or neglected something that would warrant reprimand.

"Doris Jane?" Perkins said with a chilling calmness.

"Yes, sir?"

"You're looking a little tired. Why don't you go home

early, tonight."

"But, Mr. Perkins, I—I'm not finished with the invoices, yet, and —"

"I said I'd like you to go home. Them invoices will be here tomorrow."

"You mean I ain't fired?"

"Not if you can get gone within the next ten minutes, you aren't."

"I'll go right now," she replied.

"And why are you going home early, Doris Jane?"

"Because I'm real tired, Mr. Perkins."

"I thought you were." He watched as she slipped into her coat and started for the door. "You have a nice evening now, hear?"

"Yes, sir."

Half an hour later, the sun was going down and the first stars of evening were beginning to appear. Perkins went to the window, again, and having looked so many times, already, was startled to finally see someone coming. With townspeople still working at the other shaft, he feared the possibility of a scene but saw with satisfaction that his men had already taken precautions.

The three company guards were nothing more than silhouettes as they made their way quietly to the office. They came inside and Luther—a tall, muscular Swede who towered even above Perkins—dropped the unconscious man he had been carrying over his shoulder, into a chair.

"He gave us a little trouble," one of them explained as their boss looked critically at the blood trickling from Harlan's mouth and nose. "Luther had to... well, you'll still be able to talk to him."

Perkins looked at his watch. "Shift will be over in ten minutes," he said. "Most of the men will be gone pretty quick, or helping over there with the cave-in. After it settles down, I want you boys to take him off the grounds. Still too many town people hanging around."

"Where should we take him?"

"I don't care where you take him!" he snapped. Then he pulled a handkerchief out of his pocket and mopped his forehead. "Long as it's out of sight and earshot."

"We'll teach him good, Boss," Baker promised.

"See that you do. I don't want to worry about him getting up the nerve to try something like this, again. Do it right, and I'll see to it you boys get—"

Harlan stirred and tried to focus his eyes on the shadowy forms in front of him. It was too dark to see faces, but the smell of cigars told him where he was. "Perkins—you monster—you've got eight and nine year olds down there!"

"Real pity you did that, boy," Perkins said as the mine whistle blew a loud short blast to signal the end of the shift. "Trespassing, I mean."

"I saw enough—I saw plenty! I'm going to—"

"Now, you listen here, mister," Perkins grabbed his face in a vice-like grip while the others pinned him to the chair so he couldn't move. "It doesn't make one bit of difference what you saw."

"There will be an investigation," Harlan warned.

"Like hell."

"In a federal court!" He strained against the hands that held him but they only pressed tighter, crushing his ribs against the back of the chair until he could hardly breathe. "You'll face—criminal charges, Perkins! You and anyone else that's in on it —just wait!"

"I don't wait for nobody."

"I'll go the newspapers! Not that company thing they run in Cedarville, either! I'll go to the—"

"Shut up."

"The radio! I'm going to tell every—"

"Gag him, Warren." Perkins took a few steps back while the men did what they were told, and reached for his jacket that hung over the back of a chair by his desk. "I'm going to see how the work parties are coming along. You boys take him out the back way and make sure nobody sees. I don't want to worry about him no more. Hear?"

Luther bent down and ran a rough, greedy hand back and forth over Harlan's face. "Now," he taunted with a grotesque smile, "you gonna dance with the devil, boy."

"Mr. Perkins?" Warren asked suddenly, following him to the door. "What should we do with that horse?"

"Shoot him."

50

Several hours later, the last of the work parties were gathering their things as Jared Henderson was finally carried out on a stretcher. The night was cold and crisp and so clear the sky seemed overly crowded with brightly shining stars. The first frost of the year was coming. The men could see their breath as they stood talking quietly in small groups before heading home, as Lias wandered through the crowd feeling a growing apprehension he couldn't explain.

He walked over to where Aaron was standing with his oldest son. Angus McCord looked like a replica of his father, except that he was about thirty-five years younger and his hair and beard were black.

"You seen Harlan around anywhere?" Lias asked them.

"I ain't seen him since we first got here," Aaron replied, "He wasn't in my work party."

"I seen him, all right," said Angus. "And he wasn't in no work party. Seen him wandering around the main heading just after we all went back to the shift."

"God almighty," Lias breathed. "Are you shore it was him?"

"It was him, all right." Angus bent to spit a stream of tobacco juice off to the side. "He don't exactly look like a working man dressed in them fancy suits he wears. I was gonna ask what he was doing only he was gone by the time I walked to the end of my work room and looked down the main tunnel."

"Lordy—if Perkins found that out," said Aaron, "Harlan probably got his-self escorted off company property without even getting on a work party. My guess, he's back home by now, fit to be tied."

"Harlan's too hot-headed to get off that easy," Lias worried. "He don't know when to keep his mouth shut. Besides, he's been put off once, already."

For a moment they were quiet as each man's mind filled with possibilities and absorbed Lias' concern. Aaron said, "We best stop by Doc's on the way home and make shore. You coming, Lias? Or you heading back with your boys."

"I'm coming. I sent Johnny home after the shift on account of the boy ain't up to no overtime, yet. It's all he can do to put in a full day."

"I'll ride along with you," said Angus. "Case there's trouble. Now I think on it, weren't no company guards at the gate tonight, neither."

"That's a bad sign." Aaron sighed heavily and reached into his pocket for the keys. "Up to no good somewheres."

Tom's cabin was dark.

No one answered the knock but the door was unlocked. Aaron and Angus stepped inside while Lias waited out in the car. But his churning emotions at being so uncomfortably close to Tom's place were quickly becoming overshadowed by a growing concern for Harlan. In a few minutes, the two men were back, again.

"No fire on the hearth," Angus reported. "Don't look like anyone's been home all day. Dog's gone, too."

"Doc must be out on his long circuit," Aaron figured. "Else he would've been down to the coal-works, like he always is when there's a accident."

Lias began to cough and Aaron noticed the handkerchief he held to his mouth was already so blood-covered, it was more red than white. "We best take you on home, Lias" he suggested. "You been out in this cold air too long, already."

"No, let's head for the schoolhouse. Could be he went back there."

"Ain't gonna help for you to kill yourself looking, Uncle Lias," said Angus as he glanced at him over the seat from the driver's side. "Any reason why we should let you?"

"I got a bad feeling about this." Lias returned his handkerchief to his pocket again. "I seen he was headed for trouble, last week, and didn't do nothing to—" He was interrupted by another violent fit of coughing.

Angus started the car and headed for the school.

Fifteen minutes later, their headlights cut a swath in the dark as they bounced and jostled over the play area toward the schoolhouse. There were no signs of anyone there, either. When they made a wide circle to return to the road again, the beam of light washed over the saddle and blanket Harlan kept over the low branch of a tree during the day.

"Hey –" Aaron pointed, "there's his saddle but I don't see the horse nowhere. He don't keep him tied out here, though. Maybe he done wandered off and Harlan's inside."

"He wouldn't be setting in the dark," Angus replied. "Probably just didn't take time to saddle up when he heard the whistle blow this afternoon. Kids say he can ride that horse wide open without even hanging on. He don't need no saddle."

"Better look inside anyhow," Lias said.

Angus pointed the car back toward the schoolhouse, again, and drove it close up to the porch so they could use the headlights to see by. He and his father got out and started up the steps while Lias waited in the car.

"Door's open," murmured Aaron. "Probably left in a holy fright when he heard that whistle blow."

"Got something spilled all over the floor, here. Watch your step, Pa." Angus moved inside ahead of him. "Looks like something was—sweet Jesus—- look at that!"

In a horrifying glare of light that shown through the windows, they saw Harlan's deathly still figure seated at the desk.

His hands were clasped together over a stack of papers, covered by a dark spreading blotch. His bloodied head was thrown back and his jaw slack and gaping, giving the bizarre illusion of a silent unending scream at the heavens. A sheet of white paper was stuck up against his chest with the words NO SCHOOL TODAY written in thick, sticky letters. In blood. Everywhere there was blood.

Aaron was the first to recover and move in close. "Still breathing!" He spoke in an amazed whisper. "Bring one a them blankets out of the back seat. Could be enough time left to pack him over to Granny Harper's place. If we can get this here bleeding stopped."

It was impossible to drive all the way. At the steep, winding trail that led nearly a mile down into a hollow that cut into the gnarly side of Sugar Hill, the three men made a hasty stretcher of blankets and two young saplings. With Angus in the front to carry most of the weight, and the two older men behind, they trudged along the trail for half an hour before finally coming into view of the dim lamplight from Granny Harper's remote little cabin. Though halfway up the mountain, it was at the farthest end of the Bog Hollow. They were met by two dogs the last half of the way, so, when they reached the small clearing that held the deep woods away from the cabin, the old woman was already waiting for them with the door open.

"Just me, Ma," Lias called ahead as they climbed up onto her porch. "We got us some trouble here."

"I figured it was one of you boys." She stepped aside to let them in. "Else them dogs wouldn't have took off on me like that after they heared something. What kind of trouble you got?"

Lias pulled back the blanket. She held a kerosene lamp down close to look over the crumpled, bloody body, and then gave a start when she recognized the suit. "Lias Harper—I ain't doctoring no kin of Tom Bascomb! So, you can just cart him right back to wherever you got him!"

51

"You got to, Ma— Doc's gone and I ain't gonna let this boy die!"

There was no going against Lias if his mind was made up. She turned and started for the loft room with her mouth set in a firm grim line. "You all get him out of them clothes, then," she relented. "Have to cut them off. Lias, go on out to the shed and get the wire cutters. See ifen you can't get that baling wire off from around his hands. Take your time... looks like it's cut clean down to the bone."

They brought in the long wooden table from the kitchen and set it before the fireplace. They laid Harlan down and worked over him beneath the glow of three oil lamps that were placed on the mantle and trimmed to their brightest flames. They did whatever the old woman told them to do – whether it was to get this or warm that – right down to holding two gaping pieces of oozing flesh together as she stitched them closed. More than once, one or the other of them had to step outside for a moment to quell a threatening nausea that no amount of spitting could get rid of.

Granny Harper kept on at a steady deliberate pace. It was no matter to her if this man lived or died. She began with the largest wounds first, dabbing each cut with a thick, poisonous-looking substance that had been heated on the stove. After she had painstakingly taken a hundred and twenty-eight stitches on his head and face alone, and her own back was beginning to ache with all this "bending over effort," Harlan startled them all with a sudden heartrending, convulsive sob. The three men froze.

"He's trying to come around," the Granny woman explained. "I'll give him something for the hurt so's it'll go easier on him. Lias—fetch me that lamp down to the table here and I'll use it to heat this knife." She withdrew a small paring knife from her apron pocket and placed it across the glass chimney. While it was getting hot, she went out to the kitchen and returned a few minutes later with a shallow bowl and a thin sliver of reed with a needle-sharp point.

"Hurry up, Ma," Lias urged. "Boy can't suffer like this for long!"

"Don't rush me, now!" she snapped back. "This here's pure opium. It'll work right quick once it hits the blood but I got to go slow and careful getting it in. Can't take no chances. Too many things to go wrong."

She made a clean, small cut into a vein on the back of one of Harlan's hands. Then, taking the tiny reed in her mouth, she drew up a portion of dark liquid from the bowl, eased the sharpened tip into the vein and blew gently until nearly all of it was gone. Within minutes, he was quiet again.

Three and a half hours after they had first arrived, Granny Harper had done all she knew how to do, except to watch and wait. The men gently eased the quiet form between blankets made up on a cot set into a corner closest to the fire. They returned the table to the kitchen and scrubbed all traces of blood away with strong lye soap, and finally settled down for a while to try and gather their thoughts after the long ordeal. It was nearing midnight.

Aaron sat on the hearth in front of the fire, for once looking all of his seventy-two years. "It's a sad day," he sniffed, wiping his nose with the back of his hand. "It's a sad day when hoods can do something like this to decent folk and get away with it."

"What was he thinking?" Angus filled his pipe from a small pouch of tobacco and tamped it down with his thumb. "Even a outlander ought to know you can't go up against big business that away. No matter how right you are."

"He didn't think they could hurt him," Lias eased himself into an overstuffed chair near the fire. "Thought he had nothing to lose."

"If he wanted that bad to know what was down there, why didn't he ask somebody?" Angus said.

"He's been trying ever since he got here," Aaron reminded them. "Didn't none of us feel like talking."

"I should have told him when he come to me last week," Lias admitted. "Said he was gonna light a fire under the company but I thought he meant to do it by writing a letter to the NLRB and going through legal ways. Testifying, or such."

"Well, he must have done something," said Angus. "Ain't seen the company go this far in a time and a time."

"We been letting them kick us around for a time and a time," Lias answered. "Ma? Quit fussing in that kitchen and go to bed."

"You boys need some nourishment to get home on," she called back to him. "And I'm putting fresh coffee on. Except for you, Lias. You're gonna have sassafras tea."

"I ain't neither. I'm having fresh black coffee just like Angus and the ol' man—you hear me? And I'm too tired to argue."

"Well," Angus looked over to where Harlan was laying quietly in the narrow bed against the wall. "What are we gonna do about it? Get rid of the guards? They'll just bring in more but it would at least be a eye for a eye."

"I think Harlan might have hit on something," Lias answered. "Suppose he found a crack in that company wall nobody knowed about? If we're quick we could maybe bust on through before they can patch it."

"We ain't nothing but rats in that company's grain bin, Uncle Lias," Angus objected. He still had five children at home to raise and he grew uncomfortable at the thought of another protest. "Ain't gonna do no good for us to start scratching on them walls, again."

"You want to let them keep us rats forever?" Lias challenged. "They picked our bosses, our Laws, and even our Mayor. We let them start picking our teachers and we ain't just gonna be living like rats all our lifetime—we're gonna start breeding rats! The mess will go on forever."

"Lordy!" Aaron shuddered. "That sends the shivers right to my bone!"

"Way I see it," Lias went on, "This boy done us a favor. It's sort of like we been woke out of a sound sleep by somebody hollering fire. Maybe we don't like how he hollered. But we got to put out the fire."

"Just how are we gonna do that?" Angus asked.

Lias reached for his own tobacco and began rolling himself a cigarette as he thought for a moment. "First we got to call for a Gathering of the Clans. Get everybody together as soon as we can before winter sets in."

"You got something particular in mind?" Aaron asked.

"Yep."

"Well, they all gathered for your daddy back in 'twenty-eight. I reckon they'll come for you, too."

"They'll come." Angus looked at Lias with a knowing twinkle in his eyes. "If for no other reason than he done struck nothing but terror in these hills for the past thirty years."

"Coffee's hot." Granny shuffled in with the pot and several mugs on a large platter. "And I got some cold meat and biscuit-bread to go along." She handed a mug to each man and then returned to the kitchen for the food.

"Now look at that!" Lias in disgust. "Mine's sassafras!"

"Ah, drink it up, Lias," Aaron advised. "You ain't gonna win, nohow, and we're way late for home already."

"I reckon I'll stay here and help Ma watch," Lias said. "Least till we know if he's gonna live or die. Will you stop by and tell Ceely for me?"

"Shore, I don't mind," Aaron replied. "But what about Bonnie Rae? She's gonna want —"

"Tell her to stay put or there's gonna be trouble," her father warned.

"Lias, them kids was made for each other. Can't you see that?"

"She stays home."

"What if he don't pull through?"

"Wouldn't help none to have her watch."

"Don't he deserve something?"

"I'll do everything I can for him. I'll stand in till Doc gets back. I'll keep him here, deep in Harper land, and set my brothers to watch so the company don't get at him again. But he can't have my baby, Aaron. If he comes out of this, he'll want to be taking off for the outside. And I don't blame him. I'll even help him go. But he shore ain't taking her with him. That's where I draw the line."

He set his empty mug on the hearth edge, and tossed the end of his cigarette into the fire. "He's a good man, all right, but he's a furiner any way you look at it. They never stay."

"Doc stayed."

"And he crossed me."

"I don't think he never meant —"

"Leave it lay, Aaron."

52

For Harlan, there was a time of shapes and shadows and voices too far away to be understood. Sometimes it was dark—and in that dark—lurked a fear so powerful it snatched his breath away. Sometimes he floated peacefully through half shadows, high and drifting, like gray dawn breaking but never quite breaking through. There were kind faces and tender gestures that came and went through darkness and sun, darkness and sun, and sometimes his head pounded so painfully, his entire body trembled under the strain.

And he dreamed.

He dreamed of a valley that seemed to stretch out endlessly, where Prince was running wild and free against the sky... his dark mane flying... flying. The horse came close a few times, prancing and whinnying the way he did when he wanted Harlan to come out of the schoolhouse and go home.

Then there were angry jeering voices and that continuous racking pain. His hands were tied with something that cut like razor when he moved—he couldn't get away from it. Why didn't they just kill him? He couldn't take anymore. "No more!" he moaned over and over again. "No more!"

Lias listened to the tortured pleading for a moment and then got up from the supper table. "Sounds like he's coming around this time, Ma."

"Could be the fever's broke, then." She got up to head for the stove. "About time. Any longer and I'd be worried it went to the brain. Go on in, Lias, and I'll get some more mixture ready."

Harlan's eyes opened slowly and moved over the unfamiliar surroundings with a mounting dread. When he saw the shadowy form approaching him, his breath came in short, quick gasps and he cried, "No—don't—"

"Harlan," Lias put a steadying hand on his shoulder, "It's all right, boy. Ain't nobody after you no more."

"Lias?" he whispered tentatively, "Lias!"

"Take it easy, now."

He lifted a trembling hand that was criss-crossed with dark stitches around the wrist, and clutched weakly at the older man's shirt to draw him closer. Lias bent down to listen to the hoarsely spoken, grief-stricken words. "They—they shot Prince! Lias—they killed my—" The voice dwindled into such sorrowful heartfelt weeping that Lias felt his own throat beginning to tighten.

"I'm right sorry, boy," he replied quietly. "I'm shore sorry to hear that!"

"Like he was nothing! And he took so long to —to—" A violent shudder passed through him and his body began to shake. Before he lost the fleeting hold on consciousness, he could hear strange rising cries. Terrible sounds that followed him down and down to a frightening darkness.

They were his own.

"It's starting, again," Lias said as his mother came up beside him with the shallow bowl and the reed. "Knocked him right out. What's that mean, Ma?"

"I don't rightly know." She reached for Harlan's hand and searched for a vein she hadn't already cut before. "But I'm afeared—the way it sets him to shaking this away—it might could be something permanent."

Lias didn't say anything. He walked over to the hearth and

picked up the poker to stir the coals before adding another piece of wood to the fire. Instead, he stood motionless for a long time, just staring into the dying flames.

"You know, Lias," his mother observed, gently touching a cool wet cloth to Harlan's bruised head as she spoke, "I ain't seen you take on this way since the night you run that car of yours off the mountain and Gordie McBride lost his leg. You done stayed here nigh onto a week, remember? Kept his family in winter meat for... I disremember... how long did you do it for?"

"Still do," he replied quietly.

"Well, you done growed up with Gordie McBride and I reckon them boyhood feelings run purty deep. But I can't figure what this stray pup of a outlander done to get under your wing. I shore can't figure that."

"I let him walk head on into this thing, Ma. Because of who he was. Seemed he was standing like fire for everything that beat me. And he was getting a hold on my family, too. Just the way Doc done. Told myself I weren't gonna fall for the same thing twice, and I.... I shore could see it coming with Harlan."

"Didn't see it coming fast enough, looks to me like," she observed.

"I seen it all right. So, I told him enough to scare him, pushed him a little toward home because I knowed he wasn't staying anyhow. Decided to let him flounder for a spell, only..." Lias jabbed at the fire with a vengeance, put on another log and tossed the poker aside.

"Only the car went over the cliff," the old woman finished for him, settling into her rocker, near the roaring blaze.

"He didn't scare! I give him a peek at the devil and what's he do? Instead of running for home, the kid hollers war—charges head-on all by his-self—- and hits hell wide open!" He shook his head, as if he still couldn't believe it. "I never meant for nothing like that to happen."

"Don't mean you have to let him into the family, Lias."

She reached for the pipe she carried in her apron pocket. "He ain't no kin of ourn."

"I ain't gonna let him in." He took the pipe to fill and light for her as he talked. "But the boy don't have nobody else, Ma. Doc's likely off till the first snow."

"Doc don't deserve nothing from this family!" She said the words so vehemently the wispy ends of her white hair that stuck out from beneath her hat trembled. "I don't understand you that way, Lias! My boy's gone—and your pap—"

"Don't start in on that, Ma." He handed the pipe back to her with a thin wisp of fragrant smoke wafting up from the bowl. "Harlan didn't have nothing to do with them things. It's in the past."

"It ain't never gonna be in the past for me! I might as well tell you here and now…" She bit down hard on the pipe stem, as if it were a tonic instead of a treat. "I'm tending him only on account of you brung him!"

"I know."

"Don't pleasure me none to have any kin of Tom Bascomb's in my house. Even if it was God."

"Don't you think I want him gone, too?" He sat down wearily on the hearth and felt the comforting heat of the new blaze absorb into the back of his dark flannel shirt. "But he opened my eyes to some things I needed to look at. That ought to be worth something."

"Whatever it's worth," she snapped, "I reckon it'll take the rest of your lifetime to pay."

"I said, I'm gonna help him," he insisted. "Not take him in."

Granny Harper got to her feet with a sudden need to do something peaceful, like clearing her dishes away in the kitchen.

"You hear me, Ma?" Lias called after her as she shuffled away from him. "I'm not gonna bring no furiner into the family, again!"

"You already done it, Lias," came the reply.

53

Lias stayed at the little cabin in Bog Hollow until Harlan could sit up and feed himself and no longer thought every approaching shadow was another company guard. When the stitches were finally removed, Lias carefully shaved the still tender places of his face with a straight razor, leaving a dark mustache that covered the worst of the longest scar. The effect was startling. The once smooth features took on a more rugged handsomeness, and the long dark hair and mustache set off the pale blue eyes with a magnetic intensity.

Lias helped him dress in clothes that had belonged to his brother, Buck. They were typical mountain attire that consisted of a plaid shirt over long cotton underwear, jeans, and a leather hat for outside. Afterward—from all outward appearances —Harlan looked like any number of men who had been born and raised in Cedar Creek. But on the inside he was shattered.

The painful spells, though they had become less frequent, had not let up in their intensity. Two and three times a day, they racked his entire head with almost unbearable suffering until the soothing effects of the opium dulled his nerves. His lack of resistance to fight off the attacks upset him more, and the debilitating moans he was reduced to before the strong drug took over, filled him with shame. Granny Harper seemed to make him wait longer each time, holding back the desperately needed relief with a grim, immovable firmness that he was at a loss to understand. He wanted to leave her harsh looks and that little cabin in the dark, deep woods, but he couldn't. He did not think he could live without the small shallow bowl and reed the old woman so constantly brought to him.

It was different with Lias. In him, Harlan found a kind of acceptance he had never known. A kind that did not depend on his actions or who he was. He did not have to earn it. With it came a compassion that went beyond the mere duty of one man helping another. There were strong feelings between them that he couldn't quite place. Where had they come from? These feelings that showed up in little ways.

In the way the older man stayed up with him at night when the spells were especially bad. Or like pouring his coffee when he was shaking too much to pour his own. Or by simply talking about the weather after Harlan had just gone to emotional pieces before the opium took effect.

It was nine long days before Lias finally decided it was time to go home. Each morning, the thick heavy frost had lingered a little longer on the barren branches of bushes and trees. Any day might bring the first snow and he did not want to be here when Tom arrived. Someone along his route home might have told him already and he could be on his way even now.

Nearly everyone on the ridge would know by now.

For over a week, Aaron and three of his sons had combed the hills and hollows for miles around to announce the Gathering that was to be held at the schoolhouse the following evening. Harlan was well enough to take care of himself, now, and Lias only stayed on longer because the young man still seemed to need him somehow. Yet, seeing him improve a little more each day began to ease the weight of responsibility and Lias was anxious to get back to his family. Until now, he had seen no one but Big John, who had visited several times, delivering news and messages and special food that Celia had sent along.

Waiting for him on the evening he left, Lias sat in the overstuffed chair, smoking a cigarette while Harlan lay stretched out on the hearth rug, staring up at the ceiling. The old woman was already in bed. Not that she was in the habit of retiring so early: she still only spent as much time with Harlan as she was forced to.

"I reckon you'll be wanting to head back to Richmond, now," Lias began the serious subject casually.

"There's nothing left for me in Richmond," Harlan replied.

"Wherever it is you were headed, then," Lias corrected himself. "I reckon you'll be wanting to get on with it."

"I was waiting for a visa clearance to China. I got an approval to run a small refugee school on the Burmese border. But it's in a war zone."

The news caught Lias off guard. Did this man have nothing better to do than run from one desperate situation to another? After a few moments of—once again—trying to figure out Harlan Fleming, he gave up and said the first thing that came to his mind. "I heard on the radio the President was calling all Americans to come out of them places."

"The missionaries are still there. For a while, anyway. The mission board waived the restrictions because I'm already familiar with the customs and the language. I grew up there. Stayed until I was ten."

"When's this here clearance supposed to come through?"

"Anytime. But I took the position in Cedar Creek on the understanding that I would complete the entire year." He turned tortured eyes toward Lias. "I would have finished out the year."

"You started something good, Harlan," the older man's voice was comforting. "Well see it gets finished."

"Lias..." He sat up and leaned back against the hearth with his forearms resting across drawn up knees. "They said they'd kill me if I didn't get out of Cedar Creek."

"Nigh onto killed you anyhow. You done a brave thing, going against them on your own like that. Derned foolish. But brave."

"I wasn't brave! I groveled and begged! I even said I was sorry!"

"You didn't mean it."

"I did when I said it. I lost every ounce of self-respect I ever had! If I can't even stand to face myself in a mirror anymore, how can I face anybody else?"

"Might seem that way now," Lias reassured, "But I reckon after a time, when you're starting your new life in China…"

"I can't go to China, now. What good would I be like this? What good am I to anybody, like this?"

"Few days ago, I weren't so shore, neither. But you're starting to hold your own."

"Only because of this!" He turned the backs of his hands toward Lias to expose the tiny, scratch-like cuts they were covered with. "How do you explain these to a school board? Much less the elders of a church!"

"Never put much store in that church and elder business, myself. What a man does is between him and his Maker. Way I see it, that there opium's a Godsend when you're suffering a killing pain. It can see you through. You need it now—all right—but it ain't always gonna be that way, Harlan. And Ma's been at these things for a long time. She knows when to take it away."

"Take it away?" He felt suddenly worried at the thought. "I can't get through one of those things without it! You tell her that, Lias, she'll listen to you! Will you tell her before you leave tonight?"

"She knows what she's doing."

"She does, and she'll just let me die!"

Lias got to his feet and tossed the end of his cigarette into the fire. "I don't deny she's against you but she promised to do everything she could to make you well. And she will. My brothers are close by, they'll look in, now and again, to make sure."

"I wish you weren't leaving."

"Gathering of the Clans tomorrow. Every man over fifteen from here to the Wind Ridge ought to turn out. That's a lot of people gonna pick up where you left off."

"Don't leave yet, Lias."

"Boy—I've got a family to take care of. Now, this is Harper land—this whole, deep holler. I got five brothers and their families living round about it, and don't nothing come or go without them knowing. You're safe as long as you want to stay. And when you're ready for that train, I'll—"

"I don't want any train!"

"What do you want, then?"

"I want my kids out from under that hill!" he said with a fervent stubbornness.

"I'm working on it."

"And if I can get well, I want my school back, again."

"Ain't you had enough, yet?" Lias picked up the poker and began to jab at the fire with a restless impatience. "Them company boys know just what they're doing—that's why they're hired for! You weren't killed on account of they didn't mean you to be. But I'm telling you, if you keep pushing things you ain't gonna be that lucky, again. Is that what you want?"

"I want you and I to be on the same side," the young teacher confessed quietly. "And most of all..." He reached out and clasped the rough, work-worn hand without turning his head to face him. "Most of all I want to thank you for everything you've done. For being my friend and treating me like one of your own. Even when we disagreed. You're a good man, Lias Harper."

It was impossible—after the many days of physical care and concern Lias had already given him— not to respond. He returned the handclasp with a spontaneous, genuine affection, and suddenly—in that moment—realized the same thing his mother had sensed the first night he was here.

Harlan Fleming had won him over.

He sighed irritably at himself. "Another derned furiner! I hope I ain't gonna live to regret it."

"You won't," Harlan assured. "I'll stand by whatever you decide. I'd even stay in Cedar Creek, Lias—if I get well. And if I do…"

Their eyes met and held.

The last thread of contention between them was being weighed in the balance, and both of them knew that the decision of that moment would be final. Whatever words Lias Harper was about to pronounce, he would stand on for a lifetime. The pause was long and uncomfortable.

"Please," Harlan whispered.

Lias pointed a warning finger at him and said emphatically, "Boy—don't you never—never—cross me!"

"I won't," Harlan promised quickly, "I swear it."

"Well, all right, then." He walked across the room and reached for his jacket and hat that were hanging on a peg near the door. "I reckon it's settled. I'll let you know how the Gathering comes. And… I'll send Bonnie Rae."

"Not yet," he protested just as quickly, though he could hardly contain the sudden wave of relief that washed over him. "Only if I get well. I don't want her to see me like this. I don't want anyone to see me like this! Especially Bonnie Rae."

"Might be a time and a time before you're rid of them spells altogether, Harlan," Lias spoke the words honestly. "Truth is, it might could be—"

"I'll wait."

54

Two days later on a Sunday afternoon, Big John Harper made his way along the steep winding trail to his grandmother's cabin. He climbed up on the sagging wooden porch, made a mental note to fix it for her next spring, stomped mud from his shoes, and stepped into the warm inside.

"Hey, Granny —" he called out cheerily toward the kitchen where he could hear her banging pots and pans with an unusual energy, "you got enough for one more at supper?"

"I got enough for the whole bunch if I could ever get them all out here at once. When you gonna bring that new bride of yours out to visit your old Granny?"

"Soon as I can." He tossed his cap onto one of the hanging pegs at the door and sat down at the table. "I'd have brung her today if things was like usual around here." He cast her a calculating glance as she came to set a cup of coffee in front of him. "Are they getting any more like usual?"

"No, they ain't." She heaped three teaspoons of sugar into a cup for herself and sat down at the table across from him. Whenever this grandson looked at her that way, she couldn't tell him anything but the truth. "And speaking of such, you seen Hoddie around out there anywhere?"

"Hoddie? Nope. Ain't seen him since the sugar party.

Why?"

"Because." She took the pipe from her mouth that had long since gone out and stashed it in the pocket of her apron. "He's been sneaking around this cabin like as if it was a haint! I hollered at him, a while ago, to come in and eat with us but he run off like a scairt rabbit. I just can't figure it. Hoddie's been visiting me once or twice a week ever since he could climb a fence. What do you suppose got into the boy, Big John?"

"Probably just trying to catch a look at Harlan without getting caught. Eight years old, a feller can set a heap of store by his teacher. Especially one like Harlan. Hey—where is he, anyhow? Got some things I want to tell him about."

"Out in the shed I expect." She got up suddenly, left her coffee untouched, and returned to the pie she had been making with renewed fervor. "Probably in the little loft place over the goat pen."

"What's he doing out there? Milking's over till spring, ain't it?"

The old woman didn't reply.

Big John set down the coffee he had been sipping on and studied her carefully. "Granny," he said, "you ain't been having words with him, have you?"

"I'm baking him a right fine apple pie, here. Would I be doing that if we was having words?"

"I reckon you'd be doing it after you had words," he guessed. "What were they about?"

"What do you think they was about?" she snapped. "I done took him off the opium, that's what. Last night was the first and he was fit to be tied. I give him laudanum but they's only traces of it in there, and it don't do nothing like the other. He had a spell coming on a while ago, and—well—we had words. He lit out for the loft. Ain't seen him since."

"I reckon I best go on out there."

"Don't think he'd want company."

"Well..." He crossed the kitchen, fairly filling the little room with his height and presence and hardly had to raise his arm to open the cupboard above her stove. "Sometimes…" He lifted a brown clay jug from the top shelf, "Company comes calling unexpected and a body just has to make the best of it." He flashed her a reassuring smile and headed for the door.

The little goat shed that stood behind the cabin was chilly inside even though it was built stout and strong. Must be loose boards somewhere, Big John mused. A white, silky-coated goat lifted her head from the oats she was munching to watch him enter, and gave a friendly "baaa" in recognition. "Howdy, Annabelle," he whispered as he passed.

He could hear muffled moans and labored breathing before he began to climb the ladder to the narrow hayloft above her. "Harlan?" he spoke gently and placed a careful hand on the trembling form. "It's me—Big John. I brung something that'll help. Come on, now, take a swallow or two of this."

Without looking to see what it was, Harlan reached out trembling hands toward the proffered jug and drank desperately. Suddenly, he was choking and gasping on the fiery liquid, and— though he had never tasted mountain whiskey before—he knew exactly what it was. He shoved the jug back toward Big John.

"Oh—oh—Lord, it hurts!" He clutched his head in his hands and lay back in the hay, again.

"Come on, take her down, boy," Big John slipped a forearm beneath Harlan's shoulders and raised him up again, as if he had been a child instead of a grown man who was fairly tall and broad himself. "Try again. Ain't no use to fight alone if you don't have to."

Harlan drank.

Twenty minutes later, the worst was over and the trembling was fading into a deep tiredness. He lay with his eyes closed for a while, knowing John was there but unable to look at him. "Well," he finally spoke quietly, "now you know what I've been doing for the past two weeks."

"Shoot," came the gentle reply, "you're doing a heap better than the last time I seen you during one of these."

"When did you see me?"

"I been here a couple times. Shore was a intolerable wait through the first two days. Thought maybe you wouldn't pull through. Bonnie Rae's been half out of her mind, Harlan."

"I don't want her here."

"Her and Daddy been going round and round about that. But she's staying put. So far, anyhow. I had to tote her back once, first night she heard. But that was natural."

"She came here?"

"Naw, I caught up to her halfway. All the kids been asking for you, too. Had to close down the school." He looked for long moments at the incredible change that had taken place in a man who now seemed to resemble some legendary embodiment of every ridge runner that ever lived and died on the mountain. Must be the clothes, he thought with a near reverent amazement… and wondered fleetingly if something of his Uncle Buck's spirit had come back with the wearing of them.

Then he wondered what kind of man this was who could so give himself up for the miseries of others. Suddenly, he had to know. "What made you do it, Harlan?" He finally ventured. "When wouldn't none of us do it ourselves."

For a long time there was no reply.

After a while, Harlan sat up slowly and looked over at the magnificent man with his striking good looks, sitting only a few feet away from him. His feet were propped up on top of the ladder, and his back rested casually against the wall. "I guess I didn't realize what I was up against," he said at last.

He looked out the little open window beside them, where a cold draft was blowing in, and could see nothing but tree-tops. "Something came over me when I found out there were more than just the older boys down there. I had no idea there were so many young ones. Did you know that, John? They're using them to pick coal out of slag heaps all day long."

"Yep."

"Doesn't that tear at you?"

"Not like seeing one gunshot for helping his folks in the

whiskey business."

"Tom told me they will shoot at children," Harlan admitted. "But I had a hard time believing it of law officers."

"Well, they do," John's voice bore a trace of bitterness at the thought. "Lost one of my own cousins that way, a while back. Ten years old. Shot by a revenuer when she tried to warn the folks."

"Such a little girl!" Harlan was shocked.

"Holly June Harper. You got one of her brothers in the school. Hoddie."

"Hoddie's sister? John, I—"

"Little angel of a thing that loved everything purty. Never even knew what hit her. Liked to killed her mama to lose her. She ain't been the same since."

"I don't know what to say." He shook his head miserably. "Except that there's got to be something we can do about all this. Something!"

"Well," John picked up the brown jug and took a long swallow himself before answering. "Daddy come up with a plan that's like to make your head spin. Laid it all out at the Gathering, last night."

"Were there many people there?"

"Nigh onto every man in the county. Excepting my wayward brother that's making and running whiskey somewhere on this mountain this very minute and too ashamed to show up."

"I'm sorry to hear that, John."

"You and me both. But you should have seen Daddy, Harlan. It was just like in the old days. Shoot, he shore can turn a crowd if he's a mind to."

"What's the plan? And what if they don't get behind it?"

"They'll get behind it," he assured. "Makes sense. First thing we're gonna do…" He took another drink and sat for a long moment without saying anything.

"Is…" Harlan prompted, beginning to warm to the news.

"Is call a strike. Nobody's going to work come Monday."

"Thank God!" Harlan whispered. And then emphatically, "Oh, John—John! It's the right thing to do, you'll see."

"Had me go down and post notices up all over Cedarville about holding a town meeting next week. Got something up his sleeve for that, too, but he ain't telling just yet. Anyhow, the shot's been fired and it's anybody's guess where it'll hit. No matter how things go, though, it shore is good to have him back. I'm obliged to you, Harlan."

"I don't know what for."

"It's all on account of you, that's what for. You got to him, boy. You're the first to do that since... well, since a time and a time."

"I 'd like to see him at that town meeting."

"Ain't no reason why you can't."

"Yes, there is."

"Listen, here. After Daddy told your story at the Gathering, ain't a man in Cedar Creek wouldn't protect you with his life, Harlan. Me included."

The words caused a feeling of inadequacy and despair to flood over the young teacher. He looked away, started to run a self-conscious hand through his hair, and covered his eyes instead. He felt his emotions rising to the surface and for a moment was afraid he might break down.

"Hey," Big John said gently, "Granny was rustling something up in the kitchen when I come—- looked like a pie. Let's go on in and have some."

"You go. She could use the company."

"Don't think she'd cut into it unless you was there, since she made it for you."

"She couldn't have." Harlan looked back at him. "Not after what I said to her before I came out here. She must have seen you coming."

"Nope. It's for you, all right. But, just out of curiosity, what did you say to her? Couldn't have been too bad if it earned you one of Granny's pies. They're famous around these parts."

"I told her the truth," he said with a sudden fierce conviction. "I told her she was a hard-hearted, bitter old woman who doesn't mind seeing people suffer— maybe even enjoys it! Especially when it happens to be an outsider."

"Lord almighty, Harlan," Big John was shocked at such words coming from a man he thought so refined. "Shoot, you didn't really say that to her, did you?"

"I've said worse than that between last night and today. She's just plain stubborn! Won't give an inch."

"Not with opium, she won't."

Harlan was startled that he knew but the surprise only lasted for a moment before the sudden need to confide in someone made it fade. "I thought I was going to die last night, John! And if I had—she would have just sat right there and watched me!"

"But you didn't."

"That's not the point," he argued. "If I was one of the family, she would have done something about it. I begged her— begged her, John—and she wouldn't do a thing!"

"She give in once already," John explained quietly. "Had a younger brother name Ellis, way back before my time. Gut-shot during a blood war. She got to feeling pitiful sorry about the way he was suffering and she give in to him. That was near forty years ago. She ain't never give in to nobody since. And there's been a heap of others between him and you."

"What'd he do—turn into a raving opium addict and embarrass the family for the rest of his life?" Harlan's tone was cynical. "Well, maybe—considering his choices—that didn't look so bad to him."

"He died."

Harlan was stunned by the unexpected words and, once again, could find nothing to say. Why did he keep coming head to head with these things, only to find there was some dreadfully unbearable reason for them all? What kind of curse hovered over these mountains that held such a grip on every corner?

"Granny's hard all right," John admitted, "always has been. That's on account of she seen a lot of suffering in her time and most of it was her own kin. But you're wrong about her being hard-hearted. She's the kind that treats a body like kin the minute they walk through her door. Now..."

He drew himself up to his full six-feet-nine inches, and looked down at Harlan with a glimmer of the same authority he had seen in Lias. "She done baked you a pie and you best come eat it."

55

On a chilling, windswept night, a few days later, Big John climbed down out of the truck where he had parked behind the Cedarville Town Hall. Lias had taken a fit of coughing about five minutes before they arrived and his son waited patiently for him to get over it, thinking it was a bitter night for a sick man to be out in. Other cars and trucks continued to arrive as he stood there, most of the faces familiar and many of them family.

Inside, the large room was so packed with people they were standing along the walls and gathering at the back. There were several chairs up near the podium where the Sheriff and deputies were sitting. Henry Perkins was there, dressed in a clean white shirt and sitting next to Mayor Ainsley.

The tall, burly mayor was wearing an imported tweed suit. His hair was a distinguished shade of gray and curly, and it was easy to see that—even in the present hard times— he had not denied himself any luxury. He sat next to Sheriff Harrigan, the two of them commenting to each other from time to time as if an impromptu town meeting were an ordinary occurrence.

At seven o'clock, Lias stepped behind the podium and looked over the room. It was the largest crowd he had ever stood before. Feeling unnerved by the many eyes upon him, he took off his hat and surprised even himself by saying, "I'd like to start by having us all sing *America the Beautiful*."

"We didn't come here for a community sing, Harper," the Sheriff said. "Let's just get on with the civic matters and Company grievances."

"Now, isn't it just like a sheriff to want to be on the job at all hours!" laughed the Mayor, getting to his feet. "I think we could all enjoy singing that heart-moving song of our sweet country. Especially during election month! Stand up, everybody and lead on, Mr. Harper."

The hats came off, every man in the place got to his feet and there wasn't one that didn't recall the beloved words. Whether from Cedar Creek or Cedarville, whether rich or poor, they all knew the song from their young days when they still believed in those words.

And crowned thy good
with brotherhood
from sea to shining sea.

Everyone sat down. The room grew quiet and Lias looked out at the faces. "I ain't never seen either of them shining seas," he began. "But that don't worry me none. I want to know where the brotherhood's gone. I want to know which one of us here turned our backs when they dropped the first man's wage to fourteen cents a hour when they was digging and selling more coal than any other time in this nation's history!"

He paused a moment for effect, and then said, "I want to know who to blame for sending the first child under the hill when there was able-bodied men that could have gone instead. I'm gonna be the first to confess to this here community, tonight... that I did. And I'm here to make it right.

"It's a fact," he declared. "I put my name to the paper that brought in the union agents that caused us all a lot of grief. I put my own kids under the hill to try and make it through the hard times—and when that weren't enough—I made and run illegal whiskey, thinking I had a right."

Harrigan leaned toward the mayor and whispered, "Did you all hear that? That was a confession!"

"Be quiet,Earl," Ainsley whispered back. "The man isn't saying anything we don't all already know."

"It's a confession," Harrigan muttered to himself and took a small pad and pencil from his shirt pocket. "In front of witnesses and I'm going to write it down."

"Like I say," Lias continued, "I thought I had a right to do wrong, since everybody else was doing it, too. I was fooled. And who fooled me? These men up here?" He pointed to the row of officials behind him. "No, sir. I don't recollect that Perkins here ever came knocking at my door to twist my arm till I went to work for the company. And I sure never heard of no blockader taking the Laws to court for busting up his still and putting a stop to his illegal business." He rubbed a thoughtful hand over his chin. "Why, it even occurs to me that—much as I've complained about this man here," he pointed to Ainsley, "setting himself up to be mayor—"

"Now just a minute —" Ainsley objected.

"I don't recall," Lias went on, "ever having troubled myself to come down off the mountain to vote for someone else, instead. Nope.I can't in no way say I was fooled by any of these men up here. But I was fooled by something to end up under a Judas Tree like this. Well, I give it some thought. Then it come to me!" He leaned over the podium as far as he could, stared boldly into the faces of the crowd and said, "Fool's Gold."

There was a baffled silence while men tried to make a mental connection between Fool's Gold and striking for higher wages. Even the Cedar Creek people shifted uncomfortably, worrying that Lias had finally gone too far. Sheriff Harrigan— having been busy writing down the confession—missed most of what was said and was now looking around trying to figure out what was going on.

"Now, Fool's Gold," said Lias, "don't look like a lump of coal, it looks like gold. It shines like gold. And I'll vow, it's them shiny half-truths that'll get a man every time. Don't know too many men that'll fall for a out and out lie. But if there's a little bit of truth in it for a man to recognize—I swear—it'll take the majority every time!"

He smacked a fist down on the podium for emphasis. "That's just what happened here! The hard times come along, and following right behind was this rumor that the only people who was getting by was the ones that was doing a little wrong on the sly. And back in them dark days didn't nothing have a purtier shine than money. Do like the men that had it and you could have it yourself.

"Run a little whiskey, your kids could get shoes. Able-bodied man in your family gets kilt or can't work no more, put one of your boy children down under the hill to take his place. You want to run the company under the Guard System when the government says it ain't legal..." Now he turned around to look Harrigan directly in the face. "Just pay the sheriff a little extra every month to look the other way."

Harrigan got to his feet and pointed an indignant finger. "That is slander!"

"And if you want to get yourself elected into a public office," Lias finished loudly over the protest, "Just pay a poor man five dollars to vote you in!"

"I'm going to have to agree with the Sheriff," said the Mayor. "If this sort of talk is the public statement you called us all here to listen to, then—"

A camera flashed without warning, and the thought of his campaign smile twisted into an angry grimace and plastered on the front page of the morning papers, made Harrigan sink back into his seat, again.

"Please." Now it was Ainsley who held up a hand. "If the press would kindly hold off on pictures until after the meeting."

"It's the truth," Lias went on as if he were unaware of the

discomfort he was causing the officials behind him. "Every man has the right to choose if he's gonna do right or do wrong. But it's an honest-to-God lie to think doing wrong will get you anywheres! The song we just sung said the good would be crowned with brotherhood. The Bible says there ain't no peace for the wicked nowhere! So, I see it as purely logical that we'd end up with the kind of situation we got here."

"He hasn't said a logical thing since he got up there," muttered Harrigan.

"He's right," Perkins spoke up from the mayor's other side. "We didn't come to hear some backwoods mountaineer preach us a sermon on the good life!"

"I seen a lot of farming in my time," Lias said. "But I have yet to see a farmer plant his field with seed corn and then watch for a good crop of tobacco to shoot up. But—it's a fact—there ain't a day goes by no more that I don't see somebody doing wrong and waiting for some good to come out of it! If a man plants evil it shouldn't be no surprise when evil crops up all around.

"The situation we got now in this community ain't nothing more than the results of dishonesty and illegal business that each man here has been allowing to go on for the longest kind of a time!" Then his eyes shown with a fervent zeal as he declared to the citizens before him, "We done—all of us—sowed ourselves a whirlwind! And now we got to reap the storm."

He paused and even the officials behind him were quiet this time. "On behalf of the citizens of Cedar Creek," Lias finally pronounced, "I do solemnly and officially declare a strike on the *Black Star Coal Works* until such a time as the following conditions are met! First, abolition of the Guard System. Second, the formation of a employee's committee that can choose and appoint checkweighmen and foremen. Third, graduated pay raises till such time as the coal miner's wage reaches the national average."

Perkins burst out laughing.

"And finally," said Lias, "removal of all children from under the hill."

"All right," Ainsley replied as if a great weight had suddenly been lifted off him. "The statement has officially been made, gentlemen. We'll allow a few minutes, now, for—

"I ain't come to the civic matters," said Lias.

"I want to hear those civic matters," replied Harrigan.

"All right," Ainsley relented. "But we'd appreciate if you wouldn't drag things out."

"I'll get right to the point, your honor," Lias promised. "Being there ain't enough citizens in Cedar Creek to hold much bargaining power—"

"That's the first thing you said all night that makes any sense, Harper," said Perkins.

"We would like to publicly remind the company that there ain't no county roads in Cedar Creek. Therefore, in accordance with the strike, we are withdrawing the use of these privately owned roads to company traffic till further notice."

"Can he do that?" Perkins whispered to Ainsley.

"He can't do anything we can't get by, one way, or the other," the mayor whispered back.

"Furthermore, we would also like to remind the company that four miles of the railroad track laid down for the new shaft, is also on private land and will have to be moved. Use rights being denied there, too."

A murmur of surprise moved over the crowd, and hushed whispers and comments began to hum between friends.

"Now, with the situation in town being what it is," Lias raised his voice to be heard over the noise, "and due to the fact we ain't foolish enough to expect these property rights will be upheld by the local Laws, we do hereby publicly and officially announce a boycott on the town of Cedarville until such time as Judge Chamberlain is restored as rightful mayor of this county, and a man that's big enough to keep and enforce the whole law, is properly elected to the office of sheriff."

Now, an explosion of exclamation broke over the crowd.

"All right! All right!" Harrigan stood on top of his chair

and shouted to be heard above the roar. "This sham of a town meeting has gone far enough!"

"It certainly has," agreed the Mayor. "You can't declare a boycott on this town, Harper. Why, that would be like laying siege to your own city."

"*If thy right hand offend thee, cut it off!*" Lias quoted.

"How will you eat? How will you trade? The small number of people you have behind you will render the whole thing ineffective."

"Alone, we got meager fare," Lias admitted. "But by pooling our paychecks together we had enough to have over three boxcars of winter supplies sent in from Princeton to get us by on."

The Mayor rose slowly to his feet and looked over the crowd for the familiar face of a well-known railroad employee. "Sam Hodges?"

"Over here, sir."

"That true?"

"Yes, sir. Three and a half boxcars come in this morning, chuck plumb full of winter staples for Cedar Creek."

"Didn't you find that to be somewhere out of the ordinary, mister?"

"Well, I—"

"I hope you had the good sense to put a hold on that merchandise. For tax purposes."

"Lord sakes, Mr. Mayor, I never heard of such a thing!" The man's face began to redden at the accusation. "They claimed and collected it all as soon as it come in."

"As for the small number of people…" Lias turned around to look directly at Ainsley. "We had a Gathering last Saturday night and took count. We got four hundred and thirty-four, counting all them that come down out of the hills. Which don't count the forty percent we figure we got here in town that are willing to back us."

"That's ridiculous!" objected Harrigan.

Lias turned back to address the crowd. "Can I have a show

of hands from all you townfolk that got kin in Cedar Creek?"

Hands went up all over the room. When the deputy who was seated beside Harrigan raised his hand, a look of total disgust spread over the Sheriff's face.

The deputy shrugged. "Blood's thicker than water," he replied to the accusing glare.

"We're gonna tear down what's rotten in this county and start over!" Lias declared with a sudden, vibrant zeal.

A resounding wave of applause and approval went up.

"We're gonna do things right!" he shouted.

The applause grew louder and men began standing up all over the room.

"We're gonna lift up our heads and be proud of what we are, again!" he cried emphatically.

People began stamping their feet in a deafening rhythm on the wooden floor.

"Hold it—hold it!" yelled the Sheriff as the crowd went wild.

"I'm leaving." Perkins reached for the coat on the back of his chair.

"Henry, be reasonable," Ainsley tried to persuade him. "You walk out now and it's as good as admitting you're guilty."

"They got a name for crowds like this, Beauford," Perkins replied. "Back where I come from, they call them lynch mobs. See you boys later."

"Earl?" the Mayor turned to the sheriff and intoned gravely, "Do your job."

"What?"

"Are you, or are you not, the Law in this town?"

"Look at them, Beauford," Harrigan complained. "Everybody in here has gone crazy!"

"I'm telling you —you better get this mob under control and keep the peace! Call out your deputies!"

56

"Look at my deputy!" Harrigan barked back at him. "He's over there raising cain with the rest of them! No, sir. Perkins was right. Best thing to do is go home and hope it's all blown over by morning."

"Are you telling me," Ainsley accused, "after two and a half years as sheriff of this county, you don't have an ounce of influence over these people?"

"I'm telling you it would take some kind of man to get anything across to these people in the state they're in, right now. Look over there," he pointed. "Harper can't even get them to listen anymore!"

Ainsley looked over in time to see Lias motion Big John over to his side and shout something into his ear. "Who is that?" marveled Ainsley. "He's a giant! Spawned in the backwoods from all that inter-marrying, no doubt. Probably crazy as a loon!"

"Don't you believe it," Harrigan replied. "That's Big John Harper and he is no fool. Fact is, if he ever said enough to implicate himself, we really would have something!"

"Folks!" Big John's baritone voice boomed out over the crowd. "We got one more thing to announce before the meeting can adjourn."

The noise ebbed and quieted.

"The citizens of Cedar Creek," he went on, "would like to extend a offer of help to any of you, here, who ain't got kin in Cedar Creek but would like to stand with us anyhow, on account of it's your town, too. Them that's interested, can talk to Jed Farnsby at the Cedarville post office."

"Jed Farnsby!" the Sheriff moaned. "They even got Farnsby in on this!"

"Now, this meeting is officially adjourned till after elections," said Big John. Then he added with a broad, handsome smile, "And may the best men win!"

"Hey!" Someone spoke up. "Ain't nobody running against Harrigan!"

"I nominate Big John Harper!" A man in the front row shouted.

"I second that," replied another.

A look of total surprise came over John's face.

"Third," came a final approval, before a roar of applause went up.

Lias raised both hands and the room grew quiet, again. "Johnny, do you accept the nomination?"

"Well, I..."

"He does!" His father answered for him. "Now, this meeting is adjourned till a week from tomorrow. And don't nobody forget to vote!"

"Let's go," said Ainsley.

"They can't do that." Harrigan put his jacket on and started out with him. "Can they?"

"They can. But they sure aren't going to get away with it!"

"What about the pictures, Mr. Mayor?" A reporter called after them. "And what do you think of Judge Chamberlain and Big John Harper running opposite you and Sheriff Harrigan on next week's ballot?"

"I think it's a farce!" Harrigan interjected, pointing a finger at the man, just as another camera flashed in his eyes. "Now, which one of you disrespectful paper boys did that?" He blinked away the spots, only to have several other successive flashes assault him.

"Smile, Sheriff," Ainsley threw a friendly arm around the irate, younger man. "Unless you want to look like the wrath tomorrow morning on everybody's breakfast table. It's democracy, boys," he said to the newspapermen. "But we know this town's got more sense than to hand itself over to an aging has-been and some backwoods outlaw! That sort of thing might have done for the turn of the century, but this is the Age of Progress. To quote our fine President."

"When did he say that, sir?" asked a reporter.

"Well," Ainsley laughed, "if he didn't, he should have! Isn't that right, Sheriff?"

"There goes Harper!" called one of the reporters. "Let's catch him before he leaves."

"Tell me this is a bad dream, Beauford," said Harrigan, as he watched them go. "Tell me I don't have anything more to worry about this week than giving a talk at the Women's Auxiliary Tea."

"Think of it as a bump in the road, Earl. That's all it will be to look back on."

"Some bump."

"I haven't come up against a bump yet that couldn't be plowed under. You have anymore of those nice Havana cigars left at your office? I think it's time we had us a little talk."

It was late by the time Big John wound his way toward home. The bare branches of the trees were covered thick with rime ice, and he thought how they looked like skeleton arms thrust out over the road. He cast a worried glance toward his father.

"Lord, it's cold!" Lias sighed. "I'd rather have snow than just clear freezing cold like this. But I reckon we'll get home soon enough."

"You shore look wore out," his son observed.

"I admit it took a lot out of me. Went just like I thought it would, though."

"I had no idea we had that many people behind us. Weren't half that many to back us in the union wars. Where did they all come from?"

"They ain't all coal miners, that's the difference. They're Americans. Raise up the flag and the things it stands for, and I'll vow, you'll get good honest people coming out of the woodwork." He looked out the window. "It 's a wonderment, ain't it?"

"What."

"I spent all my lifetime thinking I was different from everybody. When I got saved, I felt like I was the only one could see the Light. For a while I was scared to tell too many people I seen it. But then when I finally get guts enough to speak out the truth no matter what folks think of me, I got a majority standing behind me. They ain't standing behind me actually, they're standing behind the truth. It's like truth sort of speaks for itself. And when it does, people listen. Shore is a wonderment!"

"Well, about me running for sheriff. Especially when I been against them laws for most of my lifetime. I just can't see as how—"

"Johnny, you'd be the best sheriff this here county ever had. Besides, the plan won't work otherwise."

"The plan—you mean you had it figured before tonight?"

"Shore I did. Why do you think the boys nominated you? You think candidates sit around public meetings hoping someone will take a notion to nominate them?"

"Still don't seem right."

"You think any of them others didn't get up there that way? They gathered their friends together and set it up. But don't you believe any of that bunch wake up of a morning and say, Lord, I hope I can do right, today. Ain't a one of them up on that platform tonight isn't rotten from the inside out."

"But you should have at least asked me, first," his son complained. "I mean, I'm a grown man. A married man. I ought to be making them decisions on my own."

"I didn't want you to be nervous in front of all them people."

"Still, what if I didn't want to?"

"You think I raised you up and don't know what you're made of?"

"You can't just go figuring I'd like to run for sheriff, Daddy. That's too big of a thing. Might be too big of a thing for voters, too. After the kind of life us Harpers have been living all these—" He felt the truck slip dangerously on an icy curve and competently sped up to pull out of it.

"You want to run for sheriff, John?" Lias conceded.

"Yep."

Their eyes met for a moment and they both laughed.

A tremor of excitement went through John. "Could be we might actually win something this time!"

"Might not win the battle," his father replied, "but we shore gonna win the war."

"What do you mean?"

"I mean we ain't gonna win this election. Don't expect to. Ainsley and Harrigan—Perkins, even—- had this county in their grip for too long. And they ain't gonna give up easy. Got to realize right now, that election's gonna be fixed."

"Lord, almighty." John grew serious, again. "How we gonna get around that?"

Lias pulled his collar up more snuggly around his neck and looked out the window at the frozen countryside slipping by. "We're gonna get rid of the sheriff," he said quietly. "The only way we know how."

57

The following Monday, in the late afternoon, great flakes of snow began floating down from a steel-colored sky. They were giant flakes that swirled and twirled like children playing games, spinning and chasing one another before finally touching the ground. The air all around grew crowded with the varied shapes until the playing stopped and they began to drift down heavily. They landed on the outstretched branches of pines and piled up in tiny drifts along rocky ledges of the hillside.

The first storm of winter was brewing.

As quickly as the ground was covered with white, a vast and isolating silence engulfed the little cabin in Bog Hollow. Its steep, shingled roof would shed all but a thin blanket of snow and the wisp of gray smoke rising from the chimney would be a constant reminder for miles around that everything was well, inside.

Harlan was chopping wood out in the yard when it started. He continued the chore, enjoying the invigorating tingle of new snow and the storybook beauty it draped over the rugged, wooded hillside.

"You want to catch your death?" Granny hollered at him from the doorway. "You got enough wood piled up to last me till spring thaw. Now, come on in here before you're half froze!"

"I'm tired of sitting around," he answered. "And I'll go crazy if you tell me to come in once more. It's nice out here."

"You rest that ax for a spell, young feller—do you hear? Your brains is addled enough, already."

"All right," he relented. "But I'm going to sit on the porch for a while and watch the snow come down. Why don't you come out and watch it with me?"

"My rumatiz won't abide that kind of foolishness." She went back inside.

"There's magic in the first snowfall, Granny," he called after her.

"I can see it from the window," she answered back.

The old woman closed the door behind her and Harlan sat down on the steps to look out over the hollow. About thirty feet away, the hillside pitched steeply into thick woods, and somewhere far off to the left was a swampy bog that stretched for so many miles a person could get lost in it. Some had.

Deep in the heart of that bog was where the Harper still had once been and he wondered if Joseph Lee might be out there, even now. He was wondering about that wild, young Harper who had gone openly against the family when he suddenly noticed a piece of paper lying on the corner of the step. It hadn't been there a few minutes ago, when he sat down. Harlan reached over and picked it up.

It was a piece of *Big Chief* tablet paper, covered over with the entire alphabet, penciled in a childish scrawl. He recognized the peculiar form in lettering. By the time he looked up again, a short, stubby pencil with a dull point had appeared on the edge of the step, too. Harlan reached for it. He drew a smiling happy face with sunshine rays all around it and returned pencil and paper to the edge of the step.

When it disappeared, he bent down to peer beneath the wooden porch and look for the young owner. "Hoddie," he spoke into the darkness where he knew the boy was hiding,

"Why don't you come out and talk to me for a while?"

"You look different," came the small reply. "How come you got them kinda clothes on?"

"I borrowed them. Is that all right?"

"I reckon."

"What are you doing so far away from home?"

"I live here in the holler. You ain't gonna whup me, are you, Mr. Harlan?"

"Have I ever whupped you before?"

"Nope."

"Then why do you think I would now?"

"Because Uncle Lias said weren't nobody supposed to come up here, till you say it's all right. Is it all right, Mr. Harlan?"

"It's all right," he replied. "Besides, your Granny's been worried about why you haven't visited her for so long. So, why don't you come in and see her."

First the small blonde head appeared, and then the shoulders as they wriggled out from beneath the wooden steps. Before Harlan knew it, the boy had flung his arms around his neck and declared, "I love you, teacher! When you coming back to the schoolhouse?"

"Hoddie." Harlan lifted the young boy with him as he stood to his feet to take him inside. "As soon as I possibly can."

Bonnie Rae watched from the corner of the goat shed, and her heart began to pound. It had cost three peppermint sticks and a box of crayons to bribe her young cousin to approach the teacher without permission. She was convinced that Harlan didn't really want to be left alone, no matter what he said. And she had devised a daring plan to prove it . But without Joseph Lee, she was unsure of exactly how to carry out the finer points.

She thought of sending Hoddie on ahead only after discovering, through Big John, that the boy had been keeping close watch on the cabin ever since Harlan had arrived. Now, after witnessing the spontaneous warm affection he had been greeted with, she was sure she was doing the right thing.

She hadn't planned on the snow.

It would be a cold wait in the goat shed until after dark when the lights would go out in the cabin. The family thought she was visiting John and Sarah but she had come here, instead. Not long afterward, the snow had started. Now, she stood staring at the empty porch for a long moment after they had gone inside, contemplating the startling change in Harlan's appearance.

If he had been attractive to her before, now, he looked like everything she had ever secretly dreamed of. Harlan Fleming looked like a real mountain man; the admiring kind there seemed to be a shortage of, even on the mountain. It was hard to believe this was the same man who spoke French and wore finely cut suits. The one who had asked her to marry him and go off into the world. Harder still to understand why he didn't want her to see him. In Bonnie Rae's opinion, this new Harlan was even more appealing than the old one had been.

It gave her a fluttery feeling to think of being caught up in those arms that had so comfortably been swinging the ax, or to hear declarations of love from the same voice that had so easily bantered back and forth with her bossy granny. These were things she could understand and relate to. Things she had been born and raised to admire. What could he possibly want to hide from her?

Lias had been strangely evasive in answering her questions. And when she pressed for reasons why she couldn't visit anyway—whether he wanted her to or not—she got the same reply every time. "It'd just devil him if you went when he don't want you there. Boy just needs more time," her father had said. Time for what? She had come dangerously close to admitting they had already made plans to marry. But then that might have steered things in the wrong direction altogether.

Tonight, she intended to find out what the big secret was. With Lias no longer standing between them, it could only mean that Harlan was planning to leave Cedar Creek. That he might be having second thoughts about marrying her. He had probably come to some agreement with her father and Lias was no longer worried about her running off with him, anymore.

But she couldn't bear the thought of losing him, now!

Not when he had suddenly and surprisingly become everything she had ever wanted. Joseph Lee's suggestion that night on Big John's porch had shocked her. Though she couldn't picture herself ever doing anything like that, she had come up with an idea along the same line that should get the same results. Because she knew it would appeal to the strongest part of Harlan's nature.

His honor.

Long after the cabin was dark and quiet, Bonnie Rae tiptoed onto the porch and put a hand to the door. She hesitated only for a moment. For although it had stopped snowing, a cold icy wind was blowing and she was already bitterly chilled from her wait in the shed. A soothing warmth enveloped her as soon as she stepped inside.

Harlan lay sleeping in the corner bed against the wall where she knew he would be. But seeing him so close gave her that fluttery feeling, again, and she began to have second thoughts. What if he got angry with her? But he hadn't been angry with Hoddie this afternoon and, though he disapproved, he hadn't even been angry that long ago night when she surprised him by going on the hunt.

She moved quietly to the hearth and started taking off her long leather jacket and knit gloves. Whether she was shaking from cold or pure nervousness, she didn't know. She took off her boots and leggings. The snow that was clinging to them began to melt and make half-moon puddles on the stone hearth. She took off her long wool skirt, her sweater, everything down to the thin cotton slip she wore underneath it all.

Bonnie Rae moved over to the bed in the corner and stood looking down at Harlan in the soft glow of the fire. He was sleeping deeply and she watched him for a long time before gathering enough nerve to lie down, ever so carefully, beside him. He stirred and she held her breath, afraid he might wake up. He mustn't find her here until first light. After she had slept with him all night long.

But she couldn't sleep.

Instead, she let her eyes travel over his face, lingering on the fresh reddened scars along his jaw that led down into the neck of the white, long-sleeved undershirt. Her practiced search did not miss the ones that circled the wrist that rested on top of the quilt, either. Then she saw the familiar markings on the back of his hand and realized with a sudden shock why he hadn't wanted her to come.

That sort of doctoring was Granny's last and most drastic measure. The effects of it were terrors she had only heard stories about. Why hadn't anyone told her? Joseph Lee would have if he had been home to tell. He never kept things from her the way her father and Big John did. Now, everything began to make sense.

Harlan had not only nearly died, he could still die.

Her eyes moved over him intently this time. Back to the injuries on his face, until—with a sinking feeling—she saw what she had missed, at first. There was a another scar that followed the line of his mustache, continued under his cheekbone, then disappeared into the dark wavy hair. A head wound! That was why her father had stayed so long and no "visitors" had been allowed to disturb him.

She turned quietly—imperceptibly—and buried her face in the pillow to stifle a sob. As she did, her long soft hair brushed against Harlan's cheek. He stirred at the pleasant sensation and somewhere in the haze of waking and dreaming, reached out and pulled her against him. A sweet elation flooded over her.

"Oh, Harlan," she whispered, relieved by the response and feeling a warmth of contentment she could barely contain as she nestled closer. "Harlan!"

The intimacy brought him suddenly and fully awake, only to realize with a startled surprise that he was not dreaming. "Bonnie Rae—" He buried his hands in her hair and turned her face toward his. "*Chère*—what are you doing here?"

"Please don't send me away!" She whispered fervently, as if her life depended on it. "I'll die of mortal shame if you do!"

He kissed the side of her face—not trusting himself to do more—and whispered, "Well, we can't let that happen. You're not too close to danger to change your mind."

"I wanted it to be like Ruth—in the Bible. She lay down with the man she loved, secret-like, and when he woke up and found her there in the morning, he married her."

"Bonnie Rae."

"But you woke up soon as I got here. Now, it occurs to me, you ain't gonna think so highly of me doing such a thing. Do you still love me?"

"Of course I do."

"Then why didn't you want to see me for so long?"

"I didn't want you to see me," he answered. "Not this way."

"Harlan, I never seen you look so good!"

"I'm all right for the moment. But I have terrible spells."

"Daddy says they're getting better, every day, though. And, now, since the opium's gone—"

"He told you about that?"

"I seen your hands." She ran her own softly over the top of his. "I reckon I know just about every remedy Granny has. And I know them spells must have been awful bad for her to—"

"I hate what they do to me! In one moment of stupidity, I've managed to ruin everything I ever worked for. Something I never even came close to understanding until it was too late." His tone took on a sudden note of despair. "I had wonderful plans. And I wanted to take you with me."

"Don't talk like that, Harlan—like it's over, already—don't never."

"The truth is..." He turned her face up to his. "They might never go away. If not, I have to find some way to live with them. At best, I might be able to teach school, again, but not by myself. I can't expect you to be part of a life like that."

"Thunder and hail, Harlan!" she cried with a sudden frustration, "You can't expect me not to!"

"Shhh." He pulled her head against his chest to quiet her and warned, "You're going to wake up Granny in a minute and if you're not in her bed instead of mine when she opens her eyes—"

"I love you!" She whispered back with a thump of her fist against his chest for emphasis, as if doing so might knock some sense into him. "Shutting me out ain't right! I don't care if you go stark, raving crazy ten times a day! I got to be with you!" Then feeling self-conscious at such an outburst, she added, "Even if it's only for a time. Don't you want to be with me, too?"

"More than anything, dearest."

"All I wanted was for you to want me, again."

"I never stopped, *chère*. But if you stay here much longer..." He tightened his arms around her for a few moments and breathed in the fragrance of her hair one more time. "I won't be able to guarantee your safety, anymore."

"I said I didn't mean for you to wake up. You believe me, don't you?"

"No."

Bonnie Rae's heart suddenly began to pound at the thought of losing his respect with her daring plan. What was she thinking?

"But I'm pretty sure it didn't turn out that way for Ruth, either. So, now, you'll have to marry me, honey. No matter how things work out. Under the circumstances, it's the only honorable thing for us to do."

58

By the time Tom got close to home a few days later, the storm had increased and the snow was beginning to pile up in drifts that would remain around the mountain community throughout the winter. He had spent most of his time in a remote area beyond the Wind Ridge, and it wasn't until he reached a farm on the outskirts of Bog Hollow that he first heard the news about Harlan. Was he destined to lose every single member of his own family in violent death before their time?

He headed straight for Granny Harper's cabin.

Since it was still several hours away, he did not stay long enough at the farm where he heard the news even to warm up after he had heard it. Instead, he climbed quickly back onto his mule and started out, again, though he had already been traveling for hours in the freezing weather. By the time he came to the familiar, winding trail that lead to the old woman's cabin, his nose was numb, and the edges of his beard and mustache were tinged with small particles of ice where the moisture from his breath had frozen.

Darkness crept in before he got there and, after a while, he could barely see the path in front of him. Granny Harper's dogs met him halfway, but they—having no knowledge of relational rifts—remembered him as a friend and escorted him the rest of the way. He realized he had been nodding off only after he awoke with a start and found himself still seated on the mule while the animal stood quietly in the yard in front of the lighted cabin.

The comforting smell of wood-smoke engulfed Tom as he slid stiffly to the ground and stepped up onto the porch. When he knocked at the door, Harlan answered. Without speaking, the two men moved into an embrace that conveyed their feelings of regret and concern, and the deep need to reassure themselves in one another. Harlan's years of dependency on this man who had always been able to make things right sparked an immediate sense of hope and well-being in him.

"From what they told me out at the Davis place," Tom held him at arm's length and ran a calculating finger over the dark mustache, "I wasn't sure what to expect. But it looks like you're all in one piece, as far as—" All at once he felt the jagged scar that ran fairly hidden beneath the right side of his mustache, and along the cheek bone to disappear into his hair. He followed its entire length up over his nephew's ear and across to the back of his head. "What did they do to you, son?"

"I'll tell you about it." Harlan pulled away. "But first come inside and get warm while I bed old Blu down in the shed for you."

Tom watched him disappear into the yard, then stepped hesitantly into the warmth of the cabin. He closed the door behind him and stood against it for a moment, his eyes locked with the old woman's as she sat rocking in her chair by the fire. "How long has he been here?" he finally asked.

"Nigh onto a month," she replied. "And he's still on the laudanum. Laudanum and whiskey.

"You didn't use opium?"

"I used it."

"What strength? What did you mix it with? Bloodroot? Bitterroot tea?" He wearily pulled off his hat and jacket but he dared not step up to the fire or make himself at home in this woman's house without her consent.

"Used the pure." She knew he was waiting but took her time to confirm his worst fears in the bluntest possible manner. "Cut into a vein... blew it straight into the blood."

"Lord!" he breathed fervently before turning away from her on the pretense of laying his things by the door, which were now dripping with melting snow. He stifled the response to criticize the dangerous method. Even when they were friends they had disagreed over methods. But they had never really been friends.

Yet, she had obviously saved Harlan's life in spite of her crude ways and the long years of resentment she held against him. He must not—dare not— offend her. Granny Harper got to her feet with a resigned sigh. "Come on in, Tom Bascomb. You look too done in to fight with. Hungry, too, I reckon. Want coffee?"

"I had to see him." His tone was apologetic. "But if you rather I didn't stay..."

"Set yourself down by the fire. I took into account you'd be coming. The boy's been looking for you a time and a time."

"I want you to know how much I appreciate what you've done for him. Not many people in your place would have." He hesitated a moment, then said exactly what he was thinking. "You had every right to refuse."

"I did refuse. But my boy done took to him." She pulled her clay pipe from her apron pocket and put it into her mouth, unlit. "Same way he took to you before you done turned against us."

"I never meant it to be that way, Granny. If you could only believe that!" He looked at her through tortured and imploring eyes. "I'll be sorry about it for the rest of my life!"

The familiar reference softened her a little. "God works in mysterious ways," she intoned. "You want to know some truth? I was thinking—on the night they first brung him here—on how it weren't right that my boy's gone and they brung me yours."

Tom sank down onto the hearth with a bitter remorse, suddenly feeling every mile he had traveled over the past weeks and the full weight of this burden he had carried for four years. "I'm sorry!" he whispered, again.

"So was I," she countered. "I was sorry Lias brung him. Sorry right up till he'd been here about a week. He was fighting it so hard and I just give him the remedy. He were drifting off, so plumb wore out he couldn't talk. He raised up a hand while I was leaving and I reckoned he wanted to tell me something."

She sighed and took the pipe out of her mouth, only to thoughtlessly put it back in, again. There was sudden emotion in her care-worn face and he could see it was difficult for her to go on.

"I bent down close so he could whisper." She hesitated, took a deep breath and continued with a determined effort. "I bent down to hear what he had to say. And he didn't have nothing to say! He just... put his arm around me... and he were wearing my Buck's clothes..."

She clutched her shirtfront, sniffed, and took her pipe out of her mouth, again. "And that boy of yours... he done slipped right in to my empty place just as easy as he fit them clothes! I reckon maybe I needed him nigh onto as much as he needed me. Seems that was the way of it."

Tom felt his own emotions churning and looked away from her into the fire. "Thank you," he whispered quietly. "Thank you for everything."

"Well, you're welcome to the hearth bed, anyhow. And I'll go fetch something to warm your insides with."

When Harlan came back in, the two men talked late into the night. In the weeks Tom had been gone, the tides of Cedar Creek were turning. It was not the same place Tom left that he had come home to. Harlan was not the same. Throughout the evening, Tom watched him carefully, noticing with a doctor's perception, the telltale signs that told him more about his nephew's condition than the young man was willing to admit.

By the time Tom lay down for the night on the soft, feather tick mattress on the hearth, he was barely able to contain the guilt-ridden knowledge that weighed so heavily on him. Whether Harlan's strong young body would be able to overcome such a drastic injury to the brain was uncertain. It could only be proven with time. But whether or not Tom—had he been there to intervene —could have prevented the incident from happening in the first place, would haunt him for years to come.

Harlan did not go home with him.

For once, Tom had to agree with the old woman and admit that only rest and quiet throughout the healing process could keep some unexpected crack in the skull, before it was fully mended, from finishing what the original injury had started. Meanwhile, the doctor knew an Austrian Surgeon he had worked with during the War, who had become expert in such injuries. He would immediately begin corresponding with him.

These things, combined with the still volatile situation with the company, made Harper land the safest place for Harlan to stay. And he meant to stay. So, as this first blizzard swept its way through Cedar Creek, the mountain roads became impassable and the people were enveloped in a peaceful isolation. It was one that would not be invaded by anyone but near neighbors who were within walking distance, or those who had exchanged their automobiles for sleds and sleighs.

Not only would Harlan remain here, Tom could tell just by looking at him that he belonged. The man had been drawn into the innermost reaches of this mountain clan as if he were some long lost son, returning home. And to Harlan, they were like the missing pieces of his own family, too many of whom he had lost too early to know. Now, Harlan Fleming fit into Cedar Creek in a way that was more than Tom had ever dared to hope for.

But it was bittersweet.

59

The town of Cedarville was not doing well. Everywhere, there were signs that the strike was beginning to take effect. Against all odds, Cedar Creek was becoming a thorn in the side of those who had oppressed them for so long. So, it was only weeks before Christmas, in a roadside cafe just over the county line, that Mayor Ainsley drummed impatient fingers on the blue-checked tablecloth and looked again at a large watch he carried in his vest pocket. Almost eight o'clock. The waitress came by and warmed his coffee. When Harrigan finally appeared in the doorway, he had grown impatient to the point of irritation.

"You know, Earl," he said as the man in uniform sat down across form him, "this is the kind of behavior that makes me tend to believe those rumors I've been hearing about you lately."

The Sheriff turned his coffee cup right side up in the saucer and motioned to the waitress before answering. "I got delayed on the way over."

"Seems to me you've been getting yourself delayed quite regular."

"Is that what you wanted to see me about? Because if it is..." he paused to give his full attention to the waitress.

"You all ready to order, now?" She took a pencil from her neatly pinned back hair and touched it to the tip to her tongue.

"Just pick me out something you think is good, sugar," said Harrigan with a rakish smile. "And the Mayor, here's gonna have…" he turned questioning eyes to Ainsley.

"Ham and eggs."

After she had gone, the young Sheriff looked across the table and asked, "What did you want to talk to me about, Beauford?"

"This personal war you've been carrying on," Ainsley replied. "I'll get right to the point. You're gumming up the works, Earl. I told you this whole thing would take care of itself, if we'd just set back and let it. You're not letting it."

"This whole thing is gonna take care of me if I stay sitting back much longer! What you and Perkins don't realize, is this run-a-the-mill strike of yours has turned into a major revolt! And if you think I'm gonna end up like the last sheriff of this county, you're crazy."

"So far, there's been no violence. But I'm telling you right now—if there's gonna be—it'll be because some hot-head like you set it off."

"No violence? Beauford, they're trying to get rid of me!"

"You won your election."

"I've been the victim of violent crime three times now!" he insisted.

"I wouldn't call it violent crime," the Mayor corrected him. "I mean…" he lowered his voice and leaned forward a little, "being discovered by your own deputy, in your own squad car, parked in front of your own office—"

"Beauford."

"At seven o'clock in the morning, sleeping off a drunk would've been bad enough. But finding a girl in there, too!" He shook his head shamefully.

"I never laid eyes on her before in my life."

"Earl, for situations like these, there are other excuses that would've been more believable."

"It's the truth! This old man with a gray beard came up to me after work the night before. Next thing I know, I'm being hog-tied and blindfolded by a whole bunch of them! Forced to drink moonshine or choke to death! I don't remember anything after that until Roger was banging on the window the next morning. And—I swear—I never laid eyes on that girl until she poked her head up over the back seat right then and said hello!"

"Well," Ainsley moved out of the way as the waitress set their plates on the table. "A person might be able to accept that as a possibility one time." He unfolded a napkin and tucked it into his belt. "But not over and over. And if you expect me to believe they kidnapped you and held you prisoner for two days..."

"Nobody held me prisoner. I told you. I woke up after being drugged —or something—way back in the woods. By the time I hiked out, I was somewhere on the other side of the Greenbrier River. Two counties over!"

"Old man with the gray beard, again?"

"I'm telling you, this is serious!"

"And I suppose someone's been breaking and entering the county courthouse just to stash half-drunk jars of whiskey in your office."

"My own deputies are against me. I've got a conspiracy on my hands! And I'd sure like to know what this world's coming to, when you can't even trust the people you work with."

"You know what I think, Earl?"

"What."

"I think you've been working too hard." He dipped a corner of toast into a bright orange pool of yoke and took a bite. "I think the stresses and strains of this county situation are starting to get to you. Can't have that. Now, we've got to come up with a realistic solution or—eat your pancakes before they get cold."

"Or what?"

"Or we're going to have to find someone else who can handle the stresses and strains. Sort of business we're in..." He paused to chew his food and swallow it down with a swig of coffee. "We can't afford to have someone with the reputation you've been setting yourself up for."

"Setting myself up—"

"Got to get this situation under control, Earl, before it gets out of hand. Have any ideas?"

"I've got ideas."

"Well, let's hear some."

"Next man sneaks up on me is gonna get himself shot dead, that's what."

"That's just the sort of scandal we don't need. You have to remember we're not dealing with ordinary people here."

"That's what I've been trying to tell you! They're all craftier than—"

"Craftiness doesn't concern me right now. It's their back-woods independence I'm worried about. I mean, we're talking about people that on this day in nineteen thirty-seven—the twentieth century—are still holding grudges leftover from the war days. And I don't mean the World War. I mean the Civil War. You kill one of them, and they're liable to start the revolution all over, again. We'd end up with the National Guards out here to keep the peace. Then you can bet the cat would be out of the bag."

"So, just what do you expect me to do, Beauford? Sit around and let them play their games with me? Or step down altogether and hand over my office to that muscle man of theirs?"

"I told you before, the only way to handle them is to let them hang theirselves. Now, listen to me." He shoved his empty plate back and leaned forward, again. "Time is the up-per hand in this game and we still have that on our side. I say, let them tough out the winter without work. Their supplies aren't gonna last forever. And when they run out, their tempers will be cooled. They'll be begging to get back to work. Simple as that."

"What do I do in the meantime? Sit around and smile at everybody?"

"I'm advising Perkins to spend the winter back in Chicago and I'm shutting down the company. It's just costing me money, right now, and it'll take away their security of thinking they can go back to work if things get too rough. When I open it again, next year, I want people waiting in line to get in. At any wage."

He removed the napkin from his belt and wiped his mouth. "We've been in a slump with so much over-production, anyhow. It'll be better all around to hold off until after the first of the year. From what I hear about a war in Europe, industry ought to be picking up all over again, pretty soon. We've got enough capital, we won't even miss a beat."

"What about them trying to root us out of office and take over the town? This is no joke, Beauford. Wait till you run into one of them in a back alley one of these nights."

"I've decided to take a vacation until things cool off a bit, myself."

Harrigan sighed in disgust. "Another winter in the south of France? I might have known."

"Europe doesn't have such a good climate for vacationing these days. I was thinking about the Virgin Islands."

"That's just great!" Harrigan shoved his chair back and pushed his untouched pancakes aside. "And what am I supposed to do? Stay here all by myself in the middle of an uprising and pretend I'm keeping the peace?"

"Of course I wouldn't suggest that you spend a whole winter away, but you've got enough able deputies to handle things for a few weeks, anyway. That's about all it would take for most of this to blow over. You've had almost three years of peaceful community relations, Earl. Some of it's bound to be remembered."

"Sounds pretty cowardly, if you ask me."

"Nobody's really asking you. We're level-headed business men, not reactionaries. We do what's best for the company and leave it at that. We use the civic process, we don't allow our-selves to become consumed in its fires. If Cedarville turns into a ghost town tomorrow, it shouldn't really concern us. The company concerns us. And that we still have complete control over."

"I wasn't kidding about the conspiracy, Beauford. If I go away now, that man of theirs will be sitting in my chair when I get back."

"The only way they could do that is by recall. And they'd have to prove incompetence to do it. I'm worried about that happening if you stay here and allow yourself to participate in these crazy escapades. It would be illegal for them to take over the office while you were away on legitimate business or vaca-tioning. Then we'd have the law on our side, again. So, you see, Earl, you're the only real danger to the whole situation. What do you say?"

"I'll think about it."

"Well..." Mayor Ainsley got to his feet. "Don't think too long. I'd like to know today so we can make plans. Now, look at that, it's starting to snow, again. This business of having to drive over the county line to find a restaurant that's open is ridiculous. But we couldn't have talked this openly anywhere in Cedarville."

"There's spies everywhere you turn in Cedarville, Beau-ford."

"You coming?"

"Go ahead. I'm gonna stay here and think for a while. I'll stop by the house this afternoon."

"See that you do." He reached for his hat and coat. "Try not to take everything so personally. Next year at this time, we'll be laughing over this."

Harrigan didn't reply and the Mayor started for the register to pay his bill. He looked out the window, again, irritated at the thought of having to make the long drive home in bad weather. He walked outside and a stinging blast of winter forced him to hold onto his hat and turn up his collar against it. He didn't notice the old man pass by and enter the restaurant.

He was too busy, irritably making his way to his car.

60

A few days before Christmas, the Harper family gathered for a work party at a rambling farmhouse about a mile away from the school. The old Farnsby place had been vacant for years. The last three teachers were single and preferred boarding with another family instead of rattling around in the large house by themselves. Besides that, the place was sadly in need of repairs. It was going to be repaired, now, because there was going to be a wedding in Cedar Creek.

After the spring thaw, when the traveling preacher came through, Harlan and Bonnie Rae planned to be married and set up housekeeping here on the sugar farm. It was a dreamlike place on the edge of one of the best maple groves in Cedar Creek. Years ago, it was a working sugar farm. It had been the home of a family of five boys and four daughters, whose mother had been the Cedar Creek teacher for nearly thirty years.

When the World War came along, she lost her husband, three sons, and even a daughter who was a nurse, to a war no one really understood. Ruth Farnsby moved what was left of her family into Cedarville. Now, she lived with her youngest son, who had lost a leg while serving in Italy, and who was now the town Postmaster. The farm had long since been donated to the Cedar Creek school and the residents collectively paid the yearly taxes on it.

So, when the Harpers arrived in an old-fashioned sleigh with hickory runners, drawn by an ancient family mule, it was an all-out festive occasion. They were also pulling a smaller sled, loaded down with paint, wallpaper, curtains that Bonnie Rae and Sarah had made, and a large rag rug that Celia had been working on for nearly two months. Along with plaster, lumber, and nails for any repairs that needed to be made.

Granny Harper came along with Harlan and Rafe, nearly a week before the rest of the family arrived, to oversee the cooking and act as general supervisor for the placement of furniture and the last of Harlan's personal belongings that had been sent up from Richmond. It was easier to get the furniture packed this far in during the winter months, when snow smoothed out all the rough spots in the roads and allowed large horse-drawn freight wagons with runners to bring heavy things over the steep winding roads or down into the deep gorges known as hollers. Now, with the house turned into a home, and the coming of Christmas so close at hand, there was a holiday mood that made even the repair work seem fun.

Late in the afternoon, as Lias and Big John sat perched up high on the steep shingled roof, patching a crumbling chimney, the older man's eyes wandered past the little meadow that was blanketed in winter white, to look up at Sugar Hill. The towering peak rose up high and majestic above the trees that surrounded it, losing itself in the cloud-swept sky. Big John noticed his father's gaze and deliberately kept at his task.

There was a long, strained silence between them.

"I want him home for Christmas, Johnny," Lias finally spoke first.

"Daddy, you know well as I do, what he's doing up there on that hill."

"Christmas is a day of peace. I want to see my boy."

"I promised Sarah I'd take her into town to see her folks and share Christmas supper with them. We'll stop by and see you all Christmas morning and then head on down the hill.

Don't reckon we'd be back till the day after."

"Pains me to see the family broke apart."

"He's the one that done it, ain't he?" Big John put down the tool he was working with and wiped a plaster-covered hand on his pant leg. "What do you want me to do? Stand up for sheriff and turn the other way while my little brother runs illegal whiskey?"

Lias sighed.

"I can't do it, Daddy," Big John said a little more gently. "I'd be no better than Harrigan. And if our boy don't come to his senses by the time I am sheriff..." He went back to the small chore with renewed interest, so, he wouldn't have to look at Lias when he finished the sentence. "I won't have no choice but to bring him in."

They heard the front door open and close below them and Harlan came outside. "Somebody's coming," he said.

"Angus McCord," Big John recognized the lone figure walking across the white meadow.

"I reckon he's got the news we been waiting for," Lias said. "Let's head on out and meet him."

Angus waved and gave them a friendly smile as they all neared each other. He had a blue knit scarf tied over his hat and under his chin and his cheeks were rosy red from the long walk in the cold. "We're all back safe and sound," he called cheerily.

"Any trouble?" Lias asked.

"Nope." He looked at Harlan. "Boy, you look a sight better than the last time I seen you. Well, shoot, you look like a honest-to-God American!"

"Tell us how it went, Angus." John nudged him, "Before we get back to the house. No need stirring up the womenfolk and younguns with it."

"Well," Angus began, "we followed him out of town to a little roadside place where Ainsley was waiting for him. Had to wait around till they was done talking. After the Mayor left, Pa headed in and passed up the Sheriff on his way out."

He burst out laughing. "Shoot, Uncle Lias—he done just like you said he would! Ran back in and made a derned fool of his-self in front of all them people. Said this ol' man was trying to kill him! Grabbed hold and started dragging Pa out, again. Cook and a couple other guys had to pull him off."

"How many people you think was there?" asked Lias.

"Twenty, maybe. Including the help. He was strung out just like you said."

"Aaron all right?" John queried.

"Yep. Just acted real surprised, like he never seen him before. They threw Harrigan out—gentle-like, on account of he was a Law—and give Pa a free breakfast. We was waiting for him outside, the boys and me. By the time Pa come out, we had him all took care of."

"Oh, my God." Harlan went pale. "You killed the Sheriff?"

"He ain't dead," Lias assured. "Go ahead on, Angus."

"Well, we drove north about eight days. Two days past the Canada border. Paid a French Indian twenty dollars to haul him and some supplies to a hunter's shack away up in the hills there. If he gets brave and hikes out, ain't nothing but a logging camp nearby and don't nobody speak nothing but French there. Ain't a telephone around for sixty mile. I give him a month, six weeks maybe, to get back. If he even comes back."

"Did he get any idea where he was going?" Big John asked.

"Nope. Them potions Granny give us done good. We fed him a couple or three times on the trip, but only at night unless he should pick up on the direction. Rest of the time, we kept him blindfolded. He was madder than a bull buffler, boy, but it weren't nothing we couldn't handle."

"It's a shame," Lias said, "that his wayward ways should get out of hand so soon after elections. Johnny? Tack another notice up on the Town Hall. Let it read: Due to the strange behavior and mysterious disappearance of our duly elected sheriff, the citizens of this county propose that a recall be held December twenty-seventh, nineteen thirty-seven, to appoint Big

John Harper in his place."

"What about Ainsley?" His son asked.

"I'll bet my last dollar," Lias replied, "we won't see hide nor hair of him till next spring. He thinks more logical than Harrigan does. He'll know he's been beat. For now, anyhow."

"What's to keep them from taking everything over again when they do come back? Especially after folks been out of work for so long." Angus wanted to know.

"That there's a little something else we can thank Harlan for." Big John threw a casual arm across the teacher's shoulders as they walked along. "He wrote to the NLRB before any of this started. We got a answer back last week, and–derned if we didn't get us a hearing! It's set for the early part of next summer, if we kin hold out that long. That company will be facing criminal charges for the way they been doing things."

"I'm hoping Ainsley will sell out instead of facing them charges," Lias said. "And clear out of Cedar Creek altogether."

"How come we got to wait so long?" Angus asked.

"Things take a long time when it comes to the government," Harlan explained. "They're backed up with a lot of other cases, I guess. I hope we can hang on until then."

"I got some ideas we ain't tried yet, for hanging on," Lias assured them. "And I—"

He was stopped in mid-sentence by a snowball that came flying out of the bushes a few yards away and splattered into his face with an uncanny accuracy. The assailant could have got away unrecognized if he hadn't squealed with delight and given himself away.

Within minutes, there was a war on.

61

As snowballs began to fly in all directions, everyone chose a human target and took up sides. Rafe and Lou Ellen withstood a considerable barrage in order to erect a hurried wall of snow that they pulled Harlan behind, so, the three of them could withstand any attack.

Little Sam cried out, "I don't need no one on my side but Big John!"

"You got me, boy," came the reply, and alliances were formed.

Jenny Beth—shielded safely behind her father— fashioned herself a magnificent snowball to throw at someone. When it was ready, she stepped out into the open and hollered, "Oh, Rafie—" and drew back her arm for the delivery.

But before she could complete it her brother responded with lightning speed and a mass of slush splashed into her face with a stinging, clinging cold that hung on and dripped painfully down her collar.

"That ain't—f-fair!" she shrieked, bursting into tears as she tried to brush away the cold with awkward, mitten hands. "You—you awful—"

"Now, just a minute." Lias, bent down to untie her knitted scarf.

"He ain't playing fair, Daddy!"

"Ain't no laws in this game, baby." He brushed the snow from her face and neck with the soft wool. "He'd never knowed you was there if you didn't call him."

"He's b-bigger than me!"

"Then you got to outsmart him. Now..." He wrapped the scarf around her head several times, until her face was completely covered except for a narrow slit to see through. Then he tucked the ends snuggly into her collar. "You can take anything that comes, now. Get yourself another snowball and we'll sneak up on him!"

There was a wild explosion of whooping and hollering and Celia lifted a lace curtain to look outside. She was just in time to see Lias run across the yard with his youngest daughter perched on his shoulders to hurl a lop-sided snowball into her brother's left ear at close range.

"Land sakes!" She watched as they ducked behind a stark-looking lilac bush for cover and hurriedly began gathering more snow. "Vow and declare!" She reached for her own coat hanging on a wall rack near the door.

"Something wrong?" Granny's wrinkled face appeared in the kitchen door with her pipe clenched tightly between her teeth.

"That son of yours!" Celia buttoned her new, ankle-length wine-colored coat Bonnie Rae had made for her birthday. "Is out there in that cold air, running around like a youngun!"

"He oughten to do that," the old woman worried. She pushed her hat farther back on her head and came close to look for herself. "That cold air on them lungs is the worst thing he can do to his-self. I done told him that a hundred times but it don't do no good. See if you can get him in here before he takes another spell like he had last night."

"I'll get him in here!" She went out the door with a firm determination and started across the porch. "Lias Harper!" she called indignantly. "Just what do you think you're—"

"Watch out, sugar babe!" Her husband warned as another one of Rafe's projectiles came at her with a perfect aim.

"Everybody get Mama!" Little Sam crowed rapturously, at which signal a barrage of snow came flying at her from all directions.

"Save her, Daddy—save her!" Jenny Beth hollered as Lias reached out and pulled his wife behind the bushes with them. "You're on our side, Mommie!"

"Lias!" Celia brushed the snow from her face and hair. "What are you doing?"

"Playing with my kids." He stifled a deep cough. "Ready, Jenny?"

"I'm ready!" She began to prance back and forth like a miniature soldier.

"You're coughing, already," Celia objected. "And it's getting colder every minute out here."

"One more charge." He hoisted the little girl up onto his shoulders, again.

"Lias!"

"Cut me one of them pieces of pie and I'll be in before the coffee's made."

She sighed as he started across the yard and was about to return to the house when Big John rushed at them with Little Sam perched on his shoulders, hollering like a banshee. Angus ran to intercept them and Lou Ellen jumped on his back, to rub a snowball into his black-bearded face. In the meantime, Rafe— knowing his teacher should not be doing such things consistently blocked any of Harlan's advances to join in the more physical aspects of the fray.

"Stop that!" Celia yelled as they all converged on each other. An out-and-out brawl followed, with everyone except Rafe and Harlan in a tangled heap and Lias on the bottom of the pile.

"Stop that this minute!" Celia ran to the porch, grabbed the broom they had been using to sweep snow from the doorway and headed toward the crowd with a fervor.

Bonnie Rae looked out an upstairs window where she and Sarah had been hanging curtains. "What's Mama doing out there?"

Sarah looked over her shoulder. "Looks to me like she's whupping every last one of them at the same time." She smiled, and her voice was low and musical when she asked, "Think she needs help?"

By the time they had gone downstairs and donned coats and gloves, the battle had cooled and the participants were already headed inside. Except for the young ones, who still had plenty of energy left for making snowmen and ice-angels. Granny hurried back into the kitchen to slice the pie and Bonnie Rae swung the door wide to let everyone in.

"I was worried there for a while," Lias stamped snow from his boots before he came inside, "that maybe your mama had forgot how to play." He took a handkerchief from his pocket and coughed.

Set yourself down by the fire, Lias." Celia's face was flushed and radiant from the exertion.

Bonnie Rae brushed snow from Harlan's shoulder as he came in behind them.

Why do I get the feeling you had a hand in that?" He raised an inquisitive eyebrow and helped her off with her coat.

"Me? It was over before Sarah and I even got out the door."

"I haven't done an ounce of work or play today without Rafe racing ahead to do it first, or stopping me altogether. What did you bribe him with?"

"Bribe him – why, Harlan Fleming! I don't know where you come up with such—

The door opened, again, and Rafe banged through with an armload of firewood. Seeing them still standing at the coat rack, intent in conversation, he cheerfully interrupted, "He figured it out, Bonnie Rae, but that won't make no difference. Got that sass cake in the oven, yet?"

"We better have a talk." Harlan took her by the hand and—instead of heading into the living room with the others—started upstairs.

"I ain't got time for talking," she protested, "I got a sass cake in the oven!"

"With all these women hustling around here, I'm sure it won't burn."

"Harlan, it's just you ain't near careful enough. When I seen how much you and Rafe been doing around this place all week, moving furniture and such, I figured you needed—"

"I'm not made of glass anymore, *chère*. Will you take my word for it? I'm getting stronger every day. And I can tell when it's time to slow down. You, on the other hand..." He pulled her close on the upstairs landing and slipped into French as they continued walking down the hall. *"... need to find something else to worry about besides me."*

"I have plenty to do. All these beautiful things – I had no idea!" She put an arm around his waist and clung tightly. *"I feel like I'm dreaming! I thought you sold everything in Richmond."*

"I sold the farm, not the furniture. Most of it has been in the family for years, especially Aunt Melanie's things. Coming from the 'old country' – as you say – her history goes back farther than ours. I couldn't sell any of it. Just had it stored in a warehouse in the city. This house is bigger than ours was, though. It seemed to swallow everything up."

"The Farnsbys had nine children, along with whoever else they might take in from time to time. They kept building on and adding rooms over the years. Why, there's enough bedrooms to sleep the whole family up here tonight and still have a room left empty!"

"Two rooms left empty. The kids and I are going to set up a tent in the study, have popcorn and roast marshmallows in the fireplace, and read adventure stories until late into the night. Big plans."

"Anyone else invited?"

"Closed party, I'm afraid. I have a feeling you'll be too busy with other things to look in on us, anyway."

"Can't think what with. Sarah and I made up all the beds

and I've got the whole kitchen put away already. Nothing left but to eat good food and enjoy it all. Feels like Christmas started early for me!"

"Me, too. Which is really why I brought you up here. To give you an early Christmas present."

He opened the last door in the hallway, which revealed a short set of stairs that led up into the attic. Bonnie Rae had no reason to have gone in there, today. She had already been over the house from top to bottom when she first came out, three weeks ago, with John and Sarah, to make a list of things they would need for this family work party.

Harlan softly kissed the side of her face and whispered, *"Merry Christmas, dearest, with all my love."* He stepped aside to let her precede him up the stairs.

"Law!" she marveled, with a return to English as she went, "Can't think of anything else I'd want more than what you already—"

Instead of the large empty space she had expected, with some wrapped package waiting to be opened, the great room had been divided by a newly built wall, painted white, and turned into a cozy and inviting sewing room. There was a deep window seat built into the other end, beneath a large window that looked out across the back field and toward the maple orchard. There were storage cupboards and shelves on either side of it, already filled with her own patterns and materials that her mother and sisters had organized.

An entire room just for sewing! Far away from everything else. Imagine not having to lock a door against little brothers and spread projects over beds every time she wanted to make something. Unable to say anything for a moment, she could only turn back and fling her arms around him. "Harlan! Just when I think I've got enough to last me for all eternity—oh, Harlan! If you ain't careful, you'll spoil me for certain!"

He lifted her off her feet for a moment. "Maybe that's what I have in mind."

"But how could you think of something so wonderful?

How did you know I—"

"I know you, Bonnie Rae, and that's the pleasure of it."

There was a rustling behind them.

Harlan kissed her, again, then set her down as the rest of the Harper girls crowded up the little stairway. All of them—including Granny—had been beside themselves trying to keep the wonderful secret as they had slipped in and out during the day, arranging everything just right and making sure Bonnie Rae didn't venture in while waiting for whatever time Harlan might choose to show it to her.

"Mama—did you ever see such a place?" Bonnie Rae asked.

Celia hugged her daughter. "Seems the Lord's paying you back for all them things you make everybody for just what it cost you, honey!"

"We'll have plenty of room to sew wedding clothes, now, Mama," Lou Ellen opened and closed the window-seat, gave the wheel a turn on the old Singer sewing machine, and then peered into Bonnie Rae's sewing basket, as if to make sure the familiar assortment of things was still there.

"Don't look like spring's gonna get here soon enough for this family," Granny observed, her mind still on the tender scene they had walked in on. "I reckon you all best move in till then just to help me keep a eye on these two whenever they get together!"

"You best worry about keeping a eye on Rafe and Lil Sam, Granny," Jenny Beth announced. "I bet they got half that sass cake ate, just since we been up here."

"Tarnation!" The old woman gasped and turned to hobble her way down the stairs, again. "Come on, Jenny, I ain't about to let myself get outnumbered down there!"

"Let's all go down," Ceilia suggested. "After the sweets and coffee, we'll come back and pick out some dress patterns. I'll vow, you girls should have a good start before we have to leave tomorrow."

In the living room, there was a blue and white checked,

French provincial couch and two deep blue chairs arranged around the hearth. Lias sat in the one closest to the fire and he, Angus, and Big John, were talking as the happy group descended from the upstairs. They passed by like a flock of birds winging over, and Harlan veered off to sit with the men as the girls continued on into the kitchen. A few minutes later, Sarah came in to pass around drinks.

"What's this?" Lias looked suspiciously into his cup before tasting.

"Sorry." She gave his shoulder an indulgent pat. "Granny says it's either sassafras tea or a onion poultice for you."

"I believe I'll take the sassafras," he relented. "But I want a extra big piece of pie to help me get it down." When she turned to go back in the kitchen, he tossed the contents into the fire and looked around self-consciously at the tell-tale hiss.

Big John frowned.

"I don't know what she's been doing to it lately," his father answered the accusing glance, "but it tastes like the wrath anymore. It was awful before but nowadays—"

"How long you been doing that?" his son wondered.

"Just the last few weeks. But a man can only take so much!"

John let it pass with an indulgent smile but made a mental note to tell Bonnie Rae she would have to find a different way to administer the dose of medicine Doc had given them to help keep their father's winter cold from turning to pneumonia. John had also noticed that Rafe was not having much success in misplacing his many stashes of tobacco, either.

Angus stayed for coffee and a liberal piece of pecan pie, and then left to get back to his own family. Celia put up another fuss when Lias went outside again to see him off and was so relieved to have him return in a few minutes without lingering in the bitter cold that she didn't notice Rafe leave the yard to head out toward Sugar Hill.

Several hours later, when the boy didn't turn up for supper, she carried on for a while about having to put up with another child that never told her when he was going or coming. Which reminded her that he hadn't been working since the company shut down and he was still smoking cigarettes right under her nose. At least Joseph Lee had always been polite enough to do his smoking in private.

By the time Rafe finally came back, the women were already upstairs in the sewing room. Little Sam and Jenny were constructing a tent out of blankets in the study, and Big John was talking quietly with Harlan as he lay in one of the bedrooms, waiting out another painful headache. The difficult spells were slowly becoming more bearable and he was learning to recognize signs of them coming on in time to retreat to some quiet corner until it was over.

When Rafe slipped back into the house, only his father remained in the living room by the fire. The boy sat down disconsolately on the hearth, still radiating cold from the chilled air outside.

"What did he say?" Lias tossed the end of an unfinished cigarette into the fire.

"He wasn't there, Daddy. Cabin don't look like nobody's been there for a time and a time. Still was gone, too."

A wave of despondency swept over Lias. He leaned his head against the back of the chair and closed his eyes for a moment. "Boy just learned too well," he admitted quietly. And suddenly, for the first time in his life...

He felt old.

62

Joseph Lee did not come home for Christmas. He stayed hidden deep in the hills throughout the entire winter, producing the finest grade whiskey in the county, just the way his father had taught him, and his grandfather before that. No one knew where he was. Though his product was growing in demand and appearing in abundance in the local trade, he himself was never seen. The still was moved so frequently that even the mountain boys couldn't find it. They were always looking. It was becoming something of a sport to match wits with Joseph Lee Harper.

Occasionally, a diligent search would uncover an abandoned site that had been set up so ingeniously the trackers learned from it and quickly incorporated the new knowledge into their own operations. One three week search below a stream revealed nothing until an accidental discovery proved that the necessary water had been cleverly piped to a hidden thicket several hundred yards above. Joseph Lee was swiftly developing a reputation that not only matched but surpassed the long line of Harpers that had gone before him.

In the meantime, J. Edgar Hoover was busy honing his increasingly successful organization of federal investigators into a band of cool, levelheaded professionals whose advanced systems of criminal technology were turning the department into an intelligence machine. There had been an undercover investigation going on in the county for a long time and enough evidence had finally been gathered to promote decisive action. An action that was being held at bay by a single slender thread. The advent of spring.

In early March, before any leaves had appeared on the trees and even before all the melting snow had run down the steep mountainsides to swell the streams, the wild flowers began their seasonal procession across Appalachia. Fragile dainty flowers with names like "spring beauties" and "blue-eyed grass" could be seen coming out of the woods and running down mountains. Then new leaves on the maple trees turned a bright red-orange which stood out in striking contrast against the forests that were also beginning to unfurl in every shade of green.

There were small, rarely seen frogs called "spring peepers" that could be heard in the hush of deep woods, and turtles appeared in abundance on the banks of rivers and streams. Spring came shyly to Cedar Creek, touching first the mountaintops and then spreading its gentle warmth down hillsides and deep into every hollow. The black bears were stirred and roused from their winter sleep. And in April, the children sought out the black birch saplings whose sap tasted sweet and spicy like wintergreen.

In a low crevice on the north face of Sugar Hill, all the implements of Joseph Lee's still— along with a near fortune in illicit liquor— were hidden safely away behind a false wall that was covered over with mountain clay. A half-mile below, in a tangle of woods where the still had recently been operated, stood a tumbledown shack in a small clearing with two cars wedged into it.

Joseph Lee crawled out from beneath Tate's Ford sedan and wiped a grease-covered hand on his pant-leg. Somewhere, a soul-stirring wind bewitched the late morning solitude. He couldn't feel a breath of it in these deep woods but he could hear a telltale rustling in the very tops of the tall pines. A door squeaked on its rusty hinge and Tate emerged from the shack, humming the same two bars of a movie theme song over and over.

"When we get into Princeton tomorrow," said Joseph Lee as his friend handed him a cup of coffee, "there's something I want you to do for me, Tatum."

"Just name it, Ol' Son," He opened the door on the passenger side and climbed in.

"Don't leave town without seeing a different picture show."

"What?"

"I'm sick and tired of that song."

"Well, shoot—that tune's got a way of slipping up on me just like that purty face of Jean Harlow. Mmmm! That picture was really something, wasn't it?"

"Yeah, but I could do without the song."

"Just think…" He touched a match to a freshly rolled cigarette and slouched down so he could lean his head comfortably against the back of the seat. "How Clark Gable must feel when he wakes up in the morning, knowing he gets to kiss the purtiest girl in the world over and over like that."

"He don't feel it no more, that's for shore."

"A man wouldn't never get tired of Jean Harlow, no matter who he was."

"He didn't get tired of her, she died."

Tate bolted straight up as if he had been struck. "What'd you say?" He leaned across the seat to stick his head out the window on the driver's side and look at Joseph Lee with shocked disbelief.

"I said, she died."

"But we just saw her in that picture-show last month!"

"That was a old picture, Tatum. Shoot, she's been dead almost a year."

"Gawd!" He sank back against the seat and tossed his cigarette out the open door, half smoked. "Day-em —that's awful!"

Joseph Lee tipped his cup for the last swallow of coffee, felt grounds rush into his mouth and bent over to spit it out.

"Maybe it was just a rumor," Tate suggested. "Where did you hear it? Them newspapers?"

"Yep."

"Could be a rumor, then."

"Tate, the news was all over. Where were you?"

"Shoot, I don't know. Was it on the radio?"

"Sure, a couple times."

"Must be true then, if it was on the radio. Gawd!" He shook his head sadly. "That's the worst news I heard all year."

"It ain't exactly news, no more." He set his empty cup on the roof of the car. "You know, that makes me wonder how much you're missing every time I send you into town to find out what's going on."

"That ain't the same thing."

"So, what's going on in town?"

"Nothing."

"That's what I'm talking about." He leaned his forearms on the partly rolled down window and looked inside. "Coal wars about to break loose all over, again, and you're talking about Jean Harlow. Did you know Perkins was back in town?"

"I heard something about that last week."

"How come you didn't tell me? I had to hear it from Willie Junior this morning and he don't even know what day it is."

"I didn't think it much concerned us."

"When are you gonna get it through your head that every-thing concerns us?"

"You know something, boy? You're getting to be purty dern miserable to live with. Hardly past morning and you're jumping everybody already."

"Listen, Tate."

"Why don't you go eat some breakfast."

"Let me explain something to you. Again. We need Perkins. Hear me? We need him. Because with my brother turning sheriff, we ain't got a chance not getting caught sooner or later. Soon as he gets this company thing settled, he's gonna start looking our way. And I'll tell you right now, Tatum, that big ol' boy knows every trick I do. And he can catch us."

"That why you wanted to shut down when everyone else is starting up, again? We're gonna be missing out on a lot of opportunities, boy."

"We're gonna be missing the opportunity to breathe fresh air if we ain't smart."

"Sort of hard to believe your own brother would turn you in."

"He's a changed man." Joseph Lee's tone was sarcastic. "Just like my daddy."

"Some kind of change when a man don't even stand up for his own no more."

"I reckon they think they're standing up for something better, nowadays." He straightened up again and let his eyes wander back up to the tops of the trees. "We got anything to eat in there?"

"There's some cold beans and venison left over from last night."

"Shoot." He started for the shack. "Three grown men around here and not a one of us can cook decent."

Tate climbed out of the car to follow him inside. "If you'd bring Ivy down here, we'd have us some fine eating."

"You know what happens to womenfolk if they get caught around a still, Tatum? They get shot dead right along with the men. She don't even know the locations, that's how much I tell her."

"Listen, Ol' Son, since we're shutting down, anyhow, I don't see how come we don't just take the whole lot with us tomorrow. Make a lot of money and quit this place. Start over again, somewhere's else."

"Too risky to take it all in one run. I already told you that. Besides..." He sat down at a rough-hewn table in the center of the low-ceiling room and looked into the pot at the cold, gray mass. "Dang—that's awful." He shoved it away and turned his attentions to a steady monotonous clicking coming from the far corner of the room. "What are you doing over there?" he asked of the slouched figure in the miner's cap.

"Just getting ready for tomorrow, boss man," came the reply. "So, don't get no idees."

"What kind of ideas are you getting, backwards boy?" He walked across the room to look over his shoulder.

Willie looked up at him with a disdainful expression. "I told you not to call me that."

Joseph Lee eyed the pile of two-penny nails with the heads snipped off and the wire cutters still poised in Willie's hand. He looked at the neat row of empty shotgun cartridges lined up waiting to be filled and the realization dawned on him. "That ain't for no Winchester," he accused.

"It's for my new, magazine-loading repeater shotgun," Willie replied with a grin.

"You want to drive that pilot car tomorrow, Willie?" Joseph Lee asked levelly.

"You already said I could."

"Well, you ain't gonna drive nothing if you bring either of them guns."

"You think you're the boss man!" Willie's face reddened with a sudden rush of anger. "Well, if you don't let me drive that car, I'm gonna—kill you—boss man!"

"Why don't you kill me, right now?"

"Ah, come on, you two." Tate set the pot over the coals in the fireplace.

"You hear him, Tate?" Willie got to his feet and knocked his sack of nails to the floor. "He's baiting me!"

"Can't stick up for yourself?" Joseph Lee taunted.

"He's baiting me so's he can beat the fire out of me, again!"

"Know why?" Joseph Lee asked. "Because taking you anywhere is like lighting a stick of dynamite and hoping it don't go off!"

"I ain't no half-wit!" he cried.

"Well, you shore act like one."

Ordinarily, Willie's face looked clear and oddly innocent beneath the miner's cap. But now it became distorted with a mixture of rage and frustration. "I ain't no—" he turned away from his assailant and broke into frustrated sobs.

"Leave him alone, J-Lee," Tate said. "He ain't hurting nothing."

Joseph Lee turned and strode across the little room and out into the yard, again. When he had gone, Willie Junior sent the empty cartridges across the room with a sweeping gesture, then tipped over the small table he had been working at in a blind fury. He kicked at the sack of nails and stood still in the middle of the room, trying to get his emotions back under control. Tate watched him for a few moments and then went outside. Joseph Lee was sitting on the sagging porch steps, smoking.

"He didn't deserve all that," Tate said quietly. "What's wrong with you lately?"

"I don't know. I got a cold feeling in my soul." He sighed. "Like I should have been home yesterday." He fastened his eyes on some point beyond the front bumper of the first car. "If you're so all-fired tired of me, why don't you leave."

"Well, I would if it weren't for a few things."

"Like what. The money?"

"Shore. I ain't denying that. But you know what's really got me hooked?" Joseph Lee didn't answer, and Tate leaned back against the porch rail and told him anyway. "Curiosity."

"What's that got to do with anything?"

Tate shrugged. "You're the first person I ever knowed that's right all the time. I mean it's like you got the sixth sense. It's a curiosity." He sat down beside him on the porch. "Much as I hate to admit it, I reckon you're right about shutting down, too. Everybody else'll be sweating and running from federal men—and a mountain boy turned law—and you'll be setting back with a pocketful of money and a stash of next year's whiskey turning itself prime."

"If my brother don't get me."

"Just stay out of his way. Like you been doing."

"Can't stay hid forever. I been gone six months. Now, I got a feeling like I can't get home fast enough. I miss the family. Shoot, you want to hear something don't make no sense at all? I even miss Johnny."

"Ooooweee!" Tate marveled. "You'd be hanging yourself for shore if you try going back now."

"Maybe."

"Way I see it, you—"

There was a low growl beneath the porch where they were sitting and Tate's dog emerged, staring into the trees with the hair on the back of his head raised. "Somebody's coming," Tate got quickly to his feet. "I thought you said we was—"

"Better get inside."

They hurried into the shack, took up rifles and peered out the single, broken-out window. Willie was still off in the corner but he had hastily gathered up his ammunition as soon as he heard the dog start to bark. The animal stayed at the edge of the clearing, barking fiercely and waiting for the intruder to set foot on his appointed territory.

"Call off that dog or I'll shoot it dead!" came a familiar voice.

"Well, I'll be!" Joseph Lee straightened up and started for the door. "It's the ol' man."

Tate whistled for his hound and Joseph Lee went outside just as Aaron McCord appeared in the clearing. "Shoot fire!" Joseph Lee broke into a grin as they neared each other. "I swear, Ol' Man, you are the only one on this mountain could have tracked us here!"

"I'll admit you had me stumped a few times. Lordy!" He gave his young friend an impulsive hug and was surprised at the warm response. "I been looking for a whole week!"

"You're the first face from home I seen in six months," Joseph Lee drew away from him. "What brought you?"

Aaron's smile faded and he looked into the eager blue-green eyes with compassion. "Your daddy's dying," he said gently.

A cold misery swept over him. "I been feeling like something was wrong for a couple weeks now." He turned away for a moment and tried to control the quaver in his voice. "I got to get home."

"Your kinfolk been gathering for the last week," Aaron said. "He's been asking for you. That's why I come."

"I hope it ain't too late. I got something I got to tell him. We'll go, as soon as I tell Tate."

"I heard," Tate stepped down from the porch. "What about tomorrow?"

"You and Willie just gonna have to go ahead on without me."

"J-Lee—" he protested.

"It'd be too risky to wait. You can do it. Everything's ready. All you got to do is follow the same plan as before. But I got to go, Tatum. I got to."

"I shore hope you know what you're doing." Tate leaned against the side of the shack. "All the way round."

63

They arrived after dusk. Joseph Lee could smell wood-smoke and see a countless number of shadowy figures moving around a fire that was burning in the front yard. He was out of the car before it came to a stop, pushed through the crowd, and pressed past the tangle of people in front of the door.

"Here comes Joseph Lee," someone said in a hushed voice. "Let him through."

The house was more crowded than the yard. It smelled richly of food and the table was heavy with every imaginable fare brought in by the many relatives and friends that had come from near and far to pay their respects to Cedar Creek's ruling patriarch. An isle opened up for the son to pass through and he put his hand to the bedroom door, hesitating only for a moment before he stepped inside.

The room was empty and quiet, lit by the single glow of a candle burning in a glass holder on the wooden dresser. Lias was stretched out full length on the bed, dressed in the only suit he possessed, with his hands folded peacefully across his chest and two copper pennies holding his eyes closed.

Beside him in a straight-backed chair, Celia sat dressed in black, quiet and unmoving. She looked up at her son with eyes that were dulled with sorrow. He tried to think of something to say to her, then spread his arms in a gesture of futility and looked away. She got slowly to her feet as if it took every effort and walked past him, laying a hand gently on his shoulder as she passed. She closed the door behind her and left him in the cool, dark room all alone.

There was a terrible, welling pressure deep in Joseph Lee's throat and he moved over to the chair and sat down, afraid to look too closely at the still silent figure beside him. He realized he was still wearing his hat and pulled it quickly from his head. A heavy sense of guilt began to press in on him.

It seemed that in all of his life—no matter how hard he tried—he had never been able to come through for this man. "I did try," he found himself murmuring. "I tried, Lias, but you never waited for me. You was always out there running ahead of me somewheres. I weren't bad enough for you and then I weren't good enough!" He raised his eyes from the patchwork quilt to the dark material of the suit.

He took a long, deep breath and swallowed hard. "I had something to say to you... day after tomorrow... about that night in the barn. You could have stayed, Daddy. I wanted you to. What I really wanted was…was…" He looked at the silent form of his father fully—then searchingly—as if by some inner force or strength he could will Lias to hear him.

"I wanted you to love me—just once—the way you love Johnny! Daddy…" he whispered leaning toward him."All them times you hurt me and I said I hated you, I never really did. Do you hear me? You were mean to me but I loved you anyways. I loved you!" He leaned his head on the coal-blackened hands that still smelled faintly of tobacco and cried, "I just wanted you to love me back! Why couldn't you—ever love me—"

He sat up again and sniffed, willing himself back under control. A grown man shouldn't be carrying on this way. What was wrong with him? He had come to pay his respects and say goodbye. Best to leave it at that. So, Joseph Lee bent down to embrace his father and mutter a stiff, formal goodbye. Then without really knowing why, he raised the lifeless arms and placed them around himself.

Just once.

It was customary when a man died, for the other men in his family to do the laying out. Those that had been with him during the last violent spell, left grief-stricken and silent while two of his brothers remained, along with Big John and Rafe. Harlan had turned to leave with the others when John asked him to stay, saying quietly that two months and a ceremony wasn't going to make him any more a member of this family than he was right then. Lias had wanted him near even at the end, and that was enough.

As the news spread quickly through the waiting crowd, hats came off, heads were bowed, and someone began to sing "Amazing Grace." Now that the indomitable spirit was gone, Lias' broken, disease-ravaged body looked smaller. They washed him gently – tenderly—and dressed him in his best. Celia returned when they had finished, having changed her clothes to mourning black, and was prepared to be the first to sit up with him during the wake. He would be buried the next day, but until then, he wouldn't be left without someone he loved by his side. She had not been there long when Joseph Lee came.

Big John had been standing in the kitchen and didn't see his brother come in. He was holding Little Sam in one arm as he opened the door to the back porch for Sarah with the other. "We're gonna go clean up and rest for a spell," he said to those who were gathered there. "Be back in about an hour."

One of the women seated at the table got up and reached for the boy. "Come sit with Aunt Opal, honey," she said gently.

"No!" The little boy buried his face in the strong, protective shoulder of his brother. "I want to go with Johnny!"

"He'll be all right," Big John assured. "We'll lay him down at our place." Then he noticed Lou Ellen standing beside one of the counters, looking lost and forlorn. "You come along, too, baby," he said to her.

She breathed a sigh of relief and didn't need to be asked twice.

Just as they were leaving, Rafe darted through the crowd and whispered, "J-Lee's here," before his older brother walked through the door. Big John handed Little Sam to Sarah, sent her on without him, and turned back toward the room where his father lay. He had left that room less than a half hour, ago, but it was still a jolt to see his father laid out for burial. It took a few moments for him to pull himself together.

Joseph Lee had his forearms leaning against the windowsill and was looking out into the darkness when his brother came in. He had his back to the door and did not need to turn around to know who it was. "I want to come home, Johnny," he said quietly.

"You sure took a long time to decide."

"Too long for Daddy."

"He knew you'd come around." He sat down wearily in the chair. "It's the rest of us weren't so sure. What I need know, now, is if you are sure."

"I'm sure. I can't spend the rest of my days running like a deer in the woods. Besides, I can't cut you all out of my life like that. I been too miserable." He turned around to give his brother a long and searching look. "And I ain't fool enough to think you wouldn't come after me now that you turned sheriff."

"Makes things more complicated, all right." John sighed.

"What do you mean?"

Big John sat quiet and still, thinking. The long silence caused a shadow of doubt to spread over Joseph Lee. It never occurred to him that John would say, no. He had always believed his family would take him back and stand by him—no matter what he had done—as long as he submitted to their authority. But if there were no family to work and worry for, if there was no giving or taking of love and sharing of life, where would the value of that life be? His father was dead. And this long, long silence of his brother spoke more than words.

All at once, the heartbreak and uncertainty of Joseph Lee's life began to churn inside him until he couldn't hold back the surging torrent of despair. Suddenly, that life no longer seemed worth fighting for. He leaned his head and shoulders back against the wall and closed his eyes. The realization that his own brother was going to turn him in was a crushing blow. With no sudden passion to fight—or even run —he sank slowly to the floor and gave up.

"Joseph Lee—" John tried to explain.

"Nobody waits for me."

"That ain't so. Now, just—"

"Why does everybody keep changing the rules? First we couldn't trust the Law, and now we are the Law. You all decide to change your ways and do right —and by the time I get around to changing mine— it ain't enough no more! Now, you're gonna tell me you're bound by the law to take me in."

"I didn't say that."

"I saw it in your face. But I ain't done nothing nobody else in this family ain't done before—including you!"

"Just let me think a minute."

"Johnny!" Joseph Lee covered his face with his hands as if he could forcibly hold back the tears. "Johnny, don't let them lock me up where I can't breathe. Please! I'll do what you tell me—anything— I swear it!"

"Damnit, J-Lee!" Big John sighed miserably and rubbed a thoughtless hand over his chin in the same gesture that Lias had been apt to use. "Where's the still?" he relented.

"Took apart and buried in a cave on the north side of Sugar Hill."

"Well, you sure didn't do that too soon. Federal boys gearing up for the biggest run of raids this county ever seen. The name you been making for yourself —on top of the one you was born with— they want you in the worst kind of way. What's more, they're just waiting for me to cover for you.

Boy, you got me between a rock and a hard place!"

"Tell me what to do, and I'll do it!" he cried. "But don't shut me out!"

"You're gonna have to swear off the business for good."

"I will!"

"And I mean for good—because if I hear you so much as even looked at another still, I'm gonna haul your backside down to the jailhouse and lock you up myself!"

"I won't shame you, no more."

"And you're gonna have to light out and stay hid till this here raid's over. Because there's a warrant out on you that I'm bound by law to look into. I can't do it right now, though, on account of... on account of I'm beside myself with grief. So, get."

"Can't I even see the younguns, first?"

"You especially can't see them younguns! It's one thing to slip in and pay your respects but if you do any more, I'd be out and out letting you. And if I let you, I'd have to let every last man on this ridge get away with the same thing you done. I can't do that."

"But I at least got to talk to Mama! I couldn't when I first come, on account —"

"Joseph Lee, I'm gonna turn my back and set with Daddy for a spell. And if I hear anything but the rustle a them curtains behind me, I'll be forced to do something about it! I'm sorry but that's what it's got to be."

Big John turned the chair toward the silent figure of his father, rested his elbows on his knees, and leaned his head in his hands. He heard his brother get up, walk across the room, and slide open the window. After he heard the muffled sound as Joseph Lee landed on the soft ground outside, he murmured, "Run high, boy—like a eagle. Don't let me catch you!"

Then he laid his head on his arms and cried.

64

Two weeks later, Joseph Lee was awakened out of a sound sleep by a loud persistent knocking on the door of the cabin on Sugar Hill. He climbed down the ladder from the loft that he and Ivy were using as a bedroom and reached for his rifle before opening it.

"It's me, Ol' Son," came an urgent whisper out of the dark, "I got to talk to you."

"Where you been all this time, Tatum?" Joseph Lee opened the door wide for his friend to come inside. "I was starting to think you took off on me." A soft glow fell over them as Ivy lit a lamp on the mantel and stirred up the buried coals of the fire that had already been banked for the night. Tate pulled his hat from his head and sank wearily into a chair at the table.

"You look awful." Joseph Lee set his rifle aside. "Best go on back to bed, Ivy."

"Just a minute," Tate protested. "Let her make me something to eat first, Ol' Son. I ain't ate since day before yesterday and I'm half starved."

"What would you like?" She tied her yellow housecoat more snugly around her waist and pushed her tousled hair back from her face.

"Anything that's food." He leaned his elbows on the table to rest his head in his hands.

Joseph Lee sat down in the chair opposite him. "All right, what happened? And where you been?"

"I don't know where to start. I need a cigarette, first."

"Shoot— you want a bath or anything else while you're at it?" Joseph Lee went to the mantel for a pouch of tobacco and started to roll a cigarette.

"I wouldn't mind," Tate mumbled. He cast an anxious glance over to where Ivy was slicing ham at a small counter next to the sink. "Hand me one of them pieces plain, will you, honey? I feel like I'm fixing to die."

She gave him one and it disappeared within seconds. Joseph Lee lit the freshly rolled cigarette and handed it to him before he sat down at the table, again. Tate drew in deeply and inhaled, then looked across at his friend and shrugged. "I lost everything," he said. "Everything."

Joseph Lee swore and looked away from him. "What about Willie?"

"I lost Willie on some country road about ten miles outside Princeton. He got stopped by a game warden and a state trooper."

"Tate—that's one of the oldest tricks in the book! Where were you?"

"What was I supposed to do? I had to drive right on by and leave him."

Ivy slid a plate in front of them with a few sandwiches made from freshly baked bread. She opened a jar of dill pickles, another of peaches, and returned to the little black cookstove in the kitchen corner to put on a fresh pot of coffee. The stove was new and beautiful with shiny, nickel-plated trim. Joseph Lee had brought it home for her several months ago.

"So, what happened when you got to Princeton?" Joseph Lee asked after Tate had eaten half a sandwich.

"Well," he began with his mouth full, "I got in about nine-thirty that night. Was driving down this main road real peaceful like, wondering what I was gonna do about Willie. You know —"

He reached for a pickle and looked at Joseph Lee. "I was wondering if I should stay there in town and wait for them to let him go—I knew they'd let him go—it being his first time and all. And while I was thinking on it, I see this state trooper step out of a circle of light coming from one of them street lamps, blowing on his whistle."

He shrugged, again, and chewed thoughtfully. "I stepped down on the pedal and you had that baby tuned so good it looked like he was flying backwards! Couple blocks later, another Law comes out of a little phone booth like thing and hollers. Passed him by just like the other. Half a mile down, they had a road block set up waiting for me."

He sighed, as if he still couldn't believe it. "State trooper standing out in the middle of the street holding a rifle gun up to his shoulder. It was pointed right at my head. So, I stopped."

"Tate," Joseph Lee asked in quiet disbelief, "how come you didn't get off that main road after you passed the first one? I mean, it only stands to reason—"

"I don't know why. I reckon the car was running so good, I just didn't think nobody could catch me. Just didn't think."

Ivy poured coffee for each of them and set the pot on the center of the table. There were only two chairs in the cabin and Joseph Lee slid his back to make room for her to sit on his lap. "So, that's where you been all this time?" he asked. "They took you in, then let you off on parole?"

"Nope."

Joseph Lee began to grow impatient. "Well, what happened?"

"It was worse than getting took in. I'm telling you, Ol' Son, this thing has got way out of hand! I sat there with them Laws pointing their guns at me, waiting to be brung to justice. Then one of them smiles and says, well, boy, what's it gonna be? You going to jail, or turning it over? Shoot!" He reached for another sandwich. "What could I say? I told them to help theirselves."

Joseph Lee swore again and began to roll himself a cigarette.

"I didn't mind them taking the shine, J-Lee," he said quickly. "That was fair. But they took my car! No justice a-tall! There I was—smack in the middle of Princeton—with nothing but eight dollars and thirty-five cents! Weren't enough for no train or bus-fare. I waited around for Willie a few days. Looked for him, even. But he never showed. I was broke by then, so, I come on home."

"How come you ended up here first? Bit out of your way, ain't it?"

Tate was quiet for a long time. His spoon clinked noisily against the dish as he dipped the last of the peach juice from it.

"Why ain't you been home?"

"Willie beat me back," he replied, unable to look into the blue-green eyes when he said it. "Thinks I left him on purpose. He's gone plumb crazy. Dug up our stash down the hill."

"What?"

"Says it's out and out war."

"Out and out war!" Joseph Lee fumed. "Why that—"

"He's got a regular arsenal down there, boy!" Tate spoke fervently now, as if Joseph Lee's anger had given sanction to his own. "I couldn't even get past to go on to my own place! Took a pot shot at me —lookee here—" He lifted his dark hair back from his forehead to expose a scratch-like graze. "Half inch over and it would have kilt me!"

"I've had all I can take of that half-wit!"

"He's got his little brother and a couple friends with him to keep us out. Shoot—I believe he means to sit there right under our noses and steal yours and my share both!"

This time it was Joseph Lee who was quiet. Ivy felt a restless apprehension sweep over her and got up to clear the table.

"What are we gonna do?" Tate asked.

"Tatum, I was counting on them profits as much as you," Joseph Lee began slowly. "And I ain't denying it would give me a heap of pleasure to go down there and hang that backwards boy with a new rope! But I can't."

"Why not?"

"Because the whole situation has turned itself into a powder keg, that's why. Stuck with a real short fuse. There's a raid fixing to come down on Cedar Creek any day now, and we're on the top of the list. I promised Johnny I wouldn't touch nothing to do with the business ever again, if he'd let me by."

"Well, ain't you something!" Tate breathed disdainfully. "You promised Big John. How about me promising my brother and my ol' blind Pa to keep food in the place? I told you already, we ain't got no more pension. So, what am I supposed to do? Let them end up in the poor house on account of I ain't got the brains or guts to provide for them?"

"You got other choices besides the business."

"No, sir!" he shook his head emphatically. "You got other choices. You got friends and family all over this ridge to help you out. And a good patch of bottomland besides. Me—I got nothing but myself and a little ol' shack that got built on a piece of rock barren by some relative with less brains than me!"

"Tatum—"

"I need the money from that stash —it's mine— I worked hard for it!"

"Didn't you have none you saved back at all?" Joseph Lee tamped the end of his cigarette out in a saucer.

"I put it all into the car and a few supplies to get the family by until now. All I could see ahead of us was the high life. Didn't see no reason to hold nothing back."

"I got more than I need saved back. I'll loan it to you."

"That ain't the kind of help I come for!"

"I'll give it to you, then."

"You don't understand." Tate got to his feet, feeling so suddenly and deeply offended that it was a few moments before he could speak. "I'm twenty-seven years old," he said quietly. "I lived all my lifetime on the company pension or hand outs from other folks. What I made on the hill last year, I earned! And for the first time in my life I paid my own way."

He looked at Joseph Lee with an intensity he had never shown before and said quietly—almost reverently—"I tasted a kind of pride in it. I held my head up for a little while and I seen glorious days!" He sniffed and wiped his nose with the back of his hand. "And by God almighty, I ain't never gonna take another hand-out from nobody, again!" He reached for his hat that was hanging on the back of his chair, and started for the door.

"Wait just a minute." Joseph Lee got up to stop him. "Ain't gonna help for you to go getting yourself kilt. Willie might be half-witted but that don't mean he ain't dangerous."

"Can't see as I got much choice. I aim to get what's mine, or die trying."

"You got a plan?"

"No, I ain't got no plan!" He threw his hat back onto the chair with a sudden frustration. "What do you think I come here for? I thought I could count on you! I thought this was one time when I weren't gonna have to pay the price for not being smart enough, or fast enough. Because you got enough brains and guts for both of us! I had the crazy notion we was friends!"

"Tate, if it was anything but the business!"

"I ain't asking you to get back in the business! I ain't asking you to make it, or run it. I just want you to help me get back what's already ours before Willie either gets caught, or blows it all to hail! Please, J-Lee. If for no other reason than I was there for you one time. When you needed me."

The last phrase struck deep.

"All right, Tatum." Joseph Lee sighed. "I'll get my gun and meet you outside."

Ivy felt a cold fear wash over her. "Joseph Lee," she murmured quietly at first, "you ain't really going…"

They both turned back to look at her as if they had forgotten she was there.

"Ivy," her husband assured, "it ain't nothing for you to worry over. Go ahead on, Tate. I'll be out in a minute."

Tate reached for his hat, again, and turned to leave.

"Well, if you think I'm just gonna stand here and let you go off and get kilt!" She tried to stop him as he reached for his gun. "You ain't if I got anything to say!"

"I ain't gonna get kilt," Joseph Lee replied firmly. "And you ain't got nothing you can say. Now—"

All at once, she raised the plate she had been washing and hit him with it.

"Hey!" Tate moved toward them. "Cut that out!"

She turned on the intruder with increasing fury and began to hit him, too. "Honest to God!" she cried, "I'm gonna kill you myself, Leroy Tatum! For coming here like this!"

"All right!" Joseph Lee snatched the plate from her and tossed it onto the table so hard it broke. "That's just about enough!"

"Gawd!" Tate backed away as he put a hand to his forehead with sudden shock. "She drew blood!" Without warning, Ivy picked up the coffee pot that was still half full and hurled it at him. It missed by a mere few inches, crashed into the door behind him and spattered the scalding liquid all over.

Joseph Lee dropped his rifle, grabbed her by the hair and swung her around to face him.

"Day-em!" Tate hollered angrily and slipped quickly outside.

Ivy burst into tears.

"This here's something I got to do, baby," Joseph Lee's grip melted in to gentleness as he explained. "I don't expect you to understand. But I don't expect you to shame me, neither."

"But you promised, J-Lee!" she cried. "You promised we was gonna live peaceful from now on!"

"I ain't breaking no promises. All I'm gonna do is help

Tate teach Willie Junior a lesson. I'll be back before morning."

"I got a awful scared feeling inside me," she pleaded. "I just know something's gonna happen to you!"

"Don't worry," he said. "This ain't nothing I can't handle." He let her go and bent to pick up his rifle, again.

"Joseph Lee!"

He kissed her lightly and backed away with a reassuring smile. "I'll be all right."

65

Big John Harper pulled his patrol car to a stop behind the Cedarville drug store and went inside. Ordinarily, it was closed by five-thirty. But tonight—because of a special radio broadcast—it had been re-opened between the hours of nine and eleven. It was April fourteenth, and President Roosevelt was giving his first "Fireside Chat" of 1938.

Already, a crowd had gathered. Big John walked past the counter, tucked in the back of his uniform shirt that Sarah always kept so neatly pressed for him, and re-adjusted the pistol at his hip that he had still not grown used to wearing. He moved down an isle that held large jars of rock candy, and on toward a pot bellied stove that was throwing off a comfortable, even heat.

"Evening, Sheriff," said one of his cousins who was seated along the wall, and Big John smiled.

All at once, an announcer's voice came crackling over the radio, "LADIES AND GENTLEMEN, THE PRESIDENT OF THE UNITED STATES."

"Shhh! All right, here it is," someone quieted the crowd and turned up the volume. A hush settled over them all. Then the voice of Franklin Delano Roosevelt, that had become familiar even to these hill people through his many previous broadcasts, began to address them from the large brown box on a nearby shelf. The radio—that most magical of all inventions—was like a window to the outside world.

They sat transfixed, facing the receiver as if somehow it actually contained the embodiment of that voice; while each man pictured in his mind's eye, his own version of the magnificent White House, were the broadcast was being made. A few forgotten hats were quickly pulled from respective heads and everyone listened intently.

"I HAD HOPED TO BE ABLE TO DEFER THIS TALK UNTIL NEXT WEEK," said the President, "BECAUSE, AS WE ALL KNOW, THIS IS HOLY WEEK. BUT WHAT I WANT TO SAY TO YOU, THE PEOPLE OF THE COUNTRY, IS OF SUCH IMMEDIATE NEED AND RELATES SO CLOSELY TO THE LIVES OF HUMAN BEINGS AND THE PREVENTION OF HUMAN SUFFERING THAT I HAVE FELT THERE SHOULD BE NO DELAY.

IN THIS DECISION, I HAVE BEEN STRENGTHENED BY THE THOUGHT THAT BY SPEAKING TONIGHT, THERE MAY BE GREATER PEACE OF MIND AND THE HOPE OF EASTER MAY BE MORE REAL AT FIRESIDES EVERYWHERE, AND THAT IT IS NOT INAPPROPRIATE TO ENCOURAGE PEACE WHEN SO MANY OF US ARE THINKING OF THE PRINCE OF PEACE."

Easter! John was startled. Why, this coming Sunday was Easter and he hadn't even realized. With the family still mourning Lias' passing, and the concerns he was having in town, he had lost all track of time. He cast a questioning glance toward the front of the drug store just to check, and sure enough, there were baskets done up with gaily colored ribbons and boxes of candy on display.

Well, he would talk to Sarah when he got home about doing something special for the younguns. Then he wondered fleetingly how he had gotten along so many years without Sarah. They could not help the dark cloud that had hovered over their house for so long but, now, they must do their best to get rid of it. Childhood was too short to miss the opportunity of gathering all the brightness to it that one could manage.

The word "labor" filtered through his thoughts and he realized he hadn't been listening to the speech. Now he had missed something important about collective bargaining and labor relations. The voice was outlining recommendations that were made to Congress earlier in the day and how the government could help create an economic upturn.

"...HISTORY PROVES THAT DICTATORSHIPS DO NOT GROW OUT OF STRONG AND SUCCESSFUL GOVERNMENTS, BUT OUT OF WEAK AND HELPLESS ONES. IF BY DEMOCRATIC METHODS, PEOPLE GET A GOVERNMENT STRONG ENOUGH TO PROTECT THEM FROM FEAR AND STARVATION, THEIR DEMOCRACY SUCCEEDS; BUT IF THEY DO NOT, THEY GROW IMPATIENT. THEREFORE, THE ONLY SURE BULWARK OF CONTINUING LIBERTY, IS A GOVERNMENT STRONG ENOUGH AND WELL ENOUGH INFORMED TO MAINTAIN ITS SOVEREIGN CONTROL OVER ITS GOVERNMENT..."

"Sounds like Communism to me," someone said critically.

"It don't neither," another objected.

"Why, it shore do. Big strong government—controlling everybody—if that ain't Communism, I don't know what is."

"He's talking about the people controlling the people. You ain't listening, Harve. If the governmen—"

"Shhh!" a voice near the wall objected. "You all shut up so's the rest of us can hear."

"... NOW WE HAVE PLENTY OF CAPITAL, BANKS AND INSURANCE COMPANIES LOADED WITH IDLE MONEY: PLENTY OF INDUSTRIAL PRODUCTIVE CAPACITY AND SEVERAL MILLIONS OF WORKERS LOOKING FOR JOBS. IT IS FOLLOWING TRADITION AS WELL AS NECESSITY IF GOVERNMENT STRIVES TO PUT IDLE MONEY AND IDLE MEN TO WORK, TO INCREASE OUR PUBLIC WEALTH AND TO BUILD UP THE HEALTH AND

STRENGTH OF THE PEOPLE—AND TO HELP OUR SYSTEM OF PRIVATE ENTERPRISE TO FUNCTION. IT IS GOING TO COST SOMETHING TO GET OUT OF THIS RECESSION THIS WAY, BUT THE PROFIT OF GETTING OUT OF IT WILL PAY FOR THE COST SEVERAL TIMES OVER. LOST WORKING TIME IS LOST MONEY.

EVERY DAY THAT A WORKMAN IS UNEMPLOYED, OR A MA-CHINE IS UNUSED, OR A BUSINESS ORGANIZATION IS MARK-ING TIME, IS A LOSS TO THE NATION. BECAUSE OF IDLE MEN AND IDLE MACHINES, THIS NATION LOST ONE HUNDRED BIL-LION DOLLARS BETWEEN 1929 AND THE SPRING OF 1933. THIS YEAR YOU, THE PEOPLE OF THIS COUNTRY, ARE MAKING ABOUT TWELVE BILLION DOLLARS LESS THAN LAST YEAR."

"Lordy! What's he talking about? I ain't made nothing this year—

"He's talking about everybody together."

"Everybody together—if this county's got that kind of cash money floating around somewhere, it's a downright sin we ain't got none of it! We're Americans, ain't we? Where's our share?"

"Your share is what Perkins is using to pay his road gang five dollars a day, that's what," someone else replied..

"Good Lord!"

"Shhh!"

"THE GOVERNMENT CONTRIBUTION OF LAND THAT WE ONCE MADE TO BUSINESS WAS THE LAND OF ALL THE PEOPLE. AND THE GOVERNMENT CONTRIBUTION OF MONEY WHICH WE NOW MAKE TO BUSINESS ULTIMATELY COMES OUT OF THE LABOR OF ALL THE PEOPLE. IT IS, THEREFORE, ONLY SOUND MORALITY, AS WELL AS SOUND DISTRIBUTION OF BUYING POWER, THAT THE BENEFITS OF THE PROSPERITY COMING FROM THIS USE OF ALL THE MONEY OF ALL THE PEOPLE SHOULD BE DISTRIBUTED AMONG ALL THE PEOPLE—AT THE BOTTOM AS WELL AS AT THE TOP.

CONSEQUENTLY, I AM AGAIN EXPRESSING MY HOPE THAT THE CONGRESS WILL ENACT AT THIS SESSION A WAGE AN HOUR BILL, PUTTING A FLOOR UNDER INDUSTRIAL WAGES AND A LIMIT ON WORKING HOURS. TO ENSURE A BETTER DIS-TRIBUTION OF OUR   PROSPERITY, A BETTER DISTRIBUTION OF AVAILABLE WORK AND A SOUNDER DISTRIBUTION OF BUYING POWER."

There was a general murmuring throughout the crowd and Big John, who had been leaning against the back wall, straightened up with a sudden amazement. Up until now, the speech hadn't been much more than the typical, political vagueness trimmed with niceties and patriotism to produce something of a glorified pep-talk. Now, the President had said something tangible.

If Congress really did pass a wage and hour bill that would establish a minimum wage and make it a law, then the greater part of Cedar Creek's battle with the company would be won. Could it actually happen? If the President of the United States could get Congress to pass something like that, their little town would no longer be fighting by themselves. They would have the whole country behind them. Along with the strong arm of the government to enforce their ideas. For the first time—in his lifetime, anyway—that government would take a stand with the people instead of big business. And that would be an out and out miracle.

All at once, John felt as if a light had been switched on inside him. He suddenly knew exactly what he had to do. He had to get rid of the last remains of corruption in his town and pave the way for the enforcement of the new wages and hours bill. There must be no question that this was how it was going to be when the new company owners arrived. And he was cer-tain they would arrive, just as his father had predicted.

Ainsley had relinquished his office to Judge Chamberlain and remained in the Virgin Islands. But he had sent Perkins back with a new set of company guards and a handful of out of state workers to begin construction on a new road leading into Cedarville. Rumor had it that he was paying the road gang an unheard of five dollars a day.

Immigrants and Blacks were trickling in from neighboring counties in anticipation of the re-opening of the company and the people of Cedar Creek were growing restless. John had called another town meeting, encouraging them to stand firm and assuring them of the promised hearing that was set for early summer. He had searched out those among them who possessed good bottomland and organized collective farming so that none of them would be forced to return to the company out of dire need.

They had made it through the winter, but it was well into spring, now, and things were dragging out. The people doubted that justice was strong enough to prevail. They began to worry about missing out on even the poor incomes they had before. A small company check looked better than no check at all. Big John Harper began to lose sleep at night wondering what would happen if they were right. Sometimes, he wondered if he were the only one in the world who was making a stand for what was right.

But now the very President of the United States was behind him. And if Roosevelt could persuade Congress to do right, then Big John Harper could certainly persuade the people of Cedarville and Cedar Creek to do the same. The only ones left who stood in his way were Perkins and his much-feared company guards, who still held enough sway to turn people against him.

But John knew what to do about them, now. The idea had come on him like a brainstorm. God had not allowed him to be put in this office for nothing. He would do it first thing in the morning. The sooner, the better. Just thinking about it gave him a sense of peace.

The rest of the speech drifted over the listeners, inspiring, drawing them together; challenging them to uphold something called a National Will. The words were taking hold like seeds falling into ready soil, and it wasn't until someone shook him by the arm that John noticed one of his deputies had slipped quietly up beside him.

"What's wrong Roger?"

"Sorry to interrupt." The man motioned him outside, "But we got us some trouble." They moved quietly away from the crowd and were standing by John's car before Roger explained, "Couple of federal men come into the office a while ago, with about ten state troopers. Fixing to pull off that big raid we been waiting for."

"Whose still?"

"It ain't just one. Seems it's gonna be the four biggest operators in the district. Gonna do them all in one night. They got locations and everything. Want every man and car we got to go along."

Big John felt his insides churn but it didn't show except for a slight tightening of his jaw. "How come they waited until now to let us know?" he wondered out loud.

"You know how them federal men operate," Roger slipped into the seat next to him and the engine roared to life. "Everything undercover. They didn't want no slip-ups. Big foreign looking man, name of Sergeant Mensky is in charge. Along with that Durham feller that hung around so long, last fall."

66

Joseph Lee crept around behind the little shack he had lived in such a short time ago on Sugar Hill, and pulled back the hammer on his rifle. It was dark inside but he could hear movement, so he tossed several stones onto the old wooden porch to entice someone outside. Willie slept like a cat, so he expected he would be the one to come.

No one came.

He waited a little longer and then moved quietly toward the door. He put a hand to the latch and was about to ease himself inside when a cold chill passed through him and—for reasons unknown— backed off and went over to the window instead. The rustle of movement became louder as he peered in through the broken pane. He tossed a stone inside.

When nothing happened, he struck a match and looked around. The room was empty except for a half dead raccoon that was tied to one of the wooden legs of the table, carrying on a weakened but persistent struggle to free itself. Then his gaze fell on a chair that was placed oddly in the center of the room. It had a shotgun mounted on the back, rigged ingeniously to go off whenever someone opened the door. When Joseph Lee realized how close he had come to opening that door, he broke out in a cold sweat and felt suddenly sick inside.

"Psssst! J-Lee!" Tate whispered to him from the trees a few yards away. "Come on over here, boy—"

"Shhh." Joseph Lee moved over to him. "Like as not he'll come jumping out of the bushes at us. He ain't in the shack and he's looking for blood."

"Well, come here," Tate whispered more quietly. "I got to show you something.Gawd! It'll make the hair on the back of your head raise up." Tate started back into the trees with Joseph Lee following. When they came to a small clearing, he stopped suddenly and put out a hand to hold back his friend. "There... in that thicket," he breathed.

"What is it? Did you look?"

Tate nodded. "It's Willie's car. And that awful smell gets worse the closer you get to it. I ain't looked inside."

"I thought you seen him get caught just outside of Princeton."

"I did! He was pulled over the side of the road just like I told you. Game warden was already snooping around back. Trooper must have told him to get out, because they was just opening the door when I passed by."

"That don't make sense," Joseph Lee objected. "If they took your car, stands to reason they would have took his, too." He thought for a moment. "I don't like the looks of this. Let's check under the seats and see if he's still got the shine."

"You go first, Ol' Son. My whole body's breaking out in the goose flesh. I believe we're walking straight into a haint!"

"Ah, you been listening to too many booger tales! This ain't no haint—booby trap, maybe. But it ain't no haint."

Joseph Lee led out and Tate followed reluctantly behind. When they came to the thicket, the repulsive smell had grown so strong that Joseph Lee had to pick up the end of his open shirt and cover his mouth and nose with it.

Tate pulled a handkerchief out of his pocket and did the same. "Great Gawd," he whispered fearfully, "the air all over's got cold as ice! I heard tell once, that—"

"Will you shut up?" Joseph Lee pulled a loose bit of brush

out of their way. "There it is. Willie's car, all right. Come on up close and strike a match. I want to look inside."

Tate reached into his pocket. "Our Father which art in heaven..." He struck a match on the sole of his shoe. "With a halo by thy name..."

Joseph Lee opened the back door and leaned inside. "There's blood all over the back seat, here. Hold that thing a little higher, will you? I can't reach the seat latch."

Tate leaned over closer. Joseph Lee felt around until he found the lever and raised the seat to expose the compartment he had personally packed with a hundred and eighty-seven quarts of illegal whiskey, two weeks before. An overpowering stench poured forth.

In the few seconds before the match sputtered and went out, he was confronted with the horrifying vision of two uniformed bodies in the advanced stages of decomposition. Joseph Lee backed off so fast he knocked Tate over. The two of them stumbled and staggered away, coughing and gagging as they went. They had gone several hundred yards before they finally stopped.

"Oh—Gawd!" Tate moaned, "Willie done kilt himself a couple of Laws!"

"Tate!" Joseph Lee said with a sudden urgency, "We got to get out of here! This is a set up!"

"Gawd—Gawd!"

"If these hills ain't crawling with Laws right now, they're gonna be!"

"Maybe he got away with it—it's been two weeks."

"That's what scares me. Ain't been nobody around asking questions or nothing. Even Johnny would have said something about a murder investigation. Them bulletins come in down at the office all the time. I bet they tailed him here, figuring to catch all of us. I bet they even tailed you!"

"What are we gonna do?" Tate worried. "We done got ourselves backed right up into this box canyon."

Joseph Lee thought a moment. "We ain't been here long.

If we hurry, maybe we can skin out before they get to us."

"What about Willie?"

"Willie's a dead man. I ain't gonna worry about him. He's gone stark raving crazy this time, boy. We just better hope we don't run into him before we can get out of here. Let's go!"

They did not go back the way they came. Instead, they pushed their way through the thick undergrowth in an attempt to get quickly to the safer heights of the mountain. In less than twenty minutes, they came out on a rocky shale-barren about thirty feet above a dirt road. Across it lay a small, little-known path that lead up to the other side of Sugar Hill.

Tate bounded down in a fervor, stumbling and sliding. He was about to start up the other side when Joseph Lee said, "Hold it!" in a tone that turned Tate's blood cold. He looked down the road behind him and—to his horror—saw a strange glow on the horizon. Joseph Lee signaled him back up, again.

"Now, what do we do?" he panted as he reached for a hand back up over the top. "They'll see us shore if we go that way. It's right out in the open!"

"A whole caravan of Laws gonna be cresting that rise any minute," Joseph Lee sat down quickly to pull off his boots and socks. "Get your shoes off!"

"What for?" Tate asked, though he immediately did as he was told.

"Because we're gonna get run, that's what for," Joseph Lee told him. "Worse feeling this side of hell. But we might still make it. They'll expect us to skin out through them woods but we head for the north side of the mountain, instead, hear?"

"Day-em!" Tate stood to his feet and looked up. "That's straight up, boy—can't nobody climb that!"

"We can climb it. Just follow me. Less apt to fall or make noise without shoes, so, toss them in the bushes somewhere."

There was a narrow patch of woodland they had to pass through before they got to the north face. They hurried along, pushing past thorn bushes and brambles, expecting to hear gunfire at any moment. All at once, they broke into a newly made clearing that had never been there before. They stopped abruptly. Ghostly shapes and shadows were moving around a low fire that burned beneath what they immediately recognized as their own still.

"Back up!" Joseph Lee whispered desperately.

It was too late. A dog barked, and Willie and two others spotted them. "I'm ready for you, boss man!" Willie snatched up his rifle.

"It's a raid!" Tate yelled.

The others stopped and looked fearfully behind them to see if it were true. But Willie kept on coming. Joseph Lee ran only a short distance before he turned back suddenly and lunged toward Willie with a fierce, rising anger. Baffled by the surprise, the youth lost the few seconds it took to level his gun. Joseph Lee knocked it out of his hands and pushed him to the ground.

"You brought the Laws down on us!" He grabbed him by the collar and shook him furiously. "You stinking—"

"Let him go—let him go!" Tate yelled. "Here they come!"

Joseph Lee looked up in time to see lamps and lanterns coming toward them through the trees. He turned toward the pass to the north face, only to hear the sound of men coming from that direction, too.

There was no place left to go.

He felt a cold terror shoot through him. "Ahh—we've had it!"

"We'll give ourselves up!" Tate offered quickly. "Ain't none of us here gonna get more than a parole. Long as we don't shoot first, they won't open up on us. We'll give up, and you make a run for it!"

Joseph Lee shook his head, unable to speak.

"Go on, you got to!" Tate insisted and gave him a push. "They'll lock you up shore if you don't! Now, go on!"

Joseph Lee took off like a deer into brush. Tate looked after him for a moment and then turned around in time to see Willie level his rifle and draw a bead on the back of the retreating figure.

"Willie!" He sprang for him just as he fired.

Joseph Lee went down in the same instant that he heard the gun go off. He felt a searing pain go through him and the last thing he was aware of before everything went black, was a volley of gunshots.

They rang out across the hills like the crack of mountain laurel.

67

Big John Harper knew the moment would eventually come when he would have to go against friends and family to uphold the law. But he felt miserable about it. It was a hard thing to do no matter how right it was. He could only breathe a heartfelt thanks that he would at least be spared having to go after his own brother.

Less than an hour after his deputy had come for him, seven cars filed out of town with headlights slicing through the dark toward Cedar Creek. They held twenty-three men, armed with rifles, guns and various tools needed to break up the stills. As they began the long climb up the narrow dirt road that lead to the ridge, a hoot owl hollered down at the disturbance.

John looked up in time to see it wing its way from a tall roadside pine to a safer, deeper part of the woods —then averted his eyes quickly—wishing he had not seen it. Not on this night. It didn't comfort him any to notice the bright, luminous face of a hunter's moon, either. It was only beginning to peek over the crest of the mountain, now… but it was rising.

He looked over at Sergeant Mensky. A tall man with a flat nose, and eyebrows that met to form a dark solid line across his forehead. He did not know him. Or the two other federal men in the seat behind. Durham had opted to ride somewhere else, even though he was the senior officer on the case. And with good reason. Once the initial shock wore off that the man even had the audacity to show his face around here, again, John could swear he felt his blood boil every time he looked at him.

None of the others said a word to him throughout the ride. At the box canyon, Mensky motioned him to pull over and all the cars followed behind them. When the men got out and gathered around for instructions, Big John hung back.

He had set himself to be a follower on this night. He might have to uphold the law but he did not have to tell everything he knew. This raid—planned and carried out in secret by federal men—could just as well be finished by them. And if they were so all-fired worried about him tipping someone off, they could do without his tips for them, as well. They were making a mistake just parking here like this.

Big John Harper moved back and forth along the fringes of the crowd while Mensky talked, feeling his heart begin to race and his whole body gear up to give everything he had—both physically and mentally—for what lay ahead. The same way it always had when he worked in the business, himself.

"... and come at them from the trees," he heard Mensky say, "where we'll fire a warning shot before—"

John's head snapped up. "Don't shoot." His tone was firm and everyone looked at him. "You shoot and people are gonna get killed. There ain't no need for that. Most of these are decent folks, not criminals. They'll run if we scare them. But if we catch them fair., they'll give up."

"I'll bet," someone said sarcastically.

"If you open up on them without warning," John went on, ignoring the remark, "then we're gonna have a fight on our hands."

"That's what the warning shot is for," Durham spoke up for the first time. "To let them know we mean business before anyone has to get hurt."

"That's not what it means, and you know it," John looked at him so hard and long that the man had to look away to keep his nerve.

"Admit it, Harper," Durham said, "you got a system set up with your backwoods—"

John pushed through the men that separated them so fast Durham stumbled backwards trying to get away from him. "You say one more word to me," he spoke in a chilling whisper, "and I'll kill you!"

"Keep him off me!" Durham picked himself up off the ground and threw an accusing glance at Mensky. "I told you we shouldn't have brought him!"

Mensky cast a calculating glance at the man who could reduce one of his most intimidating detectives to such outbursts, "I'm sure the Sheriff, here," he finally replied, "is more than aware of his duties before the law. So, what exactly do you suggest... Sheriff Harper."

"Surround them," John replied quietly. "Put a couple men at every escape place. Let them know we're there, and they'll give up."

"The trouble is," Mensky reasoned with the calm diplomacy that had made him a leader in the department, "How can we find these—escape places—before they do?"

"I'll tell you where they are," John said. "And if anyone does get by," he relented, "I'll go after them, myself."

The words settled the matter. But they rang through John's heart, long after he spoke them. Then a feeling crept into him that he could not shake. A ripple of disturbance in his innermost being. A warning that hummed like an instinct in every fiber of his conscious and unconscious senses. Something was wrong.

And he had never in his life disregarded that feeling before.

His response was so automatic it was almost subconscious. By the time he realized what happened, he was already moving with it. He placed men at the areas he had promised—except for the one only he knew about. He would cover that one, himself. But a shot rang out before he got there. There was a moment of deadly silence and then an earsplitting shriek of a rebel yell before the woods all around him exploded into gunfire.

No one saw Big John Harper after that.

68

Early the following morning, the deputy who had been left in charge of the office in Cedarville, looked up as the rest of the deputies began filtering in. "How did it go, Roger?" he asked the first man in. "Where's all them federal boys? You wouldn't believe it, but we got a line of blockaders downstairs already, waiting on the sheriff to get back so they can turn themselves in!"

"Are you fooling me? He said they'd do that, but I sure didn't believe it!" The deputy sighed tiredly and sank gratefully into a chair. "I'm beat."

"Have some coffee." The other opened a thermos on his desk and let the pleasant aroma of the rich brew waft over them. He looked at the rumpled, dirt-dusty uniform that was even torn in several spots. This was the officer that never had a crease out of place and always smelled like *Doublemint* chewing gum. Now his rust-colored hair was disheveled, and he had a shadow of the same color beginning to stand out on his chin.

"Well?" The deputy who stayed behind persisted. "Tell me how our mountain boy did, bringing the law down on his friends and kinfolk. He isn't dead, is he?"

"Nope. And I'm gonna tell you right now, Curtis —you ain't never gonna hear me breathe another word against that man as long as he holds this office. Ain't gonna listen to one, neither."

"He did that good?"

"Did good? Shoot, he played both sides, boy. And..." He paused to sip the coffee Curtis handed him while the other eagerly pulled his desk chair around to listen. "Didn't neither side think he was unfair."

"Where's the prisoners?"

"Federal men took them on into Princeton. Ain't but two."

"Two," the man marveled, "I thought they were gonna take four stills. Biggest bust the country ever seen at one time."

"We did. But wait till you hear this. We didn't even fire at two of them! Sheriff just had us all sneak up on them real quiet-like." He sighed, again, and shook his head as if still in awe of it. "And you know, that's just what we done. That big ol' boy knew ever last place they could run off to. We spent most of the night just sneaking around in them woods. Crawled on my belly like a animal! And Lord, if I didn't pick up four of those good for nothing ticks doing it. You know, Curtis? Them things go straight for the hairy places. Got two of them right up under this arm here, and you wouldn't believe—"

"Just go on about the raid, Roger, I've had ticks before."

"There ain't much more to tell. Only place it got touchy was the first one. They opened up on us before we thought they even knew we was there. Some crazy kid come at us firing one of them new repeater shotguns. Hurt one of the troopers pretty bad."

"He one of the prisoners?" Curtis asked.

"Nope. Mensky slowed him up with a bullet in the knee. But that boy just got wilder every time somebody winged him. Nicked two more troopers before they finally put him down. Man, he had over twenty bullets in him when we checked him over."

"One dead and three wounded. Still don't sound bad for all them stills."

"Four. There was four wounded. Other was a mountain

boy that didn't give us no trouble. He was trying to give up but caught some crossfire. Ain't hurt bad, but..." Roger's eyes flickered with the pleasure of successfully having made the man wait for the real news. "But he went on and on about that crazy kid shooting..." He paused, again.

"Go on—shooting who?"

"Joseph Lee Harper. Off in the bushes somewhere. Said he wanted to talk to the Sheriff, personal."

"You mean, you got him? Big John took his own brother down? Great God!"

"No, sir, he did not do that. Didn't none of us see him—or the Sheriff—till it was over. I thought they both lit out. But then Big John shows up right in the middle of the crowd. Been with us all along, I guess. Never did find Joseph Lee. Found a lot of blood where it must have happened, though. Left a deputy and a couple troopers to comb the area. Picked them up this morning." He sipped on his coffee, again. "Didn't find nothing. Sheriff's gonna go out looking with some mountain boys, later on, and bring him in."

"He ain't gonna bring him in. Not his own brother, he ain't. Man's one of the best trackers in these parts, and he couldn't find him? He's covering for him."

"We'll see." Roger poured himself another cup and looked out the window. The streets of Cedarville were all but deserted at this early hour.

"What about the Manifee still?" Curtis asked after a while. "I'd like to see that mean old cuss come head to head with somebody who could match him. I'll bet you didn't just pop up and tell him to give up."

"Nope, we didn't. That's where John really showed what he was made of. Man's a natural borned lawman, Curtis. Even if he is younger than us."

"Aw, I ain't blaming him for that no more. It's been a heap quieter in Cedar Creek having somebody here in the office whose word was already law out there. A heap quieter."

"First thing John said, was, this man's shrewd and dangerous. He's been to jail twice before and knows what he's running from. Said if we caught him at all, we might as well figure on a fight. And he was right."

"Nobody hurt?"

"They was all backed up against some rocks. We fired off a couple rounds, and—listen to this—the minute ol' Judd Manifee run out of shells, John charged him before he could reload. Got him in one of those bear hugs of his. Lordy, that man is strong! Mensky walked up, clapped the cuffs on him, and the whole thing was over. Just like that."

"What about the others? His boys just let the Laws take their daddy down?"

"They was scared of Big John. He told them if they moved, he'd kill Manifee dead right in front of them. There and then."

Curtis whistled and went back to his desk, again. "Never was nothing but bad blood between them two families, anyhow. But you wait. Big John Harper ain't gonna let nobody go after his brother but himself. And he just plain ain't gonna find him."

The door to the office opened, and two more deputies came in. "Be nice to go home early," one of them speculated. "After a night like this, you'd think—"

"Think, again," Big John came in behind him. "You're gonna come along with Roger and me, while these others work on the reports."

"What?" The only man who was younger than John, eagerly picked up his hat, again.

"Boys, we got one more sore spot in this county," Big John reached into his desk drawer for a box of new shells. "I figure as long as we're cleaning up, we might as well clean it all up."

"Sheriff, you said, yourself, only a mountain boy could even come near to tracking that brother of yours down."

"I ain't talking about tracking, Junior," Big John hustled the men outside, again. "We're fixing to pay us a little visit to the company. See if we can't catch us a rat."

It was mid morning when Henry Perkins looked up and saw the Sheriff's car moving toward him over the newly leveled road. Several men in the road gang stopped work and moved out of the way for them to pass. He watched Big John Harper pull the car to a stop and get out with two of his deputies. But Perkins ignored them as they came close, and went back to looking at his blueprints.

"Mr. Perkins," John said as he neared him, "I'd like to talk to you for a few minutes. In private."

The men closest to them started to move away.

"No," Perkins objected. "Whatever you got to say to me, Harper, you can say in front of my boys."

"Are you sure?"

"What do you mean, am I sure" he replied irritably. "I'm sure I got a job to do, mister, and you're wasting my time. If you got something legal to say to me, say it. Otherwise, get out."

"All right, Henry, I reckon it's your choice. I got legal business with you."

"So, get on with it."

"Looks to me like I'm gonna have to shut this operation down for a spell."

Perkins pulled his cigar out of his mouth, looked him

straight in the eye and laughed. John smiled back at him. "I figured you'd try something like that," Perkins said, turning serious. "But if you think I'm as careless or stupid as Harrigan and Ainsley, you got another thing coming!"

John looked down at him for so long without saying anything, that Perkins began to feel uncomfortable. "Go on—" He waved the cigar in a wide expansive gesture, "take a good look around you, Harper, you won't find one thing that isn't legal! Because I made sure before I started. All this land is a government easement for the use of people that own property up here—the company included, mister—none of it's private! So, as soon as we get this road through, we're gonna commence operations. Same as before. And all that crying about private roads? It won't mean nothing anymore!"

"That's interesting, Henry," John replied. "Except that ain't what I come for. The business I got with you doesn't concern the company. It's personal."

"Personal—you said you come to close down the operation. I'd call that company business."

"I just naturally figured if you was to get pulled off the job, they'd have to shut down long enough to replace you."

"Who's gonna pull me off?"

"I am. You shouldn't oughta come back here, Henry. This county's had a warrant out for you since last winter. As sheriff, it's my duty to comply with it."

"Ex ridge-runner for sheriff! If that ain't the biggest joke!"

"I'm here to arrest you for assault." John pulled a sheaf of legal papers out of his back pocket and thumbed through them. "With intent to do murder. I got eight cases on that account and men that are willing to testify to those crimes. That's just over the last two years. I ain't dug no further back, yet, but I'm gonna."

"Why, you—"

"And one account of larceny."

"Larceny—I haven't stole nothing! You got to have proof before you come around talking like that."

"You stole a highly trained Morgan horse from the government teacher, last winter," John explained patiently, "that was worth over—" He looked through his papers, again.

"That horse was on my property! I had every right to—"

"You can tell that to the judge, Henry," John said. "Right now, it's my duty to let you know that what you say here in front of these fellers can be used against you in a court of law."

"This is a joke."

"It ain't no joke," he replied. "Are you gonna come peaceful, or do my boys and me have to take you by force?"

"You better think twice before you do this, Harper," Perkins warned. "A few trumped up charges aren't gonna keep me in jail. I know my rights. I'll put in a call to the company lawyer, be out on bail tonight and back on the job tomorrow."

"We'll see."

"And if you think I'm gonna let this kind of inconvenience slide by unnoticed, you got another thing coming! I told you before you're not dealing with a half-wit. I'll get rid of you just like I did the others that got in my way. Same as I did that government teacher that came snooping into places he didn't belong."

"I wouldn't say you did such a good job getting rid of him," John said, with light coming into his eyes that made Perkins nervous. "He's been back teaching school for quite a while now. Just like he come here to do. And he's got all the younguns out from under the hill you was trying to hide from him. Fact is—way things look—seems more like it was him that took care of you."

"Well, we'll see." Henry Perkins threw the stub of his cigar aside and wiped the sweat from his forehead with a handkerchief. "Let's go if you're taking me in. Get it over with so I don't need to waste time when I got a job to do." He turned to one of the foremen standing beside him, dumb-founded. "Make sure the work gets finished, today," he said confidently. "I'll be back first thing tomorrow."

"I'll be back first thing tomorrow, too," Big John told

them. "To arrest all you company guards as accomplices in these crimes if you ain't out of the county by then. Or if you ever come back."

They started toward the waiting vehicle, with the two deputies following close. Work stopped as the men paused to watch the Boss Man being driven away in the Sheriff's car.

For a long time Perkins was quiet. He sat in the back seat beside one of the deputies while John drove and the other deputy rode up front.

Finally, he looked out the window and spoke. "What are you trying to prove with all this, Harper? You know how it will turn out. The company will start up, again. The same men will go back to work for the same wages. The same kids. That's the way things are. So, what's to prove?"

"The President's gonna pass a law against them things any day now, Henry," John replied. "That makes it all worthwhile."

"There's been laws before. Since when did they ever get in the way of big business?"

"Since the federal government made them things a criminal offense. They're starting to side with the working class, now."

"They've had them kind of laws before, too. Tried to anyhow," Perkins reasoned. "It's still up to the local counties to enforce them. Looks to me like you lose any way you look at it. It's like kicking your foot against a brick wall."

"You forgot one thing, Henry. I'm the local law, now. And I intend enforcing every regulation the government passes down to me. If big business don't like it they can go make big business somewhere else. We got along nigh onto six months without the company. I reckon if we had to, we could do without it, altogether."

"That will never happen. Not as long as there's coal to be dug out of that hill, it won't. No, sir. It'll just turn into one long war between you and the company. Between you and me, Harper, since I'm the one running things. And I'm gonna be running things. You hear me, John? Don't think this little escapade to your office is gonna change anything."

"I figured you'd feel that way," John replied. "I didn't think it would be as easy to run you off as the rest of them."

"I don't scare easy. And once I get back tomorrow, I'll—"

"You ain't going back, Henry."

"What are you gonna do? Dump me out of town, or out of state, until I turn into a raving maniac like Harrigan?" He laughed sarcastically. "I'm not the raving kind."

"Nope. I know you ain't. That's why I got a federal man waiting back at the office to take you in on charges of tax evasion. Them other crimes might be easy to worm out of but fooling with taxes, Henry... that's a federal crime. Uncle Sam don't let fellers off so easy on them accounts, if you recall. Just look what they done with Al Capone. He had more than enough money to buy his way out of it and they didn't let him get by for nothing. You being from Chicago, I thought you would've considered them things. Or were you workin for them other boys all along?"

It was quiet for such a long time that John could hardly keep himself from throwing a look over his shoulder to see the expression on Perkins' face. He was about to pull into the parking lot behind the Town Hall, and contemplated taking the long way around when his prisoner finally spoke, again.

"How did you know about them taxes? Or who I worked for in Chicago?" he asked quietly.

"I didn't," John admitted. "But I figured a man that don't think twice about committing one crime, wouldn't be bothered breaking another kind of law, neither. I knew you wasn't fool enough to get yourself tangled up in the moonshine trade. Taxes was the only other federal crime I could think of. On account of all the stories they put in the newspapers when Al Capone went down."

"The newspapers? You mean you—"

"All I needed was a confession in front of reliable witnesses. And you just this minute give it to me. Did you hear that, boys?"

"Yep," the two men who had been unusually silent up until then answered almost in unison.

"All right, all right." Perkins leaned over the seat. "You got me like a bear in a trap. I don't know where some backwoods boy like you would come up with those kind of brains. Reading the newspapers! But you got me fair and square. Let me out, right here. I'll leave town on the next train. You'll never see me, again!"

"I can't do that, Henry."

"Why not? You're gonna let the others high-tail it out of here. You let Harrigan get away. What's the difference?"

"The difference is, a wounded bear is a sight more dangerous than one that ain't. I didn't really want it this way but you just sort of hung yourself."

"Look, Harper. Just listen to me. You've always been a poor boy. How would you like it if—"

"You ain't bribing me, are you, Henry?"

"Well..."

"Lord, I hope not. That's a felony."

"A felony! You're awful free with those legal terms for somebody who's committed a few of them, himself! You're nothing but a backwoods outlaw! A pretty stupid one if you think they'll keep you on any longer than it takes to clean up your own neck of those same backwoods! They're using you, Harper, that's all."

"But I'm in now, ain't I. And it's a good thing for all us folks on the ridge. That's the glory of an elected office, Henry." John looked back and smiled a handsome, knowing smile. "Sort of works both ways, don't it?"

They pulled into the parking lot and stopped. Perkins got out slowly, feeling sweat begin to prickle along his skin at the thought that Big John Harper might have actually acquired some of that morality everyone had been talking about, lately. He stared in disbelief at the broad, strong body as it moved away from him with some unexplainable inner grace that pervaded his presence in spite of anything that came against him. Perkins had personally seen that frame move with the same kind of grace under a load no other man could carry.

"Harper, wait—"

"Bring him on in, boys," John said to his men instead of Perkins. "And Roger? Tell Grace to put in a call to Princeton and get one of them federal men back down here to pick him up. We don't want him sitting in the jailhouse any longer than he has to."

"You mean there's no federal man waiting for me?" Perkins burst out.

"Nope," the Sheriff admitted. "There ain't."

70

A quiet peacefulness settled over Cedar Creek. With Perkins gone and the threat of impending trial, Ainsley reluctantly sold the Black Star Coal Works. No longer singly operated, it became one of the many mines owned and run by the local Pocahontas Fuel Company. Rumor had it that miners fared better working for this company but that was yet to be seen. Operators were operators, big business was big business, and they had always held the upper hand in Mercer County.

A new Boss Man was sent and word was out that they would be hiring local people to continue road excavation. No one knew yet what wage would be offered. They would begin hiring shortly after the Fourth of July, and talk of having a company payday again, began to reverberate throughout the community. Harlan worried as the talk spread among his older boys at the school and Big John began to grow nervous.

On June twenty-fourth, the night before Harlan and Bonnie Rae were to be married, President Roosevelt addressed the Nation, again, in the second Fireside Chat of nineteen thirty-eight. In it, he announced that Congress had passed something called a Fair Labor Standards Act, which was commonly known as the Wages and Hours Bill. That act, which successfully set a floor below wages and a ceiling over hours of labor, also ended child labor. It became illegal to employ anyone under the age of eighteen in a hazardous occupation such as mining. Those fourteen and over could hold other kinds of jobs but only outside school hours.

The strong, protective wings of the American Constitution were spreading over the Nation, reaching even into its remotest regions in an effort to bring a heritage of freedoms back to the common workers. For the first time in many generations, the living standards of the little mountain community of Cedar Creek were rising.

Had they known in the beginning that they would not only have to survive the winter but a long period of unemployment that would stretch to seven grueling months, they might never have tried. But they did. And out of their necessity and need for each other came a strong close-knit community, reminiscent of earlier days.

The man whose first fierce outrage against injustice had shocked and shaken them from their widespread apathy had paid the highest price. The people of Cedar Creek paid him back with an acceptance he had been looking for all his life. Harlan Fleming might have only been a shadow of the man he had been when he first arrived, but Cedar Creek was a merciful land of shadows. Though he would never go to China, or fight for other injustices in far-off places, he would always be a hero at home.

It didn't matter that he sometimes had to leave his students in the middle of a lesson to wander off quietly somewhere. He had Bonnie Rae to work with him, now, and she stepped in as if she had always been meant to be a teacher. They had fifty-three students in the Cedar Creek School and between them they were introducing the first comprehensive, steady education that had been offered there in years.

The sorrows and tragedies of the Harper family had postponed their long anticipated wedding. From early spring when Lias had become seriously ill, all the way to the lovely mountain summer when they had finally but reluctantly been forced to hold funeral services for Joseph Lee.

No one had ever found the last great whiskey runner of the Harper Clan. Even Aaron McCord, known throughout the county for his ability to track down anything that could move or leave sign, was unable to locate the body or bones of his young friend. He never quit trying. There were times when the old man sat wistfully on the bank of some quiet stream and would suddenly hear a soft rustle in the deep woods around him. "That you, boy?" he would call out hopefully. "It's me— the ol' man—Lordy! I been looking a time and a time!"

Joseph Lee Harper, whose cleverness and cunning had been looked upon with admiration in his lifetime, became a legend in his death. But the community of Cedar Creek, having suffered too much pain and heartbreak, was starved for hope and heroes. Most of them chose to believe that the young Harper had gloriously outwitted them all.

Some believed he had hidden at Granny Harper's until he was well enough to hike out over the mountain and start a new life, altogether. Some were certain he had died somewhere in the hills and his spirit now roamed freely over the surrounding woods. His little cabin on Sugar Hill became another local haunt. There were even some who swore that on nights when the moon was full, a thin wisp of smoke could be seen rising, wraithlike and ghostly from the old chimney. Those brave enough to peek inside, now and again, during a broad daylight only found it dust-covered and vacant.

The popular opinion was that he was still alive, deep in the mountains somewhere, waiting for things to settle down enough to come home, again. It could happen any day. Who was to say that the same strong feelings for family that once drew him out of hiding to pay last respects to his dying father would not also tempt him to show up at his sister's wedding?

Saturday morning dawned beautifully. The sun rose up over the grand heights and spilled into the darkest depths of Appalachia, promising to make the coming day sweet and warm. Harlan walked through his new home tentatively, feeling as if it no longer belonged to him. It had been cleaned and scrubbed by a long succession of Harper women, some of whom he hadn't met before they appeared on his doorstep to carry out their plans. Yesterday, they decorated the hearth and doorways with fern and white dogwood blossoms, and it suddenly struck him that his wedding was going to be nothing less than a major event. The evidence was everywhere.

Guests started to arrive in the late afternoon. Colorful rag rugs that were brought as gifts began to appear on the floor, along with an array of crocheted tablecloths, newly made linens, and other household items. Someone brought four laying hens and a rooster, and sometime during the gathering, a baby pig was placed in the barn. Lias' older sister, Lettie, contributed a loom that had been in the family for over a hundred years.

Harlan changed into one of the suits he had worn when he first arrived in Cedar Creek: a dark wool that felt uncomfortably warm for a day like today. Then he remembered how cool this mountain air had seemed to him, last year. Food began to appear in abundance on tables that were set up in the yard, and musical instruments were already being brought out. In the meanwhile, his intense blue eyes were drawn to the road over and over again, in anticipation of Bonnie Rae's arrival.

"Take it easy, son," Tom said. "She'll get here."

His eyes twinkled with teasing pleasure and Harlan thought how good it was that he had gained a bit of weight and was beginning more and more to resemble that beloved uncle who raised him. "Am I being that obvious?" he asked.

"Your heart's in your eyes." Tom smiled. "Come on over and meet the traveling preacher. It will give you something to do for the next five minutes."

As they started across the crowded yard, one of the many children who were already playing games in every available open space shouted excitedly, "Here she comes, Mr. Harlan! Here comes the bride!"

Bonnie Rae carried a cluster of wild mountain violets and her lovely red hair beneath a delicate lace vale tumbled in wavy splendor onto the shoulders of the white dress. Celia, wearing blue and already dabbing at her eyes, looked proud and radiant.

"Let's have us a wedding!" Big John shouted as he helped Sarah down from the truck.

"Not yet—not yet!" protested his Aunt Lyla. "Granny ain't here and we can't commence without her."

In a few minutes the sound of a lone motor was heard and one last truck pulled into view with Granny Harper in the back, enthroned on her rocker. "It's Jimmy, all right," said Aunt Lyla, whose husband was driving. "He said he'd bring her if he had to hog-tie her to do it. Looks like he near had to!"

When the truck pulled to a stop behind the other cars in the yard, a tall lanky man with dark hair, who bore a striking resemblance to Lias, got out, grinning. "I got her!" He called out reassuringly to everyone. "Told her she could just as easy wait for her call to Glory, here, as anywhere else!"

"Now, we can have us a wedding," Aunt Lyla beamed. Then she looked at Big John, who was standing beside her. "Lift her down from there, John-Boy!" She gave the towering man an authoritative swat on the backside.

"Aunt Lyla—" John lifted his grandmother down, chair and all. "That ain't no way to treat the county sheriff!"

"Oh, pashaw!" She bent down to give the old woman a hug. "You come just in time, Granny. And you look so purty!"

"Bonnie Rae done sewed me a new dress," she said, although it had been impossible to persuade her to give up the old hat. "I reckon I had to wear it somewheres!"

Then, the traditional mountain wedding sprang to life. The fiddlers played and the people sang as the preacher took his place on the porch to speak the "marrying words" over the lovely young couple before him. Everyone grew quiet as the vows were exchanged. And when the Reverend finally pronounced them man and wife, Harlan kissed his bride long and sweetly, to the wild applause of their mountain friends. The crowd gathered around to congratulate the newlyweds, and the real celebrating began.

They danced and sang and ate together while the children ran around the farm with a wild abandon, laughing and chasing and catching the little pig again, and again. The men and boys, from the oldest down to Little Sam, all wanted their turn to dance with the bride. They made a sport of keeping the bride and groom separated.

Harlan and Bonnie Rae went along with the fun, dancing with every guest, but continuing to cast fond looks and smiles at one another across the crowded yard. They were allowed to rest at intervals but only long enough to sample the traditional "Methiglam," which was the fabled honey wine from the Old Country. After that, they were whisked away to dance, again.

Good food flowed from the kitchen in steady streams. Wild turkey to home-cured hams, sweet potato pies and large kettles of pork and beans. There were potato salads and hot, crisp rolls, along with a variety of pies, cakes and puddings for deserts. Everyone had brought their festive specialty. Children were left to themselves to avoid vegetables and gorge unabashedly on sweets.

When a black and white DeSoto pulled into the yard, followed by another car and a truck with braying dogs in the back, a hush started first among those outside and then spread like a darkening cloud to the house. The music stopped. Lon Durham and Sergeant Mensky got out. The crowd that had been so noisy and raucous only moments before stood silent and aloof in the presence of the intruders.

"You all remember me," Durham's voice pounded the silence like a hammer. Somewhere a baby began to cry and a young mother crooned protectively.

"By now, you all know what I do for a living," he reminded them.

71

Big John let go of his wife and moved through the frozen dancers toward the two officers. His eyes locked on Durham, whose eyes were already scanning the crowd for Joseph Lee.

"He ain't here," Big John's voice was controlled but threatening.

"I have a warrant here to search this place," Durham snapped back. "Ten federal law officers to do it and see that you don't lay a hand on me in the process."

"I said he aint' here."

"Well, I hope you don't mind if we just look for ourselves."

"I mind."

"I'm sorry, John," Mensky apologized. "But he's a criminal at large, and we had to make sure. Durham's been on the case for almost a year, and he's convinced—"

"Durham's gonna convince himself dead if he ain't careful," John warned. "I won't be responsible for what happens to him, Mensky. He's offended too many folks, here. As for Joseph Lee, there's a grave up on the hill next to my Daddy's, and we all quit looking for him a long time ago."

"There's nothing in it, Harper!" Durham said, sarcastically. "We looked."

"Why, you disrespectful—" Big John seethed.

"Now, take it easy," said Mensky. "I know this is hard on everyone. We'll be on our way as soon as we look around."

"Where's Ivy Tolliver?" Durham spoke into the crowd and held up a slip of paper. "We've got a warrant, right here to take her in for questioning. All legal."

"Ivy moved to Princeton," someone spoke up. "Away back last year."

"She went to Princeton, all right." Durham's eyes gleamed with hatred at Big John. "But according to the county records she married Joseph Lee Harper and ran off with him somewhere."

A surprised murmur passed through the crowd.

An officer stepped up to Mensky and reported quietly, "He's not here, Sarge. We've gone through the house and they're starting the dogs around the area. If he's been anywhere near here in the last few days even, they'll pick up the scent."

"Let's go, Durham," Mensky turned back toward the cars. "Sorry about all this, John, but I had to follow through. It's my job."

"You haven't seen the end of me!" Durham threatened. "I know he's still alive! And I intend to find him and that girl of his, if—"

Mensky shuffled him through a sea of somber faces and into the nearest car. The truck was parked at the far edge of the field, and dogs began to bray wildly as they were released.

"Just wait and see where all your backwoods loyalty will get you, John Harper!" Durham called out from the back seat window as the engine roared. "And all the rest of you are accomplices!"

"What's wrong with you?" Mensky reached across the shouting officer to abruptly roll up the window as the car moved off. "You know what kind of people we're dealing with, here. Too many remarks like that and we could end up having to fight our way out of here!"

"You want me to do my job, or don't you?" Durham

smoothed down his blonde mustache with a furtive glance out the side window as they left the yard. "Can't you see that big old boy's about ready to crack?"

"He's doing a good job. You can't ask more of any man."

"He's doing a good job of fooling everybody, Mensky. Including you. I've been watching these people for over a year now, and I'm telling you—"

"Keep it to yourself, I'm tired of listening."

"That's not what you'll say when I bring in your criminal. Pull over and let me drive my own car, will you? I'll find that kid if I have to—"

"Let him go, Lon. He's probably dead, anyway."

"Kid's too good to get himself killed on some fluke. He's got one weakness, though, Sarge, and I know just what it is. That's the one I'm gonna hang him with! That boy - and believe me, that's all he is—the famous Joseph Lee Harper throws all caution to the wind when it comes to family. He might have given us the slip, now, but by the time Christmas rolls around..."

"From now on, he's dead!" Mensky's voice was firm. "Just like the man said. And whatever this personal vendetta is you have against him and that girl, you better let it go. There's other counties and other cases to solve. This one's been a hornet's nest for years and I think we finally have someone whose enough on our side to change that. If we let him. And so help me God, if you weren't such a good detective—I'd arrest you for your other crimes! If you hadn't proved that girl was still alive, I would have."

"But I get the job done, don't I, Mensk," Durham replied. "That's what counts in the long run. Well, Joseph Lee Harper's not dead, either. He's somewhere close by. I can feel it! If you didn't have such scruples, we could put an end to the whole bunch of them, right here and—"

There was a sudden explosion of shattering glass beside them, and Durham slumped against Mensky without finishing his sentence.

The car swerved as the officer who was driving looked over his shoulder in shocked disbelief. He stared at the thin trickle of blood coming from the side of Durham's head. "What kind of a crack shot was that?" Then he cast a nervous glance upward along the side of the hill they were curving aroundbefore turning back in a sudden panic when he almost ran off the steep embankment that fell away on the other side. He took the next curve too fast and felt the back end of the car fishtail.

"Take it easy, Brady—" Mensky turned to look through the back window behind them but the other cars that were following were not yet in view. "Just keep on going!"

"But that big old boy just murdered him, Sarge —in cold blood! You know it was him!"

"It could have been anybody." Mensky eased the still form of Durham back against the seat and glanced out the back window, again. "Keep this car under control now. I don't think the others even know what happened."

Brady braced both hands on the wheel and let up on the accelerator. "What do we tell the coroner?" he worried.

"The truth," Mensky brushed a jagged piece of glass from the sleeve of his coat. "I'm going to say someone shot him in self defense."

For a long time after the police cars had disappeared around a bend in the dirt road, an appalling hush hung over the wedding crowd. Even the children seemed frozen in their places—their security shattered—as they waited for some reassuring word or action from the adults. It seemed like an eternity before one finally came. The sun began to set behind the mountains and fireflies started to appear for brief flashes in the yard.

"Hey!" Big John's voice suddenly boomed over the somber silence as if —like the shadows of dusk— he had just appeared out of nowhere. "Ain't this supposed to be a wedding? I believe we got us some serenading to do!"

There was an almost audible sigh of relief from everyone as he reached for his fiddle.

On this special occasion, it was not his own, but his father's. He stepped up on the porch and looked down at the cluster of people pressed in close around it... around him. He was the head of the Clan and they looked to him, now. It did not frighten him. Instead, he felt a great love for them all. His people. And it transformed him. He seemed almost godlike with his strong features and gentle eyes. First born, first loved, and—always—with that winning Harper smile.

He touched his bow to the strings as he tucked the fiddle under his chin with an almost reverent grace. The note that drifted out over the people was calm and peaceful, and reassuring. It said the earth still turned, and the sun still set every evening, and men and women still gave and were given in marriage. So, there was hope.

A pleasant murmur passed through the crowd as it fell on them and two lines formed to make a path all the way to the house from the yard. Someone began singing low and sweetly,

"Let me call you sweetheart...
I'm in love with you..."

A harmony of other voices joined in as Harlan took Bonnie Rae's hand and walked her down through the "Lover's Lane." When they reached the porch, Big John stepped aside with a smile and they turned around to wave at everyone before going inside. This was their goodnight, though the singing and celebrating would continue for many hours outside their door.

"Oh, Harlan," Bonnie Rae's eyes suddenly brimmed with tears as he closed the door behind them. "I been looking for him all day! Now, I ain't sure. If J-Lee's certain gone—I'll never believe in nothing, no more—never!"

"Mrs. Fleming," Harlan looked down at her with a tender

smile as he turned her gently toward the fireplace. He put his arms around her and whispered, "Always keep a little hope set aside for miracles."

There on the mantel, in a delicate glass vase, stood a handful of—what looked like—miniature pine branches. All crowded with clusters of the rare, yet unmistakable, white blossoms of Scotch Heather.

From high up on the Eagle Wing.

The End

"And a man shall be like a hiding place from the wind, and a shelter in the storm; as rivers of water in a dry place, as the shadow of a great rock in a weary land."

Isaiah 32:2

About the Author

Lilly Maytree is an inspirational adventure novelist who decided to prove to herself that some of the things her characters did could be done in real life. A decision that sent her careening along on a very long voyage through the Inside Passage to Alaska with her captain husband aboard a sailboat called the *Glory B.*

She eventually ended up on a faraway island that was so beautiful she never went home. She lives there on a float house, tucked into a little cove in the wilderness, with the *Glory B* tied up alongside, ready for more adventures. Which she loves sharing with readers. It has even been said that she time-travels (but that's probably just a rumor). To find out what she's doing right now, simply visit:

LillyMaytree.com

You can also get in touch with her by sending an email to: lilly@LillyMaytree.com. It might take a few days if she is adventuring far away... but she always comes back sooner or later.

Other books by
Lilly Maytree

Novels:
The Rising
Gold Trap
The Pandora Box
Neptune's Lady

The Stella Madison Capers:
Home Before Dark
A Thief In The House
Sea Trials
The Pushover Plot
Lost In The Wilderness
The Last Resort
Voyage of the Dreadnaught
(Four Stella Madison Capers)

The Complete Stella Madison Capers

Novella
Night Visitors

For Writers:
Unspoken Rules
Writing Rules!

For Parents:
The Nature Of Children
(And how to deal with it)

Behave Yourself!
Teaching children to discipline themselves.

This book was published by:

If you enjoyed it, please consider leaving a review in any of the places you like to buy books. To browse other books like this—fiction and nonfiction—visit:

LightsmithPublishers.com

We appreciate you taking the time to read. We hope you will also take a look at of the Free Ebooks we offer each month.

To get your free download of Night Visitors, go to:
LillyMaytree.com,
click the Books By Lilly Maytree tab,
scroll down until you see the Night Visitors cover,
then click on the "A Free Gift For You" button.

Happy Reading!

Thank you for reading this book! You might also like Lilly's novella *Night Visitors*.

Night Visitors is the story of how Marion Bates, a middle-aged woman who suddenly hits a catastrophe in her life, meets Dee Parker, a young investigative reporter who talks her into doing things she never even thought of before.

Sooner or later, something unexpected happens to everybody. It isn't easy to accept help—especially from strangers. But sometimes just knowing you are not alone can make all the difference in the world.

It was a time when all Marion could think about was how to keep on living. To tell the truth, she really didn't care about anything else. Which is the only logical explanation she could come up with–later–of why she jumped headlong into a life-or-death nightmare just to help her new friend out of one of her own.

Yes, this is how it all began.